# Lovers' Perjuries

or, The Clandestine Courtship of
Jane Fairfax & Frank Churchill

a retelling of Jane Austen's

## EMMA

(A Jane Austen Sequels book)

## Joan Ellen Delman

Lovers' Perjuries;

Or, The Clandestine Courtship

of Jane Fairfax & Frank Churchill

A Re-telling of Jane Austen's EMMA

by Joan Ellen Delman

ISBN : 978-0-6151-5005-5

**A Jane Austen Sequels book**

www.JaneAustenSequels.com

Acknowledgements:

I am grateful to the many individuals and organizations—too numerous to list here—whose internet sites on various aspects of British history and geography have provided me with so much useful information; and to the many authors whose books have been likewise valuable. I would particularly like to thank the gracious moderators at the Republic of Pemberley website, for all the time and energy they devote to providing an informative, stimulating and civil venue for the discussion of Jane Austen and her work. Special thanks to Kathleen, Jenny, and Linda for their prepublication critiques. Warmest thanks again to the delightful Ariel of arielcollage.com for much encouragement and support; and my deep appreciation to Edith Delman for financial assistance, and to Bob & Ellen O'Brien, Deborah Malcarne, Barbara Sandford, and Edith Delman for providing house space over the years when it was desperately needed.

# Lovers' Perjuries

## Part One

**"Jupiter from on high laughs at lovers' perjuries."**
**(Ovid)**

## Song

Love still has something of the sea
From whence his mother rose;
No time his slaves from doubt can free,
Nor give their thoughts repose.

They are becalmed in clearest days,
And in rough weather tost;
They wither under cold delays,
Or are in tempests lost.

One while they seem to touch the port,
Then straight into the main,
Some angry wind in cruel sport
The vessel drives again.

At first disdain and pride they fear,
Which if they chance to 'scape,
Rivals and falsehood soon appear
In a more dreadful shape.

By such degrees to joy they come,
And are so long withstood,
So slowly they receive the sum,
It hardly does them good.

'Tis cruel to prolong a pain,
And to defer a joy,
Believe me, gentle Celimene,
Offends the wingéd boy.

An hundred thousand oaths your fears
Perhaps would not remove;
And if I gazed a thousand years
I could no deeper love.

Sir Charles Sedley, 1639?—1701

# Chapter One

**JANE FAIRFAX WAS** born out of the short-lived union of a worthy if impoverished Lieutenant of the infantry, and a beautiful young lady of good family and no fortune. The couple enjoyed but a brief interval of conjugal bliss before the valiant officer met his end on the battlefield; the grieving widow followed him from this world within a twelvemonth. Thus at the tender age of three was Jane Fairfax made a helpless orphan, and left to the guardianship of her grandmother, Mrs. Bates, of Highbury.

To the detriment of the child's future career as a heroine, Mrs. Bates was neither a termagant nor a tippler; nor did Miss Bates, the old woman's spinster daughter, ever beat her niece, or lock her up in a cupboard. Though their pecuniary resources were narrow, and their intellectual resources scarcely less so, Jane's grandmother and aunt were thoroughly cheerful and good-natured; and from both ladies, it must be owned, the child received only such gratifications as constant affection and a meagre income could furnish. With these awful impediments in her path, little Jane soon bid fair to achieve no more distinguished a character than what a pleasing person, good understanding, and warm-hearted, well-meaning relations could engender. She was growing to be, in other words, a sweet, pretty, unexceptionable, and unexceptional girl.

An early change of circumstance, however, opened new prospects. A Colonel Campbell, under whom Jane's father had served in Spain, and whose life the young officer had once taken considerable pains to save, retired from the army; and upon returning home, he sought to repay his obligation to the Lieutenant by taking some notice of his unhappy orphan. The Colonel was married and had one child, a daughter very near Jane in age. He invited Jane to his London home for a visit of some length; and so well and

so quickly did little Miss Fairfax recommend herself to the
Colonel and all his family, that in short order they discovered her society to be indispensable to their happiness.
Before she was nine years old, she was already Colonel
Campbell's pet, Mrs. Campbell's darling, and Miss Campbell's bosom friend. Good Mrs. Bates was therefore
approached with a proposition: if she would allow her
granddaughter to make a home with the Campbells, the
Colonel would undertake to be wholly responsible for her
education and maintenance. Mrs. Bates, though far from
acute, could not but recognise the advantages to her ward
of such an arrangement. She willingly committed Jane into
the custody of Colonel and Mrs. Campbell, only reserving to
herself a little private sorrow for the loss of her dear girl.

As the years passed, Jane's connection with the Campbells afforded her little of real benefit; nothing, indeed,
beyond superior instruction, improved understanding,
broader experience, and more well-informed companions
than she would otherwise have been able to claim. It would
have been more profitable by far, had Colonel Campbell
been possessed of a desolated castle in the Pyrenees, or a
lunatic wife hid in the attic; but alas! he had neither. Moreover, Colonel and Mrs. Campbell were people of solid
judgement and sound principles. They permitted the two
girls to read, for diversion, only those novels which might
impart to their youthful minds some uplifting moral lessons. As a result, both Miss Campbell and Miss Fairfax
grew to womanhood as little given to indulge in sentimental
fancies as it was possible for any two young ladies to be.
Where they might have spent many delightful hours weeping over Mrs. Radcliffe's *Mysteries of Udolpho*, for example,
they instead applied themselves to the study of music and
drawing (subjects, it must be granted, not in themselves
despicable; for by such accomplishments many a heroine
has evinced a deep and estimable sensibility). And where
they might have passed a pleasant week sighing over *The
Miraculous Nuptials*, they instead memorised extracts from
Sherlock's *Sermons*. Very indifferent heroines, both—it cannot be denied.

In spite of this deficiency, Helen Campbell had recently
shown some promise of fulfilling a heroine's destiny, by falling in love. It was, however, an unprosperous affair. Her
beloved, Mr. Edward Dixon, was neither a gamester, a
drunkard, nor a seducer. He was not even a poet given to

interesting fits of melancholia. He was only a respectable and amiable gentleman, with an unencumbered estate in Ireland, and a comfortable competence of two thousand pounds per annum. Miss Campbell's parents, on being solicited for their approval of the match, did not compel their daughter to marry an elderly and debauched earl instead; nor did they spirit her away, under cover of darkness, to be shut up in a French convent; but rather, having already formed a high estimation of Mr. Dixon's character over a several months' intimacy, gave their consent to the engagement without making the smallest difficulty as to jointures or settlements—thereby extinguishing all of Miss Campbell's pretensions to the elevated status of heroine.

But a heroine we must have; so the task of attaining to such heights falls to Miss Fairfax. And a daunting task it is, in light of her guardians' unconscionable kindness and generosity; for in every particular save one, and in defiance of all established custom, the Campbells persist in treating their ward almost as a child of their own. That single point of deviation, however, is a material one. The Colonel's fortune (about twelve thousand pounds) can secure an adequate portion only to his daughter, and not to her friend. Fittingly, it is on that precise point of disparity that all Jane Fairfax's chance of future glory rests. By it, she is marked out for a heroine's portion of suffering, degradation, and self-immolation. In effect, she is destined to become—*a governess.*

Some of my readers, comfortably seated on well-padded sofas, enjoying the warmth of well-fed hearthfires, and sipping cups of well-sweetened tea, may at this moment be formulating in their heads a little witticism or two on the subject of governesses—doubting, perhaps, that their duties can be quite so arduous, or their positions so demeaning, as I have presumed to represent. I can only suppose such readers have never been obliged to expend their energies in the care, control, and instruction of other people's children—perhaps not even their own; and I can assure them the exertion required to discharge such duties creditably is so great, as to render the profession exceedingly disagreeable to those whom fortune has denied any other respectable means of subsistence.

But as our story begins, the time of Jane's servitude is not yet arrived. The Campbells have postponed the business again and again. More than once have they declared her too young, her health too delicate. With the forbearance of a true heroine, Jane submits to their present judgement; but she is firmly resolved to begin her new life upon entering her majority, and to this resolution the Campbells reluctantly consent. In the meantime, however, they claim the privilege of doing all that lies within their power, to fortify her for the rigours of her destiny.

# Chapter Two

**IT WAS COLONEL** Campbell's habit, during the summer months, to remove with his family from London, and make a visit of some length in a quieter corner of the kingdom. This year the seaside village of Weymouth had been chosen, ostensibly to try what sea-bathing might do for the Colonel, who was growing a little deaf; but also in hope of his ward deriving some benefit from the bracing sea air—for Jane, since childhood, had exhibited a recurring weakness of the lungs which, though far from dangerous, was now and then a matter of some little apprehension to her friends.

On arriving at Weymouth, the family took up residence in a small but well-appointed row-house. The house was admirably situated within a short walk to the sea, yet sufficiently removed from its influence to lessen the adverse effects of the strong maritime winds, against which Mr. Wingfield, their London apothecary, had cautioned them. The Colonel felt some misgivings in taking the place, lest his wife and daughter should find it altogether too cramped for comfort. But Mrs. Campbell, aware there was nothing more eligible to be had on short notice, made light of any possible inconveniences, saying she was sure they should be out of doors so much as to make any little crowding a matter of indifference; and Miss Campbell declared it was all part of the fun of being from home to be squeezed together into as small a space as possible. Mr. Dixon, having neither obligation to compel nor inclination to endure a separation from Miss Campbell, elected to join the family on their holiday, and installed himself in lodgings at a nearby hotel.

On the very morning after their coming to Weymouth, the three ladies walked out early to the strand, each to take a turn at braving the swelling breakers in one of the many bathing machines standing at the water's edge. By the end of their first week in Dorset, the entire party had already tasted all the sweets which a seaside holiday can offer. They strolled daily along the Esplanade; had visited both the assembly and concert rooms; and determined which among the various shops and coffee houses would be accorded the honour of their patronage. Harvey's Library was an establishment particularly favoured by all. Within its elegant walls, Colonel Campbell could peruse the London newspapers, and study all the significant new political tracts; Mrs. Campbell could read the latest issue of the *Review* or the *Quarterly*; and the young people could divert themselves with narratives of history and travel, or leaf through volumes of poetry and novels just published.

One day, soon after their arrival in Weymouth, Jane and Miss Campbell walked along the Esplanade with Mr. Dixon, who was speaking to them of the countryside around his home, Baly-craig, in Ireland. Though he had often entertained them in a like manner, it was a subject upon which he spoke so well, and with so much warmth, that they never heard him without interest; and as he talked now of the Wicklow Mountains, with their wild hills, heathered moors and wooded valleys, Miss Campbell felt a prodigious longing to see the beauties of a land which, in a few months time, would become her home. They had previously seen some sketches of the county, taken by Mr. Dixon himself; however, Mr. Dixon had little genius for sketching, and his renderings could convey but a vague idea of the region's grandeur. Miss Campbell, therefore, now decided they should step into Harvey's library, in hope of discovering some folio of engravings which might satisfy her curiosity.

The irony of seeking the scenic splendour of a far-off land on the ill-lit shelves of a dusty bookseller's shop, rather than remaining outdoors to enjoy the splendour near at hand, was not lost on Jane. But she was in the habit of submitting herself to Helen's wishes, which were sometimes whimsical, but never disagreeable; nor would she dream of teasing her friend about a curiosity so very natural and reasonable as that she was now expressing. So she offered no objection, and a few minutes later found herself entering Harvey's.

While the other two were engaged in their search, Jane wandered away to inspect an assortment of poetry books shelved in an adjacent corner. Absorbed in surveying the orderly volumes, she paid little heed to a gentleman who stood nearby, until he gradually made his way almost to her side, apparently intent upon the same titles she was examining herself.

Reaching simultaneously for the very same book, they exchanged embarrassed smiles; and "Excuse me," and "I beg your pardon," were politely uttered. The gentleman, in a chivalrous gesture, handed her the book, and with a slight bow and another quite disarming smile, discreetly removed himself to a little distance.

Jane could hardly fail to observe that he was a more than tolerably good-looking young man. But she also could not converse with one so wholly unknown to her, and was careful to take no further notice of him. Besides, her attention was soon claimed by her friends.

"Dear Jane—do come here and look," Miss Campbell called out. "Ned has found just what we wanted!"

"I think, Miss Fairfax, you will find these pictures quite striking," added Mr. Dixon as she hastened to join them.

Mr. Dixon held the large volume (*Picturesque Views of the Antiquities of Ireland*) open, and began pointing out to her some of the features of the scene portrayed in the first plate. It was a ruined abbey, one of many which may be found scattered all about the Irish countryside; but Jane had time only for a brief glance at its gothic towers, before her attention was drawn away again.

"I beg your pardon for intruding," an eager voice broke in. "I know I am taking a great liberty, but I could not help overhearing. Is it possible—do I have the honour of addressing Miss Fairfax, of Highbury? Granddaughter of Mrs. Bates, and niece of Miss Bates?"

Jane had turned at the initial words and, on doing so, was astonished to see the young man she had encountered a few moments earlier.

"Do you know my relations, sir?" she asked.

"By report only, I regret to say. But what a blockhead I am—I have not introduced myself! I am Frank Churchill; I believe you know my father, Mr. Weston. Perhaps he has mentioned my name to you?"

"Mentioned!" she exclaimed with delight. "You may be sure, sir, that the name of Mr. Frank Churchill is well known in Highbury. By my aunt Hetty's account, Mr. Weston, whenever he returns from seeing you in London, talks of little else for weeks afterwards; and as everyone in Highbury is so very fond of your father, the entire town looks upon you quite as one of their own—without having so much as laid eyes upon you these twenty years. Indeed, when it becomes known that I have had the good fortune to meet you, I have no doubt I shall be the envy of the whole neighbourhood!"

She paused, amazed at her own flow of spirits. Why, an impartial observer might almost accuse her of *flirting* with Mr. Frank Churchill! Mr. Churchill, however, made no accusations.

"I fear, Miss Fairfax," he said with a grin, "that your Highbury acquaintance will more likely hold your present good fortune uncommonly cheap; and with some cause, too, for I have thus far exhibited the most shameful indifference toward Highbury and all its inhabitants—though unwillingly, I assure you," he added. "But then, perhaps it is that very indifference to which I am indebted for my celebrity. I am at present an exotic—a bird from the remotest jungles of the New World. Let me but once be heard to have been physicked by Mr. Perry, or to have taken a bowl of gruel with Mr. Woodhouse; or, better still, be seen buying a pair of gloves at Ford's—and doubtless I should soon enjoy all the neglect accorded any other prosaic English sparrow."

She laughed. "So Highbury is slighted as a matter of policy. But are you quite sure you have never been there, Mr. Churchill? You seem to know it so well, I should have guessed you had lived there all your life."

"I know of Highbury only what my father tells me—which is a great deal indeed. I shall be very discreet, however," (with a mischievous gleam in his eye), "and forbear to repeat the many words of praise he has bestowed upon a certain young lady of his acquaintance. But," said he more seriously, suddenly mindful of Miss Campbell and Mr. Dixon, who were observing their exchange with some interest, "I must apologise. I am keeping you from your friends."

Jane performed the necessary introductions with a becoming flush. She then found herself at leisure to study Mr. Churchill, as he turned his attention to Miss Campbell and Mr. Dixon: telling Helen he had had the pleasure of meeting her parents on a few occasions in town; then asking them both how they liked Weymouth, whether they had much acquaintance there, and other questions such as belong to an opening acquaintance.

Jane had long been familiar with Frank Churchill's history. His father, Mr. Weston, was the eldest son of a respectable family. Lively and outgoing by nature, as a young man Mr. Weston had chosen to enter the militia, pre-

ferring an active profession to the more sedentary employ-
ments in which his brothers were engaged. Captain Weston
was a general favourite; and when Miss Churchill, of a great
Yorkshire family, fell in love with him, nobody was surprised except her brother and his wife, who had never seen
him, and who were full of pride and importance which the
connection would offend. Miss Churchill, with ten thousand
pounds at her own disposal, declared she would marry
whom she pleased; and the Churchills threw her off with
due decorum.

To Mrs. Weston the marriage was little worth the enmity
it engendered. Well might she complain of such a husband,
for his faults were grievous indeed: after the vows were
taken he proved, quite unaccountably, as good-natured,
generous, and affectionate as he had seemed during the period of courtship. Had he but lost all her money at cards, or
beat her senseless three times a day, no doubt the lady
would have doted upon her husband most tenderly. As it
was, she could not content herself with the lot she had chosen. Her ten thousand pounds, wedded to Captain Weston's
modest fortune, were inadequate to her notions of comfort.
Even as the couple lived beyond their income, she repented
and repined; and, after three years of matrimony, she died
of a lingering illness, leaving her bereaved husband with an
infant son to provide for, and somewhat diminished means
from which to provide.

Shortly before her death, however, a tentative reconciliation had taken place between Mrs. Weston and her haughty
relations. Her brother, in particular, had been much softened by the idea of the imminent loss of his only sister;
and after her death, the childless Mr. and Mrs. Churchill offered to adopt the little boy Frank as his uncle's heir. Some
perseverance was necessary—and more delicacy than was
commonly employed by the Churchills—to persuade Mr.
Weston to submit to their proposal. But the Churchills were
a family accustomed to getting their way, and Mr. Weston a
gentleman accustomed to yielding. In the end, Frank was
delivered up to Enscombe, the Churchills' estate in Yorkshire, and Mr. Weston turned his energies to repairing his
dwindling fortune. He saw Frank every year in London, and
was on each occasion pleased afresh to find him untainted
by the detestable Churchill pride. Indeed, Mr. Weston was
delighted with the fine young man his son had become.

Mr. Frank Churchill, today, was a very gentlemanlike

man of three-and-twenty. His face was not, perhaps, mod-
elled on the classical ideal; but its features were assembled
into an appealing whole, with lively, laughing eyes, and a
thoroughly bewitching smile. His person was very good, being neither too short nor too tall, and neither thin nor stout,
but with every part in excellent proportion to the others,
and forming all together a figure both manly and elegant.
His manners, too, were nearly perfect; for he possessed a
natural, well-bred ease which could scarcely fail of pleasing.
More importantly, his character, though not without flaw,
was infinitely better than the deficiencies of his education
might have given anyone reason to expect.

He was stopping in Weymouth with his aunt and uncle,
who had taken a fashionable house along the Esplanade,
with a sweeping view of the sea. They had made the journey
to Weymouth so that Mrs. Churchill, who was of a sickly
constitution, could try what sea air and salt water might do
for her health.

"We have not been here two days," he now explained to
his three companions, "but how long we shall remain is difficult to say. If my aunt finds sea-bathing of benefit (as I
certainly hope she may), we might stay till Michaelmas, or
even longer. Then again, if her complaints should worsen,
we might be off in a week. Our plans are quite indefinite."

"With the threat of a sudden departure hanging over you,
Mr. Churchill," said Helen, "I am amazed at your sacrificing
even part of an afternoon indoors, when you might be out
walking along the strand, gazing at the sea, and contemplating the sublimity of nature."

"Yes," said Mr. Dixon, laughing. "Only those of us so fortunate as to be sure our visit will be a long one, may enjoy
the privilege of slighting such attractions for an hour or
two."

"In truth," Mr. Churchill explained, "I stepped in here just
for a moment, in hopes of finding something to read in the
evening—even a circulating library has its attractions, you
know. And excepting the stars," he added with a grin at
Jane, "one may see very little of nature's sublimity after
dark."

"Your devotion to literature is commendable," said Miss
Campbell, understanding him only in part. "Still, you need
not sequester yourself with a book every night, I hope.
Weymouth is not London, certainly, but even Weymouth
has its share of evening entertainments to offer. Tonight, for

instance, there will be a ball at the assembly rooms. Might we hope to see you there?"

"I cannot answer with any assurance, as I do not know what my aunt's intentions may be. But I will come if I can, for I own there are few enjoyments more to my liking than dancing—"

Here he was checked by the sight of a servant coming towards them in great haste. Excusing himself for a moment, he went off to speak to the man. When he returned, he said with evident disappointment, "I may as well offer my regrets to you now. I fear there is very little chance of my having the happiness of seeing you all this evening. My aunt is taken ill, and I must go to her at once. I am sorry indeed."

"No apology is necessary," said Mr. Dixon. "Of course you must be with your aunt if she is unwell. And if you should find her enough improved by this evening—"

"It is most unlikely, I'm afraid."

"But we may hope for the best," said Helen. "And even if you cannot come tonight, we are certain to meet again sometime or other. Indeed, as my parents are not entirely unknown to you—may I be so bold as to ask you to take a family dinner with us at our house, on any evening you should find yourself at liberty? My mother and father would be pleased to see you, I'm sure."

Frank brightened at the invitation, and expressed his gratitude for her kindness very warmly. After accepting their wishes for Mrs. Churchill's speedy recovery, he took his leave, and departed with the servant.

"What an amiable gentleman!" Miss Campbell exclaimed after he had gone. "Did not you think so, Ned?"

"He seemed an agreeable fellow," said Mr. Dixon.

"Of course," Jane remarked, "we really know little of his character."

"But he reads a great deal, apparently," said Miss Campbell, "which suggests a mind not unaccustomed to serious reflection. And you know his father, Jane; is not his father a very respectable person? For as the twig is bent, they say, so is the tree inclined."

"Mr. Weston is very respectable indeed; but Mr. Churchill was not raised by him."

Briefly, she related Frank Churchill's history. His being taken from his father at such a young age made him an object of sympathy to Miss Campbell; while Mr. Dixon declared that the acquaintance of such a pleasant, gentlemanlike person, in such a place as Weymouth, must be deemed worth having—unless and until they knew some actual harm of him. The ladies could not disagree; and after Miss Campbell's stating once more that she hoped they would see him again soon, the subject of Mr. Frank Churchill seemed all but forgotten in the bustle of collecting and paying for the books they had chosen.

It was a subject which Jane, however, could not long forget. They left Harvey's shop and, returning to the Esplanade, seated themselves on a bench overlooking the sea. Gazing quietly on the lovely scene before her, she marvelled anew at the freedom with which she had addressed Mr. Churchill. But he was not really a stranger, she told herself. He was dear Mr. Weston's son; and she had known him, or at least, known *of* him, for many years.

Miss Jane Fairfax, as has been previously stated, was an exceedingly rational female, very little inclined to divert herself with romantic dreams or idle fancies. But it must be confessed that Mr. Frank Churchill had, for a long time, occupied a special place in her imagination; she regarded him somewhat as a kindred spirit. Like her, he had been orphaned, or nearly so, at a very early age, and raised far from his native home. Though he did have one parent still living, he was, like her, dependent on strangers. So there were points of striking similarity in their past and present, if not in their future circumstances—for Frank Churchill was his uncle's heir, and would one day be very rich. With material prospects so much more promising than her own, Jane could only hope he had been no less fortunate in the *character* of his guardians than she was in hers; but she feared it was not so. She had often heard from her aunt Hetty that Mrs. Churchill was a proud, overbearing, disagreeable woman, who ruled Enscombe, and everyone in it, with an iron will.

# Chapter Three

**FRANK CHURCHILL HAD** often regretted that his aunt's habit of commanding his time and attendance prevented his ever visiting his father in Highbury. As we have seen, however, the inhabitants of that village were well known to him by report; and he had often heard, from Mr. Weston's lips, the name of Jane Fairfax.

Though a tolerably sensible man, Mr. Weston was a generous judge of people. He liked almost everyone, and spoke with approbation of all his neighbours. Frank nonetheless supposed there must be at least a few among them not entirely agreeable; and he could not consider his father's representations with perfect confidence, though his curiosity was piqued by some of them. There was a Miss Taylor, for instance—a middle-aged spinster, of whom Mr. Weston spoke so often, and with such warmth, that Frank had begun to suspect some partiality in that quarter. There was also a Miss Woodhouse whom he praised very highly, and mentioned particularly as a desirable acquaintance for his son. She sounded like a lively girl, full of fun and high spirits, and Frank felt a strong inclination to meet her. But the sound of "Emma Woodhouse" had never held for him a fraction of the poetry contained in that simple name, *Jane Fairfax.*

He could not have fixed upon the exact moment when he first became aware of the peculiar magic in that name; but it had long exemplified to his mind every perfection of womanly grace. Miss Fairfax's beauty, her gentle goodness, her many accomplishments, he had been hearing of with growing interest for years. He had for some time wished to know this paragon, and on a few occasions he had been so fortunate as to meet her guardians, though unaccompanied by their ward; but he had been unable to further the acquaintance. The Churchills and Campbells did not travel in the same circles. Colonel Campbell's friendships were mostly those formed during his years in the army, and Mrs. Churchill had a low opinion of military men—did not like them as a class. Men of no birth or breeding, she was wont to complain, were forever being passed off as gentlemen merely by means of a *Colonel* or *Admiral* affixed to their names; and she avoided such upstarts whenever possible. Still, Frank hoped he might sometime see Miss Fairfax at the theatre, or the opera, or another public place. But their paths never crossed; and she had remained until now but a dream, a vision to animate his idle moments.

This first interview with the real Miss Fairfax had done nothing to dispel the ideal on which his mind had long dwelt. The deep grey eyes, with their dark lashes and brows—the delicate, clear skin—soft, well-modulated voice—graceful carriage—air and address—all were calculated, he felt, to inspire the strongest attachment. Why, he believed he was half in love with her already! Mr. Weston's accounts had fostered in him but one small apprehension, that he might find her reserved; and reserve was a serious flaw indeed to a young man like Frank Churchill, whose own temper was naturally open and ardent. His father had often used the word 'elegant' to describe her. Elegant! What a cold, formal word, for such warm, such womanly beauty. Reserved! She was not in the least reserved; and her unreserve was the sweeter to him, because he imagined it (however fancifully) to spring from a feeling within her—a presentiment, perhaps, not unlike his own—that some mysterious working of fate had predestined them for one another.

Such were Frank's musings as he entered his uncle's house, where he found Mrs. Churchill reclined on a damask sofa with her eyes closed, apparently asleep. Turning cautiously, he attempted to retreat without making any sound; but a floorboard creaked beneath his feet, and she called out sharply,

"Frank! Is it you? Are you come back at last?"

"I hope I did not wake you, ma'am."

"I was not sleeping; I am too ill to sleep. What can have kept you out all this time? It seems hours since I sent that dawdler off to look for you."

"I was only at the bookshop; but I would have returned sooner had I known you wanted me. I'm sorry to find you are feeling no better."

"Hmmph. It was that footman's fault, of course. He took his own time—no doubt stopping to dally with every pink-cheeked shop girl along the way. He is an idle, good-for-nothing fellow, like all of them. I would have sent Dobbs after you, but she was already gone out for me on another errand."

"My dear aunt, I am sure he came as quickly as he could," Frank contradicted her gently. "After all, he had no way of knowing where to find me."

"And you must remember, Frank, when you go out, to tell me where you are going—else how *will* anyone be able to find you if you are needed? Goodness knows I have tried never to let my ill-health interfere with your pleasures, any more than was necessary. But really, in my present state, there is no telling—. Besides, had I known you were going to the library, you might have brought me back something to read. There is little enough I can do to amuse myself in this condition."

"If you wish, ma'am, I should be happy to step out again at once, and bring back whatever you like. I am at your disposal."

Somewhat mollified, she replied, "Well, not just now. I really am not equal even to reading just now. But do sit by me, Frank, and talk to me. The sound of your voice is restful to me."

"I have a volume of Shakespeare in my room. Shall I fetch it and read to you?"

"Shakespeare? I don't think—. Oh, very well. I don't much care for Shakespeare, you know; but I suppose it makes little difference. Perhaps it may distract my mind a little."

He expressed a fervent hope that she would find it so, and hurried off to retrieve the desired book from his bed-chamber.

**JANE AND** Helen returned home to find that visitors had called in their absence. A son of the late Major Devere, who for years had been an intimate friend of Colonel Campbell's, had lately obtained the preferment of St. Alban's Church in Weymouth, and now resided there along with his sister. Miss Devere had lived with her brother and managed his household ever since the Major's death some five or six years earlier. Upon being informed of the Campbells' visit to Weymouth, the Deveres lost no time in paying their respects to their father's old friend, and were consequently seated in the parlour with the Colonel and his wife when Jane and Helen came back from the bookshop that morning.

Stephen Devere was thirty, and handsome. Margaret Devere was two or three years older; and though by custom spinsters ought to be plain, and either foolish or ill-tempered, Miss Devere was even handsomer than her brother, and was, besides, good-humoured and rational. Jane had never seen the lady before, but Mr. Devere she had met once previously: just after taking orders, he had stopped briefly with the Campbells in London before making the journey northward to begin his curacy. He was then a sober young man of three-and-twenty; she a girl of fourteen, and shy of strangers. At that time, she had hardly looked at him at all, and had made but a slight impression on *his* mind. On this second meeting, however, she looked enough to find him a civil, quiet-spoken gentleman; and he was quite forcibly struck by her beauty.

It happens Colonel Campbell had for many years har-boured a little private hope that a match might someday be arranged between his daughter and Mr. Devere. Major Devere had been a valued friend, and Colonel Campbell held his son in high esteem. Such a marriage could not be thought of, however, until Stephen, a younger son with his fortune to make, should have some prospect beyond the meagre income of a curacy in a remote part of the country. Moreover, there had been no opportunity for the young people to form any sort of attachment; and before the Colonel's favourite scheme could come to fruition, Helen had fallen in love with Edward Dixon. With few regrets (for Mr. Dixon was a man of solid merit, and, in a prudential light, by far the better match), the scheme had been given up.

Observing Mr. Devere now, as he addressed a remark to Jane Fairfax, the Colonel noted a pleasing congruity be-tween the handsomeness of the one, and the beauty of the other; and a new scheme, perhaps even surpassing the original, began to suggest itself to his mind. He could not but be aware that Jane's only chance of escaping the life of toil and mortification which lay before her, was to marry. Now, the living of St. Alban's, he had already learned from Mr. Devere, was a comfortable one; comfortable enough, certainly, for a young man to marry upon. And while the income it provided would perhaps be something less than Miss Campbell With Twelve Thousand Pounds might be considered entitled to, it would be great wealth, indeed, to Miss Fairfax With Nothing.

Colonel Campbell, however, had no taste for matchmaking. He was neither so arrogant, nor so foolhardy, as to attempt to control the destiny of his fellow human beings. It was enough to have formed such a plan in his own head, and to know that present circumstances would afford every occasion for the gentleman and lady to come to an understanding—to the mutual happiness, he hoped, of both.

# Chapter Four

**IT IS A GRAVE** misfortune for any young lady to enter a ballroom without having previously secured at least one dancing partner. Thus it was with no small satisfaction that Jane indulged the wishes of Mr. Devere, before he and his sister concluded their morning visit, by promising him the first two dances of the assembly. Since the Campbells had at present little acquaintance in Weymouth, she was pleased to be certain even of that solitary partner. Of course, Mr. Dixon could always be relied upon to save two dances for her. And she entertained a small hope that, should Frank Churchill somehow find himself able to attend the ball (though, she reminded herself, that was not very likely), she might have a third partner as well.

They met with Mr. Devere and his sister just as the lines were forming for the first dance, and Mr. Devere promptly took possession of his prize. What conversation the two had, as they moved across the floor, was supplied chiefly by Jane's exertions. The gentleman spoke little, but whether out of diffidence or reserve, she could scarcely guess. Perhaps, she conjectured, he kept all his eloquence for the pulpit. His dancing was good, however, if a trifle solemn, and gave her no cause to despise him as a partner.

"Your family home is in Derbyshire, I understand?" she asked him, when the movements of the dance permitted.

"Yes—near Bakewell."

"I have never been to Derbyshire, but I have heard much of its beauties."

"I have always thought it a fine country," he admitted.

After another interval: "Miss Campbell tells me she visited your home with her parents when she was a little girl, and that you took a great deal of trouble upon yourself, to keep her agreeably occupied during their stay."

"Oh, no. Not at all. I was home from school on holiday, you know, and had nothing else to do."

She could think of nothing more to say, and they continued in silence for some time. During one pause late in the dance, she thought to inquire how he had obtained the preferment of St. Alban's church; and here she was better rewarded for her efforts.

"The living of St. Alban's," he explained, "is in the gift of Lord Paget—whose great ancestral estate (as perhaps you are aware) lies just outside Weymouth. During my curacy in the village of Beckford, in Northumberland, I was so fortunate as to became acquainted with a very old friend of his lordship's, Mr. Reed. Mr. Reed is master of a boy's school in Beckford—an excellent man, Miss Fairfax; very good to the poor, and much beloved by his pupils. When the rector of St. Alban's passed away last year, Lord Paget wrote Mr. Reed to ask if he knew of any deserving clergyman to whom he might offer the benefice; and my kind friend recommended me to his notice."

"And do you find your present patron to be as good a man as his friend?"

He weighed his words before answering. "Unhappily, Lord Paget has been confined to his bed for some months past, and so is unable to take any active part in the affairs of the church. Lady Paget, however, has been very generous with her time, and with her—counsel."

There was that in his tone which led Jane to suspect Lady Paget's counsel was not always perfectly agreeable to him—but of course he could not be expected to say so; and the dance came to an end without his saying anything else at all. With Helen and Mr. Dixon, they returned to the others. The gentlemen were then dispatched to procure refreshments; and while Mrs. Campbell and her daughter went off to repair a small tear in Helen's gown, Jane had a brief *tête-à-tête* with Miss Devere.

"I hope you are pleased with my brother's dancing, Miss Fairfax," said that lady with a smile.

"Yes, indeed."

"It will shock you to learn that I have found him acceptable as a partner myself, on occasion; for I prefer even the disgrace of standing up with my own brother, to the horror I have just endured, of sitting down in company with all the other old maids. Though I am past the age of hope, you see, I am not yet so antiquated as to be beyond the enjoyment of dancing."

"You will forgive me, Miss Devere," said Jane with an answering smile, "if I say how very unlikely I think it that you could have any difficulty in procuring a partner if you wished to dance. Indeed, I can only assume you have rejected all such applications this evening, to afford yourself the pleasure of sitting and talking with Colonel and Mrs. Campbell."

She laughed. "The rector's spinster sister, repulsing an army of importunate beaux! What a charming picture you paint! But I must conclude you know very little of the world, Miss Fairfax, if you can really suppose it to compass such an impossibility."

Before Jane could offer any reply, the gentlemen returned, bearing cups of negus; and Miss Devere turned playfully to her brother, saying,

"You have been gone long enough, Stephen; and I daresay Miss Fairfax will refuse to stand up with you again, for in your absence I have had a chance to tell her all your secrets."

"You do not frighten me, Margaret," he said quietly, but with a smile. "First, because I know you are not serious; and second, because I have no secrets to tell."

"Then you would do better to pretend you had—or Miss Fairfax, instead of thinking you a scoundrel, will think you only very dull."

Miss Fairfax protested that she thought him neither.

"You must not mind what my sister says, Miss Fairfax," said Mr. Devere, "as you can see I do not. 'Tis only that she takes great delight in plaguing me."

"I hold it a sister's duty to plague her brother, that he may not be thrown into a perplexity when later he finds himself plagued with a wife."

"If that is your design, Margaret, you may save yourself the trouble. I have no intention of taking a wife who will plague me."

"Nor does any man, when he is a bachelor. But you have only to look about amongst your acquaintance, to see that nine husbands out of ten are plagued all the same."

"You are too severe upon your sex, Margaret," said Colonel Campbell, as his own wife and daughter rejoined the party.

"And we can have no better proof," said Mr. Devere, "than the example immediately before us: I am sure Mrs. Campbell is an excellent wife, and has never given her husband a moment's pain."

Mrs. Campbell put her arm through her husband's and

looked up at him with an affectionate smile. "I am sure my husband has never given me the slightest cause to pain him."

Miss Devere submitted cheerfully. "How very unlucky for me, that we should happen to have at hand one of the few truly happy couples in all of England! I shall therefore leave off being satirical, until I find myself in company more favourable to the exercise of my wit."

The musicians were starting up again. Mr. Devere requested a dance of Miss Campbell, and Mr. Dixon asked Miss Devere, leaving Jane without any partner. Still a little fatigued from her earlier exertions, however, she sat quietly beside Mrs. Campbell, sipping her lemonade with every semblance of bearing this great indignity with perfect composure.

It was impossible, however, that she should find herself amid so gay and animated a scene, without feeling a little disappointed by the absence of Mr. Churchill. As she sat wondering whether he might not yet make his appearance, her gaze turned unconsciously to the doors; and to her pleasure, she saw Frank Churchill himself walking towards her. After presenting him to her guardians, she inquired after Mrs. Churchill, hoping that his presence at the ball signified an improvement in her condition.

"Thank you, Miss Fairfax," said he, "my aunt was feeling rather better before dinner. Unfortunately she was so much worse afterwards as to find it necessary to send for a physician. He prescribed laudanum, which she has often taken before—and which always results in such a prolonged and heavy slumber, that I felt myself justified in leaving her to my uncle's care for the evening."

She wondered at this seeming insensibility toward the suffering of his aunt; but remembering what she had heard, both from her own aunt, and from Mr. Weston, about Mrs. Churchill's illnesses, she was inclined to pardon him for that little, understandable selfishness; and to credit him with a great deal of amiability in being so very desirous of meeting with them again.

After these preliminaries were gone through, there was nothing else to be done but to join in the dance. No spot was to be found near her friends, but they readily found another set to accomodate them.

"Now, Miss Fairfax," he began as they worked their way up from the bottom of the line, "what shall we talk about?

Have you a favourite topic of discussion for dancing—or is your enjoyment of a ball so complete as to render all conversation unwelcome?"

She told him she had no objection to talking, provided she were not out of breath, and suggested, if a more compelling subject were lacking, they could always have recourse to the weather.

"The weather! Oh, no. I should then seem just as dull to you as every other tiresome wretch you have ever had the misery to stand up with. No, we must debate a question of some consequence; by which I may impress you with the depth of my understanding, the refinement of my taste, and the brilliance of my wit. And, I must not omit to include, a *most* endearing humility."

Laughing, she observed that, with such faculties at his command, he could hardly fail of making even so commonplace a topic as the weather tolerably entertaining.

There was a necessary pause in their speech as they went down the dance; after which Jane asked, "Would music suit you for a topic, Mr. Churchill?

"I would rather listen to music than talk of it. But I suppose we might try it as a subject, since I am too stupid to think of a better."

"You are fond of music, then?"

"I am very fond of music. I have always a very great pleasure in hearing good music well played—and even in singing myself, when the opportunity offers. Whether my audience receives a similar pleasure is open to some question, for my talent is hardly equal to my zeal. Coleridge's celebrated epigram applies, I think:

> Swans sing before they die—'twere no bad thing
> Did certain persons die before they sing.

"I need not ask, of course," he went on, "whether *you* are musical. My father has often told me of the great enjoyment he has in hearing you play, whenever you are in Highbury."

"Much of the credit for my performance rightly belongs to Colonel Campbell. It is thanks to his generosity that I have been so fortunate to receive instruction from the best masters."

"But even with the best masters, application is needed to excel; and it is in application that many fail, who might possess talents even comparable to your own, because they dislike the trouble of practising."

"Practice is more an indulgence than a trouble, with such advantages as I have enjoyed."

"You are determined to refuse all compliments, I see. Well, I shall cease tormenting you with them, at least until I have had the happiness of hearing you play myself—a happiness which I hope I may be admitted to very soon."

She gave only a smile in response, as the demands of the dance silenced them once more.

"Is this your first visit to the seaside, Miss Fairfax?" he queried when they could speak again.

"I hardly know what answer to make. I have visited the seaside on several occasions; yet on every visit it seems as if it were altogether new to me."

"You feel a considerable pleasure in the sight, then?"

"I do not think I could ever grow tired of it, if I were to gaze upon it every day of my life. Such a view as the sea provides! The shifting patterns of the waves, the beautiful permutations of light, the changing colours of water and sky—these are charms one can never have surfeit of."

Frank was in eager accord with her sentiments: he, too, felt a powerful attraction to the sea. "Indeed," said he, "I can think of no sight more animating—none more apt to inspire the strongest, and the deepest feelings, both of awe and delight."

His enthusiasm was rewarded with a warm smile. After another slight pause, he inquired, "And have you ever been in Yorkshire, Miss Fairfax?"

"Never in my life. What is it like?"

"You would be pleased, I think, by the wonderful diversity of places to be seen there: the medieval streets and great cathedral at York—the bay at Scarborough—the mills of Leeds and Sheffield—deep dales and sweeping moors—derelict castles and ruined abbeys—and thousands upon thousands of... sheep," he concluded with a grin.

"But what about your own corner of Yorkshire, Mr. Churchill? What is Enscombe like?"

"Enscombe is my home, and very dear to me. If I were to try and describe it to you, I fear I should give a too-partial account."

"I would prefer a too-partial account, to a cold, objective one."

"Then I will not hesitate to tell you that Enscombe is the fairest spot in all Creation. I am only afraid you will think ill of me, when I tell you I think it even more beautiful than Highbury. However, having never set foot in Highbury since I was three years old, I am reasonable enough to admit the possibility of error."

She laughed. "I commend your fair-mindedness, sir. But can you not offer a few more—particulars?"

"Very well, ma'am. Enscombe would, I believe, be reckoned a grand old manor by most people. The park is large, and the pleasure grounds extensive. There are lawns, and shrubberies, and shaded walks—a sizable wilderness with a stream running through it, and a fine wood adjacent. Some improvements were made in my grandfather's time, but only such as enhance the natural perfections of the place, without imparting any artificial appearance. The house is also very large; but the furnishings must be abused as old-fashioned, being in the style of an earlier age. My aunt has talked forever of having everything done over, and even went so far as to order new hangings for the drawing room a few years ago; but unfortunately, want of health has prevented her doing more."

"And does the neighbourhood afford you any agreeable society?" she asked.

"Its isolation, I am afraid, is Enscombe's great fault. There are few families within easy reach (few, at any rate, whom my aunt deems admissible as acquaintance)—and I rarely see anyone of my own age. In truth, it was I who urged my aunt and uncle to come to Weymouth this summer, partly for selfish reasons. We did not go to town last spring, and I confess I was heartily sick of seclusion."

"So for all your great love of home," she said with another smile, "you are not quite heartbroken to be away from it."

"At the present moment," said he, "I am wholly content to be exactly where I am."

Here the music ended. He thanked her for the dance with a low bow, and led her back to her friends.

The rest of the assembly passed very agreeably for Jane. At its close, Mrs. Campbell added to her pleasure—and did what she could to secure its continuance—by repeating her daughter's earlier invitation to Mr. Churchill, that he should take a family dinner with them some evening. She extended the same invitation to Mr. Devere and his sister. It was a proposal in which all three were most happy to acquiesce.

# Chapter Five

**JANE WAS NOT** so entirely taken up with idle pleasures on this holiday in Weymouth, as to be lost to all sense of duty. At the earliest opportunity she left her own elegant neighbourhood, to pay a call at a much humbler establishment, in a faded part of town. The person she sought there was the sister of an impoverished old widow, a certain Mrs. Gibbs of London, toward whom Jane had performed many small acts of charity over the years. On hearing that she would be travelling to Weymouth, Mrs. Gibbs had entreated Jane to do her the great favour of delivering a letter to her sister, Mrs. Nesbit, who lived in Weymouth, and was both poor and sickly. Jane assured Mrs. Gibbs she would be happy to perform the errand, and promised furthermore to provide the invalid with any assistance in her power.

The history of Mrs. Nesbit was an affecting one. Her husband had died soon after their marriage, leaving her a young and penniless widow. She had consequently supported herself for more than forty years as a governess. This last fact alone was enough to rouse Jane's curiosity and compassion towards her, given her own future connection with that profession. Moreover, Mrs. Nesbit's most recent employers had used her very unkindly. On a seaside holiday with the family the previous summer, the old governess had grown too ill to perform her duties; the Albrights had discharged her at once, and left her at Weymouth without even paying her last quarter's salary. It was therefore with no common degree of interest that Jane set forth to call on her.

She walked alone to the address Mrs. Gibbs had given her. In London, she rarely went out except in company with Helen and her mother, but it had always been her custom, when visiting her relations in Highbury, to take long rambles by herself; thus she entertained no fears of a solitary walk. The weather was fine, and, not wishing to neglect any opportunity to enjoy the beauty of the seaside, she took the long way round, by the water. Her senses were fully engaged by her surroundings as she walked: her eyes surveying the curling waves, shimmering in the sun, with great pleasure; her ears attuned to the rhythmic wash of the tide, and the mournful cries of the seabirds. *Why should they sound so sad,* she wondered, *when they can spend their lives in such a glorious place as this?* She breathed in the fresh sea air with a sense of exhilaration, and delighted to feel the cool southeasterly breeze stealing through her hair and playing over her cheeks.

At the boarding house, a slatternly, middle-aged woman answered her knock. After making an impertinent survey of Jane's attire, the woman took her up to the third floor, where she rapped sharply on a battered door.

"A lady to see you, Missus," she yelled, then flung the door open without waiting for a response. A moment later she disappeared down the stairs, leaving Jane standing alone at the threshhold.

The room she looked in on was small and cheerless, and at present unoccupied. No drapes covered the one window, whose panes were thick with many years' accumulation of dirt. The walls, too, were dirty—the paper peeling in spots—the furniture shabby. There was a second room, however; she shortly perceived some movement beyond a curtained doorway, and heard a frail voice call out, "Wait just a moment, if you please."

It was a little while before an elderly woman emerged from behind the threadbare curtain which, Jane assumed, concealed her bedchamber. She hobbled out with a laborious gait, leaning heavily on a roughhewn cane. Despite the dirt of her surroundings, her white hair was pinned back into a neat bun, and her wrinkled cheeks, though pale, had a well-scrubbed look. Her serviceable black gown was worn, but looked tolerably clean.

"Mrs. Nesbit?" Jane asked, still standing out in the dingy passageway.

The woman's face betrayed some astonishment at the elegance of her visitor. "Did you wish to speak to me, Miss? Please do come in—come in and sit down, my dear. I'm sorry to have kept you waiting."

Jane entered the room and, after helping Mrs. Nesbit into a chair, sat down in another. Briefly she stated the purpose of her visit, closing the explanation by taking Mrs. Gibbs's letter from her reticule.

Tears brimmed in the elderly woman's eyes as she held the letter with trembling hands. "God bless you, my dear!" she cried. "I've not seen nor heard from Sarah in a twelvemonth! Tell me, is she well?—for I cannot wait to know."

"Quite well, but very anxious about you. She expressed her concern to me one morning; and at her request I inquired after you in Conduit Street. Mrs. Albright's maid gave me a letter for Mrs. Gibbs, which you had entrusted to her before the family left Weymouth several months earlier. She had found no chance to deliver it, as the family came to London much later than usual this year—they had not been in town a week when I called."

"Ah! 'Tis no wonder, then, I've heard nothing before this. My dear, you have made an old lady very happy today. I shall be much easier now I know all is well with Sarah."

Pleased both with Mrs. Nesbit's appearance and her manner, Jane assured her she was delighted to be able to render any service either to Mrs. Gibbs or herself, and asked if there were not anything else she might do to augment her present comforts.

"I fear, Miss Fairfax, it is too much to ask," she answered diffidently, "but it would give me the greatest pleasure if you would call on me again. I am well aware this is hardly the sort of place—nor is a sick old woman the sort of company, to tempt an elegant young lady like yourself. But I have no friends in Weymouth, and, being ill, I am rarely able to leave this house; so you would be doing me a very great kindness if you would come only once in a while."

"I should be more than happy to come; but is there no other assistance I can offer of a more—practical nature? Is there any medical person attending you? And is your landlady providing you with such other services as you may require? Please forgive my presumption in asking; but I know a little of your circumstances, and I fear you have not the help which your fragile state of health demands."

Mrs. Nesbit thanked her warmly for her interest, but declared she was adequately provided for, and was in need of nothing so much as a little cheerful society. Jane doubted, but could not press her any further. She proceeded instead to engage her in friendly conversation, learning a great deal more about her life, and about the governess-trade.

At the outset, Jane mentioned her own intention of entering that profession; and it is possible Mrs. Nesbit may have thought it right, on that account, to soften or even to omit some of the trials she had encountered in it. At all events, she made few complaints. She had been very attached to her charges over the years, and generally treated kindly by their parents. Most painful, she said, was leaving the dear ones behind, when the time came to begin a new situation with a new family. She rarely saw the children again after leaving the household, and could only imagine her boys and girls grown into men and women, perhaps with children of their own. She could not defend the conduct of Mr. and Mrs. Albright; but the young ones, though a little spoilt, had been affectionate to her, and she had hopes they would turn out well in the end.

Everything the old woman said added to the general impression of her worthiness; and there was something in the poor invalid's neat white bun and pale blue eyes, even in her very voice and manner, which reminded Jane a little of her own dear grandmother. She left the house after more than an hour's time with a firm resolve to call on Mrs. Nesbit again soon.

# Chapter Six

**ON SUNDAY, JANE** and the Campells attended divine service at St. Alban's Church, where Mr. Devere gave a sermon on judgement. Though he spoke well, and with some authority, his preaching was of a type Jane did not admire very much. His pronouncements were stern; and he talked a good deal more of sin and punishment, than of forgiveness and redemption. He did, however, conclude the service with that familiar, if little heeded, text—*Judge not, that ye be not judged*—and a reminder to his listeners that the right of judgement belongs to Heaven alone.

As they all congregated in the churchyard afterwards, Colonel Campbell discussed with the young clergyman the merits of his sermon. Mrs. Campbell ventured to wonder whether a little less severity might not be more to the purpose, particularly when speaking of those human failings to which even the best of men are sometimes prone.

"Undoubtedly, you are right, ma'am," began Mr. Devere, in a far more gentle tone than that with which he had just addressed his flock. "But—"

"But," Miss Devere interjected in a low voice, "Lady Paget, our Most Beneficent Patroness (that very imposing woman whom you may have noticed seated in the first pew) is the sort of person who does not feel she has heard a proper sermon if she has not been threatened at least half a dozen times with eternal damnation."

Mr. Devere scolded his sister for speaking with disrespect of the lady who had done so much good both for himself and for the church. As he did so, a joyful reunion was taking place in another part of the churchyard, between that same beneficent woman and a very old friend: Mrs. Eugenia Churchill.

Years ago, the two had been schoolfellows at Mrs. Jennings' Academy for Young Ladies, an establishment wherein girls of only middling gentility could acquire all the requisites of well-bred feminine accomplishment. Mrs.

Jennings' pupils were taught to dance the quadrille and the minuet, to pour tea and dispense tea-cakes, to net purses and embroider needle-cases; and learned just enough of drawing, music, and French to make them fashionable. Supplementing these important studies, the young scholars were also tutored in the more trivial subjects of reading and writing—though exhorted to limit the display of such accomplishments to an occasional perusal of the "Elegant Extracts," and the composition of short but exceedingly charming letters.

Having been early recommended to each other by a congenial sympathy of taste and temper (for both were selfish and vain; both enjoyed gossiping, and abusing the character of any person not immediately present; and both had high hopes of marrying very well indeed), Miss Caroline Baxter and Miss Eugenia Wilson quickly became intimate friends.

Their devotion to one another continued unabated, until Miss Baxter betrayed all her friend's affectionate trust by marrying *for love*. Miss Wilson was herself soon to be wed. She had utilised her own natural gifts, and the acquirements of her excellent education, to beguile the wealthy and well-connected Mr. Churchill, fifteen years her senior, into asking for her hand—and she might readily have forgiven her friend's transgression, had Miss Baxter only shown the good sense to love a man of fortune. But Mr. Quincy was poor as a pieman—four hundred a year—no house in town—very small property—home a mere cottage—lived in Ireland! Miss Wilson employed every power of reason at her command to make her friend see the evils of the match; but with reason Miss Baxter would have nothing to do. Thoroughly disgusted, Miss Wilson had no choice but to throw her over.

Remarkably, however, the throwing over had been effected without a decisive break. The newlyweds removed to Ireland immediately following the marriage, and the two ladies, instead of ending their friendship in a quarrel, simply forgot to think of one another. The point was a not insignificant one in Miss Wilson's estimation, because Mr. Quincy, though poor, had an uncle possessed of great wealth and a viscountcy—both of which, with *very* good luck (the untimely death of only three near relations would secure it) Mr. Quincy might someday inherit.

Mrs. Churchill now had reason to congratulate herself on

having avoided an explicit rupture, for Mr. Quincy had lately succeeded to the title, and to a very large property near Weymouth; and Miss Baxter of old was now The Right Honourable Lady Paget. Neither woman was aware of the other's presence in Weymouth until that afternoon at St. Alban's church, when her ladyship espied a face in which the beauty of her old friend Miss Wilson might still be faintly traced. She accosted Mrs. Churchill when the service ended, receiving at first a rather cool greeting in return. But when Mrs. Churchill, in the course of their conversation, began to understand the eminence to which her former schoolmate had risen—when she heard the frequent references to *Lord Paget*, the casual allusions to *Ashdale Park*, and *our house in Grosvenor Square*—her manner warmed considerably.

Frank Churchill and his uncle stood dutifully by as this happy reunion took place, and were in due course introduced. Lord Paget was indisposed, his lady explained with a touching sigh of regret, or he would have been quite delighted to make their acquaintance. "Poor dear Paget had taken to his bed with a painful bilious complaint several months earlier, and had not left it since,"—to Lady Paget's immeasurable satisfaction; for though she did marry for love, she had very soon discovered how dreary and disagreeable even love might grow, with only four hundred a year to sustain it.

A discussion next ensued upon medical matters. Mrs. Churchill confided to her friend the sad state of her own health, and the nature of the ailment which had brought her to Weymouth. Lady Paget, with many sympathetic utterances, urged her to consult Lord Paget's own physician, Dr. Endicott. "An excellent man. His fees are quite outrageous; but if you can afford them, you will not find a better doctor in all England."

Mrs. Churchill could not be pleased by this intimation that she was not so well able to afford the doctor's exorbitant fee as was Lord Paget. For the moment, however, she kept her irritation to herself, and Lady Paget soon turned the conversation in another direction, boasting of her devotion to St. Alban's church and its clergyman, and her great patronage of both; for she was grown remarkably devout, since first she heard herself addressed as *my lady*.

"The church was in a contemptible state when we came here," said she. "Lord Paget's late brother, I regret to say,

was not much concerned with spiritual matters, and had let
things go to a shocking degree. Luckily, the old rector died
soon after our arrival in Dorset; and I persuaded Paget he
could well afford to dispose of the living on the basis of
merit alone. Our circumstances are so very easy (truly, I am
quite ashamed when I think how much we have!)—and so I
told my poor husband. 'My dear Paget,' said I, 'with such an
immense fortune as you are now in possession of, we can
easily make St. Alban's a model for every parish in England.
For if Lord Paget with all his many thousands will not set
the example, who will?' 'Caroline, my dear,' replied he, 'I
give you *carte blanche*. Spend whatever you think right. I
leave it all in your capable hands.' "

Mrs. Churchill—divided between a powerful desire to in-
gratiate herself with so eminent a personage, and an almost
equally powerful inclination to detach a plump marble
cherub from the nearest funerary monument and beat Lady
Paget about the head with it—managed to murmur a few
requisite words of acknowledgement. Her ladyship, with a
complacent smile, continued,

"And Stephen—Mr. Devere—is so properly grateful; you
may imagine how grateful. Such a preferment! Such a valuable living, to be just given away; and he not even a family
connection! It is practically unheard of these days. But
truly, he is a gem, quite a gem. Did you not think his sermon today inspired? I knew at once he was just the man for
the post. Indeed, it was I who urged Lord Paget to engage
him," she added, not at all truthfully. "I felt we could do no
less. *I* am not one to cavil over a few paltry thousands, with
the eternal salvation of our parishioners hanging in the bal-
ance; and thank heavens! I have no need to give a thought
to money. There is still a great deal to be done, however, before the church answers all my ideas of perfection. In fact, I
am expecting Mr. James Hammond here later this week. Do
you know Mr. Hammond?"

"Hammond," the elder Mr. Churchill repeated, searching
his memory for the name.

"James Hammond!" Frank exclaimed. "The painter?"

"The very same man. I have commissioned him to do an
altarpiece for St. Alban's. It will be the crowning glory of our
little church! I am in the greatest uncertainty, however, as
to the *subject* of the painting. For weeks now, I have been
back and forth between the Plagues of Egypt, and the Tor-
tures of the Damned."

"A painful predicament," said Frank, his amusement not preventing him from eyeing Miss Fairfax, who stood at the other end of the churchyard, and idly wondering if he would have any opportunity to pay his respects to the Campbells, and to speak to her, before they departed.

"The most celebrated painter in England today," her ladyship went on. "Perhaps in the world. He is much admired by Lord Egremont, you know, and has stayed at Petworth on more than one occasion. It has taken no small sum, I assure you, to entice him to undertake the work. He is in such very great demand! But, as I said, Lord Paget and I spare no expense where the church is concerned. The very vessel of our spiritual welfare, and the spiritual welfare of all those who look to *us* for guidance! After all (as I so often remind my poor dear husband), great wealth does bring with it great responsibilities."

Here she paused; but her listeners offering only tacit agreement, she soon proceeded.

"Of course, Mr. Hammond may insist on choosing the subject of the painting himself. Your truly *great* artists, you know, can be rather touchy about having anyone to tell them their business. When I sat for Mr. Hammond earlier this year, I did find him a bit temperamental. (The portrait was magnificent, by the by; worth every guinea it cost us— and it cost a good many indeed. However, everyone says it is very like.) Perhaps it may be best to make no decision, at present, about the theme of the work."

"You are wise there," began Mr. Churchill, "Lady—Lady—"

"Paget," Frank supplied in an undertone.

"Lady Paget. Yes. I was about to say... what was I about to say, Frank?"

Frank shrugged.

"I've lost my train of thought now. But it seems to me... what were we talking of, Frank?"

"Artists, sir. Temperamental artists."

"Oh, yes. Now, I knew Randalls in my youth—"

"I think you mean Reynolds, uncle, don't you? Randalls is my father's estate in Highbury."

"Is it? Oh yes, of course. Now, I knew Randalls in my youth—"

"Reynolds, sir."

"Reynolds. But now I recall it, Lady Piggott, *he* was not at all temperamental in that way; quite the contrary, in fact—a perfectly affable fellow—thorough gentleman. That is... I believe it was Reynolds. Or was it Romney?"

"How can you be so thick-witted, Charles?" cried Mrs. Churchill. "Of course it was Reynolds! The portraits he painted of us have hung in the gallery at Enscombe these thirty years!"

"Of course you are right, my dear. Very true. You are always right. It amazes me how you can contrive always to remember so much. My wife has a wonderful memory, Lady Blodgett, quite wonderful; and a lucky thing it is for me, too," he confided with a rueful smile, "for to own the truth, I'm afraid I have been growing sadly forgetful of late."

Lady Paget smiled sympathetically, and Mr. Devere now approached them, begging to be excused for the intrusion. After the viscountess presented him to the Churchills, he inquired politely after Lord Paget. He then asked her ladyship if she would do him the honour of allowing him to introduce his friends, Colonel and Mrs. Campbell, to her.

"Why, certainly—we shall be happy to oblige you," she replied with a most becoming condescension—taking the liberty (to Frank's satisfaction, if not to his aunt's) of consenting for the Churchills as well as herself.

# Chapter Seven

**JANE SAW MR.** Devere returning to their group, accompanied by Lady Paget and the Churchills. After exchanging smiles with their nephew, her eye was quite naturally drawn to Mr. and Mrs. Churchill. She had noticed them in the church earlier, and had heard enough about them from Mr. Weston to make them an object of some curiosity.

Mrs. Churchill was somewhere between fifty and sixty, a small, thin woman (the top of her head came only to Frank's shoulder), and slightly stooped in posture. Her size and bearing surprised Jane, who had imagined her to be of a large, majestic stature. She was dressed very expensively, and would have been still quite handsome, had it not been for the coldness of her demeanour, and a habitual contraction of the lips and brow which imparted an air of ill-humour to her countenance. She acknowledged the Colonel and his party with a very chilling civility; and Jane could not help thinking that Mr. Weston, whom she had sometimes heard reproach himself for unfairly disparaging that lady among his own circle, had only spoken of her with more kindness than she deserved.

She caught herself in this reflection with a blush. Had not Mr. Devere just read them a sermon on judgement? Mrs. Churchill, she reminded herself, was ill, and the trials of illness could render even a good-tempered person irritable at times; and even if she were not so ill as she claimed to be, perhaps she did not feel as well as she might. Certainly there was that in her looks which did not convey the idea of perfect bodily vigour. Mrs. Churchill, like anyone, must have her good qualities, and Jane felt she ought not to judge someone in haste, of whom she really knew so little.

Frank's uncle was much older than his wife, and his appearance was not very prepossessing at first glance; but his manners were perfectly well-bred and gentle, and he seemed good-humoured enough. In the mildest accents, he called Jane 'my dear' when they were introduced, and took her hand most kindly.

The Churchills did not linger after this, though, had the choice been left to the gentlemen of the family, there would have been no impatience to be gone. Frank could only smile his regrets to Jane as Mrs. Churchill quickly made their excuses, and hurried her husband and nephew off to the waiting carriage.

Following their departure, Lady Paget began talking once more of her plans for St. Alban's church, telling the Campbells of the expected arrival of James Hammond. They were as much impressed by the news as she intended they should be, for they were great admirers of Mr. Hammond's work. But Jane observed with some amazement that her intelligence had taken Mr. Devere unawares: happening to look round at that gentleman while his patroness spoke, she perceived in his looks not merely surprise, but something very like alarm. Greater still was her astonishment when, seeing him thereafter look toward his sister, she turned her own gaze upon Miss Devere, and marked with wonder the trembling lip—the ashen brow—the white-knuckled hand, clutching at her brother's arm, which pronounced her to be suffering under a heavy shock! Jane felt a strong stirring of compassion for her, but without any means of putting it to use; and an almost equal measure of curiosity, without the smallest hope of having it soon satisfied.

The attention of the others, fortunately, was too much engrossed by Lady Paget's announcement to allow them take notice of the rector or his sister. Her ladyship, all insensible of the emotions she was rousing in those two breasts, proceeded to issue an invitation to the entire party to meet her distinguished guest.

"I will be giving a *soirée* at Ashdale Park on Wednesday evening, in Mr. Hammond's honour; and I hope Lord Paget and I shall have the pleasure of seeing all of you on the occasion."

Colonel Campbell, answering in behalf of his family, expressed his gratitude at being so honoured, and Mr. Dixon made his own courteous assent. Lady Paget then turned to Mr. Devere, who, though still keeping his sister's hand firmly within the crook of his arm, had by then regained his composure.

"My dear Stephen," said she, "Would you be so good as to

return with me now to Ashdale Park? Poor Paget was dreadfully low this morning, and your coming to read to him for an hour or two I am certain would be the very thing to set him up again. If you have nothing else to do, we will both be much obliged to you."

She spoke condescendingly of being obliged; but Jane gathered the request was one he could not refuse, reluctant though he must be to leave Miss Devere in her present state of distress. Whilst Lady Paget was otherwise occupied in answering a question from Colonel Campbell about the church, she heard Mr. Devere say to his sister in a low voice,

"Will you be all right, Margaret, until I return?"

Miss Devere, having recovered a little of her own self-command by this time, urged him to go with Lady Paget; but Miss Campbell, overhearing their exchange, and inferring that Miss Devere was ill, interceded.

"I'm sure you must have the headache, Miss Devere," she said, "for you look quite wan, and are not in your usual spirits. You must come home with us, and we can look after you until your brother returns. Mama," (to Mrs. Campbell), "I am sure Miss Devere is ill. Should not she come home with us?"

"Indeed, Margaret," said Mrs. Campbell with a look of solicitude, "you are not well."

"Oh, no," she replied; "I am only fatigued with standing about so long in the sun. I am sure to be better once I am moving about. A walk on the beach, with the sea breezes to cool me, will be my best cure, I think."

"Then Jane and Ned and I shall walk with you," Miss Campbell declared. "No doubt we are all a little fagged from the heat, and the walk will do us good. Do not you think that would be best, Mama?"

"I believe your brother would be most unhappy to leave you by yourself, Margaret," Mrs. Campbell agreed, appealing to Mr. Devere, who admitted he would be easier leaving her in Mrs. Campbell's custody.

"You may walk back to our house with Ned and the girls," said Mrs. Campbell, "and if you are not altogether mended by the air and exercise, then you may lie down upon Helen's bed and rest. If you do feel better, we shall have the pleasure of your company until Stephen returns. Stephen, I hope you and Margaret will join us for dinner?"

The Colonel, having just then finished his discussion with

the viscountess, seconded his wife's invitation, and the matter was decided. Mr. Devere, with a few words of gratitude to them both, left his sister to their ministrations, and set off with Lady Paget for Ashdale Park.

# Chapter Eight

**MARGARET DEVERE** politely declined Mr. Dixon's offer of an arm to lean on, and he and Miss Campbell set off toward the Esplanade with Jane and Miss Devere following. Leaving the quiet lane in which St. Alban's and its Rectory stood, they turned down a narrow thoroughfare lined with shops, all of which (it being Sunday) were dark and shuttered. Miss Campbell was talkative, looking back frequently to address the two behind; but the subject she fixed on was an unfortunate one for Miss Devere: Helen could talk of nothing but Mr. Hammond. She was quite in transports at the prospect of meeting him in person, and could not contain her excitement.

"In my opinion, James Hammond is England's greatest living painter," she said. "Having been in the north until so recently, Miss Devere, I suppose you can know nothing of his paintings. But I assure you, they are extraordinary! My parents took Jane and Ned and me to see an exhibition of his works at the Royal Academy this spring, and I thought his landscapes by far the most beautiful I ever saw. There was a series of pictures from the Lakes, which—oh! you cannot think how exquisite."

"Indeed," said Mr. Dixon. "Skiddaw and Bassenthwaite, Grasmere, Windermere, Ullswater—all on a large scale, and rendered with such truth as to make you feel almost as if you were standing before them. He has done some magnificent paintings on mythological and religious themes as well."

"I was especially struck," said Helen, "by *The Deluge Cometh*, and *Rape of Europa*—which, however, Papa said were really about the war with France. Did not you think them remarkable, Jane?"

Jane quietly assented, and Mr. Dixon added,

"His portraits, too, are far above the common. It is not merely his capturing quite distinctly the individual characters being depicted; any portraitist of moderate abilities can do as much. But Mr. Hammond's portraits convey something more; something eternal about human nature. His *Woman with Red Lilies*, for instance. Never have I seen a more perfect representation of sorrow and shame, as appeared to be welling up from the very depths of that poor creature's soul."

"And the expression of malice in his *Lady with a Spaniel!*" said Helen. "It was frightful to look on."

In their enthusiasm, the pair did not notice how little response they were eliciting from Miss Devere, or, if they did, perhaps attributed her languor to the headache. Jane, perceiving the agitation which Miss Devere was at pains to conceal, made some attempts to steer the discussion to other topics; but each time, after a brief interval, Helen returned to the subject of Mr. Hammond.

At last they reached the Esplanade, and here a little change was required. As they descended to the beach to join with the other strollers and shell-seekers, the frolicking children and stray dogs, their conversation was interrupted by the competing charms of the white-capped sea. Jane and Miss Devere each found themselves obliged to accept Mr. Dixon's offers of a supporting arm, the sand providing but indifferent footing; while Helen, sturdy and agile, walked unaided beside Jane.

Their progress was unhurried. They stopped frequently to examine the occasional cockleshell or bit of seaweed that appeared in their path, or just to stand and contemplate the beauty before them. At length they turned back towards the Esplanade.

"Is your headache better now, Miss Devere?" Helen asked.

"A good deal better," was the answer. "Indeed, the wind by the water is so bracing, I own I would like to stay and sit on one of these benches for a little while. Another hour of such a restorative, and I am persuaded I should be cured entirely."

"I should have no objection myself to staying out all day," said Helen. "But I am afraid if we are not home soon, my mother will begin to feel some anxiety on our account. We have been walking near an hour already, I am sure."

"I would not wish to worry Mrs. Campbell on any account. Still, I should like to stay. It will be best for you to go on without me, I think."

"Miss Devere, we cannot leave you here alone," said Mr. Dixon.

She was thoughtful a moment. "Perhaps if—if Miss Fairfax would be so kind as to keep me company, you both might go on ahead; and we would join you at home shortly. That is, if you are willing, Miss Fairfax?"

Jane was quite willing, the more so from the supposition that Miss Devere wished to unburden herself to her. That supposition was shortly after justified; for they had no sooner settled themselves on a bench after the other two departed, when Miss Devere began,

"Miss Fairfax, I am certain it did not escape your notice— you cannot have failed to remark my reaction—I might say, my distress, when Lady Paget was speaking of James Hammond."

"I confess, I did observe what appeared to me some agitation, in both yourself and Mr. Devere, at the mention of his name."

"Your curiosity must have been more than a little roused by so odd a circumstance! You need not be afraid to own it; in your place I should have felt just the same. Having said so much, I hope you will forgive me if I take the liberty, despite the newness of our acquaintance, to describe to you the history of my connection with Mr. Hammond. I am well aware of the peculiarity—the impropriety, perhaps—of relating what I am about to relate, to a comparative stranger. But I believe I can trust to your discretion, and to your kindness; and it would be the greatest relief to me to be able to talk of what I am feeling. If you had rather not hear it, however, it will certainly remain unspoken."

Jane could not deny a deepening curiosity in the matter; nor did she hesitate to assure Miss Devere that she felt all the compliment implied in being favoured with her confidence. She would be only too happy to hear whatever Miss Devere wished to tell, if the communication could afford her any comfort.

Miss Devere began. "Having witnessed my discomfiture when Lady Paget spoke of him, you may be amazed when I tell you it is fifteen years since I last saw James Hammond."

Jane looked her interest, and her companion continued.

"In the intervening period, I have grown enured to hearing him often talked about—such a man of consequence as he has since become! Though when I knew him, he was hardly—. Of course, in so remote a spot as Stephen and I have been residing these eight years past, I heard much less of him than would have been possible, I suppose, had we been in London or some other fashionable place. We would even, perhaps, have met again long before now. It was not the mere mention of his name, however, but rather the knowledge that he would be coming to Weymouth—that I would soon see him, which so discomposed me. But I am wandering out of all logical sequence."

Looking upward with a sigh, and then at Jane with a smile, she said, "You are a very patient listener, Miss Fairfax. I shall now endeavour to reward you by coming to the point. Fifteen years ago, James Hammond and I were deeply in love with one another."

Miss Devere here had need of a little pause before she could proceed with her story.

"I was seventeen when we met; he was twenty-three. He was then a struggling painter, with a great deal of talent, and very little money. Being therefore reduced to earning his bread by whatever means he could find, he determined on seeking a position as drawing master in some private family. By chance he was recommended to my father's notice, and soon afterwards was engaged to give me drawing lessons.

"I will not attempt to describe Mr. Hammond to you. No doubt you will see him soon enough, and judge for yourself. I will only say, he was unlike any other gentleman I had ever known, and superior to them all. He was not handsome, precisely; but he had qualities and abilities to attract any woman.

"Well, my lessons began. My previous instruction had been good; and a strong desire of pleasing him ruled me almost from the start of our acquaintance. So he found me, though hardly a prodigy, a more apt pupil than he had expected; and I soon earned his respect by my diligence in application. We spent a good deal of time together, often out-of-doors on my father's estate, walking, sketching, and conversing. We quickly discovered a striking unison in our tastes and opinions, and a similarity in our tempers; and we began to enjoy each other's company more and more. For my part, I was in love before I knew what I was about. You may guess what was my joy when, after many weeks of painful suspense, he opened his heart to me, and made a declaration of the warmest, most devoted attachment. In return, I assured him of my tenderest affection and regard.

"He proposed to speak to my father at once. But I advised—entreated him to delay. I knew my father would object to the marriage—would not think him good enough, not only on the grounds of want of fortune, but want of proper connections. Do you know anything of James Hammond's history, Miss Fairfax?"

"Nothing at all."

"His father was a cabinet-maker. In every way an honest, sober, industrious, exemplary man—but still a cabinet-maker. And he had a grandmother who had once been on the stage! Yet his family was very dear to him, and he was even proud of them. Indeed, he had cause to be proud, as well as grateful; for it was their hard work and constant sacrifice which enabled him to acquire the education of a gentleman. But they were very low; far too low, I had not a doubt, to suit my father.

"I did not wish to wound James's feelings, or to have my father wound them. So I told him only that Papa would not like me to be married so young; and that he would not allow me to marry without some adequate provision for my maintenance.

"James could not but concede the second point. Indeed he had himself concluded that our marriage must not take place until he had advanced a little in his profession, and we could be certain of something to live on. The wages of a drawing master were hardly enough to support one, let alone two; and to make a name for himself as a painter was not an end to be gained overnight. Still, he saw no reason why we should not be engaged right away. He had an unshakable faith in his own talents, and was confident of future success. Since we had already pledged ourselves to one another, why should we not declare it openly to all the world?"

Miss Devere broke off for a moment, and Jane asked, "Had you any idea that Major Devere might eventually be persuaded to the match?"

She shook her head. "None. But I was resolved within myself that I would marry James anyway, whenever we should be certain even of a small income. I knew my own little portion of two thousand pounds would be withheld, if I were to marry without Papa's approval—and though I felt it no sacrifice to forgo mere material ease, if only we could be together, still we must wait for a *something* to keep body and soul together; and who could say how long it would be in coming? In the meantime, therefore, I thought it best if we continued as we were; for we had then at least the freedom to see each other often.

"I pleaded and argued. I even, finally—reluctantly—suggested the likelihood of my father's objecting to his family connections; but he would not yield to my judgement. To carry on a clandestine affair, to maintain an engagement in secret, would be to conduct himself in a manner inconsistent with his own notions of honour, and my father, he felt, would be quite right to denounce him; but were he to declare his intentions frankly and forthrightly, he trusted my father would respect him the more for his integrity. With my own better knowledge of Papa's character, I knew he was mistaken; but I could not convince him."

"But did not you feel, too," Jane asked, "that it would be wrong to keep your engagement a secret?"

"I did feel it," she replied, "most painfully. But given the circumstances, I saw no alternative—save to be parted from James; and that was what I could not endure to think of. If he had only heeded my advice! If he had but consented to keep our attachment a secret, I am persuaded we must have found a way to be married sooner or later... by some means or other."

"But to agree to such an arrangement," said Jane, "to maintain a position of trust under false pretences, is what no man could submit to, I am sure, and continue to respect himself. And I wonder whether he should not have lost something in your esteem as well, had he done as you advised?"

Margaret shook her head. "Impossible!

"You may guess," she continued after a brief pause, "what happened next. James applied to my father, and received just such a reward for his honesty as I had predicted—though in such an instance I could not enjoy even the usual satisfaction of being right.

"In my father's eyes, James Hammond was no more than a servant, hardly to be distinguished from a—a footman, or a gardener. And for such a one to be... *meddling* with his daughter! He heaped every conceivable abuse upon poor James, who could scarcely speak a word in his own defense; nor could I. James suffered it at first with remarkable forbearance, but after a time his own anger flared, and unpleasant words flew in both directions. Papa then ordered me to my room, and I found I could not disobey: he called in my elder brother Richard to take me away, whether I would or no. I know little of what passed afterwards; only that

James was driven from the house, with threats of the gravest punishment if he ever dared set foot on the property again.

"As for me, I found myself locked up—positively locked up in my room! That evening my maid brought a message from my father, bidding me pack my things and be prepared to travel early in the morning; he would take me himself to Scotland, where I was to stay with my elder sister and her husband until such time as he saw fit to allow me home again."

"And you never saw, or communicated with Mr. Hammond again?"

"Just before I left, I managed to put a letter for him into the hands of a servant I thought could be trusted. I entreated James to follow me to Scotland, and—"

She stopped; and there was a little silence, before she concluded, "But he never came, Miss Fairfax. He never came."

She said no more, and after an interval, Jane asked gently, "Is it possible that your letter miscarried? That Mr. Hammond might never have received it?"

"It is possible. The letter may have been intercepted; or he might have left his lodgings before it could be delivered. He might even have come to Scotland, and been kept from seeing me. But it is some time now since James Hammond has attained that degree of success, which must have secured him from the need of consulting anyone's wishes in the matter but his own, and mine. He might have found me out years ago, had his attachment remained unchanged. Nothing could have stood in his way; nothing but his own indifference. And perhaps—who knows?—perhaps he never really loved me at all... or only a very little. Perhaps when my father parted us, he was glad to be free of me."

"Has Mr. Hammond ever married?" Jane asked.

"No—not to my knowledge."

After a period of reflection, Jane ventured to suggest that, though the gentleman's sentiments would appear to have undergone a great change since Miss Devere first knew him, she could see no reason to conclude his love was not real. "He was very young, after all; only three-and-twenty; and young men are not often renowned as models of constancy. He may have ceased to love after a little while. But that is not the same as having never loved."

Another interval passed; and then Miss Devere spoke

more tranquilly, saying,

"Now, Miss Fairfax, now that you have heard all this long and woe-begone history—no doubt you will dismiss me as either a thoroughly pathetic creature, or a very great fool, when I confess to you that, in spite of all the time that has passed since I last saw James Hammond... in spite of—everything—I love him still. Oh, not that I was not certain I had reasoned myself out of it long ago. Until today, I thought I had learnt quite rationally to accept my fate. I was wholly content to remain single, and to keep house for my brother for the rest of my life. I laugh to think how many times I have been heard to express my conviction, that any woman of sense, if she be not entirely friendless, nor altogether penniless, might yet have it in her power—though unmarried!—to live a satisfying life; to be frequently useful, and even, occasionally, happy! Is not this a most fitting end to all my high-wrought sentiments?"

# Chapter Nine

**MR. DEVERE,** on arriving at the Campbells' house a few hours later, was relieved to see his sister much improved in spirits. Finding occasion to exchange a few private words with her after dinner, while Miss Campbell entertained the company with a country air on the pianoforte, he had the surprise (by no means a disagreeable one) of learning that her recovery was owing largely to the kindness of Miss Fairfax.

Miss Campbell soon afterwards surrendered her instrument to Jane—was in fact hurried off by Mr. Dixon, a man of considerable knowledge and taste in music, who openly admired the superior playing of Miss Fairfax even beyond that of Miss Campbell. Had that young lady been of a jealous temper, this preference might have been a source of discord among them. But Miss Campbell had all the artless confidence of a well-loved child, without that excessive self-importance which often arises from a faulty degree of parental indulgence; for the Colonel and his wife were far too wise to confuse spoiling with love. They had taught their daughter always to give her best effort to anything she undertook; and had instilled in her a belief that, so long as she *had* done her best, she could have no reason to feel ashamed of the result, even where there existed no extraordinary aptitude or accomplishment in which she might justly take pride. So she played happily to those who were willing to listen; knowing her performance, if not exactly capital, was quite as good as most. And she cheerfully acknowledged the pre-eminence of Jane's talents, and heard her sing and play with an appreciation nearly as great as Mr. Dixon's, and entirely untainted by any feeling of resentment or ill-usage.

Even Mr. Devere, who had little natural taste for music, was compelled to listen with attention while Jane performed, and to feel he had never enjoyed any performance half so much. Complimenting her upon it later, while the table was being placed for cards, he also took the opportunity privately to thank her for her assistance to his sister.

"The history of my sister's connection with Mr. Hammond," he said in a low voice, "is one I should not like to have generally known. Even the Campbells, you perceive, know nothing about it. But I am sure Margaret may safely trust to your discretion, Miss Fairfax; and it will do her good to have some better confidante than myself."

"I cannot doubt, Mr. Devere," said Jane, "that your own affection and understanding are of the first importance to her. But if I can render her any service by means of a sympathetic ear, I shall be very glad."

After a moment, she added, "May I ask how long Miss Devere was banished to Scotland, after this unfortunate affair with Mr. Hammond?"

"Nearly two years," was the reply.

"Two years! That is a long period. But she was living with her sister, so perhaps she did not mind it."

He shook his head. "I am sorry to say there were no pleasures in her exile, which could at all have compensated her for its duration. My eldest brother, too, at about that time got himself into a serious scrape, which—I will not trouble you with the details; but which occasioned Margaret some unpleasantness at his hands, and was a most severe trial to my father as well. She and Richard have been less than friendly ever since. Indeed, it was for that reason she left home and came to live with me, after my brother came into the property.—But you must not imagine, Miss Fairfax, that my father was an unkind or a tyrannical parent. His actions, though they may seem harsh, were guided by a genuine anxiety for Margaret's welfare."

"You thought his actions justified, then?"

He hesitated before answering. "I think he might have erred, perhaps, in sending her away for so long. Still, as regards Mr. Hammond, I would have you understand that my father was only trying to protect his daughter from a man who appeared in his eyes a villain."

"You met Mr. Hammond yourself, did not you?" she asked. "Did you think him unprincipled, or mercenary?"

"He did not strike me so, particularly. However, I was not intimately acquainted with him; and I was but fifteen then myself. At all events, I cannot condemn my father for acting as he did. I beg you will try to look at it from his point of view: Mr. Hammond was placed in a position of some trust in our household; and he grievously abused that trust, by seducing the affections of a girl too young to know what she was about. Her youth must be her own excuse; and her sex, too—for we cannot expect a woman to possess the same powers of judgement that a man is given by nature, especially in such matters as these."

Jane forbore to observe that she knew more than a few men to whom nature had apparently forgotten to grant any such gift. She did, however, take the liberty of suggesting that Miss Devere's judgement, in this instance, would seem to have been proved correct.

"Yes," said Mr Devere. "What you say is true, Miss Fairfax. But at that time, you will comprehend, Mr. Hammond had nothing, absolutely nothing; and though he is now a very successful man, his success was by no means inevitable *then*. I am quite ready to believe there was no ill intention on his part; but I am equally sure a gentleman ought not to take on the responsibility of a wife and family, until he has secured the means of supporting them."

"No, I am sure he ought not," Jane agreed. "However—"

She had been about to offer her opinion that, though a marriage or even an engagement were deemed imprudent under such circumstances, there might yet be some way of handling the matter with more consideration given for the *feelings* of the those concerned; one which might allow even for the possibility of a future connection, should circumstances change. But she hesitated for fear that such an opinion might offend him, as being a criticism of his father—which, in truth, it was. She was inclined to feel Major Devere had dealt too harshly, both with his daughter, and with Mr. Hammond. Yet relating to this affair there might be many particulars unknown to her; and perhaps there had been good reasons for the Major to act as he did. She hardly knew what to think, and therefore thought it best not to say too much.

Fortunately, her conversation with Mr. Devere was here interrupted by the others, who were calling on them to settle a debate over what to play. Miss Devere and Mr. Dixon favoured Speculation, while the three Campbells all preferred Commerce. Jane and her companion both casting their votes for Commerce, they were thereafter required to suspend their talk and join in the game.

# Chapter Ten

**ON THE FOLLOWING** day, finding herself with an afternoon completely disengaged, Jane took the opportunity of paying another call on Mrs. Nesbit. To her surprise, the old woman greeted her in a state of agitation.

"Oh, Miss Fairfax—what do you think has happened? My dear boy is here. Here at Weymouth! After all these years— my own dearest boy! I am in such a state of happiness, I can hardly tell you! All of my troubles are at an end now. *He* will look after me!"

"But I thought, ma'am," said Jane, "—was I mistaken?—I thought you had no children of your own."

Mrs. Nesbit, making an effort to speak more intelligibly, explained that the young man she spoke of was not her own son, but one who had been under her care some years ago; she had raised him from three to twelve. He had been her very favourite of all her charges, and had been devoted to her in his turn. Had the good Lord seen fit to bless her with a child of her own, she said, she did not believe she could have loved him any more than this darling boy.

"And now, this morning," she said "I have met with him again, quite by chance—and after so many years! He is staying at Weymouth with his family. Oh! such a fine young gentleman he has turned out! But it really is the most amazing circumstance we should meet, for I so rarely go out of this house, Miss Fairfax, as you know. However, I was feeling a little stronger this morning, and the day was so very lovely, that I was tempted just to go down and sit by the water for a quarter-hour—I do get weary at times of being always shut up indoors—and I had not been sitting five minutes, when he came along. I did not know him at first, but was just thinking to myself, as he walked past, what a very handsome young man he was; when, to my astonishment, I found him turning back to look at me—approaching me—taking up my hand with the fondest affection—!"

She could say no more for the present, as tears of joy

stopped her words. However, she soon composed herself a little, and continued,

"Before long he observed that I was unwell," she said, "and he insisted on escorting me home. I would rather have prevented it. I knew it would distress him to see how I had been reduced to living. But indeed, with so much unaccustomed exertion and excitement, I was feeling very weak just then, and I found I could not refuse. And when he saw the shabbiness of the house—the negligence of the landlady—the condition of my apartments—well, Miss Fairfax, you may think how angry he was! He cursed the Albrights for their neglect—scolded me for not having written to ask his help—and reproached himself for not having known, somehow, that I was in need of it! He is gone out this moment, to find me better lodgings. He says he will not suffer me to stay in this house another night!"

This story was highly interesting to Jane. "He must be a remarkable young man indeed," said she, "to remain so steadfast, after years of separation, in an attachment formed at so young an age."

But it was not long before Mrs. Nesbit, under this irritation of happiness, began to feel its ill effects. Jane therefore helped her to her bed, administered some lavender drops, and urged her to try and subdue her emotions a little—if not for her own sake, then for *his*. Her representations of what the young man would feel, if he returned to find that his very wish of relieving his old friend's suffering had in fact only increased it, had the desired result; and after a short interval, Mrs. Nesbit fell into a doze.

Jane went back into the sitting room, more than a little curious to behold the hero of this interesting tale. She had hardly time to consider whether it would be quite proper for her to remain until he returned, when her deliberations were interrupted by a knock at the door. Great was her astonishment, when she opened it, to find herself face to face with Frank Churchill!

Her first thought was that she must be wanted at home, and that he had been sent to fetch her; yet his astonishment at seeing her there appeared quite the equal of her own.

"Miss Fairfax!" he cried.

"Mr. Churchill!" she exclaimed.

He was the first to recover himself. "Where is Mrs. Nesbit?" he asked.

"In the other room."

"I did not know you were acquainted with her."

"I have known her but a short time."

"Oh."

There was another brief silence. Then,

"Miss Fairfax," he said more collectedly, "I know not what chance, or what good angel, has brought you here today; but it is a piece of good luck I could hardly have hoped for. I have just been out, you see, looking for more suitable lodgings for Mrs. Nesbit; and I believe I have found a place that will answer, but I dare not trust to my own judgement—for we men, you know, have not a very nice sensibility about papers and furnishings and the like. I thought I might bring her to examine the place herself, but I was in some doubt lest the exertion should prove too much for her. However, if I could persuade *you* to come with me, and give your opinion (if you have no other pressing engagement, that is), I would look upon it as a very great favour indeed."

Jane's astonishment could only be increased by this speech; and it was several moments before she could sufficiently overcome it to make him any reply.

"Mr. Churchill, are *you* the gentleman—is it possible you are the former charge—the young man whom Mrs. Nesbit told me of this morning?"

He assured her it was so, and she could doubt no further—though surprise would linger a little longer. She had just managed to express her willingness to undertake the task he proposed, when they heard a stirring in the other room, and Mrs. Nesbit, somewhat refreshed from her brief nap, emerged.

"My dear boy," she cried. "Have you returned so soon? I ought to have been up when you arrived, to introduce you to Miss Fairfax."

"You were not needed, ma'am," he said, hastening to help her into a chair. "Miss Fairfax and I are already acquainted."

"Can it be so?"

"Indeed, we danced together the other night, at the assembly ball. Did not we, Miss Fairfax?" he added with a smile at Jane. Then to Mrs. Nesbit again: "She is from Highbury, you know, where my father lives."

"But I thought you lived in London, Miss Fairfax! Indeed, I know it is so, for how otherwise could you know my sister?"

Frank made a brief explanation, Jane herself being still too astonished by this turn of events to be able to say much to the purpose. Instead, she only listened quietly to the conversation of the other two, observing with a great deal of interest the conduct of Mr. Churchill towards his former governess. His behaviour to Mrs. Nesbit, though exhibiting his characteristic liveliness, was infused with so strong a measure of solicitous affection and respect, as could not but raise him materially in Jane's esteem.

Before long, he suggested they ought to start on their errand. Though the house they were going to inspect was only a short way off, there was no time to waste if they were to see Mrs. Nesbit resettled that day, as he wished. As they walked, Jane could not refrain from remarking on his extraordinary devotion to his former governess; and it took little prompting on her part to extract from him a full account of it.

"Only recollect, Miss Fairfax," he related, "what my situation was, when I first came into Yorkshire. I was not three years old. I had been told that my mother was gone, and was never coming back again. I was taken from my father, from my home—in short, from everything familiar—and sent to live far away, in a place I did not know, with people I had never seen before. My earliest days at Enscombe were spent in the most abject misery! My uncle I saw little of then, and my aunt was a figure more likely to inspire awe than affection, especially in one so young; and the nursery maid, in whose charge I was initially placed, was an ill-tempered young woman. After some months, however, she did me the great kindness of quarreling with my aunt, and got herself discharged—and Mrs. Nesbit was engaged as governess to take her place. You may readily conceive what my feelings were, on finding myself in the custody of such a tender-hearted, motherly sort of woman. Was it possible, under such circumstances, that I should not be soon as dearly attached to her as if she were, indeed, my mother? And is it any wonder I should still feel towards her the deepest affection and gratitude, for years of kindness and watchful care? I am only ashamed to have you know how I have neglected her till now. But I was just twelve when I was packed off to public school, and she was sent away from Enscombe—"

"No one could possibly blame you for Mrs. Nesbit's present distress," said Jane, quite moved by his narrative.

"And the pains you are taking to help her now must dispel all censure. Truly," she persisted, as he shook his head with a smile. "Your care of her is worthy of praise. There are not many, I think, who would act as you have done, in a like situation."

He offered some words of protest, really feeling there was nothing extraordinary in his conduct. His attachment to his former governess was something which, to his own mind, might reflect a great deal of credit on Mrs. Nesbit, but certainly none on himself.

"But by all means," said he, laughing, "turn it to a merit if you can. I am sure I have few enough, if the truth were known."

It was Jane's turn to protest; but they had arrived at their destination, and had now something else to think of.

# Chapter Eleven

**JANE GAVE HER** unqualified approbation to the lodgings Mr. Churchill had chosen. The house was small, but solid and well-maintained, its location quiet. The landlady, Mrs. Roberts, a respectable widow of middle age, lived on the drawing-room floor with her married daughter. The daughter's husband was a seaman, and seldom home; so Mrs. Brown resided with her mother, and helped with the necessary cooking and cleaning—an arrangement which provided each with welcome companionship. Martha Brown was a plump, cheerful, talkative woman, something like a younger version of Jane's own aunt Hetty. An elderly gentleman (a retired clerk) rented the top floor, and was the only other inmate of the house.

The rooms Frank intended Mrs. Nesbit to occupy were on the ground floor. Though not large, they were, like the rest of the house, clean, bright, and airy. He had thought these apartments best, he explained, because Mrs. Nesbit would then have hardly any stairs to deal with; and at the back, the house opened onto a small, sheltered garden, where on fine days she might sit out of doors, under the shade of an old beech tree.

Jane could not see the smallest deficiency in any of it. The terms being reasonable, Frank closed with Mrs. Roberts at once, and gave her two weeks' rent in advance. After informing her he would return a little later with her new lodger, he and Jane left to report to Mrs. Nesbit on the success of their mission, and to help her prepare for the removal.

As they stepped down to the pavement, however, they felt the wind blowing harder, and from a different quarter, than it had done before. Looking up at the sky, Frank said, "I do not think a storm is imminent, Miss Fairfax, but perhaps, to be safe, you had better return home now. I will have no difficulties in getting Mrs. Nesbit resettled; it is only a matter of packing up her belongings, which are very few, and hiring a chaise to carry her to the new lodgings. No doubt I can have her snug in her new quarters and be home myself, before I am missed."

"Before you are missed! But you must have been gone for hours already, Mr. Churchill. I own, I did wonder your aunt could spare you so long, for I had the impression she was— that is, being unwell, I thought she usually required your attendance."

"It is often so," he agreed. "But the severity of her condition varies a good deal at different times; happily, she has been somewhat improved of late. Today, indeed, she was feeling well enough to hazard an afternoon of shopping— and she cannot bear to have me with her when she shops," he told her with a grin, "for she says I fidget her to death!"

A strong gust suddenly blew up a little tempest of dust on the pavement, and they both looked skyward once more. The clouds were thickening.

"Perhaps you are right," Jane said, "I had better go, if you really do not need me. Mrs. Campbell will be uneasy if I am out in the rain."

He assured her he could manage very well without her. "Only allow me to tell you again, before you go, how grateful I am for your help. I really did not like to rely on my own judgement in such a matter."

Not wishing for any more thanks, Jane would have been off at once, but he detained her a little longer. "I hesitate to make this added request," he began. "It will sound very odd to you, I know; but I must ask you not to mention to anyone our meeting today at Mrs. Nesbit's."

She thought it very odd indeed. "I do not understand."

"Rest assured there is no evil design in my wish for secrecy. It is only—may I be perfectly open?"

"Yes. Of course."

Stepping a little nearer to her, he continued in a lowered voice, "If, by the Campbells, or any other person, it should somehow get round to my aunt—if she should hear of my errand here today—it mortifies me to admit that she would likely put it out of my power to be of any further assistance to Mrs. Nesbit."

"Is it possible," cried Jane, "Mrs. Churchill can feel anything but pride and pleasure, to know her nephew has behaved so generously toward one in need?"

"It is more than possible. In truth, my aunt is rather jealous of my time and attention; particularly where it is bestowed on anyone she considers an inferior. She would not object very strenuously, I suppose, to my spending the afternoon with a duchess. Or a commoner with twenty-thousand a year," he amended with another wry grin, then immediately grew serious again. "But a penniless old governess! No, Miss Fairfax; it would not be permitted. My visits here must be kept secret."

Jane was irresolute. She felt what he asked of her was wrong. Yet it must be true that his aunt would react as he foretold, or he would not ask it.

"Very well," she agreed at last. "I will keep your secret, Mr. Churchill."

On an impulse, he took up her hand and raised it, just for an instant, to his lips; the moment he released it, she turned from him and darted away down the street. She arrived home just as the first drops of rain had begun falling from the sky.

# Chapter Twelve

"**THANK GOODNESS** you're home," said Mrs. Campbell when Jane entered the sitting room of the Colonel's house. "I feared you would be caught in a downpour. But you look flushed, my dear. I hope you have not taken a chill."

"Not at all. I have only been hurrying to get in before the rain started."

"And not a moment before time," Mrs. Campbell observed, turning her gaze toward the large bow window, through which a hard rain could now be seen driving across the pavement in sheets.

"Papa is waiting for you in his study, Jane," said Helen. "He has something he wishes to speak to you about."

"There is nothing wrong, is there?" asked Jane. Her ready apprehension was of some bad news from Highbury.

Helen and her mother here exchanged glances, and traces of smiles in their faces relieved Jane's immediate anxiety. "Nothing wrong, I should say," Mrs. Campbell replied. "But we will let the Colonel tell you himself."

The smiles were plainly visible now, and Jane, in increasing perplexity, excused herself to go to Colonel Campbell. Standing outside the door of the small chamber he had adopted as his study, she stopped briefly to compose herself. The meeting with Frank Churchill had left her in a perturbed state of mind, and she needed time to reflect on what had happened. But Colonel Campbell was waiting; so the problem of Mr. Churchill, and her promise to him, would have to keep a little while longer.

The Colonel did not come to the point at once, but asked if she had had a pleasant visit with her friend. With some consciousness, she replied that she had.

"I have been thinking of the matter," said he, "ever since you first told me of Mrs. Nesbit. From your description of her character and condition, it does not seem right to me that she should be living in such mean circumstances, and without proper medical attention. I would like to offer some assistance, if I might."

"Oh!" cried Jane. "That is so kind of you—so very kind! But it is not necessary now."

Perceiving some agitation in her manner, he said uneasily, "Why, my dear, what do you mean? The old lady is not—she has not—?"

Here, already, was just the eventuality she had been dreading when she agreed to keep Mr. Churchill's secret. Would it be possible to fulfill her promise without lying to the Colonel?

"Oh! no, sir. No. Mrs. Nesbit is well. I only meant that she is not in need of your assistance, because—someone else has come forward to assist her."

"I am glad to hear it; very glad. But who can this someone be? I thought, other than yourself, she was quite without friends here in Weymouth."

"Yes, she is—that is, she was. But by a remarkable chance, she met today with—a gentleman—one of her former charges. He has taken it upon himself to remove her to better lodgings, and to see to it that she has whatever else she requires."

"Well! What a fortunate occurrence! You must be pleased by such a turn of events."

"Yes. Indeed, I am. Very pleased, indeed."

Surveying her face, he asked in a tone of kindly solicitude, "Is there anything wrong, Jane? You do not seem quite yourself."

"Oh, no. There is nothing wrong. I am a little tired, I suppose. If there was nothing else you wanted, sir, I should like to go up to my room and rest before dinner."

She rose then to go, assuming the Colonel's desire to assist Mrs. Nesbit had been the object of their conference; but she quickly resumed her seat at his bidding.

"There is another matter, Jane," he recommenced. "Since you are fatigued, I will not tease you with circumlocutions. Stephen Devere came to see me today. He asked my permission to pay his addresses to you."

When she made no reply, he continued, "This comes as a surprise to you, I see."

"I am... beyond surprise," she managed to say.

"I confess, his application took me a little by surprise as well; or at least, I had not expected it so soon. But that he should wish to court you, I think a most natural thing—the most natural thing in the world."

There was an interval of silence while he allowed her to grow more accustomed to the idea.

"Have you nothing at all to say, my dear?" he asked finally.

"I do not know what tell you, sir. I can say nothing against Mr. Devere. He seems to be a—a very respectable gentleman. But I do not feel—that is, I do not think I would like to marry him."

The Colonel removed his glasses, rubbed his eyes, and replaced the glasses on the bridge of his nose. "Painful as it is to me, Jane, I feel it my duty to remind you that your only alternative to having eventually to earn your own bread, is to marry. For that reason alone, the match would make me personally very happy. But the fact that Major Devere was my good friend, and that I think very highly of his son, makes it in every way a most gratifying, a most eligible arrangement. Stephen's proposal, despite your want of fortune, testifies to his disinterestedness. May I ask if you have any fixed dislike, either to his character, or... to his person?"

"No, sir. But I hardly know him."

"Ah! and I believe that is the problem. Precisely the problem! I thought you might feel this was being rushed on you a little too precipitately. I said as much to Stephen. But he has been waiting some time for the means to marry, you know; and having obtained them, and having seen a woman he likes, he is a little impatient, I suppose, to mount his attack. And I think it no great fault in him—no great fault at all, given the prize he aims at.

"Now you know, my dear, that Mrs. Campbell and I have long looked upon you almost as a daughter. Our only care is for your happiness. I would never urge you to marry against your inclination. All I ask is that you do not make up your mind too hastily. Give yourself time to know him better. I think, if you do, you will find him a gentleman quite worthy of your regard."

"I am willing to be better acquainted with Mr. Devere; only I do not wish to be giving any false hope. I should not like to be the means of injuring him."

"A man who goes forth into battle, my dear, always runs the risk of being struck down. As the son of an officer of His Majesty's army, Stephen knows that as well as I do. But leave it to me, Jane. Leave it all to me. I will explain your sentiments to him. You will not give him either a yea or a nay just yet; but you *will* give him a chance—a chance to win your affection?"

"I suppose so, sir. If you think it right."

After she left him, Jane excused herself to Helen and Mrs. Campbell, pleading a headache. It was no falsehood. Climbing the stairs to the solitude of her bedchamber, her temples throbbed, and her emotions were in a painful tumult. She told her friends she intended to rest, but rest was impossible. Instead she walked, pacing back and forth across the tiny room, while she meditated on the strange events of the day.

Mr. Devere wished to marry her; and he had not known her a week! Reason could hardly comprehend it. She might have resented, as many young ladies would, that the gentleman had made his proposals to her guardian rather than to herself. But in truth, she was relieved he had spoken first to the Colonel. Had he declared himself to her, she was sure she should have been completely overset. It would be awkward enough whenever they should meet again; and she supposed that would be soon.

As Colonel Campbell had so regretfully reminded her, she must, before long, either marry, or become a governess. In fairness, therefore, both to herself and to Mr. Devere, she could not dismiss his proposal without due consideration. It was an eligible one, certainly. The Colonel was in a position to vouch for the soundness of the gentleman's character; and the station of a clergyman's wife, with its many opportunities for usefulness, was one suited to her disposition. She had already the beginnings of a friendship with his sister. And she did think him handsome—though *that* was scarcely a qualification of the highest consequence to her, for wherever she felt a regard, she always thought a person well-looking. But his offering for her on so short an acquaintance bespoke, to her refined sensibilities, a want of delicacy which did injure him a little in her opinion. Nor was he a man, she felt, to be easily or quickly understood. That he was a good man, she did not doubt; but the finer points of his nature were as yet unknown to her; and unlikely to be penetrated, she believed, except by a long acquaintance.

It was in the company of Miss Devere that he appeared to best advantage. His affection for his sister was pleasing to see, and her vivacity seemed to bring out in him an anima-

tion not otherwise evident. Jane herself, though, was not of
the most animated disposition; and with her, Mr. Devere
was more sedate. She had often thought that *some* opposition of temper might best promote the happiness of both
partners in the married state. Mr. Devere would do better,
perhaps, to choose a wife a bit less solemn than he was
himself. And Jane could not but be aware that *she* was
more lively, more engaged, in the company of a man like
Frank Churchill.

The comparison would obtrude, though she might wish to
avoid it. There was an exuberance in Frank Churchill, a
playfulness of spirits delightful to her. More importantly,
she had lately received proof that his affections, wherever
bestowed, were of the warmest and most enduring nature.
She had also seen evidence, today, of what she believed to
be the great defect in his character: deviousness, she could
only term it. It was a flaw which she had always considered
of the gravest sort. Yet knowing what she did of his circumstances, she found it hard to condemn him for at times
employing those little stratagems and half-truths, in which
she suspected he was all too practised.

And while Mr. Devere seemed little more than a stranger
to her, she and Mr. Churchill seemed somehow to have advanced, in the same brief span of time, to a considerable
degree of intimacy. Their meeting each other today so unexpectedly, and unbeknownst to their friends, added greatly
to that persuasion of a special bond existing between them,
which Jane had often imagined; and his asking her to keep
his secret for him had done more, perhaps, to fix her
thoughts upon him, than all his attractions of person and
manner might have done over a longer acquaintance.

Still, she acknowledged as she perched on the edge of her
bed, it would be folly to fall in love with Frank Churchill;
madness to entertain any hopes of him. Even if he should,
one day, come to feel for her something beyond mere
friendly regard, his aunt would never allow him to indulge
such feelings. Mrs. Churchill would not, by his own account, suffer him to spend an afternoon with a penniless
former governess. How fiercely, then, might she oppose herself to his marrying a penniless future governess?

No, it could never be. And certainly she was not in love
with him as yet; but she did feel even now in some danger.
Did she not owe it to herself, and to her friends, to subdue
whatever was excessive or imprudent in her partiality for

Frank Churchill—and to view Mr. Devere with an unprejudiced eye, and a disengaged heart?

There was a gentle tapping at the bedroom door, and a
moment later Miss Campbell's head peeped in.

"Are you feeling any better, Jane?" she asked softly.

"Do come in, Helen. Yes, I am a little better."

Helen walked in and sat down. "Well?" she said.

Jane gave her a bewildered look. "You are not usually so
half-witted, Jane! I want to know what answer you mean to
make to Mr. Devere's proposal, of course."

"Did not your father tell you?"

Receiving a negative reply, Jane repeated the substance
of her interview with Colonel Campbell. She was in a state
of some suspense, whilst Helen deliberated silently for a few
moments; when, to Jane's relief, she pronounced her to be
acting very wisely and properly.

"I do share my father's good opinion of Mr. Devere; and I
think he will make you an excellent husband, if you find
you can love him. But it is quite natural, before taking such
a step, that you wish be sure of your own feelings; and
there is no reason at all for haste. It is often said, you know,
'Marry in haste, and repent at leisure.' Of course, it is also
said, 'Marry first and love will follow.'"

"Perhaps I am being over-sentimental, Helen; but if I am
to marry, I should like love to come first. And do not you
think—does not it strike you a little odd, that Mr. Devere
should have declared himself so soon? We have spent all of
two evenings and a part of one afternoon together in company! Is it possible he can know his mind so quickly?"

"Darling Jane! The only thing that strikes me odd is that,
beautiful, clever, and good as you are, you do not immediately receive an offer of marriage from every gentleman you
meet! I cannot conceive how it was that Ned, after seeing us
both together, should have been so nonsensical as to fall in
love with me; though I am very glad he did, of course."

"It is no mystery to me that he did," said Jane, laughing,
"for you are the dearest girl in all the world! And if I could
but believe Mr. Devere and myself to be as perfectly suited
as you and Mr. Dixon are, I should give him my hand most
happily."

# Chapter Thirteen

**THE RAIN CONTINUED** all night and through the better part of the next day, preventing any visits from either Mr. Churchill or Mr. Devere. Jane was thankful for the reprieve, and resolved on using it to prepare herself for the inevitable rencontre; for they were all to meet again on Wednesday at Lady Paget's party. By that time, it was to be hoped, she would have her emotions under such good regulation as to be able to encounter either gentleman with equanimity.

The event proved somewhat different from her expectation. Mr. Devere presented himself at the Campbells' house on Wednesday morning, and was shown directly to Colonel Campbell's study to learn his fate. After being informed by that gentleman of the outcome of his suit, he requested the favour of a private interview with Miss Fairfax. She received a summons from the Colonel which obliged her to leave off reading her aunt Hetty's letter, containing all the latest news from Highbury, to hear Mr. Devere's petition.

"Miss Fairfax," he began when they were left alone, "I pray you will allow me to speak just a few words to you on this subject, and then I shall consider it as closed, until such time as—as I may have better reason to believe its renewal welcome to you."

Having received her quiet, if somewhat reluctant assent, he continued with a little smile of mortification, "Do not be alarmed, Miss Fairfax. I mean only to apologise for what must seem to you the rashness of my declaration. I assure you, my sister abused me up and down for my stupidity when she heard of it. And indeed, if my blundering has caused you any distress—I am heartily sorry for it—and I hope you will forgive me."

It would have taken a harder heart than Jane possessed, to withstand such a plea as this; and, having granted him the pardon he sought, she readily shook his hand, liking him rather the better, it must be admitted, for his embarrassment.

"Now, Miss Fairfax," he resumed with a little more self-possession, "I am also charged with a commission. Margaret begs you will do her the very great kindness of accompanying us to the party at Ashdale Park this evening. Lady Paget will send a carriage for us; and we could call for you at whatever hour you name. I have taken the liberty of asking the Colonel if he would permit you to join our party; and he has no objection, if the plan is agreeable to you. I need hardly explain to you why your coming with us would be of the greatest comfort to my sister."

Jane understood his meaning; and in view of the circumstances, and having no reason to fear a further urging of his suit, she was not unwilling to accompany them. Having fixed upon a time, they amicably concluded the interview, and he departed.

At the appointed hour, Lady Paget's carriage pulled up before the Colonel's house. Miss Devere was unusually silent during the ride to Ashdale Park, but her discomposure was evident. On entering the manor house, they were shown into a large and richly-furnished drawing room, where a number of people were already gathered. Many of the guests were known to Mr. and Miss Devere and greeted them with civility, exchanging a few words before returning to their own companions. Others continued to arrive. Two liveried footmen, carrying delicacies on silver trays, circulated through the room, treading softly on the thick carpets. Jane and her friends stood, waiting for the lady of the house and her distinguished guest to appear. They did not appear, however; and after a time Mr. Devere determined to go in search of Lady Paget. He returned shortly.

"Her ladyship will be down soon," said he, "or so the butler informed me. But Mr. Hammond is not here, Margaret— nor is he looked for this evening. So you may breathe again."

Miss Devere did indeed appear relieved, and said she was; but Jane was sure her relief could not be unmixed with disappointment. There was no time, though, to know more of her sentiments. Lady Paget entered the room a moment later, with smiles for her guests as she made her way toward Mr. Devere and his companions. Her smiles vanished the instant she reached them. Making no greeting, waiting for no polite inquiries as to the health of her ailing lord and master, she began a tirade upon the character of Mr. James

Hammond.

"So," she said in a low voice to the rector, just nodding to the two ladies at his side, "he is not coming! I suppose you know it already. Have you ever heard of anything so ill-mannered? I need not scruple to tell *you*, Stephen, I am extremely angry. All the trouble I have gone to, and the expense! Not that I regard *that* in the least; I could spend ten times as much without a thought. But the servants have been all slaving away; why, Pierre has been baking pastries for three days in preparation! And then a note arrives, just a short while ago—the briefest of notes, and as cool as you please, saying he is delayed in Oxfordshire; cannot say how soon he will be able to get away! No explanation, hardly an apology for his rudeness! But of course, what else can one expect from such a person? He is not of any birth or breeding, you know. His father was a brick-layer, or some such (heaven knows what!); and blood, as they say, will tell. But it is too provoking. Really, I have half a mind to offer the commission to Mr. Turner. Or perhaps Lawrence, or West, would do as well. Mr. Hammond is very much mistaken if he thinks himself the only painter of any ability in the world. There are any number just as good—or nearly so," she said with a little less certainty. "Still, it would be such a thing for our church, to have a James Hammond hung over the altar. It sounds vastly well, does not it? I must think on it further. In the meantime, Stephen, you will accompany me whilst I greet my guests? Dear Paget is too ill to come down, poor man; so I rely upon you to do the honours of the house in his stead."

And with neither compliments nor apologies to Miss Devere and Miss Fairfax, she led him away.

Jane could think of nothing to say in consideration of such ill-breeding, but Miss Devere was at no loss for words. Though indignant, she spoke them in an undertone for her brother's sake.

"I do so cordially detest that woman. Call my brother by his Christian name, as though she had known him all his life! And what is she, that he should hop to her bidding as if he were no better than a galley slave? If you only knew, Miss Fairfax, how many times, when he has wished to be out doing some good among his parishioners, he has been summoned to Ashdale Park; forced to relinquish all his benevolent designs, and submit himself to my lady's pleasure! It is thought that Lord Paget has behaved toward him in a most liberal and condescending manner, by granting him the living of St. Alban's; and I suppose," she admitted, "he does owe her ladyship some measure of complaisance on that score. But if he is to hold his office only at the cost of his self-respect and independence as a man—I, for one, think it costs too dear."

"Is he so entirely at her command?" Jane asked.

"Indeed, you can have no idea. And it is not as though, having once bestowed the living, she could have it taken away again at her whim. The bishop would have something to say about *that*. No, his position is perfectly secure. In truth, it is his own fault that she rules over him as she does. He is altogether too mild, too tractable. He dislikes to be at variance with anyone."

"I am sure it is very much to his credit," said Jane. After a thoughtful interval, she added, "I suppose there are few men so perfectly independent, as to have the power of disregarding all whims and humours but their own. The man who earns his bread must please those whose patronage he seeks. And," (her thoughts perhaps returning to Frank Churchill) "the man who will inherit his fortune must please those from whom he hopes to gain his wealth—he must purchase his future independence, by present submission."

Margaret, appearing scarcely to have heard her, said, "But I wonder why James did not come?" Care for her brother's dignity seemed to fade away as new ideas arose. "Do you think he may have heard of my being here, and wished to avoid me?"

"It is impossible to know," Jane replied.

"Having witnessed my distress at the prospect of meeting him again, Miss Fairfax, I am sure you will understand my feelings. I fear to see him, and yet—oh! I long to see him, too. I was bitterly disappointed once before, when I expected him, and he did not come. And now, fifteen years later, again he is expected, and again he does not come! Does it not seem a cruel trick, to disappoint me thus a second time?"

"But in this case," said Jane, "the disappointment will be only temporary, I think. Lady Paget said merely that Mr. Hammond's visit was delayed, not that it was given up."

There was another pause, before Margaret resumed with more of her customary spirit,

"And the way she talked about him! Calling *him* ill-mannered! She, who cannot open her lips without mentioning her immense wealth, and her *dear Paget*—who is about as dear to her as that potted geranium at your elbow. She is not fit to launder James Hammond's linen. And she had best not speak to *him* so disparagingly of his family, or she might be required to hear something to the purpose about her own antecedents. I daresay she will not find *him* so ready to bend to her will—unless he is a very great deal altered from what he once was.

"But," she resumed in a less confident tone, "perhaps Stephen will have found out something more from her. I shall ask him later."

After a little pause, and partly to change the subject, Jane asked, "Who are that gentleman and young lady talking with your brother and Lady Paget now?"

"Oh! it is only Mr. Lodge, and his daughter Mary. Mr. Lodge is an attorney; he handles law business here in Weymouth for Lord Paget."

Her liveliness returned as she proceeded to describe the family. "Mr. Sidney Lodge is a most pious gentleman. Each of his sons is named for one of the apostles. His intention, I believe, was to produce a complete set of twelve; but the sainted Mrs. Lodge had the great good fortune to be carried off by a fever after only five. The five Lodge boys you will hear universally condemned as a parcel of little knaves. The reputation is very well-deserved. Mary is the eldest child, and the only daughter, just out of the schoolroom—rather pretty, in a girlish sort of way. She is very young, but there is no harm in her. I have befriended her somewhat these several months past, for she has a great deal to put up with at home; and I am glad to be able to offer her a little respite now and then by inviting her to the Rectory. She idolises my brother—hangs upon his every word, and can hardly be in his presence without turning pink all over. It is quite amusing to watch. Stephen, of course, being as insensible as most men, has not an idea of her feelings."

As she spoke, the young lady in question left her father's side, and made her way across the room to where Jane and Margaret were standing.

"Oh, Miss Devere, how do you do? I am so glad to see you!" she began in a rush. "I thought we should never be able to come tonight, for I had to dress and do my hair over twice! I meant to wear my spotted muslin, you know, instead of this sprigged, for it is newer; but just as we were about to leave, the boys came running in, and Andrew tugged so at my sleeve that he tore it, and Matthew pulled the combs from my hair, and John and Peter and Bartholomew set up such a stamping and hallooing, that I thought it would be the death of me—Papa looking on all the while and laughing, as if he thought it an excellent joke!"

"I am sorry to hear it," Margaret said kindly. "But you are here now, and the sprigged muslin becomes you very well, even if the spotted is newer. But you have not met Miss Fairfax, I think."

She performed the introduction, and Mary looked quite abashed as she said, "I hope you will excuse my going on so, Miss Fairfax; but really I am so vexed, you cannot conceive—unless you have a great many brothers yourself?"

"I have no brothers at all, or sisters either—though my friend Miss Campbell is quite in the place of a sister to me."

"No brothers at all!" she marvelled. "You must count yourself very lucky!"

"I have not been used to think it an especially fortunate circumstance; but I allow it may be luckier to have no brothers, than to have brothers so provoking as you describe."

"Now, Mary," scolded Margaret with a twinkle in her eye, "You must not generalise! I have four brothers myself; and though certainly I have known one or another of them to be positively beastly on occasion, I can attest that at times even a brother is capable of being tolerably agreeable."

Mary's face was overspread with a deep rose hue. "Oh! to be sure. I was not thinking of Mr. Devere. But he is so very kind, and good, and—"

She stopped short, and her cheeks would have turned even pinker, had such an effect been possible; for at that moment, Mr. Devere himself, accompanied by Mr. Lodge, was seen coming towards them. Mr. Lodge was about five-and-forty, and not altogether bad-looking: an Englishman of the ruddy, beefy, well-fed variety; but a man possessed of no extraordinary acquirements, or charms of address. He was rather unctuous in manner, particularly so when addressing Miss Devere, to whom, Jane thought, he was at pains to recommend himself. Mary, now that Mr. Devere had joined them, spoke not unless spoken to, appeared fascinated by the pattern of the carpet (towards which her gaze was most frequently directed), and continued rosy in complexion as before. Mr. Devere must needs be insensible not to notice her infatuation; yet so it seemed.

The Campbells and Mr. Dixon soon came in, enlarging their own party. Mr. Hammond's absence was then thoroughly canvassed among them, before Miss Devere brought the discussion to a close by declaring, with somewhat of forced gaiety in her manner, that the gentleman's failure to materialise was no doubt merely a scheme, intended to increase the popularity of his work by heightening the air of mystery surrounding his person; and that they should do best to thwart him in this object, by according him not another moment's consideration.

Mr. and Mrs. Churchill entered the room soon afterwards, in the company of their nephew. The three were promptly claimed by Lady Paget, who was eager to triumph over her old friend with introductions to the more important personages present, including two peers of the realm, the member for the county, and the second richest gentleman ("only excepting dear Paget, of course") in the neighbourhood. Jane entertained a small hope that, after a time, Frank Churchill might come over to join their own group, but he seemed tethered to Mrs. Churchill's side. So far as she could tell (though she did try not to make a study of it), he did not even cast a glance in her direction; and despite her very prudent resolution to be more guarded where he was concerned, she felt keenly disappointed. She had expected this evening would hold a great deal to interest and, perhaps, to gratify; but suddenly the party seemed to her quite wearisome and flat.

# Chapter Fourteen

**THE FOOTMEN WITH** their trays had not come around since the Campbells' arrival, and Helen and Mr. Dixon, who had eaten only a light dinner in deference to Lady Paget's French cooks, soon excused themselves and went off in search of refreshment. Some time afterwards, Jane saw them go out onto the terrace; and the stuffiness of the room and the tedium of the affair eventually drove her to seek relief out-of-doors as well.

Amid the other scattered guests who had come out to enjoy the evening air, she lingered to admire the prospect spread out before her. The lush gardens were bathed in the glow of a moon newly-risen: their diverse forms and textures were marked out by the play of light and shadow, their brilliant colours all transfigured into a muted counterpoint of ebony and silver. The night sky was clear, and faintly spotted with stars. Above the river and the hills in the distance, a few graceful, iridescent wisps of cloud floated serenely.

At length she descried Helen and Mr. Dixon sitting together on a bench at the far end of the garden. Knowing they had little opportunity to be alone together, she chose not to disturb them; and, after a last look at the beauty of the moonlit landscape, she turned to go inside. She met Frank Churchill coming out.

"Miss Fairfax!" said he. "I have slipped away on purpose to find you, and to ask how you are. I was very much afraid," he continued in a low, eager voice, "after we parted the other day, that you had not been able to reach home without being soaked through."

It was fortunate that Jane had so firmly resolved to be sensible about Frank Churchill, or she might have found it difficult to respond with a proper dignity in the face of his warmth.

"Thank you. I am very well. I got in just as the rain was beginning, and did not get wet at all."

"I am relieved to hear it," he said. "And I am pleased to be able to report to you that Mrs. Nesbit is now comfortably settled in her new home, and finds the society of Mrs. Roberts and her daughter most agreeable."

"I am glad indeed," she replied, smiling. "I hope I shall have the pleasure of calling on her again soon."

"I know she will be delighted to see you. She has already expressed to me how grateful she is for your kindness in visiting her."

"She owes me no gratitude. It is your kindness, Mr. Churchill, which has done everything for her," said Jane, for a moment quite forgetting her intention to maintain a polite reserve, as they stood smiling at one another.

"I have some other news," he said shortly, "that I think will interest you as well. I had a letter from Highbury today, a letter from my father. And it seems that—"

"Mr. Weston is going to marry Miss Taylor."

"Yes! How did you guess?"

"It is no guess. I too had a letter from Highbury this morning; and my dear aunt was so overjoyed with the happy tidings, she could hardly keep her pen to any other topic. Let me offer you my congratulations."

"Thank you. Do you know the lady very well? My father has spoken of her before, of course; but I would like a more unprejudiced description than may be obtained from a man in love."

"I have known Miss Taylor most of my life; and I can assure you that, whatever your father has said of her, he cannot have said too much in her favour. She has a hundred good qualities. Indeed, were the man in question almost any other than Mr. Weston, I would think he could not be half good enough for her."

"This is praise indeed! Miss Taylor was governess to Miss Woodhouse, I believe?"

"Yes. And if she could be admitted to have any fault at all, I suppose it might be that she is rather of a too mild and yielding disposition to exercise authority with ease, as a governess must. But that trait will not serve her ill in marriage, I think; for is not a mild and yielding disposition a woman's best qualification for matrimony?" she said, only half in jest. "Truly, Miss Taylor cannot but make an excellent wife, even to a much more troublesome husband than Mr. Weston ever could be."

"My father is a man with few defects of character."

"None, certainly, which could occasion any real pain or uneasiness to his wife."

After a little pause, he ventured, "But you cannot think Mr. Weston's son quite so—exemplary, as Mr. Weston himself?"

Jane hoped the evening shadows would cover her confusion, as he continued, "I was almost afraid to see you this evening, Miss Fairfax; afraid of what you must be thinking—how you would judge me. I know my asking you to keep my visit to Mrs. Nesbit a secret must have seemed to you very wrong—you are so scrupulous yourself. It shocked you, I am sure it did."

"I confess, I am not in the habit of keeping secrets, Mr. Churchill. And I dislike anything of concealment, or—"

"But my circumstances are such, that—. I know it must seem strange to you, that a grown man of three-and-twenty has not more power to command his own affairs; but believe me, I should never have dreamt of imposing upon you, had it not been absolutely necessary."

Though she could not regard his behaviour as otherwise than wrong, she felt it only fair to acknowledge the difficulties which drove him to such extremities. Having received something like a pardon, his anxious look metamorphosed to an irrepressible grin as he asked,

"Then you do not think me quite a perfect scoundrel?"

Once again, she was compelled to return his smile as she admitted, "No—not quite a perfect one."

They talked a little more of Miss Taylor; then with a lively air he said, "Well, Miss Fairfax, now that you have enlightened me so thoroughly as to the many excellencies of my father's bride-to-be, will you oblige me still further, by acquainting me with her *protegée's*?—for I own to feeling a great curiosity about Miss Woodhouse. My father tells me she is a very beautiful and accomplished young lady. But good heavens! What a contemptible wretch I am, praising one young lady to another! How can I ever hope to redeem myself after such a blunder?—Might I be forgiven, do you suppose, if I hastened to assure you (having never heard either you or Miss Woodhouse perform) that I think *your* playing vastly superior to hers? And (having seen neither your pictures nor hers) that I consider Miss Woodhouse's drawings are nothing in comparison to your own? Yes," he concluded with a self-satisfied nod. "I think *that* must soften you, ma'am, if anything will."

While she would have been quite content had he shown no interest in Miss Woodhouse whatever, Jane could not but be diverted by his banter. "Oh, indeed, sir," she replied, laughing. "I am only too honoured by your compliments. And pray, allow me to say that the elevation of your taste is exceeded only by the depth of your sincerity."

He laughed in turn; after which they revisited the subject of his father and Miss Taylor, till interrupted by a servant coming out to announce the start of the entertainment. A performance, by an ensemble of musicians brought in from London for the occasion, was to commence in a few minutes. Jane parted cordially from Mr. Churchill, then walked off to frighten Helen and Mr. Dixon out of their garden retreat and back into the house.

It was a delightful concert. Delightful, at least, to those whose sole requirement was that the music be not so loud as to prevent their talking throughout; but for those who could claim any real powers of discrimination—for those who actually listened—it was disappointing. The musicians were by no means first-rate, though they *were* from London, and their hire *was* so exorbitant, and 'had dear Paget not been so very rich as he was, he could not have afforded them'. But Lady Paget, with no real liking for or knowledge of music, was perfectly satisfied in having provided such an expensive entertainment for her guests.

Frank Churchill was among those who had not found much to admire in the performance; and it needed all his powers of invention to furnish the flattery demanded by Lady Paget, on the niceness of her taste, and the dimensions of her purse. After gratifying her wishes in this respect, he applied those same powers to the gratification of his own. He had not lived with his aunt so long, without discovering that hers was essentially a contrary nature; and that it was at times possible to obtain her permission for doing just what he wanted to do, by affecting a dislike to doing it, and feigning a willingness to be guided by her wishes. Moreover, he had learned to take a kind of private amusement in these little dissimulations, to lighten the sense of gravity which might otherwise have oppressed him, under the trial of having so perverse a woman as Mrs. Churchill for his guide and guardian. Thus it was that, her ladyship having left them to receive the compliments of her other guests, he turned to Mrs. Churchill and said,

"Aunt Eugenia, I wish to consult you on a matter of some

delicacy."

Gaining her attention with this preface, he continued, "I have been wondering whether it would appear rude in me not to go over and pay my respects to Colonel Campbell and his wife. I have met them twice since we have been at Weymouth; at the church, as you know, and also at the assembly. I met the young ladies once, too, at the circulating library. I really have no wish to forward the acquaintance, but now it is begun, I rather fear it would look too particular if I did not speak to them. So I thought it best to ask your opinion—you are so very astute in these matters. How would you advise me?"

Mrs. Churchill, softened by this flattering picture of her powers of discernment, and by his submitting the question to her greater sagacity, deliberated a few moments before dispensing her opinion.

"In general, Frank, I should not like to see you get onto an intimate footing with such an inferior set of people. But I suppose, under the circumstances, it will be impossible for you to escape the acquaintance. In London, to be sure, you might go months without meeting them again, and that would be an end to it; but it is one of the evils of a watering place such as this, that one is forever falling in with second-rate society. Even Lady Paget thinks the family worth noticing, as you see (all a part of her strange infatuation with that young clergyman, I suppose; they are *his* friends). And perhaps you may find it desirable, occasionally, to seek some diversion and society from home—to relieve the tedium of always catering to the conceits and humours of a sick old woman."

Frank, in due form, exclaimed at her use of the word 'old' to describe herself, and protested he should never think her companionship tedious. "Yet I may be finding myself more at liberty than I like, now you have been reunited with your old friend. No doubt the viscountess will wish for a good deal of your company; and I foresee you will find it expedient to have your visits without the encumbrance of a third. *My* presence will be quite unwelcome to you both."

"How unlucky it is," said Mrs. Churchill, "that none of Lady Paget's children are here just now. If her younger daughter were not newly married, for instance, or if the elder had been single—I'm certain you would have found either altogether charming. And were the future viscount not embarked upon a tour of the Lakes just now, I have not a doubt (though he is rather younger than you, being just turned eighteen) that the two of you would have got on famously. Such society you would have found more to your liking, without question."

"Oh! yes—without question."

She paused to give a sigh of regret before stating with evident distaste, "All things considered, my dear, I think you may as well go and exchange a few courtesies with those people—however little pleasure you are likely to derive from the connection. Such are the little sacrifices one must occasionally make to the demands of society."

Having been thus edified by his aunt's wise counsel, Frank hastened at once to profit by it. The Campbells greeted him with a pleasing lack of ceremony, and the Colonel invited him to take one of the chairs lately vacated by Mr. Devere and his sister, whose attendance had been claimed by other acquaintance. Mrs. Campbell asked him how he had liked the performance; and he was happy to discover their opinion was in complete accord with his own.

"To speak truly," Colonel Campbell declared, "we would have done better, much better, to have stayed at home and heard these two young ladies perform."

"That is a pleasure I have been desiring for some time, sir," said Frank, "for I understand Miss Campbell is a great proficient; and of Miss Fairfax's accomplishments in music I have long been informed."

"Even so," said Mr. Dixon, "whenever you do hear Miss Fairfax play, I think her abilities will impress you. You will find they have not been done justice to."

Miss Campbell seconded his sentiments, and Jane pleaded with a smile, "I beg you will not put overmuch confidence in the praise of such partial friends, Mr. Churchill, or I shall be too frightened to play a note in your presence."

Colonel Campbell reminded Frank of his promise to join them for a family dinner. "Then you shall have a chance to listen for yourself, and form your own judgement."

"Thank you, sir. I would be very happy to come." He turned then to Mrs. Campbell. "Would tomorrow be convenient, ma'am?" he asked, and received her ready assent.

"Excellent. Excellent," said the Colonel; adding to his wife, "And we must have Stephen and Margaret as well, my dear; then we shall be quite enough to be lively. Ah! there they are now. I will ask them before we go in to supper."

Frank saw no reason, at that time, to regret the addition

of Miss Devere and her brother to the company; a larger gathering might afford him an opportunity to speak privately with Miss Fairfax. His acceptance of Colonel Campbell's invitation, however, was given not only for the sake of seeing her again (though that motive was a powerful one), but as well out of a genuine liking for the entire party. He was very fond of society, but the habitual retirement in which he was obliged to live, on his aunt's account, did not often furnish much; and seldom any so agreeable as the Campbells and their friends. Colonel Campbell and his wife he found both sensible and amiable. Their daughter, though plain like her mother, and not nearly as clever, was yet as artless and good-natured a young lady as he had ever met. Mr. Dixon was likewise plain, and perhaps not a man of remarkable gifts—but he, too, was sensible and affable. Miss Devere was amusing; her brother an unexceptionable person. And Miss Fairfax, of course, was lovely beyond description.

After a few more minutes of conversation, supper was announced, and Frank returned to his aunt and uncle. Approaching them, he assumed an air of dismay.

"I am afraid, aunt Eugenia," he said as he gave Mrs. Churchill his arm to lead her in to the dining room, "I have somehow been betrayed into accepting a dinner invitation from Colonel Campbell for tomorrow evening. It was much against my inclination; but the man pressed me so hard, he left me no way to refuse, without being positively rude. And remembering your good advice, and the possibility of offending Lady Paget if I were to slight any persons she had deigned to notice, I thought it best to submit. However, I shall be glad to get myself out of the engagement, if you can but give me a plausible excuse."

# Chapter Fifteen

**PERSUADED HER NEPHEW** would have little pleasure in the party, Mrs. Churchill made no opposition to Frank's joining the Campbells for dinner on the following evening. He arrived punctually at the Colonel's house, and was followed in almost immediately by Mr. and Miss Devere.

The party at Ashdale Park was the first topic of conversation, when they were all seated together in the parlour. The subject of Mr. Hammond's absence was raised again; but Mr. Devere steered the talk into another avenue, by asking Miss Fairfax her opinion of Mr. Lodge and his daughter.

"I did not speak to either one long enough to form a very definite idea," said Jane, "but Miss Lodge seems a pleasing, artless sort of girl, and her father a respectable gentleman."

"I sat across from that young lady at supper," said Colonel Campbell with a chuckle, "and was chiefly struck by the immense quantity of food she consumed—enough to provision a regiment! Such a slight wisp of a girl, too."

Miss Devere laughed. "It is indeed a remarkable sight, to witness the violence with which Mary Lodge can attack a shoulder of beef, or a hindquarter of pork. I once saw her devour three venison steaks at dinner, with half a loaf of bread besides—and top it all off with four raspberry tarts!"

"On those occasions," said Mr. Devere with a thoughtful air, "when we have dined with Mr. Lodge and his daughter at their home, the boys were provided for in some other part of the house, that we might enjoy our meal in peace. But in the regular course of things, I gather Miss Lodge must contend against her five unruly brothers for a share of the food; and I have no doubt she is often obliged to satisfy herself with such crumbs as escape their clutches."

"Good heavens!" Mrs. Campbell exclaimed. "Why, the poor child must be half-starved!"

"Very likely," said the Colonel. "Very likely, indeed. It is no wonder, then, that she eats as much as she can, when she has the chance. My dear, why don't we have the girl over to dine with us sometimes, while we are at Weymouth?

"I should very much like to, Colonel, if her father does not object.—By the bye, Margaret, you never mentioned to us that Mr. Lodge was an admirer of yours."

"An admirer of mine! Did you deduce *that* from his manner of addressing me?"

"I thought he made his admiration clear."

"What is clear to me," she said, "is that Mr. Lodge has been unable to find a governess who will bear with his darling boys for longer than a fortnight; and he hopes, by marrying, to secure them a more permanent keeper—a job Cerberus himself would decline to undertake. Perhaps he imagines a single woman past thirty must be delighted to accept any establishment that comes in her way. But if I am the prey he has in mind to trap for such a purpose, I'm afraid he must be disappointed."

A brief silence followed; then Helen proposed, "I wonder if we might have a little music before dinner?"

"Indeed," said Mr. Dixon. "I was about to suggest it myself. Miss Fairfax, you will not refuse to favour us by sitting down to the pianoforte now? Mr. Churchill must be impatient to hear you perform, after all he has heard of your ability; and I own I would like to see what you have been able to make of those pieces I brought over the other day."

Frank, shocked at Mr. Dixon's tactlessness, thought Miss Fairfax must be distressed by so open and decided a preference for her playing over her friend's. But she only quietly assented to his request, and moved to the instrument; while Miss Campbell, to his amazement, exhibited not the smallest inclination to take offence. And as Mr. Dixon's behaviour toward both ladies was, in every other respect, exactly what it should be, Frank concluded this odd circumstance must be proof of nothing beyond the gentleman's surpassing love of music, and the perfect amity and confidence subsisting among them all.

Jane began with 'Robin Adair', entreating Miss Campbell and Mr. Dixon to supply the vocal part, as the song was a particular favourite of the latter. They complied most obligingly; and though their execution was not marked by any conspicuous genius, the duet was far from irksome, for Mr. Dixon had a good deal of taste, and Miss Campbell was not altogether wanting in it; and their own enjoyment in the performance was readily communicated to their listeners. Jane's accompaniment was flawless, and the close of the piece was greeted with enthusiastic applause.

If music be indeed the food of love, Frank Churchill
tasted much that evening both to charm his palate, and to
nourish his passion. It was only after a few more Irish airs,
however, when Miss Campbell and Mr. Dixon sat down
again, that he partook of the most ambrosial fare. Miss
Fairfax sang—in a voice so clear, so fluid, and so achingly
sweet, that the sound could have melted the most hardened
villain in Christendom. It had wanted only a little to convince Frank that he was very much in love with her; and
scarcely had she got through a single verse before the business was accomplished.

He listened spellbound through the first two songs; but
the third being one he knew well, he could not resist stepping up to the instrument, and mingling his own voice with
hers. His mellow tenor and her supple soprano were extremely well-matched, blending together in a delicious
harmony, and giving great pleasure to their listeners. Of listeners, however, he was perfectly unconscious. He could
think only of her: of her angelic voice—of the lovely gaze she
lifted to his in delighted surprise, when he began to sing
along with her—of the shy confusion with which she turned
back to the keyboard, upon perceiving the eloquent glow in
his eyes—and of the delicate rose tint which lingered upon
her cheek for some time afterwards.

The hour of dinner arrived. Being detained by the compliments of Miss Campbell and her mother on his fine voice,
Frank lost the opportunity of giving Miss Fairfax his arm
into the dining room, and Mr. Devere won for himself the
coveted place beside her. Frank bore it pretty well, though;
trusting that, as they were but a small group, the separation could not make any material difference in their
intercourse. At all events, it was a happiness to him merely
to be situated within her vicinity—if he could not talk, he
could look; and that was happiness enough for the present.

About midway through the meal, however, sensations
more disagreeable arose. He began to perceive something
beyond ordinary civility—something of gallantry, almost, in
Mr. Devere's attentions toward her. It was discreet and re-
strained, consistent with his accustomed demeanour; but
(Frank could not deceive himself) it was gallantry nonetheless. The rector addressed himself more often to Miss
Fairfax than to anyone else, and always with an air of gentleness and complaisance suspiciously lover-like. Whether

Miss Fairfax received his gallantry with any satisfaction—
whether she even recognised it as such, Frank could not so
easily determine.

There was more music after dinner, for Miss Campbell
must also have her turn at the pianoforte. At the conclusion
of her second piece, Mr. Dixon begged Miss Fairfax to sing
again. To this Mrs. Campbell objected, out of concern for
Jane's throat, and Mr. Dixon was compelled to yield. Miss
Campbell suggested dancing, and Mrs. Campbell vouch-
safed to play for the young people's amusement as long as
they wished. The proposal was taken up with enthusiasm;
however, Frank had then another disappointment to endure. He watched as Mr. Devere led Miss Fairfax onto the
floor for a lively country dance, while he must content himself with the rector's sister. But the first change of partners
found him standing up with Miss Fairfax himself, as Mrs.
Campbell played a captivating waltz!

At the end of the dance, the clock struck eleven, and he
was forced to recollect that he would be expected at home;
but he did not leave without first receiving from the Campbells a very kind and most gratifying invitation to join their
family party again, whenever he should have a disengaged
evening. He walked home along the Esplanade with a step
tolerably light, and feelings more buoyant still; for there is
nothing to animate the spirit like the first stirrings of new
love—and the cheerful hope of its being hereafter returned.

With a lively, social temper, Frank was no stranger to the
art and sport of flirtation; but he had never been in love before—and so potent, so intoxicating was the feeling, that it
seemed to justify every sanguine expectation, and render
every impediment to happiness inconsequential. He was indeed assailed by a little pang of anxiety now and then,
occasioned by the remembrance of his possible rival, as well
as the rather larger obstacle of his aunt's certain disap-
proval; but he was too far in love to grant much scope to
sobering reflections. He was not blinded by his condition,
for he could yet savor, as he skirted the beach, the sight of
sands gleaming white in the moonlight; he could admire
how the moon illumined the foaming surf as it rushed to
embrace the shore. But to all uneasiness and doubts he
closed his eyes, as sins against his new-fledged love.

His uncle was sitting alone in the parlour when he got in,
and called out to him as he passed by on his way upstairs.

"Is that you, Frank? Are you still up?"

Frank entered through the open door. "I am just come home, sir."

"Just come home? Bless me! I thought you'd gone up hours ago. And were you really out all this time?"

"I went out to dine, at Colonel Campbell's house."

"Campbell... where have I heard that name before?"

"You were introduced to the Campbells after church on Sunday; and they were at Ashdale Park last night."

He nodded his head. "Oh, yes. Yes. A widower, I think he was?"

"No, Colonel Campbell is a married man, with one daughter—and a ward, Miss Fairfax."

"Oh, indeed. I cannot recall them very well. But I hope you had a pleasant evening?"

"Very pleasant. Is my aunt retired already? I hope she is not ill."

"She went to bed some time ago, with a headache—or was it a backache? Well, she was suffering frightfully, as she told me several times herself; though as uncomplaining as ever, dear lady! You must always remember to be good to your aunt, Frank, for she has a great deal to bear with."

With a solemn look, Frank took a chair near his elderly uncle. "I hope you do not think me often remiss in what is due to my aunt—or to you, uncle."

"No, no. Not at all. You have always been a good boy, Frank. My memory is not what it once was, you know; but I am not apt to forget how often you have sacrificed your pleasure to ours. Eugenia and I look upon you quite as our own son; and I am sure no son could have shown more affection and respect to his parents, than you have always shown to us. Only one thing could be wanting to make our joy complete; and that is, that you should find a young lady worthy of you—and give us a daughter to love as well."

Frank was quiet for a moment before he ventured, "Sir, I fear that you and my good aunt, in your kind affection for me, may have conceived too grand an idea of the sort of lady I might hope to attach."

"Nonsense, dear boy! You are my heir. I have never made any secret of that fact. You will inherit Enscombe, and an income little short of ten thousand a year. You bear the name of Churchill. Churchill blood runs in your veins. These virtues alone would entitle you to a great deal—as I have no doubt Eugenia would attest, if she were here; for she is very knowledgeable about such things, you know.

She has often confided to me the hopes she has for you."

Frank hesitated again. "I am honoured by my aunt's good opinion, but—I fear that, in her partiality, she rates my claims too highly."

"Come, come, now, you are too modest! Considering your personal qualifications (and I'm sure I speak without prejudice, when I say you are as handsome and charming a fellow as any miss is likely to meet with), I really am inclined to think your dear aunt not at all extravagant in looking for you to make a very brilliant match. Eugenia believes you have a right to aspire even to a daughter of nobility; and I daresay she will hardly be satisfied with less."

# Chapter Sixteen

"**I FOUND IT** altogether a pleasant evening," Helen declared later that night as she twisted curl papers into Jane's dark hair. Their maid having been given leave to visit her ailing grandmother for a few weeks, the two young ladies had no one to wait upon them at Weymouth, and were temporarily serving one another in that capacity. "I like Miss Devere and her brother very well; and Mr. Churchill grows no less amiable upon further acquaintance."

"They are all very agreeable," Jane agreed.

Helen scrutinised her countenance in the mirror, and said mischievously, "But I wonder whether you have not begun to find one of them *particularly* agreeable?"

Jane, thinking of Frank Churchill, was startled by the question. "What do you mean?"

"You needn't look so frightened! I only meant to tease you about Mr. Devere. But if it makes you uncomfortable, of course I will have done at once."

"I do think it will be best, Helen, to say as little as possible about—about that subject for now. When I have had more opportunity to be acquainted with Mr. Devere, I daresay I shall be glad to talk unreservedly. But until then, you may trust I have not forgotten what you are hoping for. I know that you all wish me to accept Mr. Devere; and I will oblige you if I can—"

"Jane, you goose! How can you speak so? You cannot imagine I would wish for anything but to see you happily settled, in a home of your own; you know how I have always hated the thought of your going out as a governess. But you mustn't think I would ever press you to marry someone you dislike—nor would my parents."

"Dearest Helen! I am so grateful for the friendship you have always shown me—for all your kindness and solicitude. I know you want only what would be for my good. But I must confess to you that—that I am a little afraid of my own cowardice. In dread of the future that awaits me if I do

not marry, I sometimes fear I may be tempted to wed for...
*mercenary* reasons. I hope I will always have courage
enough to keep me from doing what I feel would be wrong;
and I think to marry without love a great wrong indeed. But
at times, I do doubt myself. I doubt my strength of will—and
I tremble for my own weakness."

To acknowledge so much, Jane felt as a considerable relief; for she had never owned to her friend—had only lately
fully owned to herself—the trepidation with which she
looked forward to her intended fate. Helen's quick, affectionate response must soothe, must comfort, though it
could not remedy the ills of her situation. Jane only wished
she might be perfectly open, and talk as well of her unfortunate partiality for Frank Churchill. But she was ashamed
to admit how great an influence she had already allowed
him to gain over her, knowing as she did what little good
could come of it—and knowing that Helen, and the Colonel,
and Mrs. Campbell, all favoured Mr. Devere's suit.

She was still worrying over it the following morning as
she set out after breakfast to pay a call on Mrs. Nesbit. She
remembered, with a secret delight which she hardly knew
how to reason away, the duet she had sung with Frank
Churchill the night before, and the waltz they had danced
together; and she felt uncertain whether she most hoped or
feared to see him again today. When, upon arriving at Mrs.
Nesbit's, she found that lady sitting quite alone in the little
sheltered garden at the back of the house, disappointment
and relief came in about equal measure.

Mrs. Nesbit was pleased to see her, at any rate; and Jane
soon learned that her new friend was already improved in
health, as well as in spirits. Mr. Churchill had arranged for
her to be examined by an apothecary, whose prescription of
warm baths, and an embrocation to be applied twice daily,
had been of immediate benefit. She was also receiving every
possible attention from the landlady and her daughter: the
latter, it turned out, had a little experience as a nurse, and
was able to administer all the assistance Mrs. Nesbit required, along with a good deal of cheerful society.

There had been just time for these particulars to be
communicated, when the garden gate swung open behind
Jane, and she heard footsteps crossing the grass. She did
not turn; but she knew it was Frank Churchill even before
he called out,

"Ah! Good morning, Mrs. Nesbit. I see you have already

one friend here; I have brought you another. Good morning, Miss Fairfax."

Returning his greeting, she was obliged to look round at him, and was surprised to see that he carried a mewling gray kitten in his arms. Jane was very fond of animals; and in compassion for the tiny forlorn kitten, her self-consciousness vanished. She got up at once from her chair, and went over to caress the kitten's soft fur.

"What an adorable little puss," said Mrs. Nesbit. "Where did you find him?"

"I found him at the mercy of a disreputable pack of boys, who evidently think it fine sport to torment a small defenseless creature," he replied. To Jane, he added, "After the account we heard last evening, Miss Fairfax, I think you will not be too astonished to learn that these young savages bore the surname of *Lodge*. When I came upon them, they were tossing this poor little fellow about among them, pulling at his whiskers and swinging him by the tail—"

"My goodness—how dreadful!" said Mrs. Nesbit.

"I confess it was all I could do to keep from giving each of them a sound thrashing. But I remembered how you always used to say, ma'am, that repaying cruelty with cruelty only begets more cruelty; so I settled for giving them merely a very stern lecture (which I wish I could say had any effect), and taking their plaything out of their hands."

"Poor thing!" said Jane. The kitten was crying piteously, despite the safety of his present situation, and she ventured to suggest that he might be hungry.

"Of course! How stupid I am. Mrs. Nesbit, do you think your landlady might be willing to provide a saucer of milk for our friend here?"

"Why, certainly," she said, putting aside her needlework. "I can just run in and ask Martha Brown—"

"You can run! No, ma'am, I should think not. You will stay right where you are, thank you, and I will do the running—that is, if Miss Fairfax would not mind taking custody for a minute?"

Jane gave her consent readily, and he transferred the kitten into her arms. Looking up at him as he did so, she was discomposed to encounter an earnest gaze, and a handsome face very near her own. A moment later he turned away, and disappeared into the house.

"Do bring him here, Miss Fairfax," said Mrs. Nesbit. Jane obeyed, taking a seat near her. "There now, little one," the old woman murmured as she leaned across to rub a finger soothingly under the kitten's chin. "You are quite safe; no one will hurt you here. And you shall have breakfast presently."

Jane cradled the animal against her breast and gently stroked the top of his head. His mewling soon ceased, and he began to purr contentedly under the influence of their caresses.

"Sweet creature!" said the old woman. "He puts me in mind of a little cat young Master Frank—that is to say," she corrected herself, "—Mr. Frank Churchill—had when he was a boy. He had wanted a dog—a big, burly, loping sort of dog, you know, that he could run and tumble with. He was such an active, adventuresome child, always roaming over the hills and dales around Enscombe, and there were no other boys his age in the neighbourhood; or rather, none whom Mrs. Churchill thought it fit for her nephew to associate with. She was by no means an easy woman, I must say. But she was terribly fond of him; and I verily believe that, given time, he could have talked her into almost anything. However, she thought dogs dirty, and full of vermin, and would not hear of his keeping one. When he was old enough to shoot, she said, he might have a pointer or two for sport; but not before.

"He was terribly disappointed. Then one day he found a young tiger cat, half-starved, out behind the stables; and, after a great deal of pleading and persuading, she finally agreed to let him keep it. My heavens, that cat was attached to him! It used to follow him everywhere. A dog would have been a better companion for him, to be sure—but he loved the cat, all the same. That was his way; he was always taking care of some little injured mouse or abandoned nestling. He had so much love in him, he could never find creatures enough to bestow it on. I don't say he was the best behaved child that ever was. He could get into mischief the same as any other boy—or indeed more, at times; but he truly was the sweetest, most affectionate little soul!"

Such testimony was hardly calculated to recall Jane to a detached appraisal of Frank Churchill's virtues and faults; and when he returned shortly afterwards, bearing a brimming saucer of milk, she deemed it best to devote herself to watching the kitten hungrily lap it up.

"My dear," said Mrs. Nesbit to him as he took a seat beside Jane, leaning back comfortably and stretching his long legs out in front of him, "I was just telling Miss Fairfax about that tiger cat you had when you were a boy. Do you remember?"

"Of course," he replied, smiling. "You know I never forget old friends."

"I have been trying to think of his name, but I cannot for the life of me remember it."

"Hercules."

"Hercules!" Jane exclaimed, once again failing to maintain a dignified reticence. But it did seem an odd name for a cat!

He nodded, grinning. "Mrs. Nesbit had been reading me the story of the Argonauts, and the quest for the Golden Fleece. I fancied myself as Jason, and needed a bold and daring second to share in my adventures. So—"

"Hercules," she said, smiling back at him.

"Whatever happened to him?" asked Mrs. Nesbit.

"Why, my aunt told me he ran off, after I went away to school. In search of Hylas, perhaps," he suggested with another irresistible grin.

"And what name would you bestow on that tiny mite, I wonder," said Jane, gesturing toward the kitten.

He narrowed his eyes and studied the animal, who had finished his meal and was now sitting by Jane's feet, batting at the hem of her gown. She scooped him up in one hand— he was hardly bigger than her hand, and as light as an atomy—and deposited him in her lap. He pawed at her skirt a few times, then curled up for a nap.

Frank reached out and stroked a gentle palm across the kitten's striped fur. "What would you think of the name... Zeus?"

She could not help laughing. The idea of this diminutive kitten, no doubt the runt of the litter, owning the name of Zeus—supreme ruler of Olympus—lord of the sky—god of the thunderbolt! The others laughed too, and there was altogether such good feeling and good fellowship among them, that she could not regret having thrown off her reserve.

They all agreed that the kitten (who, whilst his fate was being decided, slept on peacefully in Jane's lap) should be henceforth known as Zeus. As to his future residence, Frank confessed he had brought him to Mrs. Nesbit in the hope that she would grant him asylum.

"My aunt does not take very kindly to animals, as you may remember. And I know firsthand, ma'am," he added, grinning again, "what an adept you are at caring for strays and orphans."

"Indeed, I should be delighted to have him. He will be good company for me—unless, of course, Miss Fairfax wishes to take him?"

Jane declined the offer with thanks, admitting that cats gave her friend Miss Campbell the sneezing fits.

"It is settled, then," Frank declared. "Mrs. Nesbit, you will keep him, and Miss Fairfax and I will come here to visit you both."

All too soon, Jane found it necessary to inform her friends that she could stay no longer. Making over the still-slumbering kitten to his new mistress, she rose to depart.

"I do so hate, Miss Fairfax," said Mrs. Nesbit, "to see a young lady like yourself go walking out alone. I am sure Mr. Churchill would be happy to see you home—would not you, my dear?"

"With the greatest pleasure, if Miss Fairfax will allow me."

"Thank you; thank you both. You are very kind. But it is not in the least necessary. I am quite accustomed to solitary walks, and it is but a little way."

"I should say it was near a mile to Colonel Campbell's house from here," said Frank.

"Oh, no—hardly more than half a mile, I think. But, in any case, I am not going to Colonel Campbell's. I am only going to St. Alban's Rectory, which is nearer still. Miss Campbell and her mother are to meet me there."

"St. Alban's!" said Frank, frowning. "You are going to call on the Rector and his sister, I suppose."

"Yes. That is, we are to call on Miss Devere, but I do not expect Mr. Devere will be there. No doubt he has parish duties to attend to in the morning."

"You are familiar with his habits," he remarked.

"Not at all; I was merely conjecturing. Is it not common, after all," she appealed to Mrs. Nesbit, "for a clergyman to spend his mornings so?"

"Of course, my dear; I'm sure it is. Now, we mustn't keep Miss Fairfax from her other friends—if," (turning back to Jane) "—you are quite determined to walk unattended?"

Jane again assured her no attendant was necessary for so short a trip; and bidding them both adieu, walked the short distance to St. Alban's Rectory without incident.

# Chapter Seventeen

**AT THE RECTORY,** she was informed by a servant that Helen and her mother were not yet come, and that Miss Devere was within the church, decorating it for the Lammas service. Stepping across to the church, Jane's attention was drawn by a gentleman approaching from the opposite direction, and it needed some effort to keep herself from staring at him—though had anyone asked her why, she could not very well have explained it. He was neither very short nor very tall; nor was there anything remarkable in his dress or bearing. His countenance might easily have been dismissed as undistinguished, save for his eyes, which, even at this little distance, were arresting both in their colour (a very pale blue), and in their expression. His otherwise prosaic appearance was thus preserved from insignificance; and withal there was so singular an air about him, as produced an almost irresistible effect.

The doors to the church were propped open to let in the breeze. Jane entered and was greeted by Miss Devere, who was occupied in tying stalks of wheat into small sheaves, representing the bounty of the first harvest, and placing them around the church. Jane admired the little tableau already assembled on the altar, employing loaves of bread and an artistic arrangement of flowers, leaves, and fruits to signify the blessings of the season. Margaret herself was dressed in a faded green gown, its long sleeves pushed up almost to her elbows. Her thick plaits were bound back carelessly, with little bits of leaf and petal clinging to them here and there.

"Miss Devere," Jane remarked, smiling, "You look like some mythical vegetable spirit, transported from Arcady."

Laughing, Margaret drew a hand across her brow to sweep off the untidy wisps of hair, and said with a flourish, "Behold Demeter, goddess of the—"

"Corn," said a man's voice.

She had stopped in midsentence, startled by the sight of

someone at the open door; it was this person who supplied the concluding word. Jane turned round, and discovered the speaker to be the same gentleman she had observed outside the church a few moments before. Margaret uttered a single syllable; and though it was spoken in the faintest of whispers, the hush of the church allowed Jane to distinguish it—"James!"

Here at last, then, was the famous Mr. Hammond—so much talked of, so eagerly anticipated! Jane felt she ought to have known him at first sight, by that indefinable quality which radiated from him like electricity. Perhaps it was merely the reflected glow of fame; but she suspected it was something more elemental, and intrinsic to his character— the dazzle of genius, to eyes more accustomed to behold the ordinary.

He walked toward them and bowed. His expression was impenetrable, but Miss Devere's agitation was plain. Distractedly, she smoothed the front of her gown with her hands, and tugged her sleeves down over her wrists. Neither of them spoke for what seemed to Jane a long interval, though it was not half a minute. He was first to break the silence, addressing Margaret with cold formality.

"Miss Devere—it is still Miss Devere, I believe; is it not?"

Margaret nodded, her tongue tied, and another silence threatened to engulf them. Despite the want of an introduction, Jane took the liberty of addressing Mr. Hammond herself—an irregular proceeding, certainly, but Miss Devere appeared to have forgotten what civility required. Under the circumstances, Jane could hardly blame her for her insensibility.

"I think, sir, you must be Mr. Hammond," she began. "Lady Paget told us you were coming to paint an altarpiece for the church. Are you just arrived in Weymouth?"

"I got in yesterday evening," he replied, his eyes still on Margaret.

"You come from Ashdale Park, then?" Jane asked.

"No," he said, with an effort redirecting his attention toward her. "Miss—?"

"Oh! I beg your pardon. I am Miss Fairfax."

"I am not come from Ashdale Park, Miss Fairfax; but Lady Paget is to join me here shortly."

"I thought I understood from her ladyship—or was I mistaken?—that you were to be staying at the Park."

"I have taken lodgings here in town. I prefer to have my

time to myself. There are too many social duties forced on one at a great house—it interferes with the work. I sometimes rise to paint at the first light of dawn; or I may stay up half the night sketching out ideas, and sleep most of the day. To conform to anyone else's schedule does not suit me."

"Perhaps that explains," said Margaret, finding her voice, "why you kept her ladyship and a houseful of guests waiting for you to appear the other night. But being such a celebrated personage, no doubt you consider yourself exempt from the dictates of common courtesy; and a dash of bad manners can only enhance that air of—*originality* with which you like to impress your adoring public. We have only ourselves to blame, if we are so foolish as to assume you will come when you are expected."

Mr. Hammond appeared both confused and annoyed by her taunt. "My father, Miss Fairfax," he explained pointedly to Jane, "was taken ill shortly before I was to leave for Weymouth. For that reason my arrival was delayed."

Margaret's only response was a mortified, "Oh!"

"And may we hope, sir," Jane hastened to interpose, "by your delay being a short one, that your father is now recovered?"

"He is, for the time being—I thank you. But the doctor informs me there is little chance of a lasting recovery."

"Oh! I am so sorry," said Margaret with instinctive sympathy.

"I am exceedingly grateful for your kind concern, ma'am," he replied in a biting tone.

An awkward silence descended once more. Jane, feeling very much an intruder, thought of excusing herself and returning to the house to wait for Helen and Mrs. Campbell (indeed, she wondered what had become of them, for it must be well past noon); but she doubted whether Miss Devere would wish to be left alone with Mr. Hammond just now. Her vacillations were put to an end, however, by the entrance of Lady Paget—who had evidently forgiven the painter for having spoiled her party.

"My dear James," she cried, "Here you are at last!"

She nodded carelessly at the two ladies. "Oh, Miss Devere—Miss—. I had not noticed you. Now James, what is this foolishness in your note," (waving a folded sheet of paper) "about not staying with us at Ashdale Park? You must know I have had a very handsome suite of apartments made ready for you. I will not hear of your stopping at an hotel."

"I am sorry you should have been put to any needless trouble, Lady Paget; but I have already engaged a set of rooms nearby."

"You may give them up as easily, I am sure. Oh, you needn't give a thought to the expense, if that is your concern. I promise you, Lord Paget will be happy to recompense you for whatever little advance you have paid out. It would be quite absurd, in our position, to quibble over such trifling sums."

"His lordship is most obliging. But I prefer to make my own arrangements; and I mean to stay in Weymouth. It will be more convenient."

"But it would be shocking to disappoint poor Paget! He was quite counting on you to enliven our little family circle, you know; for he has been sadly dull of late, poor man. And I myself had planned various—"

"It is useless, ma'am," said he, "to debate the question further. I am quite comfortably settled at Regis House, and there I intend to remain."

She gave a little sigh of resignation, perhaps thinking to herself, "Genius will have its odd notions." Mr. Hammond then turned the conversation to the subject of his work; and Jane had to admire how adeptly he managed so formidable a woman as Lady Paget. He must have had a good deal of experience dealing with such individuals, she supposed.

"I noticed as I came in," said Mr. Hammond, "a vacant building across the yard. An old carriage house, I would guess?"

"Yes," said Lady Paget. "It belongs to the Rectory. However, as the rector does not keep a carriage, it is empty just at present."

"I wonder if I might get in to look at it? Once we have agreed upon the painting for the church, I mean to set up a studio here at Weymouth to execute my commission; and I think it might do very well for the purpose, with a few improvements."

Margaret gave a little exclamation of surprise, and Lady Paget cast a glance at her. "You and your friend may go, Miss Devere," she said with a dismissive gesture. "We do not need you."

"I believe," said Mr. Hammond, with careful politeness, "that my arrival has prevented Miss Devere from completing her task here; and no doubt she is anxious to return to it. If you would be so good, ma'am as to make the necessary arrangements for me to inspect the carriage house, I shall be happy to meet with you at Ashdale Park—and Miss Devere may finish her preparations without further interruption."

Margaret, matching his cool civility, proposed to quit the church herself, and to postpone her occupation until such time as she should not be in their way.

Mr. Hammond with equal courtesy declined the offer. He put an end to the discussion by making a courtly bow to the two young ladies, then extending his arm to Lady Paget and escorting her from the church.

Some time passed after their going, before Margaret's voice broke the stillness of the summer afternoon.

"Oh! how is it possible," she cried, "that I should be less wise at two-and-thirty, than I was at seventeen!"

It had indeed been an unfortunate scene. Jane, with no words of comfort to offer, deemed it best simply to allow Miss Devere to speak her own feelings without check.

"Perhaps you will tell me, Miss Fairfax, that I should not have said to him what I did? And you would be in the right. I ought to have held my tongue. But how could I have known about his poor father?

"And then, his manner was so provoking—so cold—so distant and polite—to me, who was once everything to him! He seemed quite angry and contemptuous; and yet, what reason has he for anger or contempt? It is I who have cause to resent—I who am the injured party.

"And to think I have actually been imagining—hoping for a renewal of our former attachment! How foolish, to think that feelings so long dead, could be, or should be, revived. He has certainly made his indifference abundantly clear.

"My only wish now, is that I might never see or hear of James Hammond again!"

Jane, who was not at all convinced that the gentleman's manner bespoke indifference, observed, "It would appear, however, that Mr. Hammond is likely to be fixed in Weymouth for some time to come; and if he is, I think you can hardly avoid meeting him frequently, however little you may wish it. Perhaps it would be wisest to draw no conclusion from his behaviour at present, but rather to wait for some further illumination as to his sentiments."

There was a pause while Margaret considered this suggestion. "You think, then, that there is some hope? That I ought not to despair?"

"I cannot advise either hope or despair; but only patience."

"Patience! Ah, Miss Fairfax," she acknowledged with a smile, "I am afraid patience is a virtue with which I can boast but a nodding acquaintance."

# Chapter Eighteen

**WHEN HELEN AND** her mother finally arrived at the church, it was nearly an hour past the appointed time. To Jane's surprise, Mary Lodge accompanied them, her countenance bearing the marks of tears recently shed. In their walk to the Rectory, as Helen related, they had stopped at the chemist's shop to purchase some tooth powder; there they had met Miss Lodge. After a little chat, Mary had just turned to leave them, when Mrs. Campbell observed that a large quantity of cloth had been cut from the back of her skirt, leaving a considerable expanse of linen undergarment exposed to public view. Mary, having dressed rather hastily, had not noticed the deficiency. She was mortified beyond expression at the discovery, and naturally suspected some one or another of her brothers to be responsible.

The other two ladies had then walked her home, Mrs. Campbell lending Mary her shawl to drape over the gap. At Mr. Lodge's house, they found the boys out in the back garden, engrossed in a game of exploring. The head of the eldest, playing the part of a Bedouin sheik, was veiled in a flowing headdress unmistakably fashioned from the fabric of his sister's gown. They had cut up the dress to use in their game on a previous day, and had not seen fit to confess the crime to their sister. Instead, they had watched her leave the house that morning in the spoiled gown, thinking it a very good joke indeed, and on her return were vastly entertained by her distress. The more she cried, the more they laughed; until finally she ran into the house in hysterics, with Helen trailing after her to furnish what comfort she could.

"I gave the strongest reproofs possible to those boys," Mrs. Campbell now explained, "but they showed not the smallest compunction for what they had done! So Helen and I thought it best to bring Miss Lodge here with us, Margaret, after she had changed her gown—to get her away for a little while."

"You were quite right to do so, Mrs. Campbell," declared Mr. Devere, who, unnoticed by the others, had entered the church while this story was being told.

Mary coloured deeply as he approached her. "I am truly appalled, Miss Lodge," he continued. "This is no mere boyish prank. Your brothers have gone too far this time, and I intend to speak to your father very seriously about this incident. Indeed, as I find you in such good hands here, I shall go to him now—directly."

"Oh! thank you, sir," she managed to say, though she could not look up to meet his eyes.

"I would have spoken to Mr. Lodge myself," said Mrs. Campbell, "had he been at home. However, as rector of the parish, no doubt you are the properest person to broach the matter with him. But they truly are very bad boys, and something *must* be done about them."

"They are odious, beastly creatures," cried Mary, "and I hate them!"

"My dear Miss Lodge," said Mr. Devere gently, "You must not hate your brothers, even though they may seem to deserve it. Boys at that age can be a great trial, I know. But thankfully, they generally outgrow such behaviour by the time they are young men; particularly if they are taken well in hand. I daresay they will begin to be quite conformable in a few years, however disagreeable they may seem at present."

After conferring a little further with his sister and Mrs. Campbell, Mr. Devere left, and Margaret proposed that they should all remove to the Rectory for some refreshments. "For I am sure, Mary," she said very kindly, "you will be much the better for a little cold meat and cake."

Accordingly, they adjourned to the house, where Mary's plight, and the possibilities for rectifying it, were generally discussed among them while they ate. Margaret proposed that Mary should pay a visit of some weeks at the Rectory; and Mary was at once plunged into all the happiness that the promise of release from present miseries, and the prospect of future delights—in continued daily intercourse with the object of her girlish worship—could furnish. Mrs. Campbell, however, checked her rapture by expressing some doubt as to the propriety of a young lady's being the houseguest of a single gentleman in no way related to her.

"But my brother is so little at home, Mrs. Campbell," said Margaret; "and whenever he should chance to be here, I shall undoubtedly be present myself to serve as chaperone. Surely Mr. Lodge, who is not overmuch concerned with Mary's welfare, will find nothing to object to in the scheme."

Mrs. Campbell conceded the point, insofar as it appertained to Mr. Lodge; but it was not Mr. Lodge's objection that concerned her. Rather, it was the young lady's reputation in general that she was anxious to preserve. She had some anxiety with regard to Mr. Devere's reputation as well; for it was incumbent upon a clergyman to avoid even the appearance of impropriety.

Helen, with her usual good will, suggested Miss Lodge might stay at their own house for an indefinite period. Mrs. Campbell, though uncertain they had any place to quarter a guest in tolerable comfort for more than a night or two, thought this a better plan in other respects. Unfortunately, the house had no spare bedroom, and there was not space enough either in Helen's room or in Jane's for an extra bed. Both declared themselves ready to give up the tiny sitting room they shared, if it could be made to accommodate Miss Lodge, or to share a bed themselves if it could not. Thus it was eventually settled among them that Mrs. Campbell should write to Mr. Lodge that very evening, inviting Mary to stay at the Colonel's house; and, subject to her father's approval, the Campbells and their ward would have the pleasure of her company for at least a week or two, or until some better arrangement could be thought of.

It was not surprising that, amidst all the solicitude about Miss Lodge, Miss Devere found no occasion to mention to her friends that Mr. James Hammond had arrived in Weymouth, or that she and Jane had spoken with him; and Jane, thinking it best to leave the matter to Miss Devere's discretion, said nothing of it herself. It struck her remarkably odd that she—who in her entire life had never had one secret to keep!—should now find herself keeping two: Miss Devere's connection to Mr. Hammond, and Mr. Churchill's to Mrs. Nesbit. What was known in confidence, of course, could not rightly be revealed; but secrecy was neither natural nor comfortable to her, and fervently did she wish all need for it might soon be at an end.

**JANE NOTICED** a little irritation in her throat that evening, and by morning it had developed into a bad cold, which forced her to rest for the next several days. For a day or two, her head ached too much even to read, or to write letters, or to do anything at all but lie back limply in her bed, and let her thoughts drift to any pleasant subject they could fix on. They were perhaps fixed on Frank Churchill more than was quite prudent; but it was mere idle daydreaming, she told herself, and could do no harm.

She soon learned from Helen that, contrary to expectation, Mr. Lodge had declined Mrs. Campbell's invitation to his daughter—most likely (as Miss Devere interpreted it) because he found it inconvenient to take upon himself the various domestic duties usually performed by Mary in her nominal role as mistress of the house. Jane expressed her regret; but Helen assured her Miss Devere had not given up, and with Mr. Devere's help was trying to devise some other plan to separate Miss Lodge from her incorrigible brothers.

Jane was compelled by her illness to miss church on Sunday, but she persuaded her friends to attend without her, assuring them she expected to sleep most of the day. Left to herself, she divided the morning between dozing upon the sofa, and writing a long letter to her aunt Hetty, and pretending she was not thinking of Mr. Frank Churchill at all.

When the Campbells returned, she heard the news of Mr. Hammond's being come to Weymouth at last—though, as he had not attended church either, they still had not seen him with their own eyes. Here Jane felt it necessary to acknowledge that she and Miss Devere had met him on the previous Thursday. Helen, amazed that Jane could have failed to communicate so significant an event, jokingly wondered whether she had sneezed the wits quite out of her head. Jane excused her own remissness as well as she could, attributing it to the fuss over Miss Lodge, and to her own subsequent illness. Her friend then proceeded to inquire minutely into Mr. Hammond's appearance, bearing, speech, manner, &c.; and though Jane provided what intelligence she felt authorised to give, it was hardly enough to satisfy Helen's curiosity.

During the week that followed, friends called at the Colonel's house to inquire, as Mrs. Campbell reported to Jane, after her health: Mr. Churchill once, and Mr. Devere twice.

By Wednesday she was enough recovered to receive Miss Devere and Miss Lodge in the small sitting room, which they had hoped to make over to Miss Lodge's use. Margaret was keeping Mary with her as much as possible, and had taken her from home on one pretext or another nearly every day.

"Stephen had a long talk with Mary's father," Margaret explained to Jane and Helen, "but he found it hard going to make any impression on Mr. Lodge, who insists the boys are simply high-spirited—"

"That is just what Papa always tells me," said Mary, "whenever I complain of their behaviour. 'They're just high-spirited,' he says, 'and I shouldn't like a pack of namby-pamby boys with no spirit in 'em, by George!' "

Margaret, only partly suppressing a smile, continued, "At any rate, my brother did persevere; and Mr. Lodge was at last obliged to agree that the boys had been growing rather worse of late. Some recent misconduct of theirs has cost him not only a good deal of embarrassment, but some money, too—which circumstance, I gather, helped my brother considerably in gaining his point. Stephen thinks a tutor of the right sort might reform them; and with their father's permission, he has taken it upon himself to inquire of his old friend, Mr. Reed, the schoolmaster from Beckford. He is confident Mr. Reed will be able to recommend some suitable person to teach them."

"It is wonderfully good of Mr. Devere," said Mary, "to take such pains. But I cannot conceive anyone would willingly undertake to teach such odious creatures."

"The problem may be merely, as Stephen says, that they have never been properly managed."

"Properly managed—oh! no," Mary agreed. "They have never been managed at all."

"It is indeed kind of Mr. Devere," Jane remarked, "to take so much trouble upon himself."

"But it is just what I would expect of him," said Helen.

"Mr. Devere," cried Mary, "is everything that is kind, and good, and—and Miss Devere, too, has been most—oh! Miss Devere, I nearly forgot! When I was speaking to Mr. Devere yesterday, he recommended I should read something called 'Blair and Fordyce'. I did not like to admit my ignorance to him, but I have never heard of 'Blair and Fordyce'. Do you know what it is, and where I might get a copy? Is it a novel, perhaps?"

"A novel!" Margaret exclaimed. "Goodness, no—nothing half so agreeable. They are only books of sermons. I am afraid you would find them very dull, Mary."

"Surely not. Whatever Mr. Devere recommends could not be dull. Do you think, after we leave here, we might stop at Harvey's, so I can—oh, but I have not any money with me. Perhaps your brother has a copy he would not mind lending me; yet I should so like to surprise him—"

"I believe," said Jane, "there is a copy of Blair's sermons in the house. Is not there, Helen?"

"Yes, I saw it in the bookcase just the other day."

"Oh, Miss Campbell! Do you think your father would be willing to let me borrow it?"

"I'm sure he will. We shall go and ask him this moment."

Their absence on this errand gave Jane an opportunity to ask Miss Devere, whether she had seen anything more of Mr. Hammond since last Thursday?

Margaret shook her head. "He did not come to services on Sunday—but of course you have already heard as much from the Campbells. However, my brother met him in the church once, taking some measurements. It seems he does indeed mean to use the Rectory carriage house as his studio. There have been workmen about, hammering and sawing, since last Friday; and I believe James—Mr. Hammond, I must remember to call him—Mr. Hammond has been coming and going a good deal to direct the work. Twice I have seen him from an upstairs window of the Rectory as he was leaving. But we have not met."

"Did Mr. Devere have any conversation with him?"

"Only polite nothings, so far as I am aware. Stephen says very little on the subject; I think he does not like to talk of it, for fear of distressing me. But I am not so fainthearted now, I hope. As you said the other day, we cannot avoid meeting while he remains at Weymouth. So I have settled it within myself that—if it is right for us to be reconciled, we *will* be reconciled. And if it is not—well, perhaps I shall marry Mr. Lodge after all, and find my happiness in tenderly mothering his poor, darling, motherless little boys. The best mothering, in their case," she concluded laughingly, "consisting of a most affectionate box on the ears—to be administered daily!"

# Chapter Nineteen

**JANE WAS NOT** long recovered from her cold, when Miss Devere and Mrs. Campbell devised a plan for the improvement and relief of Miss Mary Lodge. Besides the obvious evils of her situation, the young lady's education (they both agreed) had been pretty much neglected: she was pronounced to be frightfully ignorant in history, theology, art, and literature. They could not induce Mary's father to resign her entirely to their custody; but they hoped, at least, to provide her both with amusement and instruction, by directing her in a course of reading designed to elevate her understanding, and by taking her on various short excursions to points of cultural importance within the near environs of Weymouth.

Their first trip was to Portland Isle, a place well fitted to their purpose. From fine white Portland limestone had the magnificent dome of St. Paul's Cathedral, and many other distinguished edifices, been hewn; it might serve, therefore, to usher in a review of diverse architectural styles. Portland Castle, a coastal fort surviving from the reign of Henry VIII, might inspire an informal lesson on that period of English history. And the Portland bill lighthouse, with its modern illumination and lens, could be expected to prompt a discussion on scientific topics.

They were all to take the ferry over to Portland. The gentlemen would bring their horses across with them, and a conveyance would be hired on the island for the ladies. Colonel Campbell, happening to run into Frank Churchill on the day before the proposed outing, invited him to join them. In reply, Frank promised that he would ride over to Portland and seek them out, should he find himself at liberty; but uncertain as ever of his aunt's acquiescing in any inclination of his own, he begged they should not wait for him if he failed to appear.

The weather was favourable. Frank Churchill did not appear, but the others set off after breakfast, and were soon afterwards pacing Portland's sunswept banks in search of 'holy stones'. According to Mr. Wiggins, the local guide who attended them, these pebbles, bearing natural holes pierced by the forces of Nature, were thought to bring good fortune to any who found them. But while looking for the stones, Mr. Wiggins jestingly advised, they must also be on the alert for a glimpse of the giant 'Veasta,' the fabled creature—half fish, half sea-horse—reputed to inhabit the nearby waters.

None of the party saw anything of the legendary monster, however; and Mr. Devere was the only one among them to find a lucky stone. Though wishing to tender that article to Miss Fairfax, he determined, after consulting privately with his sister, to offer it to Mary Lodge instead. Certainly, he could not have bestowed it on a more grateful object; nor could he have bestowed it more profitably for his own ends.

Had he given the stone to Jane, as he was first disposed to do, the gesture would have been very nearly thrown away, for it must be confessed that her thoughts, up to that time, had been mostly concerned with the absence of Frank Churchill—wondering what kept him away, and whether he would join them later. But Mr. Devere's presenting the stone to Miss Lodge made an impression on Jane which proved to his advantage. Shame, not jealousy, was the reason. She did not look more benevolently upon him because she feared he might be transferring his affections to another. Rather, his simple act of generosity served to recall her to a sense of his worthiness, and to her promise to Colonel Campbell that she would give the young man a fair opportunity to attach her. With an inward rebuke, she determined once more to put Frank Churchill out of her head, and attend to improving her acquaintance with Mr. Devere.

The day was not lacking in opportunities to do so. At Portland Castle, their first destination, Jane, Mary, and the Deveres were for a little while walking apart from the others; and she listened thoughtfully as he recounted for Miss Lodge the history of Henry the Eighth and Thomas Cromwell: how between them they had brought about England's separation from Rome, broken up the monasteries, appropriated their riches for the crown, and made the King supreme head of the English Church. Jane could not help admiring the gentleness and patience with which he answered Mary's many questions.

"Good heavens, Mr. Devere!" Mary exclaimed, astonishment prevailing over her usual shyness in that gentleman's presence. "Surely you don't mean to say that—that such an infamous character was the founder of our church!"

"No; not precisely—"

"But did you not just tell me that King Henry the Eighth had—*six* wives?"

"He did. That is true—"

"And that he had two of them beheaded, though they were by all proofs innocent, simply because he did not... *like* them?"

"Well, yes. One might put it that way—"

"And did you not say he nearly ruined the country by waging improvident wars, and then tried to make up the loss by seizing the property of the monks, which did not belong to him? And that his break with Rome was prompted, not by religious feelings, but mainly by his wish to divorce his first wife, and marry Anne Bullen; with whom, as Miss Devere says, he had already done—" (her cheeks now flaming) "—what he ought not to have done?"

"Indeed. Indeed," he replied, turning a little pink himself. "You are a most attentive pupil, Miss Lodge. I cannot deny that Henry the Eighth was not an—exemplary monarch, in many respects. In truth, I can say very little in his vindication, save—"

"Save," said Miss Devere with a laugh, "that his shutting up the monasteries, and leaving them to the ruinous depredations of time, has been of infinite use to the English landscape, in rendering it picturesque—which probably was the true motive for his doing it."

Mr. Devere directed a look of mild reproach towards his sister. "To call him the founder of our church, however," he said, "would not be precisely accurate. He did expedite the separation from Rome. But dissatisfaction with the Roman Church was already widespread by that time. And other than detaching us from Rome, Henry the Eighth brought few substantive changes to the church. Those were instituted under his successors—Edward the Sixth, who replaced the Latin services with English, and introduced the earliest version of our liturgy; and Elizabeth, who established the Thirty-nine Articles, which are the cornerstone of our faith."

"Then Queen Elizabeth," Mary concluded, "is really the true founder of our church. *She* must have been a model of piety and rectitude, I suppose."

Margaret chuckled. "Without question," she agreed, "despite an unfortunate tendency (inherited from her royal sire) to repay the tender devotion of those nearest and dearest to her, by tenderly severing their heads from their bodies."

Mary, looking rather shocked, asked, "Is *that* why King Henry was so determined to get another heir—to prevent his daughter from inheriting the throne, because she had a wicked nature? And yet it would seem, from what you have told me, she was only doing as he had done himself. Oh, dear! It is all so very confusing."

"I believe, Miss Lodge," Jane put in, "that Henry's unwillingness to have Elizabeth succeed him to the throne was due rather to her sex, than to her character—that he believed, as many others did before him (and as many do still), that women lacked the faculties necessary to govern."

Mr. Devere nodded. "Which is generally the case, of course. But Queen Elizabeth, whatever her defects, did rule for nearly half a century, and, on the whole, ruled well; confirming that the influence of royal blood is so great as to countervail even against the inherent weaknesses of the female intellect."

These observations could not go unchallenged by his companions, or at least, by such of those as would dare to challenge him. Mary could not have summoned courage enough to defend her sex against his disparagements, whatever her private opinion; but the hapless gentleman was roundly abused by his sister for making so ridiculous a statement. Even Jane, though expressing herself with less pungency than Margaret did, felt it necessary to declare her own conviction that the capacity to rule was pretty evenly divided between the sexes; and ventured to ask him, with a smile, "whether he would not allow that his own sister might acquit herself very creditably in the House of Commons—or that Mrs. Campbell would make a capital Minister of the Cabinet?"

Few men could have the fortitude to persevere in the face of such opposition. Mr. Devere returned Jane's smile, and made her a gracious bow of submission; only conceding as they walked on, however, that "there were of course exceptions to every rule."

Margaret again took up the gauntlet; but Jane had done. She did not think her own opinion on this question likely to be swayed, and Mr. Devere appeared quite fixed in his; and she had no pleasure in argument. At all events, they were soon rejoined by the others, and after proceeding to where the horses and carriage were in waiting, the entire party set out for the Bill.

The lightkeeper gave them a cordial welcome and ushered them through both the lighthouses, pointing out the most interesting and unusual features of each. In the new higher light, he particularly directed their attention to the lens, and the two rows of Argand lamps, which in 1788 had been the first of their kind to be installed anywhere, and which were still the best illumination made by man. Their light, he told them proudly, could be seen at a distance of more than eighteen miles.

He also entertained them with a little history of his family's long association with the lighthouses. His great-grandfather had been appointed the first Lightkeeper in Portland in 1721; and the office had been passed from father to son ever since. He spoke in reverential tones of the visit paid to the lighthouse by King George in 1791, when His Majesty was yet in his right mind (mostly), and he himself but a youth; and he regaled them, too, with tales of smugglers, storms and shipwrecks.

From Portland Bill, they were next to repair to St. Georges for refreshment; but the broad, sweeping vistas offered by the high vantage of the lighthouses, surrounded on three sides by water, gave many of them a strong desire to survey, from a closer perspective, those spectacular prospects which their present location afforded. Miss Campbell and Mr. Dixon, in their eagerness, fairly flew across the stony ground to a granite ledge which jutted out over the sea. Jane accompanied them, thankful she had worn her sturdiest half-boots, and Colonel Campbell and his wife followed in a leisurely manner at some distance. Still farther back, Mr. Devere attended both his sister, and Miss Lodge, who was ill-shod for traversing such rugged terrain, and in need of all the steadiness a gentleman's arm could furnish.

Where the thin stratum of low vegetation yielded to the shelf of rock beneath, Helen and Mr. Dixon clambered nimbly down onto the stone outcropping. Mr. Dixon then turned back, offering his assistance to Jane, but she declared her intention of remaining where she was. He rejoined his lady, and together the pair made their way to the water's edge, and as romantic a scene as any two lovers could wish to behold.

Jane walked over to a nearby boulder and leaned against it, meaning to rest until the others should catch up to them, and to give her full attention to the breathtaking sight of the opposing tides, clashing in turbulent confluence before her. If the picture of a happy couple standing side-by-side, against a backdrop of jagged rocks and leaping spray, suggested to her mind any foolish thoughts of absent gentlemen, she might console herself with the knowledge that it was probably no more than might occur to any other young lady so affectingly situated.

Her reverie, whatever its character, did not last long; for suddenly she became aware of someone seated on the ground, in front of the boulder she was leaning on. She had just begun, instinctively, to move away, when she recognised him: it was Mr. Hammond. He noticed her at the same moment; and setting aside the pencil and drawing pad he had been occupied with, he scrambled to his feet. He made her a bow so low as to make her suspect there was some mockery in it, and to give her the idea of his being rather vexed at the intrusion. Nonetheless—

"Good day, ma'am," he said, politely enough.

"How do you do, sir. I apologise for disturbing you; I had not realised there was anyone here. I am only waiting for my friends—"

She made a gesture indicating the direction in which the remainder of the party could be seen advancing towards them. With a sigh he seemed to resign himself to further interruption; and, shaking off all traces of annoyance, he smiled at Jane, and said he hoped she would do him the honour of presenting him to her companions.

"I would be most happy to," she said. "But two of them are not unknown to you—Miss Devere, and her brother."

"I should be pleased to meet with them," he replied in some confusion, bending down to gather up his drawing materials. When he stood up again, he had recovered himself sufficiently to remark, in a tolerably easy voice, "You have a fine day for sight-seeing, Miss Fairfax."

"And you a fine spot for drawing. Miss Devere and I were agreeing a little while ago that we should like to come back another time, and attempt to capture a little of its beauty in our sketchbooks. You are doing some studies for the church painting, perhaps?"

"As a matter of fact, I am not. When I am employed on a work of large scale, I find it helpful to stop from time to time, and draw something altogether unrelated, that I may afterwards return to the project with a fresh eye."

He had just concluded this explanation when they were joined by Colonel and Mrs. Campbell. The necessary introductions were made, and Colonel Campbell engaged Mr. Hammond in friendly conversation. Helen and Mr. Dixon coming back soon afterwards, the Colonel presented them to Mr. Hammond; mentioning, as the Deveres and Miss Lodge approached, that they were shortly to be married.

"My condolences to you both," Mr. Hammond offered drily to the couple.

The Colonel remarked with good humour, "You must be a bachelor, sir. You speak like an enemy to matrimony, as bachelors generally do."

"Between the marriage knot or the hangman's knot, Colonel," he said, "I don't know that I wouldn't rather prefer the second."

Margaret, making a little cough then, drew Colonel Campbell's attention, and he introduced her and her two companions to Mr. Hammond. His surprise that the Deveres were already known to Mr. Hammond, prevented his noticing the awkwardness with which the acquaintance was acknowledged on either side; and he soon recollected that Mr. Hammond had been working on a painting for the church, by which means, he satisfied himself, they had previously met. Returning then to the discussion which their arrival had interrupted, he bid Mr. Hammond account for his statement, that he would prefer hanging to marrying.

"Gladly, sir," that gentleman replied. "When a man is delivered up to the hangman's noose, he may be certain his misery is nearly at an end. When he surrenders himself to matrimony, he may be certain it is but just beginning."

"Cleverly put, sir," said the Colonel with a chuckle. "Cleverly put. I cannot share your opinion; but I think you might find an ally here, in Miss Devere. What was it you were saying at the assembly the other night, Margaret? That nine out of ten husbands were plagued in their choice of a wife?"

All eyes were turned upon her as she said, "You must have mistaken me, Colonel. I believe what I said was, that nine out of ten women were plagued in their choice of a husband."

"What—only nine, madam?" asked Mr. Hammond.

"Only nine, sir. There is always one in ten with the good fortune to escape having any husband at all."

"Margaret, you are like a Beatrice to this gentleman's Benedick," was Mrs. Campbell's amused comment. "I suppose next you will say, 'you would rather hear your dog bark at a crow, than a man swear he loves you.'"

"So I would, Mrs. Campbell; so I would. The blandishments of men in the pursuit of love are, to my ears, hardly distinguishable from the barking of dogs; and a dog, I have observed, be his neckcloth ever so well-tied, and his morning coat ever so well-fitted, is yet a dog," she concluded, favouring the painter with an arch smile.

He returned the smile; saying, "While a cat, though bedecked in muslin and lace, can yet scratch; and cat's tongue is a dish too tart for my palate."

"Cat's tongue!—Perhaps, sir, you fear you will be licked?"

"Indeed, ma'am—by a cat with nine tails."

"A cat has nine lives, but only one—"

"Hold—hold!" cried Colonel Campbell, laughing. "'Where did you study all this goodly speech?' If the pair of you can play at tragedy as well as you do comedy, you will rival Mr. Kemble and Mrs. Siddons, to be sure! But if I am not much mistaken, there are those among us too hungry to give your performance the attention it deserves. So, Margaret—if you will leave off for the moment, and apply your talents to persuading Mr. Hammond to give us the pleasure of his company to lunch—I will promise you a better audience for the second act, afterwards."

"As you know, Colonel," she replied, "tragedy is not to my taste; but I do confess to a liking for such delicacies as an inn larder may provide. And if Mr. Hammond has an appetite for aught but farce, most earnestly would I entreat him to attend us to St. Georges—and satisfy himself with whatever fare he loves best."

Miss Devere had issued to the gentleman what might, by the satirical manner in which it was tendered, be taken more as a taunt than an invitation. But there was a charm in her manner, too, that softened its sting; and Mr. Hammond found himself quite equal to the lady's challenge, and with a complaisant air consented to accompany them.

His own horse being tethered nearby, he joined the gentlemen in their ride to the inn. The ladies, travelling in the carriage, had so much to say respecting this chance meeting with Mr. Hammond, that the magnificent sights they had been so recently viewing were all but forgotten. Margaret, indeed, said nothing, but her eyes and cheeks were glowing. Mrs. Campbell declared herself very much pleased with Mr. Hammond, and made some compliments both on his person—which, though not really handsome, she admitted, was yet not at all unprepossessing—and on his manner, which to her mind showed both intelligence and affability. Helen said he quite answered all her own expectations, only that she had thought to find him more aloof and arrogant—as, they must allow, he had some right to be. But she, her mother, and Jane agreed, that he was not at all haughty in his bearing, and was altogether more amiable than a man of his genius and fame might be expected to be.

Miss Lodge, released from the restraint she had felt in the company of the gentlemen, was emboldened to speak.

"My father," she imparted in a confiding tone, "says that Mr. Hammond has had *intrigues* with half the ladies whose portraits he has painted! It was even rumoured the Duchess of R—— was ready to leave the Duke for him, but he broke it off."

A chorus of disapprobation—of *absurd!* and *for shame!* and *my dear Miss Lodge!*—greeted her remarks. Miss Devere, with dismay writ rather too plainly in her countenance, could only stare at her in astonishment, but the others were vocal in their remonstrances.

"Your father ought not to be repeating such idle gossip to you, Miss Lodge," said Mrs. Campbell, "nor should you believe it, either. I hold it very unlikely in general that tales of this sort can be true—or," she found it necessary to add, in strict honesty, "that they are not in most cases at least greatly exaggerated."

"Mr. Hammond," said Helen, "I am sure is much too good, and much too sensible, to have done anything wicked or dishonourable."

"And surely," said Jane, "we ought not to believe half of what we may hear spoken against a gentleman so celebrated as Mr. Hammond is; for I cannot but imagine that the great success he enjoys might provoke a good deal of malice, in those less favoured by fortune. No doubt his conduct is liable to all manner of misrepresentation, from those who envy gifts they will never possess."

"It is often so, without question," cried Helen. "Did not Pope say something to that effect, Mama? Something about a conspiracy, or a—a confederacy of dunces, I think. Do you recollect?"

"Indeed I do, my love: 'When a true genius appears in the world, you may know him by this, that the dunces are all in confederacy against him.' But I believe it was Swift, dearest—not Pope."

With these words, the carriage pulled up in front of the inn; and it was a much subdued Miss Devere who alighted along with the others. She was not alone, however, in having undergone a transformation during the short ride to St. Georges. Mr. Hammond, too, when the party reunited, seemed markedly altered, towards her if not towards her friends. With them he was yet easy and unreserved; but he seemed disinclined to any further exchange with Margaret— did not speak to her, except as required by common civility, and then only with a manner conspicuously distant. Jane wondered what could have brought about so striking a change, and pitied Miss Devere under such a mortification.

But so little suspicion did any but herself and Mr. Devere have of a prior connection between Margaret and Mr. Hammond, that both the lady's chagrin, and the gentleman's coldness, went unremarked by the rest of the company.

# Chapter Twenty

**FRANK CHURCHILL WAS** not in the best of tempers. Life with his aunt for several days past had been particularly trying: Mrs. Churchill had suffered an aggravation of her chronic complaint, and her nephew had been much pressed to satisfy all her querulous demands. He spent the better part of the week sitting with her, talking to her, reading to her—doing whatever he could do to keep her in spirits; and at last her symptoms began somewhat to abate. This morning, indeed, she had been so much improved as to induce him to hope that he might have a few hours at his own disposal. She was expecting an early call from Lady Paget, and he hoped he would not be wanted.

At the last minute, however, a note came from Ashdale Park, asking Mrs. Churchill to pay a visit there instead. Though complaining of the imposition, she resolved on going, and insisted Frank should accompany her. He first endeavoured to persuade her she would be well taken care of with her maid and a footman to attend her, and that he would merely be in the way; but he quickly saw her mind was made up, and his attempts to change it only increasing her irritation. Thus did he resign himself, as he had often done before, to sacrificing his own wishes to hers—and rather than join a congenial group of friends and a certain enchanting young lady in a party of pleasure, he passed an irksome morning in the company of two women, in whose conversation there could be nothing to amuse—nothing to interest or inform—nothing to charm or delight. Never had it cost him so great a struggle to submit cheerfully to his aunt's will.

Mrs. Churchill, when they returned home, announced her intention of resting for an hour or two in her room; and Frank solicited from her the favour of an afternoon's liberty. With an air of exceeding self-denial—and showing, by the expression of her countenance and the tone of her voice, how little pleased she was with the request—she at length deigned to release him; and he had not heart enough even to make a decent counterfeit of being ready to stay if she wished it. Before she could have time to change her mind, his horse was ordered, and he departed in haste.

But discovering Miss Fairfax and her friends proved no easy task. He had neglected to ascertain from the Colonel their planned route, and rode from one end of Portland to the other without finding them. Finally he learned from the lightkeeper, that they had been at the Bill more than an hour earlier, and were gone to have lunch in St. Georges. By the time he arrived at the inn, he was heated and cross, and almost regretted having come at all. Most likely those he sought had already gone, and he would have had a long, hot ride to no purpose.

Fortune, however, was kind. The landlord informed him that Colonel Campbell and his party were upstairs, in one of the private dining rooms. The certainty of seeing Miss Fairfax again, after so long a separation (for it was fully eight days since they had last met, at Mrs. Nesbit's) put him at once into a better humour; and his mood was still more improved by the hearty welcome he received. They had nearly finished their own meal, but assured him they were in no hurry at all, and perfectly willing to wait while he partook of anything he liked from the collation of cold meats, fruit, and sea-food still on the table.

Making a quick survey of the assembled group, he observed with satisfaction that his rival, Mr. Devere, was not among them. To complete his happiness, there was but one vacant seat at the table, next to Miss Fairfax herself; and with the encouragement of a blushing smile from that young lady, he did not hesitate to place himself at her side.

A small cloud did soon appear to dim his sunshine a little. Mr. Devere, who had left the room only to see about their horses, returned, and Frank learned that he had already had the felicity of sitting next to Miss Fairfax through the length of their meal. Still, Frank Churchill was not a man to dwell on clouds, where blue sky was in view. He had the upper hand at present. He was in the midst of eating when Mr. Devere came in, and the clergyman could not, in common politeness, disrupt his meal to reclaim the seat, though Frank politely offered it. Another chair must be found for him, and he must content himself with sitting by Mrs. Campbell instead.

As for Jane, she had been at once pleased and discon-

certed to see Frank Churchill enter the dining parlour. She
was not prepared for the degree of embarrassment she felt
in meeting him again—meeting him, too, in the presence of
others—after having indulged rather too freely in such idle
daydreams as she had, in the weakness of her indisposition, been giving way to. She found she could scarce meet
his eyes, or say anything to him at all, without feeling she
was betraying herself at every moment. It seemed impossible he should not sense what wild flights of fancy had been
occupying her mind! She feared, besides, that the Colonel,
or Mrs. Campbell, or Helen, so well as they knew her, would
mark her discomfiture, and question her; or that Miss
Devere, so acute an observer, might perceive what she was
feeling and find it necessary to drop a hint to her brother,
advising him to withdraw his offer for her hand.

Their next destination was the ancient Rufus Castle. Mr.
Wiggins had obtained from Mr. Penn (the Governor of Portland, and present owner of the property) permission for
their party to survey the castle ruins, and to walk over the
surrounding land. Jane, however, found she could not muster sufficient interest in the crumbling edifice to attend to
the various details Mr. Wiggins was imparting, relative to
the structure he called "The Bow and Arrow Castle". Had
she been allowed simply to look, and to enjoy its picturesque charm in silence, she might have gazed on the ivy-
covered walls with considerable pleasure. But the pompous
speech of their guide, though it raised a smile of amusement at first, after a short while grew tiresome. To hear him
expound on the history of the castle—how it had been built
perhaps in the eleventh century by King William Rufus; how
taken in the twelfth by the Earl of Gloucester; how abandoned probably in the fourteenth; walls of Portland stone,
seven feet thick; southern walls rebuilt by Mr. Penn; new
bridge added after the Norman style; &c., &c.—for such a
lecture she had no patience at the moment. She was more
in need of quiet solitude, to calm the violent flutterings
within her breast. Drawn by the the old graveyard of St.
Andrew's Church, which she could just descry in a notch
below the castle, she stole away from the others and gin-
gerly made her way down a rough flight of stones, cut into a
scrubby hillside of tufted grasses, gorse and stonecrop, and
dotted here and there with stunted tamarisk. A multitude of
small moths, common on the island, flitted about her as
she descended.

The surviving walls of the ruined church were draped in a tangle of vines and weeds. These had crept into the untended graveyard as well, prompting in Jane's mind a host of melancholy reflections on the impermanence of all things earthly. Even adamantine stone, it seemed, was no match for the natural forces of wildness and decay: the older markers were broken or crumbling, obscured by vegetation, or worn and illegible. On others, however, names and dates were yet visible, with touching outpourings of artless grief and hope inscribed beneath. On one the blazon of a skull and crossbones was plainly discernible.

She had always felt a peculiar attraction to old graveyards such as this, though she would have been a little ashamed to own it to anyone. Perhaps it was because she had lost both her parents at an early age. Or perhaps it was simply that they reminded her so poignantly of the fleetingness, and hence the preciousness, of life. It filled her with a kind of hushed awe, to walk among the weathered, mossy stones; to think of those who had been, and were no more; to imagine how they had lived, and how they might have met their deaths: with terror, resignation, or relief. Wandering now through the peaceful burial ground—the derelict church alongside, with the ruined castle keeping guard above, and the rush of the sea against the shore below—she could not help thinking, with a strange sort of bittersweet yearning, that it would be a fine place to spend eternity.

After a little time, she perched upon a remnant of the low stone wall and gazed out at the broad expanse of water, where sun-spangled waves rolled peacefully off to a distant, hazy horizon. She could not comprehend her own waywardness. Until recently, she had considered herself a quite solid, steady, and sensible young woman. But since she had been at Weymouth, it seemed as though 'something of the sea,' something of its restlessness and wildness, had entered into her—had pervaded her so entirely, that she hardly knew herself.

She could not any longer be deluded as to her feelings for Frank Churchill. He *was* dear to her; perhaps, very dear. And perhaps he might care for her, too, at least a little. Her heart murmured that he did. But regardless of the feelings of either, any nearer tie between them was manifestly impossible: Mrs. Churchill's jealousy, ambition, and pride, stood squarely in the way. Frank knew it as well as she did; nay, better. Common sense, and her own pride, told Jane it was vain to allow herself even to hope. She must cease to think of him, save as a friendly acquaintance. And if she found she could not accept Mr. Devere as a husband—if her feelings for Frank Churchill precluded any other attachment—she must enter upon the profession which had been chosen for her by those older and wiser than herself. There was no future for her, in which Frank Churchill could play any material part; and her duty to herself, and to her friends, was to school herself to accept it.

Such resolutions are easily made, of course; and more easily broken, as Jane already knew, and would now be made to know again: for Frank Churchill had invaded her retreat.

"I see, Miss Fairfax," he called out as he approached, "that you were as enthralled with Mr. Wiggins' discourse as I was."

She found herself at a loss to reply, and only smiled shakily in response. He seated himself beside her on the stone wall, and for a time neither spoke. At last it occurred to her to inquire after their mutual friend.

"I very much regretted," she began, "that my cold should have prevented my paying any visit to Mrs. Nesbit this week, though I do hope to call on her tomorrow. Have you seen her again yourself? Is she well?"

"I have been to see her but once, since I had the good luck of meeting you there last week; and there was time only for a flying visit, I am afraid. My aunt has required my attendance almost constantly of late. But I can at least assure you that Mrs. Nesbit—and Zeus—are very well."

"Has Mrs. Churchill been ill? I should be sorry to hear she is not finding the sea air of any benefit to her."

"Thank you. She has, in fact, been rather ill; but she was a good deal better today, and I flatter myself the amendment will prove a lasting one."

There was another, longer period of silence. Then, with a sigh, and something of a dispirited air, he asked her,

"Have you ever wished to travel, Miss Fairfax?"

She smiled. "I thought I *was* travelling. I have never been to Weymouth before this summer, nor to Portland."

He shook his head. "No, I mean—have you ever wanted to leave England? Have you ever wished to go abroad?"

"It would hardly do for me to dwell on such wishes, Mr. Churchill, if I had them; for I cannot expect it will ever be in my power to indulge them. You know from Mr. Weston, perhaps, what I am to become? That I have been educated to be—a governess?"

He nodded solemnly. "I had heard of it. But it may be that—that you will find yourself in a family that travels, and so have an opportunity of travelling with them."

"That is possible, I suppose."

After a pause, he continued, "Or perhaps, Miss Fairfax—perhaps you will not end up a governess at all.—Perhaps you will marry instead."

"Perhaps," she said softly, looking away; and adding, still more softly, "But I do not think it very likely."

"Would you not rather marry, than be a governess?"

With a good deal more energy than circumspection, she exclaimed, "I shall not marry merely for the sake of—an establishment!"

He regarded her with a penetrating eye. "You would marry only for love, then?"

They were venturing upon delicate subjects; and rather than make him any reply, she bent down to pluck up a little bit of wild thyme growing at her feet. She pulled it absently through her fingers, over and over, releasing a whisper of its savory fragrance into the air.

"I confess," she said after a minute, "there is one place I have always felt a secret desire to visit—a place I have read about, and seen pictures of—yet I cannot quite believe it to be real. Can you guess where?"

He was thoughtful, and she feared he might be still intent upon the topic she had hoped to divert him from. But at length he grinned and named, "*La Serenissima*—Venice."

"Yes!" she said, all amazement. "But how—?"

"A city whose domes and towers rise up out of the sea! A city whose streets are made of water! No clattering of carriage wheels on cobblestones, no clicking of pattens on pavement. Only the quiet plash of the gondoliers' paddles, gliding placidly along the Grand Canal; and the soft murmur of waves, lapping sleepily against the marbled walls of ancient palaces."

"Have you been to Venice, Mr. Churchill?"

"Only in fancy. It is a place I too cannot believe to be quite real—for it seems to me a world of such enchantment as could exist only in dreams. I am not sure I should like to go there. The reality might not live up to what I have imagined."

"Oh, no!" she cried. "I am sure it must be just as you describe! Oh, what could be more wonderful than to see a place from the realm of dreams, made substantial? How could such a place be anything but magical?"

In a low voice he replied, "I know I should find Venice magical indeed, if I could but see it—"

He broke off abruptly, and in some confusion. Another brief interval of awkward silence passed, before he renewed the subject in a lighter tone.

"But where shall we go, Miss Fairfax, when we grow tired of Venice?" he asked; adding hastily, "I and my—travelling companion? Where shall we go, when I have done scribbling as many very bad sonnets on 'the azure-tinted Adriatic' as I can invent, and require some fresh scene to inspire me? Shall we go south, to gape at the antiquities of Rome? Or perhaps north, to marvel at the mountains of Switzer-land?—for I own, high mountains, like the sea, do hold a great attraction for me."

"From Venice," declared a voice just behind them, "you must go to Florence, of course."

They were both startled by the sound, and turned to see Mr. Hammond drawing near them.

"I beg your pardon. I could not help overhearing," he said. "Forgive me for intruding, Miss Fairfax, Mr. Churchill. I came down for a closer look at the old church. But had I had any idea I should be interrupting a *tête-à-tête*—"

Jane felt her cheeks grow hot, wondering how much he had heard, and could not think what to say.

"Oh, you are not interrupting anything at all," said Frank coolly. "I came away to escape from Mr. Wiggins' prosing, only to find Miss Fairfax had anticipated me. And being embarked on one expedition, we naturally fell to talking of other, more distant places we should like to visit."

Mr. Hammond chuckled. "It would seem our guide has inspired in each of us the same idea of flight. No doubt our ranks will increase, as one by one our friends fall victim to the power of Mr. Wiggins' eloquence."

He had no sooner uttered the words, than Jane observed Miss Devere making her way down the hill. Mr. Hammond noticed her too, and frowned. Jane then asked, if he had ever seen Venice himself?

"Venice?—yes, indeed. And Florence, and Rome— Milano—Pisa—Naples. I went to Italy in the year two, after the Peace. I stayed mostly at Florence, but I travelled from there as much as I could. There is hardly a corner of the place without its share of treasures, and I wanted to see them all. In fact, there was such a great deal to see in Italy, I'm afraid I never got as far as Switzerland, Mr. Churchill. But I did visit Lake Maggiore, in the Italian Alps; and I can readily affirm to you, those mountains are sublime."

"Miss Devere," Frank called out to that lady as she drew near them. "Perhaps you will settle an argument for us, now you are here."

"An argument, Mr. Churchill!" she said gaily, with no sign of her earlier agitation, "And on such a day—for shame!"

"It is a very friendly argument, I assure you. We were only debating whether, if one had a chance of visiting the Continent, it would be better to go to Rome, or to Switzerland? Neither Miss Fairfax nor myself have been anywhere outside of England, so wecan have no decided opinion. Mr. Hammond has spent some time in Italy, and speaks of it with enthusiasm; but at the same time seems to suggest that Switzerland may be well worth seeing also, though he has never been there."

"Where is the argument?" said she. "If I were to go, I should certainly want to see all of Italy, and Switzerland too. And the Rhine, and the Danube—Vienna—and oh! so many places. It would be foolish to miss anything on such a trip."

"An admirable plan, Miss Devere," said Mr. Hammond irritably. "But perhaps some travellers might not be so rich as to be able to go everywhere they pleased."

She laughed. "Myself included. Indeed, I never have been out of England—except to go to Scotland, which hardly counts for anything. But why this talk of Italy and Switzerland, gentlemen? Are there not beauties enough here, at this moment, for us to enjoy? Miss Fairfax, do not you think this another spot we must return to, with our paints and easels?—though to do justice to such a setting, I own, might be too great a challenge for ordinary genius like ours. Perhaps," she said with a playful smile at her former lover, "Perhaps Mr. Hammond would advise us to leave such scenes to greater talents, and not expose ourselves to the ridicule of our friends by attempting them."

"Rock, sea, sky," he remarked. "Only a little skill, Miss Devere (less, indeed, than I know you to possess) might manage to make something charming from these elements. But if you are so easily frightened off by the opinions of others—by all means, you had best not undertake it."

To this last statement, he seemed to give a very particular emphasis. Jane was at a loss to understand what he meant by it; and, judging from Margaret's puzzled look, her friend was equally in the dark.

Beginning to feel they must be missed by the rest of their party, Jane now suggested they go back up to the castle; but the other three showed no inclination for it. Miss Devere proposed they should instead descend to the cove below, and her proposal was taken up with alacrity. On the path, however, they were reunited with their friends, who were just coming down with the same intention. The entire group descended together; and Jane could take some comfort in having escaped being discovered, by anyone other than Mr. Hammond, in a *tête-à-tête* with Frank Churchill—though when she asked herself, by what justification she could feel contented to have thus deceived her dearest friends, she could form no answer upon which it was not mortifying to reflect.

# Chapter Twenty-One

**THOUGH HER MIND** was much engaged with Frank Churchill, Jane also felt some curiosity respecting the sudden reverse in Miss Devere's manner. She therefore listened with no small interest when Margaret privately communicated to her, later that day, her thoughts about Mr. Hammond.

"I had a little time during Mr. Wiggins' lecture—for I am sure I did not listen to a word of it—to consider the situation," she began. "And my present view is, that whatever scandal Mr. Lodge may care to publish (and are we to credit the information of a man who would repeat such shameful tales to his own daughter?), it cannot be disputed that James Hammond has remained single these fifteen years—despite, I cannot doubt, many opportunities to connect himself well in marriage; for he is now rich and successful, and his society much sought after.

"Now, I am not so vain as to suggest it is solely for my sake he has not married; nor that he came to Weymouth with any idea of renewing our old passion. But it *was* a passion, Miss Fairfax, of no common variety. However much he may believe such sentiments to be past, they might yet have power over him; and in examining his behaviour, I cannot think myself altogether self-deceived when I say that I think they *do* influence him. His conduct, studied objectively, really does not appear to me of a sort likely to proceed from indifference."

"I have had the same thought myself," said Jane.

"And is it not curious, that he has chosen to remain here at Weymouth to do the painting for St. Alban's? Does he not have a studio elsewhere? And would it not be more usual for an artist, upon taking a job of this sort (after visiting the place, of course, to inspect it, and so forth)—would it not be more usual for him to return to his own studio to execute his commission?"

"I am not much acquainted with the habits of artists,"

said Jane, "but I would indeed suppose that the more common practice."

"Yet he is to remain here, working in the Rectory carriage
house, until the painting is completed. I can only conclude
from this, that he must have some very particular reason
for doing so.

"It does appear," she resumed after a moment, "that he
feels some resentment towards me, which I confess I cannot
understand; unless it stems merely from my unfortunate
remarks when we first met in St. Alban's. But I mean to find
out the reason for it. And I feel certain that, whenever I do, I
will find there is some feeling of love remaining—or returning. I know I am a good deal older than I was when James
and I first fell in love; but he is older, too; and I am not yet
so withered and wizened, I hope, that I must expect to be an
object of disgust to him."

"Decidedly not," Jane agreed with a smile.

And over the weeks that followed, Mr. Hammond gradually became one of their circle. He joined them, when he
could spare time from his painting, on some of their day-
time excursions; and spent more than a few evenings in
their company as well, whether they met at Colonel Campbell's house or at the Rectory. Indeed, Jane began to
wonder that he *could* spare so much time from his work;
and, despite a bearing towards his former lover which was
more often cold than otherwise, she too was inclined to attribute his behaviour to a reawakening of passion.

According to Miss Devere (who seemed to be spending a
good deal of *her* time looking out of the Rectory windows),
he came to his studio at first light nearly every day, and
generally remained there for several hours. Overhearing him
one day mention to Colonel Campbell that he commonly
took nothing but coffee before leaving his rooms every
morning, Margaret on the next day (as she later reported to
Jane) walked into the carriage house at half past ten, and
invited him to step over to the house for refreshments.
Without the smallest effort at civility—not troubling even to
put down his brush—he waved her away, grumbling at the
interruption, and stating quite crossly that he was not in
the least hungry.

Little daunted, she did not oppose him, but immediately
turned and walked out; and returned a short time later,
carrying a small platter of bread, cheese, and fruit.

"If Mahomet will not come to the Mountain," she announced, setting the food down on a table near at hand, "then the Mountain, I suppose, must go to Mahomet."

He looked up from his work, asking dryly, "Does not that proverb go the other way 'round?"

"Oh! yes," she replied. "But I thought you might take offence at being characterised as a mere agglomeration of clay."

Disarmed in spite of himself, he laughed, and thanked her with a more gracious air; admitting, a little sheepishly, that he was in truth very hungry, or he should not be so peevish. He came away from his canvas then and, seating himself before the little table, without further speech consumed all she had provided.

She, meanwhile, took the opportunity to get a look at his painting. It was as tall as he was himself, and wider than it was tall; but the composition was at a very early stage, so she could not make much of it. She ventured to ask, what was the subject of the picture? The expulsion from Paradise, he answered. How long did he expect it would take to complete, she inquired? Some months, was the vague reply.

It became her habit, after that day, to bring a tray to him at the carriage house every morning—having reasons of her own for not sending a servant to wait upon him, as she should otherwise have done. For the most part, he seemed little inclined to converse on such occasions; and at times, finding it inconvenient to stop what he was doing, would only gruffly direct her to leave the food and let him eat when he would. At other times he was more friendly, and on one occasion allowed her to stay and talk with him while he ate. But they never touched upon the one subject everpresent to her own mind and, for aught she knew, to his also.

Despite Margaret's professed love for Mr. Hammond, in the interactions between the two Jane often saw evidence of a residual anger on both sides, which periodically displayed itself in exchanges of caustic wit. Oddly, both Miss Devere and Mr. Hammond seemed to take a perverse kind of pleasure in these games of verbal thrust and parry, and often seemed, if only fleetingly, more amicable than usual at their conclusion.

Mr. Hammond joined their party in a trip to the Wishing Well at Upwey, and in another to the ancient earthen fort called Maiden Castle. He also went with them to see the swans of Abbotsbury; on which outing Miss Devere, with dark eyes dancing and fair cheeks dimpling, insisted they

must stop at the little chapel of St. Catherine, "whither all
desperate spinsters like myself journey to pray for a husband—and desperate wives for widowhood." To which Mr.
Hammond retorted by inquiring of Mr. Dixon, "whether he
had heard of any chapels hereabouts, where bachelors
might go to pray for the continuance of their celibacy?"

They met him once at the Theatre, in company with Lady
Paget, and once at the assembly rooms, by himself. There,
he even deigned to dance with Margaret—but did not request her hand until she was the only lady of their party left
without a partner, giving altogether the impression that he
asked her against his will, and only because civility demanded it. As the dance proceeded, though, he seemed to
thaw somewhat; and there was even one exquisite moment
(as she told Jane afterwards), when she fancied he was
looking at her quite in the old way. But when the dance
ended, he appeared of a sudden to recollect himself, bowed
over her hand, thanked her coolly for the dance, and said
not another word to her the rest of the evening.

Jane danced with him too, and found him a very agreeable partner: he danced well, and when he spoke, had little
to say but what was informative or entertaining, or both.
Miss Devere's name was not mentioned between them, as
he seemed determined to avoid speaking of her, and Jane
had not the courage to try it. But his glance was often
turned in Margaret's direction; and at one point he grew so
distracted with observing her as she danced with Mr. Lodge
(whose conspicuous attentiveness to her he could hardly
fail to remark) that Jane had to recall his mind to the
dance.

That the inconsistencies in Mr. Hammond's conduct
arose out of an attempt to resist Miss Devere's attractions,
Jane was disposed to infer—partly from a consciousness of
something similar, if less marked, in her own manner towards Mr. Churchill. What reasons Mr. Hammond might
have for opposing his own inclination, she could not imagine; for surely there could be no such obstacles to his
marrying Miss Devere, if he wished to, as existed between
herself and Frank Churchill.

She was surprised and relieved to find that neither Helen
nor her parents seemed to notice anything strange in her
behaviour. But perhaps the absorbing interest of Helen's
approaching marriage to Mr. Dixon, which was to take place
early in October, may have contributed to make them all a

little less observant than usual.

She was now beginning to know Frank Churchill very well indeed. Each meeting brought a better understanding of his tastes and talents, and a deeper appreciation of his merits. His defects of character, on more intimate acquaintance, proved neither greater nor fewer than she had first estimated them; yet somehow they were coming to seem less grievous.

He was frequently with them. His aunt's condition continued to improve, allowing him a good deal more liberty than he had previously been able to command, and he chose to spend much of it with Jane and her friends. At informal evening gatherings, he and Jane sang many duets, and in the assembly rooms they often danced together. She also saw him several times, quite by chance, at Mrs. Nesbit's, where they could talk more unreservedly; and she never witnessed unmoved his bearing of respectful affection towards his old governess.

Even when he was not present, Mrs. Nesbit talked of him endlessly, finding in Jane no unwilling listener. The old woman furnished added insight into Frank's character, by what she said about his aunt. Frank himself was not much given to complain about Mrs. Churchill (for which forbearance Jane honoured him); but from the little that he did say, united to what she had previously heard from Mr. Weston, she surmised that life at Enscombe was anything but comfortable for him. Her conjectures were confirmed by Mrs. Nesbit, who, in his absence, occasionally related to her circumstances which hinted at Mrs. Churchill's selfishness, obstinacy, and bad temper; followed always by a commendation of all Frank's good qualities: his affectionate nature, his sweet temper, his engaging manners, his lively spirits, his cleverness, his thoughtfulness—and on and on, till Jane could hardly recollect that she had ever thought him possessed of a single fault.

She was troubled also—troubled and elated—by a growing certainty that Frank loved her. Before her friends, he never distressed her by any indelicate particularity of manner; but when they were alone, there were hints and allusions, the meaning of which she could not mistake. Knowing the futility of such sentiments, she must wish he would express himself less warmly.

On one occasion after meeting at Mrs. Nesbit's, for instance, he walked with Jane for a part of her way home.

They talked quietly together, as they walked, about the recent marriage of Frank's father, Mr. Weston, and the former Miss Taylor. But then the coming marriage of Miss Campbell and Mr. Dixon was touched on, and Mr. Devere, who was to perform the ceremony, was mentioned. After some pointed intimations which made her exceedingly uncomfortable, Frank finally asked her outright, whether Mr. Devere was paying his addresses to her? Unable to meet his eye, she acknowledged that he was.

"Paying them, with your permission?"

"Mr. Devere is—a very worthy gentleman," she said falteringly, "and it was Colonel Campbell's advice—that is, the Colonel felt—that I should allow Mr. Devere an opportunity to—to endeavour to win my regard."

"And do you always do as you are told, Miss Fairfax?" said he, an uncharacteristic bitterness in his voice.

She could hardly fail to understand his meaning. That he might not mistake *hers*, she told him plainly, "When a person like Colonel Campbell—whose judgement I respect—whom I know to be interested only in my welfare—is so good as to concern himself in my affairs, and offer me the benefit of his superior understanding—I confess, I do not dismiss his counsel lightly."

This reply silenced him, for the moment; but he remained in no cheerful mood, and they parted company soon afterwards.

Mr. Devere, meanwhile, in keeping with the promise he had given her, did not tease her with any repetitions of his earlier declaration. His attentions, however, grew more marked. Persuaded, as she now was, that her deepening attachment to Frank Churchill must make it impossible for her ever to be honourably wed to another, she felt she ought in fairness to give Mr. Devere his dismissal. Yet she did not like to disappoint the hopes of Colonel Campbell, who was in every way a father to her, if there remained even the smallest chance that she might be able to fulfill them without compromising her own sense of right. Neither could she entirely forget that, should she not marry, there would be no other course open to her than to become a governess—though she hoped, in making her decision, that she would not be *greatly* influenced by such a consideration.

Decide she must, however; and before very long. Mr. Devere, patient as he had shown himself thus far, would soon tire of waiting for her, and might wisely resolve on making another choice. He had been of late a good deal preoccupied with amending the worst evils of Mary Lodge's condition; and though he remained apparently oblivious to her devotion, Jane did not think the poor girl's affection altogether hopeless of a return. For when first a gentleman begins to interest himself in the misfortunes of a young lady, who has great need of his kindness, his assistance, his instruction, and his guidance; who has great need of being rescued from a very disagreeable situation; and who is really rather pretty than not—is it not inevitable that the gentleman will sooner or later end by being very much in love with the young lady? And indeed, how better to rescue such a young lady, than to marry her?

At present, however, Mary Lodge was to Mr. Devere simply a member of his flock, in want of his help. In mid-September, his old friend Mr. Reed, the schoolmaster, found a suitable person to take the position of tutor to Mary's brothers, and the clergyman at last prevailed upon Mr. Lodge to engage him. Thus Mr. Morton, the tutor, arrived in Weymouth to see what he could do towards making the Lodge boys into something tolerably civilized.

Jane first saw Mr. Morton when she and Helen were out walking one afternoon with Mr. Dixon, Miss Devere, and Miss Lodge. They met him on the beach taking the air with his charges, whose conduct seemed already the better for his influence. He was a short, thick-necked young man, with the general appearance of a bulldog, but with a gentle, soft-spoken demeanour quite inconsonant with his looks. He was skilled in the Greek art of wrestling, Mary reported to them later, and had some knowledge of pugilism as well—both of which, as Mr. Dixon remarked, must come in very handy when dealing with his new pupils.

"Aye," said Miss Devere, laughing, "and a well-sprung birch rod, too!"

# Chapter Twenty-Two

**AT THE START** of October, an incident occurred which proved to be of great significance to Jane. Wishing to give the young people a special treat, Colonel Campbell hired a small yacht to take their entire party, including the Deveres, Mr. Hammond, Miss Lodge, and Mr. Churchill, for a sail out of Weymouth Bay.

The day dawned in a mizzling rain, and it looked as if they might have to defer their excursion to another day—a gloomy prospect, when their remaining days together were so few. By the time they had done breakfasting, however, a brisk, fresh wind had sprung up which soon cleared the rain away, leaving behind a wide blue sky and a corresponding expanse of sparkling blue water beneath. They had risen early, and were on the quay and ready to embark at half past nine. No sooner had they boarded than the sails were unfurled above their heads, and they were gliding smartly out of the bay.

Jane leaned over the railing of the boat, gazing at the dancing waves and listening with but half an ear to the conversation of Mr. Dixon, who stood next to her, and Helen, who stood by his other side. The rest were variously dispersed around the deck. Mr. Devere, Miss Lodge, and Mrs. Campbell were at the opposite railing, enjoying the sight of Portland's rugged limestone bluffs to the west. Frank Churchill was up in the prow with Colonel Campbell and the captain, talking of sails, masts and rigging. Margaret Devere had placed herself near the stern; and Mr. Hammond, who had followed her to that spot, stood nonetheless a little apart from her, in pointed silence.

Jane took in a deep breath of the fresh sea air, and released it in a mournful sigh. A certain melancholy feeling she often experienced at this time of year—the departure of summer, the end of the long, bright days—was much intensified by a sobering consciousness that her life was soon profoundly to change; and not, so far as she could foresee, for the better. Helen, her dearest friend and constant companion since childhood, was about to be married, and would soon be living far away in Ireland. Who could say when they would meet again? The time was drawing near, too, when she herself must leave the happy existence she had known with the Campbells, and enter on a far bleaker one. And Frank Churchill would return with his aunt and uncle to Enscombe: in all likelihood, she would never see him again. The life she had been living for so long must come to an end, and a new life, a life of unremitting toil and self-denial, must begin. She looked into the future, and saw nothing but hardship, loneliness, and loss.

Late on the previous night, she had at last determined to refuse Mr. Devere. No absurd hope of marrying Frank Churchill clouded her judgement. She knew there could be no such marriage, even if he wished it; but loving him as she did, she could not do otherwise than decline Mr. Devere's offer. She was sorry for it, very sorry. He was a most deserving gentleman, and she wished she had been able to return his affection. She had grown fond of Miss Devere, too, and felt it would have been easy, had things turned out differently, to love her as a sister. But he was too good a man to be sacrificed to a woman whose whole heart he did not possess. She waited only for an opportunity to tell him so, and, once she had spoken, would make her decision known to Colonel Campbell as well. She would obtain a position as a governess, as had long been planned, and embark upon a path of duty and subjection. It was what she had been educated for, what she had always expected. Why then should the very idea of it now fill her with such dread?

Absorbed in such thoughts as these, she was scarcely aware of a loud creaking sound behind her, and voices calling out; then something hit her hard, square across the shoulders, knocking the breath out of her. With a sudden rush of terror she felt herself pitching forward over the railing, and in another instant would actually have tumbled head first into the water; but something, or someone, had caught hold of her, and was pulling her back into the boat.

She stood stunned as the others came crowding in around her. They looked at her anxiously, speaking in worried tones, but dazed as she was she could not at first reply to their solicitous inquiries. Someone—Frank Churchill— brought up a seat for her just as she felt her legs giving way beneath her, and she sank down onto it with relief. Finally, Mrs. Campbell drove them all away, and she and Helen administered what curative they could with comforting words, caresses, and aromatic vinegar. When she was a little revived, she asked what had happened.

"Oh!" Helen exclaimed, "it was shocking indeed—my heart nearly stopped from fright! I suppose one of the men must have lost hold of a rope, or a cable, or something. Anyhow, a boom, or a spar, or whatever they call it, some way or other got loose, and swung round, and hit you from behind. And but for dear Ned's having the presence of mind, thank God! to catch hold of your skirt, and pull you back in, you would have been swept clean overboard, and into the sea!"

Had she been a young woman of a superstitious bent, Jane might have been tempted to view this incident in the light of an ill omen, or at least as the work of some malevolent angel, intent upon injuring her. Being too rational, however, to clothe in sinister meanings what appeared no more than an unlucky accident, she was a great deal more inclined to feel grateful for having been so providentially delivered; and as soon as she could speak intelligibly, she asked her friend to bring Mr. Dixon to her, that she might thank him for his alertness in saving her.

There seemed no more pleasure in the outing for her friends now. Colonel Campbell would have ordered the boat turned back to shore at once, but Jane protested she was well, and could not wish such a lovely day spoiled on her account. Eventually she persuaded him; and, after a little while, the party began to recover its spirits. Around twelve o'clock they all went below for refreshments. It was about this time Jane first noticed that Mr. Devere seemed to be avoiding her; and somehow, though she could hardly account for it, she received a conviction that he was arming himself to renew his proposals. *Very well*, she thought. She would give him her answer, and have done. No doubt it would be painful; but it would be for the best.

Despite such prudent reflections as these, she found she could not look forward to the interview with Mr. Devere, or to the subsequent explanation with Colonel Campbell, with anything like ease. It was impossible, however, that Mr. Devere should open the subject today, before so many witnesses—or even on the next day, the morrow being Sunday. By her calculation, then, she was safe until Monday; and, though knowing it was unwise to put off a disagreeable duty, she could not but feel glad of the delay.

Late in the afternoon, the vessel was turned about, and they headed back to Weymouth. The sun was sinking as the boat slowly drew towards the harbour; the darkening vault of the sky, now muted by clouds, was covered all over in soft hues of blue and violet, save for a single streak of brilliant orange, where the setting sun cut a narrow, fiery slash just above the horizon. The waves, too, were darkening around them, though tipped by a golden radiance. Jane stood at the railing, not far from where Mrs. Campbell and Miss Devere talked together quietly. She turned her head and, with a little start of surprise, discovered Frank Churchill at her side.

"Tis an affecting picture," he said. "Does it not bring to your mind Wordsworth's *'mighty waters rolling evermore'*?"

She murmured a word of assent.

"You are very quiet, Miss Fairfax," he remarked after a little pause, observing her with an earnest gaze. "You are not suffering any ill effects from your accident, I hope?"

Attempting to reply with more composure than she felt, she smiled up at him and said, "None of consequence, Mr. Churchill. I daresay the rest of you were more overset by it than I was. In truth, it was all over so quickly, and I was so benumbed with surprise, I hardly knew what had happened."

"It was a frightful—a terrible moment! If you had really come to any harm—!"

Breaking off abruptly, he cast a conscious glance toward the other two ladies, standing nearby, who, however, remained engaged in their own conversation. His countenance was still solemn as he resumed, "But I fear you will not be the better, for having been at first unconscious of the danger you were in. It is likely you may suffer some delayed mischief, from such a shock as you have received."

"A little bruising, perhaps, I must expect," said she, as lightly as possible, "—but no more serious consequence, I am sure."

He continued for a few moments to regard her intently, until she found it necessary to look away. The sky was nearly dark now, and for a time they stood side by side at the railing, neither speaking, but each tremulously aware of the other's presence. Then, feelingly, and in a voice so low she almost wondered if she had only imagined the words, he began,

"My dear—dearest Miss Fairfax!—If only—"

He stopped again. What could it mean? Was he about to
make a declaration? She was seized by a strange, giddy
mixture of joy and alarm. Breathless, she waited for him to
speak again. But the conversation of Mrs. Campbell and
Miss Devere, she perceived, was at that very moment sus-
pended. He apparently perceived it too; and concluding in a
very different tone, he said,

"If only... you will take a little extra care, Miss Fairfax—I
cannot doubt any injury you have suffered will be mended
in a day or two."

The boat was soon afterwards scudding briskly up to the
wharf, and there was a bustle as their party prepared to
disembark. The hour being late, they did not linger; but expecting to meet again at church on the following day, they
made their farewells, and went their separate ways.

JANE WAS sitting in the parlour with Helen and her
mother later that evening, when she first noticed a little
stiffness and aching in her shoulders: the bruising she had
apprehended was beginning to make itself felt. Mrs. Campbell advised that, directly she had taken her supper, she
should have Helen rub some liniment into her back, and go
early to bed. Jane, thinking that a dose of solitude might do
as much to ease her painful reflections, as a dose of liniment to ease her aching muscles, agreed to follow Mrs.
Campbell's prescription.

Before long, however, a knock was heard at the front
door; and a few minutes afterwards, Jane was summoned
by Colonel Campbell to his study, where once more she was
asked to grant Mr. Devere the honour of a private hearing.
In supposing he could not speak before Monday, she had
greatly underestimated the violence of his ardor. She was
much perturbed; and was, for a few moments, tempted to
plead indisposition, and ask for a deferral. But another
moment's deliberation determined her not to put it off, for
his sake as well as for her own.

To spare Mr. Devere the mortification of making his offer
in form, she would have preferred to announce her decision

at once. But she knew not how to begin; and he had worked himself up to such a pitch of courage as made any beginning on her side unnecessary—indeed, impossible. She stood silent, her head bowed and her eyes downcast, as he pleaded his suit.

"I am conscious, Miss Fairfax," he commenced, "that in requesting this interview, I am going back on a promise I made to you some weeks since, in this very room. But the danger in which I saw you placed, only a few hours ago, has served to remind me quite forcibly of—of the unknowable nature of God's will—of how life may be taken from us in a moment; and I feel it would be foolhardy to delay any longer. I do not wish to press you unreasonably. But I feel there has been sufficient time given for you to know your own mind. My feelings—my admiration and devotion—are unchanged—are only stronger than they were. I have no expectations, however. I am prepared to bear my fate with resignation, if resignation be necessary—as I more than half fear it will be. At all events," he concluded, "I believe it will be best—best for us both—to settle the matter one way or the other."

Here he paused; and she forced herself to look up—to speak—to make herself intelligible if she could. She quite agreed, she said, that the question was best resolved at once; and with many sincere expressions of gratitude, esteem, and regret, she gave him to understand that she could not accept him.

He said little in response—offered no argument, expressed no sense of resentment, made no accusations of ill-usage. He only stated his own regrets that the affair had not ended differently; said he should always feel towards her a true regard and friendship; and wished her well. His voice betrayed no particular emotion, but that he was hurt by her refusal, she could not doubt. His behaviour, however, was altogether generous and gentlemanly, and such as could only serve to make her feel his claims more strongly—and to wish, more than ever, that she could have loved him.

She remained in the study for several minutes after he departed, striving to regain some degree of tranquillity. In a little while, Colonel Campbell came in; and she was saved the trouble of explaining how matters stood, by his assuring her that Mr. Devere, before leaving, had apprised him of all. The Colonel's kindness quite overpowered her, and in his paternal embrace she sobbed out all the tears she had been endeavouring to suppress.

"There, there, my dear," he said, "It is quite all right, quite all right. I will not be severe upon you. Indeed, it would have been a fine match for you; and I wish you might have liked Stephen well enough to accept him. But you must do as you think best. We will say no more about it—not another word—and there's an end to it."

Some readers may wonder that Colonel Campbell, on his ward's refusing an offer so patently desirable, did not demand to know whether she was cherishing any prior attachment which prevented her from accepting it. But the Colonel reposed a good deal of faith in Jane's judgement and probity, and in her affection and respect for himself; and he believed that, had she any such reason for rejecting Mr. Devere's suit, she would likely have owned it to him at once. Moreover, he had the wisdom to perceive that if any prior attachment *could* exist without his knowledge, it must be one which Jane herself knew to be either ineligible, or hopeless of a return. In such a case, he relied upon her to struggle against and conquer it; and until she had succeeded in doing so, he deemed it altogether right that she should not engage her self, where her affections were not— perhaps could not be—engaged as well.

Helen and Mrs. Campbell were equally philosophical. It was really too bad Stephen had not been able to attach her, Mrs. Campbell remarked to her husband, especially in light of her having no other secure provision for the future. But after all, there was no hurry about the future; she need not go out as a governess tomorrow. They would be returning shortly to London, where there were always eligible gentleman to be met with. Who could say what the future might hold for her?

And Helen, rubbing liniment into Jane's back before she went to bed, said she was sorry for Mr. Devere's disappointment—but of course, if Jane did not love him, it could not be helped.

"It may be all for the best in the end, you know," she observed, "for if you *had* married Mr. Devere, you and I would have been settled in different countries, and I should hardly ever have seen you. But now you can visit Ned and me in Ireland next summer, when my parents come—and we will see if there is not a good husband to be got for you from among Ned's neighbours at Baly-craig!"

# Chapter Twenty-Three

**WHEN FRANK CHURCHILL** arrived at home that same evening, he was surprised to find his uncle pacing the drawing room, an expression of anxiety on his face.

"Frank!" he cried when he perceived his nephew in the doorway. "Thank goodness you've come back. What a commotion is here—we are all in an uproar!"

Frank was at that moment rather preoccupied with his own thoughts. Without any real uneasiness, he asked whether his aunt were taken ill again.

"Ill! Bless me, she was in such a state! She is gone to bed some time since—"

"Has the doctor seen her?"

"Lord, no, dear boy. What could the doctor do for her, in such a condition?"

Frank was wrenched from his abstraction with a jolt. "Uncle! Is it so serious as that?"

"Serious! I should say so. We are to leave Weymouth!"

"Leave Weymouth! But—I do not understand, sir. If my aunt's health is so much deranged, how can she think of travelling?"

"No, no. It is not her health. Didn't I tell you? She has had a quarrel with that Lady—Lady—oh, you know the one I mean, Frank—"

"Lady Paget?"

"Yes. Well, there was a great row about something or other, and the end of it is, that she says we must leave Weymouth right away—first thing tomorrow!"

"Tomorrow!"

"Aye! She says she will not bide a moment longer. I did try my best to dissuade her. After all, travelling on Sunday, you know, and that sort of thing. I was certain she would repent of it, and so I told her. 'It won't do, Eugenia,' said I, 'it simply won't do.' But she would not hear reason; and I dared not push too far, for she was truly in such a state! You know, my dear boy, how your aunt can be sometimes.

The very best woman in the world, Eugenia is; but she does have a little propensity, on occasion, to be just the slightest bit... quick-tempered."

"And we are really to leave tomorrow?"

"Directly after breakfast. Unless *you* can persuade her otherwise. You must try, Frank—aye, do. You always hit on just the right thing to say to her, somehow. I am quite useless at the sort of business, you know—only manage to provoke her the more. But you will be able to soften her, if anyone can."

Frank could hardly comprehend so sudden a turn. "I beg your pardon, uncle; I am so stunned, I cannot think just now. But I will meditate on what can be done. And in the meantime, sir—perhaps you should go to bed yourself. You look fatigued."

The elderly man nodded his head wearily. "It has been a trying day. You will be up awhile yet, in case she should wake, and need anything?"

"Oh yes. Good night, sir."

Precisely how much sleep old Mr. Churchill enjoyed that night, the reader may be left to conjecture; it is certain, however, that his nephew did not get any. A thousand thoughts whirled round in his head to prevent it, almost all of them centred on Jane Fairfax. Despite Mrs. Churchill's determination that he must marry a woman of wealth and rank, Frank had come perilously close to declaring himself to Miss Fairfax that very day. In truth, it was only the presence of her friends which had kept him from making a full admission of his love; and being now at leisure to reflect on the question, he felt not the smallest doubt as to his own wishes. Of Miss Fairfax's sentiments he was uncertain, yet more than tolerably hopeful: that she was not ill-disposed towards him, he was convinced; and if her affections were not his own already, he judged his chances good to win them in time.

But if he could not find a way to quiet Mrs. Churchill's anger, there would be no time. If she persisted in her intention of leaving Weymouth, he would be parted from Miss Fairfax so soon as tomorrow, and perhaps forever—without even a farewell! And yet what would it avail him, had he all the time in the world? It was impossible his aunt could ever be induced to accept Jane Fairfax as the future mistress of Enscombe.

Was he ready then, he asked himself, to risk every expectation of wealth and property for her sake? To defy his aunt, that he might marry the woman he loved?

The conclusion he arrived at, after much sober deliberation on the subject, was: *Yes.* For Miss Fairfax, he would willingly forfeit Enscombe, and the large fortune which attended it, should forfeit be required. To be sure, he loved great houses, and fine stables, and grand estates—but he loved Miss Fairfax better.

A rupture with his aunt, though, would of necessity separate him also from his uncle: a man for whom he felt the warmest attachment, and to whom he owed the deepest gratitude. Such an estrangement would, he knew, break the old man's heart. His own mother had been summarily banished from Enscombe by the rancour of Mrs. Churchill, for defying her injunctions and marrying his father. Could he doubt that any disobedience in a like form would earn him the same fate?

*But was a rupture inevitable?* Of a normally sanguine temper, Frank wished to believe that a means must exist by which he might marry Miss Fairfax, and at the same time retain the goodwill of his guardians—if he could but discover it. Yet, though he knew himself in many matters to have great influence with his aunt, in this one matter, most important of all, he could not trust to his power over her; and the longer he considered, the nearer he came to despair.

He went down to breakfast early in the morning, to find Mrs. Churchill unpersuadable on the subject of leaving Weymouth. He had often beheld her in a temper, but seldom had he seen her as angry as she was on this occasion. He could do nothing to pacify her. He could not even ascertain from her the precise nature of her quarrel with Lady Paget. She would only say that she had been grossly insulted, in a manner not to be borne.

Whether he would or no, then, he must leave Weymouth—leave Miss Fairfax. Frame it how he would, there was nothing to be done. He was not his own master; he was subject to the will, the whim, of another.

Nonetheless, by employing all his powers of address—by representing to his aunt what she would suffer in setting out so immediately, after all the fatigues of preparing for their removal—in truth, by a judicious mix of deference, flattery, and clever management—he at length gained the one critical point of postponing their departure until Monday. Now, at least, he could look for a chance to slip away sometime during the day, and try to see Miss Fairfax.

**JANE HAD** awakened, that morning, stiff and aching from the accident of the previous day, and it took very little pressing from Mrs. Campbell to persuade her to stay at home while the others went to church. She really did feel out of sorts; and (she could not but admit to herself) she had rather not see Mr. Devere again so soon. They would both benefit, she believed, from a little period of separation.

She was therefore quite alone, when she was startled by a pounding on the front door. Her initial impulse was to ignore it: all the servants were also at church, and she had rather not go down herself. Who could be calling on a Sunday? They must be knocking in error. Yet there was something importunate in the forceful rapping; and after a moment, she got up to look out at the window, where perhaps she would be able to see who it was, or what was wanted, without the trouble of going to the door.

All she could see at first was an arm clad in a grey coat. Then the caller stepped back from the door and, looking up toward the windows, looked directly at her. It was Frank Churchill! With her mind racing, and a too-familiar flutter in her breast, she slowly made her way down the stairs. She could not receive him, of course, with all the family and even the servants out of the house. She wondered, indeed, why he was not at church himself. Still, it would hardly do to leave him standing on the front steps; she would just go down and speak to him for a minute.

"Miss Fairfax!" he exclaimed when she opened the door. "I did not expect—that is—is there no servant within to answer the door?"

"They are all gone to church."

"Oh! It is Sunday. I did not recollect."

He appeared exceedingly distracted. She wondered why, and waited for him to explain himself.

"I have not much time," said he. "I must be back presently. I am come—to bid you goodbye."

"Goodbye?"

"My aunt has decided we are to leave Weymouth—

tomorrow."

"Tomorrow!" After a little stunned pause, she said, "Is not this very sudden, Mr. Churchill?"

"It is my aunt's way to do things quickly, when she has once made up her mind."

After another, longer interval, he began again, "May I ask you to convey my regrets to the Campbells, and to our other friends here in Weymouth?"

"Yes, of course. But they should be home in a little while; will you not come back later? They would be sorry to miss you."

"I am afraid it will not be possible."

"And Mrs. Nesbit? You will find time to see her before you go, I suppose?"

"Mrs. Nesbit!" he cried. "Good God! How could I have forgotten? I *will* try to see her—but I fear—there is so much to be done, and I must not stay away too long; and—. I beg your pardon, Miss Fairfax. This removal has come upon me so unexpectedly, I hardly know what I am about."

Jane was not feeling at all tranquil herself. She had known she would not be enjoying Frank Churchill's society very much longer, but she had not thought the end would come quite so abruptly.

"If it would be of any help," she finally managed to say, "I would be happy to carry a message to Mrs. Nesbit—"

He caught at this proposal, and asked if he might come in to write a short note for her to take to his old friend, in case he should not have an opportunity to see her before he left. It was a request so perfectly reasonable, she really could not refuse. They went up together into the parlour; and while he sat at a small desk composing a brief letter to Mrs. Nesbit, Jane sat on the sofa attempting to compose herself.

It often happens that, in the expectation of some unpleasant event, we endeavour by the exercise of reason and will to prepare ourselves for what we know to be unavoidable; and, after an arduous struggle, we satisfy ourselves we are ready to meet adversity with a calm and rational resignation. We are thus the more distressed to discover, when the anticipated calamity occurs, that all our equanimity and wisdom are flown; and that we are in precisely the same state of distress which would have attended us, had the misfortune taken us completely by surprise. From the beginning of their acquaintance, Jane had accepted that no good could come of allowing herself to feel more than a friendly regard for Frank Churchill. She had often reminded herself of the obstacles which stood in the way of any nearer connection between them. She had wisely prepared herself for the inevitable parting. But only now that it was arrived was she to comprehend the futility of attempting to prepare for unhappiness. She would never see Frank Churchill again; and the certain knowledge of that fact made her as wretched as could be.

She was hardly conscious of the time passing; hardly aware that Frank had finished his letter, and left it folded on the desk, with a generous enclosure of money for his old nurse; hardly knew he had crossed the room and seated himself beside her on the sofa, until she felt her hand taken up in his—heard his voice addressing her—saw the glow of warmth in his gaze as he began pouring out his love. He spoke, if not with eloquence, with an impassioned fervor which wholly overpowered her. In a manner so little like his usual polished ease, and, in consequence, so much the more disarming, he talked of feelings which had been growing from the very first moment of their acquaintance. He had for some time been aware, he admitted, that she was becoming every day more dear to him; but he had not realised how dear, until threatened with parting from her; had not fully comprehended the depth of his attachment, until his aunt's plan of leaving Weymouth had last night burst upon him so painfully.

"I am the most accursed fellow!" cried he. "Circumstanced as I am, my life is not my own. I know I have no right to speak—no right to ask. But I cannot bear to leave Weymouth—to part, who knows for how long—without telling you—in short, without obtaining some assurance—"

He trailed off mournfully, unable to continue in the face of her silence; but after a long hesitation he took up her hand again, saying,

"Miss Fairfax! You are too good to let me go away in such a miserable state of uncertainty. Only give me, before I leave, some token—some sign, whether my feelings are returned—?"

There was another long hesitation. Then her brief, barely audible reply:

"They are,"—and without warning she found herself taken in an ardent embrace which left her nearly breathless.

She soon drew away. He did not attempt to hold her, but again took possession of her hand. "You will allow me, then," he said, "to write to you from Yorkshire? And you will write back?"

"Write to you!" she exclaimed. "Do stop and consider, Mr. Churchill—consider what you are asking. To agree to a correspondence would mean—would signify that—that we were entering into an engagement."

"Yes!"

"Are you saying—do you believe you can obtain your aunt's permission for us to marry?"

"Yes. That is... I believe we will be able to marry, eventually. For now, though—for now, I own, it is impossible." He shook his head. "For now, the knowledge of our engagement must be kept only between ourselves."

"A secret engagement!" she cried. "Oh, no—I cannot! To deceive the Colonel, and Mrs. Campbell, and Helen, and—and everyone! It would be wrong—so very, very wrong. I could not consider—you should not even ask it."

"I do ask it. I must."

"And yet—have you any reason to think Mrs. Churchill will ever be persuaded to give her consent, to a match between—between the acknowledged heir of Mr. Charles Lewis Churchill, and—a penniless nobody? You know yourself that is how she will view it. You will never overcome her objections."

"But chance occurrences may be in our favour. In time, my aunt may relent—or—"

"Or, in other words," she concluded, "*We must wait for her to die.*"

"No! I did not mean that."

"What other possibility is there?"

"I do not know," he admitted. "I only know that—that I shall go mad if I cannot have the promise of hearing from you—of knowing how you are, and what you are thinking, and feeling. Of knowing that—that your affections are unchanged."

"My affections are not so easily changed, Mr. Churchill," she said quietly.

"Oh, I am a dog to doubt you! I know you have the truest, most constant heart in the world! Only—"

"Only—?"

"Only, here is Mr. Devere, paying his addresses to you—a man I would be a fool not to see is a thousand times more deserving than I am; who has the approbation of your guardians; and, perhaps, in time—"

"After the admission I have just made," she said with a conscious blush, "You cannot think I would accept the proposals of any other man—should they be offered."

"No—of course not. Forgive me—I spoke without thinking. It is simply that I cannot bear the prospect of—of what may prove a long separation, without at least the consolation of a regular correspondence. To be able to write to you, and to receive your letters, would make it seem more as though— as though we were not so entirely removed from one another, even if we should be a great many miles apart."

Jane could not think clearly enough just then to make him any reply; and there was a little intermission, before he spoke again, somewhat more cheerfully,

"Well, do not give me an answer now. I will write you when I reach Enscombe, and I will trust to your affection—I will leave it to your charity, whether you will return me any answer. I know you will have compassion on me! You will allow me to write, will not you—dearest Jane?"

He spoke the name, and the endearment which accompanied it, without reserve; and with a look of such irresistible appeal that, though she made no promise to write herself, neither did she issue any absolute injunction forbidding him to write to her. Moreover, the tender expression which filled her eyes just then seemed fully to justify his confidence that his letter, when received, would not go unanswered.

One further indulgence he begged her to grant before they parted: that of hearing his Christian name from her own lips. Tremblingly, she complied; in recompense of which, he stole a kiss from those same lips—stole another—and was gone!

**END OF PART ONE**

# Lovers' Perjuries

## Part Two

**"At lovers' perjuries, they say, Jove laughs."**
**(Shakespeare)**

# Chapter Twenty-Four

**TO ENSURE THAT** Frank's letter would come directly into her own hands, Jane began walking alone to the post-office every morning before Helen was up, explaining to her friends that she felt the early exercise to be of benefit to her health. *Oh, how easily,* she reflected with dismay, *one falls into habits of deception!*

Before the letter came, she was fully resolved she should not answer it; but once again, where Frank Churchill was concerned, her strongest resolutions were a fragile armor at best. In his heartfelt expressions of the happiness he felt at having secured her affection—in the repeated assurances of his own warm affection for herself—there was such a bewitching mixture of playfulness and earnest, as brought before her with perfect clarity all the liveliness, sweetness, and charm of the writer. What defenses could long withstand such an attack?

His letter was a lengthy one, comprising not only those avowals already mentioned, and some entertaining descriptions of the more interesting scenes and incidents of his journey northward; but also an appraisal of their predicament, and the likeliest way of extricating themselves from it. He had given the matter a good deal of thought, he said, and had arrived at a plan which he hoped would meet with her approbation.

"You are probably aware," he wrote, "that my father was formerly engaged in trade with his brothers (my Weston uncles) in London. The profits of that enterprise yielded him the comfortable independence which he now enjoys; and though he has no longer any direct share in its management, he still has many business connections in town, of whom at least one or two, I am sure, would be willing and able to assist me, if I chose to enter into the same line. Even by this means it would be some time before we should be able to marry; but as I do not want either energy or talents to apply to such an undertaking, I hope it may not be *too* long; and if you, my dearest Jane, are prepared to wait, I would make every exertion, do everything in my power to succeed in it."

Of how thoroughly in earnest Frank Churchill was, when he proposed exchanging the luxurious easy-chairs of Enscombe for the grim austerity of a London clerk's desk, I leave it to my readers to determine for themselves; though I for one am perfectly convinced of his good intentions. Can anything indeed be more plausible, than that a young man, wanting neither spirit nor intelligence, and who has lived all his life under the oppressive yoke of a selfish, ill-tempered relation, should be ready, on the least encouragement, to loose himself from her control and become the master of his own fate? In fact, Frank had long been yearning to break free of his restraints.

Still, he would rather gain his independence without the loss of his uncle, were it possible; and he even believed that, if he said nothing to his aunt of Miss Fairfax, it might *be* possible. With judicious handling, Mrs. Churchill might be brought in time to view this scheme of business as an impulsive freak—one which, if opposed, might take root, but if indulged, would soon be abandoned. He could but try to make her think so.

Jane sent her answer to this letter (for of course such a letter *must* be answered) by return of post; addressed, as he directed, to Miss Frances Cramer, in care of Maltby & Son, Saddlers, Barnstock, Yorkshire. She praised his generosity, thanking him again and again for being ready to sacrifice so much for her sake. But though in his letter he had made no mention of how his relationship with Mr. and Mrs. Churchill must suffer, should he resort to such measures as he suggested, *she* could not be ignorant as to the likely consequence of any such proceeding.

"I cannot bear," she wrote, "that, on my account, you should relinquish the fortune and position you have been brought up all your life to expect; and I think it wisest to wait, for a little while at least, before taking a step which I fear must create an irrevocable rupture between you and the relations who have raised you almost as a son. I cannot doubt that your own sense of gratitude and affection for Mr. and Mrs. Churchill would make such a rupture exceedingly painful to your feelings."

As for herself, she assured him, she was perfectly content to wait. She now considered their engagement as quite fixed. She had not the smallest apprehension as to his faith and constancy; and she trusted he felt not any with regard to her own.

Thus did it come about that Jane Fairfax was engaged to Frank Churchill, without the knowledge or sanction of her guardians, or his, or any other person whatever. Her admission of love had been the work of a moment: with his hurried departure from Weymouth, there had been no time for proper reflection. Now the remarkable state of affairs in which she found herself was the subject of ceaseless, sobering reflection; yet no amount of reflection seemed to bring her to any satisfactory conclusion. The future, near and distant, was shrouded in haze—shadowy, unpredictable, and unsettling.

She moved through the next three months in a kind of restless abstraction. Less than two weeks after the Churchills left Weymouth, Helen Campbell became the wife of Mr. Dixon, and sailed with him for Ireland. By a considerable effort, Jane was able to appear, up to that time, almost tolerably like herself. But despite the necessity of maintaining a bearing of composure before others, it was impossible she should not, in solitude, be sometimes overcome with feelings of guilt, anxiety, and remorse; impossible—when she thought how she was deceiving those so deservedly dear to her—that she should not give way to tears. She felt deeply that she had done wrong to enter into this engagement; was doing wrong in maintaining it. Yet Frank Churchill now possessed her whole heart; she loved him too well to give him up.

Margaret Devere's ill-fated love affair with James Hammond came often to her mind now: how Mr. Hammond had refused to deceive her father, and the price both had paid for his integrity. Fifteen years of separation and estrangement! She recalled, too, her own suggestion to Miss Devere, that Mr. Hammond should have lost something in her esteem, had he agreed to keep their engagement secret; and Margaret's reply—'Impossible!'

Certainly Frank's willingness to risk, on her account, both his inheritance and the affection of his guardians, could only increase her regard for him; and her own plea, that he would not be precipitate in provoking a breach with the Churchills, had been offered with the best of intentions, and with his welfare in view. But her heart misgave her when she recalled another remark she had made to Miss Devere—that no man could submit to a clandestine engagement, and keep his self-respect. What if Frank, by following her well-meant advice, should sink in his *own* esteem? Yet, when she thought of all he stood to lose if he confessed the engagement to his aunt, she could not urge him to do so.

Continued concealment, however, made her own situation more difficult, for she had months ago declared to her guardians that she would go out as a governess once Helen's marriage had taken place. She even proposed, in her reply to Frank's letter, that perhaps it would be best if she proceeded with that plan, as there was no telling how long it would be before they could be wed. Frank, however, was steady in opposing such a measure—would not hear of her doing any such thing—felt it a reproach to himself that she should even think of it. So she was required to postpone seeking employment, to some indefinite future time; and she felt the inconsistency of her behaviour.

An excuse was found for it, though, in the evidences of weeping often discernable in her face. A little emotion over their daughter's departure the Campbells expected, in view of Jane's attachment to her; and she did feel the want of her friend's society acutely: at least some of her tears were, indeed, shed for Helen's sake. But in the stubborn persistence, for many days, of a pink nose and red-rimmed eyes, the Campbells saw only the symptoms of a cold, and ample justification for deferring any inquiries after a situation. They could not allow her to take on the rigorous duties of a governess, they said, while her health was so indifferent. When they returned to London, they would call in Mr. Wingfield, the apothecary, to see what he could do for her; but she must not think of leaving them until she was perfectly well again.

Happily, during the brief remainder of their time at Weymouth, Jane saw little of Mr. Devere. Miss Devere she received with some trepidation, on the day after declining the rector's offer of marriage. She was rather afraid lest Margaret should be angry with her for not accepting her brother's proposal. Instead, her kind forbearance was so painful to Jane, that she would almost have preferred open enmity; comparing Margaret's sympathetic candour with her own duplicity, she felt she deserved no less. When, at their last meeting, she agreed to correspond with her, she did so with an inward reluctance. To repay such generous confidence with secrecy and reserve seemed but a compounding of her sins. It might fairly be supposed that Margaret Devere, of all people, would understand the need for Jane to conceal her engagement; but there was small comfort in the knowledge.

Nor did she reveal the secret to Mrs. Nesbit when, on the day before leaving Weymouth, she called to bid farewell to the elderly woman. She had earlier delivered Frank's message, and had been, at that time, sorely tempted to confide in her. Mrs. Nesbit, she knew, could have no opportunity to betray their trust, nor, still less, any inclination to do so. But though the temptation to unburden herself was great, she kept her own counsel. Mrs. Nesbit was so very fond of Frank, and held him in such high regard, that Jane did not like to say anything which might make him appear to her in an unfavourable light.

At the end of October, she returned to town with Colonel and Mrs. Campbell. London was thin of company at that season, and Jane was glad to find their engagements very few. The Campbells, too, felt some relief in this interval of quiet, after the flurry of activity and emotion surrounding their daughter's marriage and departure. Jane continued her early walks to the post-office, but needed now no fresh justification for her anxiety to fetch the letters: with her dearest friend off to Ireland, and another, albeit newer, friend at Weymouth, as well as her relations in Highbury, sixteen miles distant, letters were naturally of great importance to her. Mr. Wingfield pronounced her cold very trifling, and gave his opinion that the air and exercise could do her no harm, and might in fact do some good; so no objection was raised to this daily errand.

Helen soon wrote from Baly-craig, and Jane was gladdened to read that she found her new home very comfortable, and the surrounding countryside enchanting. Ned had given her a saddle horse as a wedding gift, and the newlyweds rode out together nearly every day, Ned introducing her to all the most picturesque spots in the neighbourhood. Everything, she wrote, was just as he had always described it to them. And dear Ned himself was just as he had always been, only now more dear than ever:

"How many novels I have read, in which the heroine is courted by a seemingly respectable, charming, and tender gentleman, only to find him turn cruel and vicious once they are wed—remember Miss Betsy Thoughtless, and odious Mr. Munden! That such circumstances sometimes do occur in life, as well as in novels, I cannot doubt; but I think I can say with perfect security that I shall never know aught of such misfortunes myself."

And unwilling as Jane had been to engage in a correspondence with Miss Devere, she nonetheless found herself reading Margaret's first letter with considerable interest as well.

"Weymouth is grown quite dreary, Miss Fairfax," she reported, "since all our friends have deserted us. About a week after you left, an express came for Mr. H. informing him that his father was taken ill again. He set off at once for his parents' home in Oxfordshire, and has not been back this fortnight. Nor (as my brother hears from an indignant Lady P.) is he expected to return anytime soon. Stephen has been so absorbed in his work, spending more time even than before in looking after the poor and sick of the parish—and of course, as much as ever doing *my lady's* bidding—that I do not see much of him either. So 'here I sit, like *imp*atience on a monument.' I can find nothing to do with myself but mope about the house; and were it not for the society of Mary Lodge, who calls frequently (and seems nearly as listless as myself), I believe I should be very dull and weary indeed.

"Miss Fairfax, I see you shaking your head. 'Cannot the lady make herself useful,' you ask yourself, 'by affording some assistance to her brother in his good works, instead of grumbling to *me* of her dullness and weariness? Cannot she pick up her brushes and pallette, and paint? Cannot she at least procure a few overlong novels from the circulating library, rather than weary her friends with such tiresome complaints as these? Does this thick-witted woman possess not a single resource of her own, with which to occupy her time?'

"These are all perfectly right and sensible questions to be asked. At the moment, however, I am afraid I have not any sensible answer to make to them; but I think you are sufficiently acquainted with my history to deduce, from among my aforementioned grievances, the true cause of my lassitude.

"But I must not give way to self-pity. I must have a *something* to amuse myself with, until J. comes back; and afterwards, too—for even when he returns to Weymouth, I cannot depend upon our having that regular intercourse together, which we enjoyed before our circle of friends was so sadly diminished. By way of diversion, then, I have determined to make a match between my brother and Miss L.

"Oh dear. You are shaking your head again, Miss Fairfax. But do not despair of my understanding. I do not mean to interfere *very* much. On *her* side, indeed, no interference is needed. And as for Stephen—well, I shall only arrange a *very* few accidental *rencontres*, and drop, perhaps, a *very* few circumspect hints—and then I shall sit back to watch and enjoy, and await the inevitable. I do think it high time my brother should take a wife, and furnish me with a few nieces and nephews to dote upon. And though he might once have fixed his thoughts upon a *certain* young lady, I believe he may, by a little judicious management, be eventually led to think almost as much of *another*."

Jane blushed on reading this allusion to herself; and though she did, in fact, shake her head over his sister's sportive scheming, she also could not repress a small hope that Miss Devere's matchmaking might prove successful—and thus release her from the guilt she felt, whenever she thought of her former suitor.

A second letter from Helen arrived, not quite as cheerful as the first. She was still perfectly content with 'dear Ned'; but Baly-craig was proving more isolated than she had anticipated. With the colder weather, she and her husband could not ride out as much as they had done before, and she was growing already a little weary of rustication. There were but few houses within an easy distance for visiting, and none seemed likely to offer any opportunity for real intimacy. One great manor house could be glimpsed even from their own garden, but the family of an earl was too grand to take more than formal notice of a mere Mr. and Mrs. Dixon. In another house lived a very elderly couple; in a third, a middle-aged widow in poor health. The Vicarage was perhaps the nearest dwelling, and the vicar, Mr. Axelrod, did seem most pleasant; but he was a single gentleman, and had not even an unmarried sister or aunt to keep house for him. Helen, so long accustomed to regular female companionship, and good society in general, missed her parents and Jane dreadfully.

It had been previously arranged that the Campbells and their ward would come to Ireland for a visit the summer following Helen's marriage. But Mr. Dixon, seeing his wife's spirits so much affected by their absence, now proposed that they should hasten their journey. The joint appeal of Mr. and Mrs. Dixon for an early visit was so insistent—was pressed with so much affection and regard—that Colonel Campbell was soon almost decided that they would make the trip in January rather than June.

Frank, meanwhile, was also growing impatient to see Jane again. That their engagement had no fixed term, he wrote her, was bad enough; but to have no hope of being with her at any period in the foreseeable future, was a positive torment. He had been puzzling endlessly over how they might contrive to meet. Was it possible she could find some excuse to go to Highbury? He had been wishing for some time to pay a visit to his father, and now that Mr. Weston was newly married there was even more compelling reason why the visit should be paid. Up to this point, it must be owned, his attempts at persuading Mrs. Churchill to allow him to go to Highbury had been unavailing; but if he could have the promise of Jane's being there to inspire him, he would redouble his efforts to obtain his aunt's consent for the journey. Moreover, with such an inducement in view, he was certain he should prevail!

# Chapter Twenty-Five

COLONEL CAMPBELL'S carriage advanced slowly along the road from London. There were treacherous expanses of ice along the way, owing to a heavy fall of rain and sleet the day before, followed by a freezing overnight, so the coachman drove his horses forward with particular care. Within the carriage, Jane was tightly bundled against the cold. She had no companion on the sixteen-mile journey to Highbury, save for her thoughts. These, however, were sufficiently absorbing to prevent her feeling any tedium in her solitude.

A letter from Frank, just before Christmas, had brought the happy news that Mrs. Churchill was at last reconciled to his spending a week with his father, provided a certain family who had been invited to visit Enscombe in January were put off—and Frank was confident they *would* be put off. As a matter of form, his letter explained, the Braithwaites were invited to Enscombe once every two or three years; but as his aunt had an uncommon dislike to the whole family, they were always put off in the end. Without question, he would be in Highbury by the second week of January!

On the strength of this intelligence, Jane had proposed to her guardians that she should spend a few months visiting her own relations in Surrey, rather than accompany them to Ireland to see Helen and Mr. Dixon. It was fully two years since she had last been to Highbury, and though, as she told Mrs. Campbell, she had been looking forward with a great deal of pleasure to visiting Baly-craig, she might not find another opportunity of seeing her aunt and grandmother again for some time.

The Campbells, though sorry for their daughter's sake as well as their own, could not but acknowledge the justice of Jane's request to give to her own family connections some part of what might be her last months of liberty. In addition, as she had not altogether recovered from that little indisposition first evidenced around the time of Helen's marriage, they believed a few months spent in her native air (generally reckoned a particularly wholesome one) might do much to strengthen her for the trials of her future life.

Thus were matters settled, when another letter from Frank arrived to throw everything into disarray. The Braithwaites *were* put off, but Mrs. Churchill could not spare him; not at present, at least. Still, he remained confident he would be able to come soon—perhaps in February. He was mortified to disappoint Jane, and mad with frustration himself; but it could not be helped.

Frank or no Frank, Jane was now obliged to go to Highbury; preparations were too far advanced for an about-face. Except for Helen's sake, however, she did not regret the necessity. Truly, she would be glad to see her dear grandmama and aunt Hetty again, and all the old friends and neighbours of her childhood. She did feel some misgiving: what if Frank should not be able to come at all? Yet he wrote so reassuringly, and with so much affection, that she could not but rely on him to find some way to arrange it.

Whether or not he *ought* to arrange it, was at times a more troublesome question. She told herself that the simple fact of their being privately engaged could not be so *very* wrong—though her conscience declared that keeping silent on a point of such significance, among those with whom, in the past, she had been always perfectly open, could hardly be regarded as right. But most important, she reflected, was to be certain no one should be materially injured by their concealment. All would be well, so long as she maintained a careful reserve towards anyone who might be a potential suitor—and there were not likely to be many such in Highbury. It did not seem probable she should meet with anyone new there; and it seemed even less probable that any gentleman with whom she had long been on merely friendly or even indifferent terms, should suddenly wish to attach her.

And if Frank also took care to avoid raising the expectations of any young ladies he should happen to meet, she ventured to hope no real harm could come of their secrecy. There was little danger of his exciting such expectations in Yorkshire: by his own accounts, the Churchills saw almost no one at Enscombe. In Highbury, however, continual prudence on his part would be required. There he would naturally be an object of great interest to all; and considering his singular attractiveness, both of person and of manner, she feared he would find it all too easy to ensnare any number of female hearts, if he were not very careful indeed.

She need not be uneasy, however. Given the exceedingly delicate nature of their situation, he would of course be circumspect. There could be no need of any anxiety whatever on that score.

When the carriage had got a few miles beyond Kingston and she found herself nearing her destination, Jane began to look about her with more attention. Soon they came around a long, sweeping curve, and Donwell Meadows came into view; she could just discern the low, rambling silhouette of Donwell Abbey, seat of Mr. Knightley, in the distance beyond. A little farther, and they passed the lane which led out to Hartfield, the estate of good-hearted old Mr. Woodhouse and his daughter Emma. Then they were driving through the populous, prosperous village of Highbury—down the broad High Street, past familiar houses, offices, and shops, past the Crown Inn, and Ford's—and pulling up before a rather ordinary two-storied brick house; wherein, on the drawing-room floor, was the very moderate sized apartment in which the aged Mrs. Bates and her daughter dwelt.

Aunt Hetty must have been watching from one of the casement windows, for she was down the stairs and out the front door before Jane had time even to step down from the carriage. She greeted her niece with a welcoming embrace and a rush of words.

"Jane—dear, dear Jane! How good it is to see you! I have been looking out for your carriage ever since we finished our breakfast, though your grandmama kept telling me you could not possibly arrive before twelve. 'Now Hetty,' said she (if she said it once, I am sure she said it a dozen times)— 'Now Hetty, you know Jane cannot possibly be here before noon,'—and I knew it was so, but I just could not keep my mind to my work—and so I told her! But now here you are at last, and after all, it is only a little past noon; and looking—do stand back a bit, dearest, and let me see how you look. Oh, goodness me! I am afraid you are rather thinner than you were when you were here last—and it is quite two years since your last visit, you know. You are paler too, I believe! But we will revive you by and by—we will nurse you up until you are well as ever. If need be, we will call in Mr. Perry. The expense will not be thought of, and I daresay—

but the journey must have tired you; I did not allow for that at first. You will be better when you are rested, to be sure. Oh look! There is Mrs. Ford in front of her shop, waving to us. Good Mrs. Ford! She sold me a fine piece of gray woolen last week—at a very good price, too. I thought to make it up for your grandmama; her dark blue is getting so shabby! Come up now, Jane. Here is Patty; she will direct the man about your trunks. You have not forgotten Patty. Here she is, Patty—here is our own dear girl, come home at last! Do come inside, Jane, this cold will do you no good; though, your coat does look very warm, indeed—watch, there is a little ice just there! A good, thick melton; but not so soft as the gray I bought for Mama. I do not think you had it when you were here before, did you? That shade is so becoming on you! Remember that little step at the turning—take care—it is very dark. Now, I think, Jane, you will be very glad to see your grandmama again."

They entered the neat little parlour, and elderly Mrs. Bates welcomed her granddaughter with every mark of an equal, if less effusive, affection. Mrs. Bates was the widow of a former vicar of Highbury, tidy, unpretending, and respectable. Her husband's death had left her in greatly reduced circumstances, and she and her daughter now lived in a very modest way. Their poverty was made less austere by the possession of some very good articles of furniture, plate, &c., surviving from that more prosperous time; and by the generosity and goodwill of many kind friends and neighbours in Highbury, who regularly sent them gifts of fruit, game, and other handsome provisions; and who afforded also that constant, congenial society, without which their lives would have been bleak indeed.

Mrs. Bates was a very old lady, almost past everything but tea and quadrille. Her days were occupied chiefly in dozing; at intervals, she employed herself with a variety of needlework. For a woman of such advanced years, her vision (with the aid of spectacles) was good, though her hearing was failing—or rather, Miss Bates believed her mother's hearing was failing, owing to a habit the latter had acquired, in self-defence, of turning a deaf ear to her daughter's perpetual chat.

Miss Bates was a general favourite in Highbury, though she had neither youth, beauty, wit, nor wealth to recommend her. Her popularity was a consequence of nothing more than her own happy temper: she loved everybody, was interested in everybody's happiness, saw all of their merits, and none of their faults; thought herself a most fortunate creature, and surrounded with blessings in such an excellent mother, and so many good neighbours and friends, and a home that wanted for nothing. The simplicity and cheerfulness of her nature, her contented and grateful spirit, were a recommendation to everybody, and a mine of felicity to herself. She was a great talker upon little matters, full of trivial communications and harmless gossip.

Both Mrs. and Miss Bates now urged Jane to sit by the fire to warm herself, and rest from the fatigues of her journey. But Jane had been sitting all the way from London to Highbury—was tired of sitting—had much rather be moving about. So the trunks must be opened, and the gifts brought out. Jane had ornamented new caps and embroidered new workbags for them both, and had knitted a warm scarf for Patty, their faithful maid-of-all-work. There was also a large new shawl for Mrs. Bates, a wedding gift from Mrs. Dixon, purchased at Weymouth.

"Helen hesitated some time in making up her mind," Jane said, "for there were three others of a similar type. The Colonel rather favoured an olive. But Mr. Dixon finally decided her on this gray, as being both the prettiest, and the most serviceable."

"And he chose very well indeed," said Miss Bates. "This will set off the new gray woolen just perfectly—do not you think so, ma'am?" (to her mother) "I do admire Mr. Dixon's taste. Indeed, I have always thought very highly of Mr. Dixon, ever since the service he rendered you at Weymouth, Jane, when you were out in that party on the water, and would have been dashed into the sea if he had not caught hold of your habit. We are so grateful to Mr. Dixon! I was telling Miss Woodhouse of it just the other day, when she was so good as to pay us a visit. It happened we had a very good sweet-cake (I am sorry there is none left, Jane, you would have liked it very much) and Mrs. Cole had just been here, and had been so kind as to take a piece from the beaufet, and say she liked it very much; so I ventured to offer some to Miss Woodhouse and Miss Smith, and they very obligingly accepted some too; and Miss Woodhouse complimented me upon it; and I daresay Miss Smith enjoyed it very much as well, though she was so very quiet, she did not say whether she did."

"You mentioned Miss Smith in your last letter," said Jane.

"I do not believe I know her."

"No—I do not think you two have ever met. But Miss Woodhouse is lately become a great friend to Miss Smith— Miss Harriet Smith, which quite surprised us at first—did it not, ma'am?" (again to Mrs. Bates) "—for Miss Smith is only a parlour-boarder at Mrs. Goddard's school, and not the sort of young person I should have expected Miss Woodhouse to show any particular attentions. But I imagine she was quite forlorn after Miss Taylor married Mr. Weston. By the bye, you must remind me to tell you all about the wedding, I am sure I could not have done it justice in my letter. The wedding breakfast was at Hartfield, you know—the drawing room filled with flowers from the Donwell hothouses, and the table spread with such a quantity of delicacies as I never saw; and the wedding cake—! But what was I speaking of? Oh, yes—well now, Miss Woodhouse, you know, has been always accustomed to Miss Taylor's companionship, and I fancy must have found her new solitude rather unpleasant; for her father, I think (dear, good man as he is!) cannot be a very lively companion for her; and so I gather she sought to supply something of the deficiency, by taking such kind notice of Miss Smith."

"I should be surprised myself at such an occurrence," said Jane, "but that your explanation makes it seem perfectly reasonable. What sort of young lady is Miss Smith?"

"Oh, a very pretty, and very pretty-behaved young lady, of about seventeen I should say. It was rumoured not long ago that young Robert Martin, who rents the Abbey Mill Farm of Mr. Knightley—a very agreeable, sensible sort of young man, is Mr. Martin; Mr. Knightley always speaks so highly of him! By the bye, Mr. Martin did me a very great service last month—did not he, Mama?—when I was coming home from paying a call at Hartfield, and I had the misfortune to turn my ankle in a ditch along the side of the road. It was but a slight turn, not at all serious—but if you will believe me, I really felt at first I should not be able to walk for the pain. It was a cold day, too, and not a soul anywhere to be seen! I had just begun to wonder what was to become of me, when who should come along but young Robert Martin, on his way to the Crown; and, upon my word, he took me up in his wagon and brought me all the way home, and even insisted on helping me up the stairs, though I could just as well have called for Patty to do it—and saw me seated in this very chair, before he would leave me."

"It was a kindness, indeed," said Jane. "You wrote me word of it at the time."

"Did I? I had quite forgotten. Well, it was rumoured that Mr. Martin was quite thoroughly smitten with Miss Smith; for she is the very intimate friend of his two sisters, you see, and spent two months with the family at the Abbey Mill Farm last summer; which I daresay is when Cupid's arrow first struck him; and it was believed she was not at all disinclined toward him—or so Mrs. Goddard thought, and Miss Nash, too. Everyone said it would end in his marrying her. However, nothing came of it. Perhaps, since her being taken up by Miss Woodhouse, he might think she was too much above him, to venture making her an offer; for one cannot suppose it likely she would refuse such an eligible suitor. Confidentially," (lowering her voice almost to a whisper) "she is the natural daughter of somebody or other, whose identity is a great secret; known only to Mrs. Goddard, and kept, so I understand, even from Miss Smith herself. She came to Mrs. Goddard's as a pupil several years ago; but having completed her education last spring, has since stayed on as parlour-boarder. She is a very sweet girl, however. Her manners are very pleasing, and her face exceedingly pretty. But no doubt you will meet her soon yourself, for I told Miss Woodhouse we were expecting you, and I am sure she means to call at the earliest possible opportunity, and welcome you back to Highbury. Such an old friend as she is to your grandmama and me!—and to you, too; or as much as she could be, given that you have been mostly living in London these dozen years, and have seen so little of her. And whenever she does call, I daresay she will bring Miss Smith with her; for they are always together now."

# Chapter Twenty-Six

**THE WOODHOUSES** had been settled for several generations at Hartfield, the younger branch of a very ancient family. The landed property of Hartfield was inconsiderable, being but a sort of notch in the Donwell Abbey estate, to which all the rest of Highbury belonged; but their fortune, from other sources, was such as to make them scarcely secondary to Donwell Abbey itself, in every other kind of consequence; and the family had long held a high place in the consideration of the neighbourhood.

Since the marriage, seven years earlier, of her elder sister Isabella, Highbury could boast no lady equal to Miss Emma Woodhouse in the united virtues of beauty, birth and fortune. This supremacy Miss Woodhouse had never yet found reason to deplore; for she was very fond of being always first in company, and of having generally the power to do what she liked. Her gentle, indulgent father possessed neither the wish nor the will to command her. Where her father failed, her mother might have succeeded; but she had died when Emma was very small, and her place had been supplied by an excellent woman as governess, who had fallen little short of a mother in affection. Even before Miss Taylor had ceased to hold the nominal office of governess, the mildness of her temper had hardly allowed her to impose any restraint; and the shadow of authority being now long passed away, they had been living together as friend and friend very mutually attached, and Emma doing just what she liked; highly esteeming Miss Taylor's judgment, but directed chiefly by her own.

Yet Miss Woodhouse was by no means wanting in admirable qualities. She was liberal and compassionate to the poor and the sick; she was also devoted to her elderly father—a man whose gentle tyranny many might have deemed oppressive—and spared no exertions to secure his comfort. And though possessed of considerable beauty, she seemed but little occupied with it. She attached, perhaps, a too great importance to the distinctions of rank; and it was owing to this that her interest in Harriet Smith had excited some astonishment among her neighbours. Miss Bates had in fact accounted for the intimacy very well: when Miss Taylor left Hartfield to become Mrs. Weston, Emma was forced into solitude, and found it not at all to her liking. Miss Smith was perhaps not so clever or accomplished a companion as her friends might have wished for her; but she must have a *someone* to walk with, to converse with, to have at hand for any little project or pursuit she might choose to undertake; and Harriet Smith, with great natural sweetness and modesty, and a delightful willingness to be guided in everything by Miss Woodhouse, was more than acceptable to her. So Emma justified the friendship, by assuring herself of the undoubted gentility of Harriet's father; and by formulating a benevolent if indefinite plan for improving Harriet's mind, through a great deal of useful reading and elevating conversation.

Miss Woodhouse and Miss Smith were among the first to call on Jane during the week that followed her return to Highbury. Due to the nearness in their ages—and from a similarity in elegance, beauty, and talents—it was commonly assumed, by those who knew them, that between Jane Fairfax and Emma Woodhouse there must exist a very strong mutual regard, moderated only by the circumstance of Miss Fairfax's being so little in Highbury. The reality, however, was that Jane and Emma had never got much beyond that outward show of friendly courtesy which civility demanded. Jane's visits to Highbury had never extended beyond a month or two, since she left it to live with the Campbells; and Miss Woodhouse seemed always so firmly fixed in the center of her own circle, that it was difficult to make a beginning. Her manner, moreover, was condescending, towards both Miss Bates and her niece. Jane might have excused the affront on her own account, but she must resent any slight to her beloved aunt. In truth, she herself felt at times a little ashamed of that lady's inexhaustible speech. Her embarrassment, however, was always directly swept away in a flood of self-reproach, for she knew how thoroughly good a creature her aunt really was. Yet Miss Bates's effusions conspired to keep her from saying much whenever the two young ladies met, creating an impression in Emma's mind that Jane was reserved—disgustingly, provokingly reserved.

Jane had long suspected that Miss Woodhouse thought her reserved, and disliked her for it; but she had not the least suspicion that it was a dislike grounded partly in jealousy. Miss Woodhouse, after all, was by no means without abilities. She played and sang—drew in almost every style—and had made more progress both in drawing and music than many might have done, with so little labour as she would ever submit to. But steadiness had always been wanting; and in nothing had she approached the degree of excellence which she would have been glad to command, and ought not to have failed of. Though ever conscious of her own superiority in fortune and situation, she could not be blind to Jane's superiority in accomplishment; nor could she be deaf to the outpourings of admiration and praise for Miss Fairfax which were perpetually on the lips of all their joint acquaintance.

"One is sick of the very name of Jane Fairfax," Emma had complained to her friend Harriet Smith one day, a few weeks before Jane's arrival. "Every letter from her is read forty times over; her compliments to all her friends go round and round again; and if she does but send her aunt the pattern of a stomacher, or knit a pair of garters for her grandmother, one hears of nothing else for a month. I wish Jane Fairfax very well; but she tires me to death."

Given such sentiments as these, it might be expected that Miss Woodhouse would make little effort to promote an intimacy between Jane and herself; but other feelings were at work, too, opposing her inclination. A desire to preserve the good opinion of her friends, particularly of Mr. Knightley (one of the few people who could see any faults in Emma Woodhouse, and the only one who ever told her of them), induced her to call on Miss Fairfax soon after her arrival. And then her own sense of justice—which, on first seeing Jane again after a two years' absence, obliged her to acknowledge to herself a real admiration for her beauty and elegance, and a genuine pity for the future of toil and submission which all that beauty and elegance was destined to—compelled Emma to invite Jane and the two Bates ladies to spend an evening at Hartfield.

If Miss Woodhouse's calling at their home threw Miss Bates into a little bustle of politeness and gratitude, an invitation to Hartfield (though extended, for Mr. Woodhouse's sake, tolerably regularly) pitched her into a very whirlwind of agitation and joy. Their humble rooms were too small to contain such busy energy. She ran to Mrs. Goddard's to borrow a pair of gold buckles for her shoes, and to Ford's for fresh ribbon to trim Jane's gown. She flew about the apartment, worrying over what Jane should wear, lamenting that she had no maid to dress her hair, apprehensive that she might not be well enough to go, and anxious they should not keep Mr. Woodhouse's coachman and horses waiting for them a moment. Then, safely inside the carriage, it was, "Jane, where are my gloves?—I cannot have forgotten my gloves!—oh, here they are, just beside me on the seat.—You have your spectacles, ma'am, have not you? Are you sure they are in your reticule?—Jane, dear, put this sheepskin over your lap—you will catch your death of cold!"

As mistress of her father's house, Miss Woodhouse was always at her most gracious and attentive when entertaining guests at Hartfield; and Jane had never known her so affable as she was in welcoming them that evening. Old Mr. Woodhouse, too, greeted them very kindly, and after inquiring with his usual gentleness and solicitude after her health, and assuring her he should always be very happy to see her at Hartfield, settled himself by the fire and listened contentedly to the conversation, feeling no need to contribute to it beyond occasionally questioning one or another of his visitors as to whether they were too warm or too cold, and urging them to move closer to the fire, or farther from it, as the case required.

There were two other guests present beside themselves: Miss Smith, and Mr. Knightley. Though Miss Smith had accompanied Emma in calling on her at her grandmother's house, Jane had been able at that time to discover little more than that she was, as Miss Bates had described her, an uncommonly pretty girl, fair, blue-eyed, plump, and rather quiet. She talked with her a little now, and found her artless, sweet, appealing—and rather ignorant. Thus far it appeared that Emma's friendship had been of little use in enlarging her mind.

Mr. George Knightley was a frequent visitor to Hartfield, being not only a very old and intimate friend of the Woodhouse family, but particularly connected with it, as the elder brother of Isabella's husband. He was a sensible, vigorous, well-favoured man, of about seven or eight-and-thirty; a man of talents, well-read and well-informed, with an exemplary character, an excellent understanding, and a benevolent heart. He was a great favourite with the Bates

ladies, whom he always treated with the utmost consideration and kindness. Jane thought him equal even to Colonel
Campbell in merit; and he liked and admired her exceedingly.

"I am sorry you did not come to us a little sooner, Miss
Fairfax," he said to her, when Emma was gone out of the
room for a minute, and Miss Bates was chatting brightly of
inconsequential matters to her mother, Mr. Woodhouse and
Miss Smith. "If you had, you would have met my brother
and sister here. John and Isabella were down from London
for a week at Christmas time; Isabella asked after you. I
gather you saw nothing of them in town last autumn?"

"I did not have that pleasure, I regret to say. She and Mr.
John Knightley are well, I hope—and the children too?"

"Yes, very well, thank you. I have a new niece, you
know—little Emma, born last April."

"Oh! yes—let me congratulate you. My aunt wrote of it.
She was very happy to receive a visit from Mrs. Knightley
last month, with all the children. She said little Henry and
John were so much grown since their last visit, she should
not have known them."

"They are fine boys, active and healthy. Their mother is a
little inclined to coddle them—but in that I suppose she is
not much different from most mothers who are fond of their
children; and I do not think the children are the worse for
it. John's more rough-and-tumble sort of affection prevents
their being too much protected or overindulged."

Miss Woodhouse now returned to the drawing-room, and
Miss Bates began talking to her and Mr. Woodhouse of her
anxiety for Jane's health. These remarks, delivered in a
somewhat louder voice than she had been using formerly,
soon caught the attention of both Jane and Mr. Knightley.

"You cannot imagine, Miss Woodhouse, how little she
eats! Upon my honour, it is scarcely enough to keep a bird
alive! Why, she had no more than three quarters of toast
this morning, with just the tiniest dab of butter. 'My dear
Jane,' said I, 'you must take more than that, or I cannot
think how you shall live until dinnertime! Take a little of
this sausage—or, if you have not a taste for sausage, here
are some excellent poached eggs,'—fresh eggs they were,
too; fresh this morning. Mrs. Cole was so kind as to send
them over, after I had mentioned to her yesterday that we
had none. Mrs. Cole is truly an excellent neighbour; but
then I am sure there is no one with such good neighbours

as we have been blessed with—isn't that right, ma'am?" (to her mother) "Such generosity as we are always receiving from the Coles, and from Hartfield, and Donwell! We never want for anything. But as I was telling you—it really is frightening, how little Jane eats. You would be quite shocked, Miss Woodhouse, if you saw it. At dinner last night, she had nought but one thin slice of mutton; it was so thin, I declare, you could almost see through it!—and though there was plenty to go around, and I urged and urged, she would have no more, and would take only the littlest spoonful of the stewed carrots, and just a very little helping of pudding besides. 'My dear Jane,' said I—"

"Emma," cried Mr. Knightley, perceiving his companion's embarrassment, and knowing well how little pleased their hostess would be by such a speech, "Emma, I hope you and Miss Fairfax intend to favour us with some music tonight. It is so seldom, ma'am," said he, turning to Mrs. Bates, "that one can have the good fortune of hearing two such accomplished performers in one evening. I should be sorry to lose the chance, for who knows when it may occur again?"

Jane looked at him gratefully. Miss Woodhouse, glad to be spared the necessity of listening to any more of Miss Bates's chatter, was quick to take up the hint.

"Oh! yes, Miss Fairfax! It is so long since we have had the pleasure of hearing you. You play and sing so beautifully! I hope you will oblige us with a long concert. My father, I know, would consider it a particular treat—would not you, Papa?"

"Indeed," the old gentleman responded with ready civility, "Let me entreat you, Miss Fairfax."

Jane was not sorry to be pressed. There was no piano in her grandmother's small apartment, and she had not had any opportunity to play since she arrived in Highbury. She was soon seated at the instrument (a very fine one) and rendering the opening measures of a familiar Italian song. When she concluded it, the performance was warmly applauded by all her audience, and she was begged to continue. Even Miss Woodhouse was kind in urging her to go on, so she complied with little demur. Indulging both herself and her friends, she played a few pieces more; till, beginning to feel that Emma must be growing impatient to have her turn, she declared that she was tired, and could play no longer. She then took her seat among the others, and listened with attentive interest to Miss Woodhouse's performance.

Though Emma Woodhouse had never attained that degree of mastery in music which Jane herself possessed, her singing style was charming. She had a good deal of taste and spirit, and could accompany her own voice quite creditably. Moreover, she knew her limitations too well to attempt anything beyond them. Jane heard her two songs with real pleasure, and afterwards told her so; but Miss Woodhouse, she thought, seemed not altogether gratified by her compliments.

From that point, the evening seemed to lose some of its bloom. The music ended, it was time for tea. Conversation resumed, and the muffin was handed round.

"Miss Fairfax," Emma began, taking Jane aside to escape another of Miss Bates's protracted speeches, "I understand from your aunt that you were at Weymouth last summer with the Campbells—that you met Mr. Frank Churchill there, and were a little acquainted with him?"

Jane felt a small inward tremor as she replied, "Yes; a little."

"I quite envy you," said her companion. "He was expected here, you know, after Christmas. All Highbury talked of nothing else for a fortnight, and Mr. Weston was sure he would come. I did think his judgement might be relied upon; but in the end, we were disappointed. I have been hearing so much of him of late, I confess it has given me the greatest curiosity to see him! And on Mrs. Weston's account, of course," she added hastily, "I am particularly anxious to know more of him. I thought perhaps that you, as a disinterested observer, might be able to supply some more solid intelligence of him."

In spite of her agitation, Jane could hardly suppress a smile at this suggestion. That she should be applied to, for a disinterested opinion of Frank! However—

"I do not know that I could tell you very much," she said.

"Is he a handsome gentleman?"

"I believe," she faltered, "I believe he was commonly reckoned a very fine young man."

"Was he agreeable?"

"He was—generally thought so."

Jane, growing increasingly uncomfortable, hoped Miss Woodhouse would inquire no further; but she persisted:

"But was he a sensible man? A man of talents—of information?"

"At a watering place," said Jane, "or in a common London acquaintance, it is difficult to decide on such points. Manners are all that may be safely judged of, I think, under a much longer knowledge than we have yet had of Mr. Churchill. I believe everybody found his manners pleasing."

With this, Emma was forced to be satisfied. Or, rather, dissatisfied, for her frustration at obtaining no further particulars, and her annoyance with Jane for not supplying them, were but ill-concealed. She proceeded to ask several more questions concerning Weymouth, the Campbells, and the Dixons; but the alarm already raised in Jane's mind was so great, that she hardly knew what replies she made in return.

# Chapter Twenty-Seven

**HOWEVER MUCH MISS** Woodhouse might be annoyed by Jane's evasions, they did not provoke her so greatly as to make her forget what was owed to Mrs. Bates and her family, or to her own consequence in the neighbourhood. The very next morning, a whole hindquarter of Hartfield pork, fresh-killed, was delivered to the Bates's house, compliments of Mr. Woodhouse and his daughter. The unexpected gift came directly after breakfast, and cast aunt Hetty into another little flurry of elation and activity. Nothing would do but she must go at once to Hartfield, to express their gratitude in person; and Jane must accompany her.

Jane had been out already that day, as she continued her custom of walking to the post-office every morning before breakfast. She had been painfully disappointed to find no letter from Frank awaiting her. He had not written for several days, and she was more than a little anxious to hear some word from him; his silence, she feared, could augur no good. In some abstraction, therefore, she put on her bonnet and pelisse, and waited dutifully in the passage for her aunt to come out. The door was ajar, and, though attending but imperfectly, she could hear Mrs. Bates instructing her daughter to convey her best regards and thanks to Mr. Woodhouse.

"His generosity really quite oppresses me," said the old lady. "But Hetty, I wonder whether we have any salting-pan large enough for Patty to salt the leg?"

"I will go down and see, ma'am," Miss Bates replied, stepping out onto the landing. "If we have not, no doubt Mrs. Goddard would be happy to lend us one. But I will just run down now and ask Patty—"

"Shall I go down instead, aunt?" Jane offered. "I think you have a little cold, and Patty has been washing the kitchen."

"Well, my dear, and if that were any reason for me to keep away, I'm sure it must be doubly so for you. But in fact, I am quite well. I have not got a cold. My throat is always a little rough in the morning, you know. I will be just a minute, and then—"

She was interrupted by the ringing of the doorbell, and Patty, immediately afterwards, brought up a note from their friend Mrs. Cole. Mr. Cole, the note said, had just received a letter from Mr. Elton, the vicar, announcing his engagement to a lady at Bath, by the name of Miss Hawkins!

Hartfield, the pork, the salting pan—all were forgotten in an instant. On such joyous intelligence Miss Bates of course could not keep silent; it must be immediately discussed, examined, and speculated over with her mother and niece. Jane had not much to say on the subject. She had never seen the Reverend Philip Elton, though she had often heard her aunt speak of him. He was, it seemed, an affable young man whose looks and manners were much admired, especially among the intimates of Miss Bates. He had taken the living of Highbury less than two years ago, and had quickly ascended to the very zenith of popularity. All the teachers at Mrs. Goddard's school, as well as the elder pupils, were wild for Mr. Elton. The Coles and Perrys, Otways and Gilberts, invited him so often to dinner it was said he need never eat alone if he did not wish it. He was frequently asked even to Donwell and Hartfield. For the past month, however, he had been at Bath, and Jane could only conclude he must have found the holiday to his satisfaction: in but four short weeks, apparently, he had met, wooed, and won fair lady.

Mrs. Bates was pleased to hear of Mr. Elton's engagement. "I always hate to think of the poor old vicarage without a mistress. But there is little else to be said, I suppose, until we know more of the young lady."

Miss Bates thought a good deal else might be said; and after declaring her conviction that any lady chosen by Mr. Elton must be charming indeed, would have gone on saying it without end had not Jane reminded her of her intention to call at Hartfield. They soon set off together; but as Miss Bates was not at all unequal to walking and talking at the same time, her observations and conjectures continued as they descended the stairs and stepped out to the street.

"Well, well. Just think, Jane—a new neighbour for us all. Miss Hawkins of Bath. I daresay she will be a very charming neighbour. Quite a romance! Only four weeks; he left just after Christmas.—Miss Hawkins, of Bath. She must be very beautiful.—I did used to think Mr. Elton might choose some young lady from Highbury. In truth, I even had some suspicions—this is just between us, Jane—but I once fancied Mr. Elton rather admired Miss Woodhouse! And indeed, Mrs. Cole gave me a little hint of it, too, some weeks since. Not that I thought there was the smallest chance of—. He is the worthiest of men, I said, but—! On the other hand, one could hardly blame him, if he should have raised his sights—; and her manner to him was always so very complaisant. But I am not at all quick about such matters. I never did have any talent at prophecy. Oh! there is Mrs. Ford, looking out at her window. I think I will just step across for a moment and tell her the happy news. She will certainly be interested to hear of it. A new bride at the vicarage! What a fine addition to her business it will be; no doubt the future Mrs. Elton will wish to make some changes to the house—new hangings, linen, and the like. Though, now I think on it, perhaps she may bring her own linen. Still, she is sure to want any number of new things; a bride always does, you know. You will not mind if I just run over to tell Mrs. Ford, will you, Jane? I shall not be half a minute."

Jane made no objection, though the half-minute stretched to ten; neither did she object when her aunt proposed looking in on Mrs. Gilbert for an instant, to impart the news to her; nor when she suggested their taking a little detour, to carry the report to Mrs. Otway. In fact, Miss Bates published the story so generously, that three-quarters of an hour flew by before they finally reached Hartfield; and upon their arrival, they found that Mr. Knightley had come in just before them.

"Oh! My dear sir, how are you this morning? My dear Miss Woodhouse—I am quite overpowered. Such a beautiful hind-quarter of pork! You are too bountiful! Have you heard the news? Mr. Elton is going to be married!"

Chancing to look at Emma as the news was delivered, Jane was surprised to see her give a little start, and a little blush, upon hearing it! Could it be that Jane was not the only young lady in Highbury with a secret? *Was it possible Emma Woodhouse was in love with Mr. Elton?*

Jane had been endlessly hearing of the vicar's affability and good looks. 'Her manner to him was always so very complaisant,' her aunt had said. There was even a something in Mr. Knightley's almost-sly smile at Emma, as the matter was being discussed, which did seem to suggest some little intrigue. Yet if Miss Woodhouse *had* fallen victim to Mr. Elton's charms, was it likely he should prove immune to hers, and choose to wed another? Emma Woodhouse was not only beautiful and clever, but very rich. How many gentlemen would spurn such a prize, if attainable? Her ignorance of Mr. Elton, and her imperfect knowledge of Miss Woodhouse, made it impossible to judge.

'I had formerly fancied Mr. Elton rather admired Miss Woodhouse,' aunt Hetty had also told her. Perhaps, then, Mr. Elton *had* offered, and Miss Woodhouse had refused. Such an occurrence did seem more probable—and could quite reasonably explain the meaning of that start, and that blush...

But all this was fruitless conjecture. Whatever Miss Woodhouse's sentiments might be, she concealed them well: after that first instinctive reaction, she quickly entered into the conversation with all her usual liveliness, leading Jane to surmise that, if her inclinations *had* been disappointed, the disappointment could not have been too deeply felt. And if it were Mr. Elton who had suffered, his sufferings clearly were not of such a nature, or of so immoderate a degree, as to make him unsusceptible of consolation. Some mystery Jane felt there must be at the heart of the matter. However, it did not appear she would learn the truth any time soon; and as the others talked of Mr. Elton and Miss Hawkins, her mind reverted to the mystery which concerned her more nearly.

Not six months ago, news of an engagement formed after only a four weeks' acquaintance would have astonished her; she would have judged such precipitance imprudent at best. Now it served merely to remind her of her own precipitate engagement, and to turn her thoughts back to Enscombe. Why had not Frank written? Had he begun to regret his impetuous proposal? Was he sorry, now, that he had ever thought of her?

She chided herself for these suspicions. There was sure to be a very good reason for his silence. She tried to imagine what it might be, but was soon startled out of her reverie by her aunt's addressing a question to her. It was necessary then to abandon her musings, to take part in the conversation, and to appear to feel more of curiosity about Mr. Elton and Miss Hawkins than she actually felt. She must have played her part rather ill, however; for after a time, Miss

Woodhouse said,

"You are silent, Miss Fairfax—but I hope you mean to take an interest in this news. You, who have been hearing and seeing so much of late on these subjects, who must have been so deep in the business on Miss Campbell's account—we shall not excuse your being indifferent about Mr. Elton and Miss Hawkins."

"When I have seen Mr. Elton," she replied, "I dare say I shall be interested—but I believe it requires *that* with me. And as it is some months since Miss Campbell married, the impression may be little worn off."

Here Miss Bates commenced another lengthy commentary, at the end of which she determined it was time to take their leave. She intended to stop by Mrs. Cole's on the way—"I shall not stay three minutes,"—but she urged Jane to go directly home, for the weather was threatening, and grandmama would be uneasy.

Mr. Knightley was leaving with them. He had business in Highbury, he said, and offered Jane his arm back into the village. She accepted it readily—she felt far more at ease with Mr. Knightley than she did with Emma Woodhouse. As they walked back together, he talked principally of his own concerns: he was a local magistrate, and also kept in hand the home-farm at Donwell, so the chief of his conversation was devoted to legal and agricultural matters, such as many young ladies would find very dull. But Jane, though living mostly in town, was a country mouse at heart. She had a strong affection for Highbury, and an interest in all its affairs; and had therefore always some question to ask, or some observation to offer, on anything touching the welfare of its inhabitants.

They parted company most cordially in front of the Crown Inn. A few drops of rain struck the pavement as she covered the remaining short distance to her grandmother's door; where, once within, she received an agreeable surprise: Mr. Weston and his wife were up in the parlour with her grandmother. They were come particularly to see Jane, and having been assured that she would return shortly, had resolved to wait. They had been sitting with Mrs. Bates about ten minutes when she came in.

Though she had known both Mr. and Mrs. Weston for many years, she greeted them with some consciousness. Mrs. Weston offered an apology for not having called sooner; she had been a little unwell for several days past. As she spoke, however, the glow of happiness evident both on her own countenance and on her husband's, led Jane to suspect her malady to be of a sort calling rather for felicitation than condolence. No disclosure was made, however; and Mr. Elton, quite naturally, was the first subject which succeeded the usual round of 'How-d'ye-dos'. Mrs. Bates had of course told them the news when they came in, and the three of them had been discussing it since. When Mr. Elton's happiness was disposed of, Mrs. Weston asked Jane a few civil questions about the Campbells, Mrs. Dixon, &c. Weymouth was named. Then Mr. Weston, suddenly recollecting, said,

"Why, I nearly forgot, Miss Fairfax—you were at Weymouth last summer, when Frank was there; he wrote that he met you. Well now, you must tell me what you thought of my son. Is not he a very fine fellow?"

Jane could not help smiling at his manner of soliciting her opinion, and with her reply gave him, undoubtedly, more satisfaction than she had given Emma Woodhouse on the same point. "Indeed," said she, "he seemed a very amiable young man."

He nodded and smiled in agreement. "That's right, that's right. I knew you would like him. And you would have seen him again here—he was supposed to come to us after Christmas, you know. But," (in a lower voice), "a certain lady, whose will is supreme at Enscombe, prevented it. For Frank's sake, I would not speak ill of Mrs. Churchill. But, just between ourselves, she is not a good-tempered woman; she is of a jealous disposition, and likes to keep Frank to herself."

Here Mrs. Weston placed a gentle hand on his arm, and he resumed his usual hearty tone. "My good wife has passed all this winter in dread of the first meeting, though I have assured her time and again that she can have no cause to be at all uneasy—for she is sure to like Frank; and I have not the smallest doubt that he will value her just as he ought. I trust *you* did not find my son so very frightening, Miss Fairfax?"

Another smile. "No—not very frightening at all."

There was a little pause; then Jane asked, with as indifferent an air as she could muster, whether Mr. Weston had heard anything from his son lately?

"Not too lately," was the cheerful reply. "But then, he does not generally write often. Young men are the unsteadiest of

correspondents, you know—they have always something
better to do."

"Frank sent me quite a lovely letter," his wife put in, "just
after Mr. Weston and I were married. I formed a very favourable impression of him from that."

"Well, well, have no fear; we shall get him here yet, my
dear. And after all, it will be much better to have him in the
spring—the weather will be more settled; and very likely he
will be able to stay a good deal longer then, than if he had
come earlier."

**THOUGH THE** thoughts and hopes of Jane Fairfax, and
those of Mr. and Mrs. Weston, might be often fixed on
Frank Churchill in the days that followed, Highbury in general seemed to have forgotten him entirely. Mr. Elton and
his bride were the prevailing topic throughout the village;
and the future Mrs. Elton was by some means discovered to
have every recommendation of person and mind; to be
handsome, elegant, highly accomplished, and perfectly
amiable. After a week, the exultant bridegroom himself returned to Highbury, though for so brief a stay that Jane
had no opportunity to meet him. She did not, however, escape hearing a full history of the rise and progress of his
courtship, as related to her aunt by Mrs. Cole: the hour of
introduction; the accidental *rencontre*; the dinner at Mr.
Green's; the party at Mrs. Brown's; smiles and blushes rising in importance; consciousness and agitation richly
scattered; the lady so easily impressed—so sweetly disposed—so very ready to have him! He had gained his point
with the most delightful facility, the most gratifying rapidity.
Her Christian name was Augusta (charming name!) and she
could boast, among her many distinctions, an independent
fortune of so many thousands as will always be called ten.
She was the youngest of the two daughters of a Bristol mer-
chant, lived in Bristol, and spent part of every winter in
Bath. Her elder sister was *very well married*, to a gentleman
in a *great way* near Bristol, who kept *two* carriages! It was
an alliance of which Mr. Elton might be justly proud; and,
as the couple had only themselves to please, and nothing

but the necessary preparations to wait for, there was a general expectation, when Mr. Elton set out for Bath again, that when he next entered Highbury, his bride would be with him.

But the affairs of Mr. Elton and Miss Hawkins, however greatly they might fascinate her neighbours, could affect Jane but little. She persevered in her daily errand to the post-office; and though still no letter came from Frank, her other absent friends, at least, did not forget her. One morning, there was a packet from Ireland, containing letters from both Helen and her mother; and another day, one from Weymouth, in Margaret Devere's hand.

Mrs. Campbell's letter was brief—only to describe the very warm reception she and the Colonel had met with from their daughter and son at Baly-craig. They were delighted to find Helen so comfortably settled:

"While the house," she wrote, "is not terribly large, the rooms are spacious and airy, and well fitted up. The grounds, though not extensive, are charmingly laid out, and give a lovely view of the mountains beyond; and the situation of the place is altogether wholesome and invigorating. Certainly, we might wish to have them settled nearer to us; but in all things else, we can have nothing whatever to complain of. Mr. Dixon's tenderness and consideration for our dear child is unvarying; and the affection and respect he has shown to the Colonel and me, is what even a son of our own could scarcely exceed."

Helen wrote in excellent spirits. With her parents at Baly-craig, she was content, and had nothing to wish for but that Jane should come to complete their party:

"I am not so selfish, dearest Jane," said she, "as to begrudge this little interval given to your own relations, when I have been so happy as to have you nearly to myself for such a long time. But as my mother and father plan on being with us a good while, I am sure you will not think it too unreasonable in me (or will readily forgive me if it is) to hope you will be able to come to us perhaps in six or eight weeks' time. Nothing could please me more; and Ned adds his own wholehearted entreaties to mine—and says I must assure you that you are very welcome to stay at Baly-craig for a twelvemonth if you choose!"

Here was kindness indeed, which Jane hardly knew how to value enough. Reading it, she could not but shed a tear or two over the great distance which separated her from so dear a friend. As she folded up the letter—though only to have the pleasure of unfolding it, and reading it over again later—she gave a little prayer of thanks, that Helen had found such a husband as she thoroughly deserved; and ended it with a wish that no misfortune should ever come to cloud her joy.

Margaret Devere's letter began in her usual style. James Hammond, she wrote, had returned for a week (during which time she saw almost nothing of him) and was then called back to his father again:

"Lady P. is in quite a taking, and talks of getting another painter to finish the church picture. It is all nonsense, of course; she would no more think of crossing him than of flying to the moon—for even with all her wealth, she must know she was *very* fortunate to engage him.

"I am occupying myself as best I can, meanwhile, with my little matchmaking scheme—which has lately received material assistance from an unexpected quarter. Young Mr. M., tutor to the Lodge boys, is grown quite enamored of their sister, I find, and turns nearly as pink in her presence, as she does in my brother's! Stephen, however (thick-witted fellow!) had not remarked the young man's infatuation—so I just ventured to drop a small hint of it to him; and he seemed not above half pleased with the idea!

"I was just now interrupted in my writing by Lady P., who called here looking for my brother. She had some unhappy news to communicate: a letter came from J. this morning, informing her of the death of his father. Poor man! He must be much affected by such a loss—his attachment to his family is deeply felt. My heart does grieve for him!

"His return to Weymouth, of course, will now be further delayed, as he must settle his father's affairs, and attend to his mother who, I collect, is rather unwell herself—unhappy woman! Lady P.'s complete want of sympathy for their distress, by the bye, was typically insufferable: 'His father's affairs!' says she with a sneer, 'I'll wager the old man hadn't fifty pounds to his name!' It was all I could do, Miss Fairfax, to keep from throwing her out the nearest window!"

# Chapter Twenty-Eight

**AS DAY AFTER** day passed with no word from Frank, Jane's anxiety mounted to alarm, and each new story she invented to account for his continuing silence was more tormenting than the last. At times she doubted his affection. But (she argued to herself) if he did not love her, why should he say he did?

One morning in early February, she took her usual walk to the post-office before breakfast, greeting the post-mistress with a cheerfulness she did not feel. She was amply rewarded for the effort, however, by the answer to her inquiry:

"Indeed, Miss Fairfax, I do have something for you this morning. My, what a quantity of letters you do get! And from such far-flung places, too—Weymouth—Ireland—and one today from—where was that now?—ah yes, here it is," (briefly examining the postmark before handing it over to Jane), "Yorkshire."

Though the handwriting appeared oddly wobbly, a glance sufficed to satisfy Jane that the letter was indeed from Frank. "Thank you!" she said, struggling to conceal her agitation as she paid out the postage. "Thank you kindly—and good day to you, ma'am."

Once outside, she hesitated. The letter must be read at once: whatever it conveyed of good or bad, she must know it now; she could not bear any further delay. If she went directly home, aunt Hetty, perhaps, would engage her in a lengthy discussion of some little matter; then grandmama might require her assistance with some small task or errand; and so, with one thing and another, she might be kept in agonizing uncertainty for half the day. Inwardly, she upbraided herself for selfishness; but (Heaven forgive her!) she *would* be selfish. Instead of turning back to her grandmother's house, she walked in the opposite direction, towards Donwell, and out across the Donwell meadows. At the meadows' edge, by a rippling stream rimmed with birch trees, she found a dry seat on a fallen trunk, whose white bark felt rough and papery beneath her fingers, and eagerly opened her letter.

Dearest, (it read)

What must you have thought when you heard nothing from me for so long? Did you think I must be gone to the Devil? Or did you only wish me so? If my silence has occasioned you a moment's uneasiness, I deserve all the reproaches you can heap on me; but I hope, when you hear my explanation, you will acquit me of any intentional fault.

About two weeks ago my black mare saw fit to disagree with me, on the matter of a little ditch that I wished her to jump; in consequence of which, I received a little injury to my right hand that made me positively unable to grasp a pen for several days. Except for the slight wrenching to my hand, however, and a bruise or two elsewhere (and of course, the *far* more painful blow to my pride), you may rest assured I am quite unharmed; but as there was no one who might write for me, to whom I dared entrust our secret, I was compelled for a time to appear guilty of the grossest neglect.

Moreover, though my hand is now nearly mended, I have been absolutely prevented all this week from getting away to send a letter to you, owing to the unexpected presence of company at Enscombe (the profoundly stupid Sir Basil Morley, and his very silly wife)—and my aunt's insistence that I should remain in perpetual attendance to help entertain them. They will be gone to Scarborough in another day or two, I believe; but I shall certainly find some way to send this to you today or tomorrow, even if it means I must condescend to the basest trickery to do it!

I hope this too-brief letter finds you altogether well; and trust you will admit no doubt that I am, as ever, your own,

F.

I pick up my pen again to tell you that my aunt has finally given her permission for me to go to Highbury—indeed, by the time you receive this, I should be already on my way! I hope you will think the news some small amends for any unhappiness you might have suffered on my account. I have no time to say more now, but will write again from the road so you may know exactly when to expect me. —F.

What happiness, what reanimation, what comforting re-assurance was contained in these lines! Frank was well—he loved her—he was coming soon! She looked up from her let-ter and saw the sun beaming gold over the freshly greening meadow; perceived a soft sweetness in the air she had not noticed before. Sparrows chittered brightly from the hedges, and there were tender little buds on the tips of the birch twigs, just beginning to swell. She read over Frank's letter a second time, and a third, all the while relishing the gentle radiance of the morning; then she walked back to Highbury with a buoyant step.

At home she found that her aunt and grandmother had been a little worried by her prolonged absence. She excused herself as best she could by saying that the day was so lovely and the weather so mild, she had been tempted to take a walk out to the meadows.

"Such a beautiful morning, aunt Hetty! You must go out yourself, if you can. The hazel is already in flower, and the daffodils are poking their green heads up out of the ground. Spring will be here before we know it!"

"Why, I declare—you are in excellent spirits today, Jane! Your colour is much improved too, if I am not mistaken. Do not you think so, ma'am?"

"Decidedly," said Mrs. Bates.

"Well, I have always said there is nothing like the air of Highbury for healthfulness. I knew it would soon put you right. If you had all the money in the world, I am sure you could not find a better air anywhere—or more obliging neighbours, either. Here has Mrs. Otway just sent us over some trout while you were gone, Jane, which Mr. Arthur caught this morning—we will have them for dinner. Mr. George Otway has a little cold, her note said. I do hope he may recover quickly, and that his brother may not catch it. Such pleasant young men—Mr. George Otway and Mr. Ar-thur Otway. It is delightful to think what a number of excellent young men there are everywhere nowadays! The two young Mr. Otways—Mr. Richard Hughes—Mr. Dixon—and of course, Mr. Frank Churchill. I wonder when he will come to Highbury to pay his father a visit? Mr. Weston thinks it will be soon; but Mrs. Weston seemed doubtful. Did you notice, Jane, what a charming hat Mrs. Weston had on the other day? I thought something of the sort would be very attractive on you; though not in that shade of green. I do not think green flatters you, my dear—it does not suit your complexion. A dark green perhaps, but not a pale. Though there is such a pretty bloom in your cheeks today, that I daresay—yes, I think, if you continue as you are, you might wear even the pale green to good advantage."

Another letter from Frank soon came, this time from Oxford, to tell Jane he would be in Highbury by the following evening! She was a little concerned to see the direction on the outside written as unevenly as it had been on his previous letter; and initially feared his injury had been worse, perhaps, than he acknowledged. The letter within, however, was written in his usual even hand—and indeed, now that she thought of it, the same had been largely true of the first letter, though it passed her notice at the time; and upon reading *this* letter, she learned he had in fact disguised his writing designedly on the outside of both letters. He was writing to his father as well as herself, he explained, and had been anxious lest the post-mistress, if possessed of a sharp eye—as post-mistresses often are—should mark the sameness of the hand on either letter, and guess at their secret. His unsuccessful attempts to write to her directly after the accident, using his left hand rather than the disabled right, had been of great use in suggesting to him this manner of disguising his writing.

Doubtless he was wise to have taken such a sensible precaution against discovery; yet his explanation provoked in her some very uncomfortable feelings. While waiting uneasily for some word from him, her scruples of conscience had been driven away by anxiety. Now that her anxiety was relieved, her conscience reasserted itself, and the sense of shame she felt in deceiving her friends returned in full force. Yet at the same time—how she did long to see him!

But there was still more in this letter to disturb her, apart from her qualms about his handwriting. He had finally obtained his aunt's permission to go to Highbury, it seemed, only because a certain Mrs. Rowley, their nearest neighbour at Enscombe, was about to receive a visit from a sister and niece, of whom Mrs. Churchill did not approve.

"Mrs. Rowley," he wrote, "married greatly above her station in both fortune and connections, and her sister, Mrs. Trent, is rather low, and not at all wealthy. When Mrs. Trent and her daughter visited Rowley Park last spring, my aunt suspected the two elder ladies of plotting a match between Miss Trent and myself; and my dear aunt is persuaded that this latest visit is arranged solely for the purpose of accomplishing that end. Miss Trent, you see, is tolerably pretty—though by no means the most beautiful young lady of *my* acquaintance; and when she was here last May, my aunt felt I was not so cool to her as I ought to have been. She imagines me quite disposed to like Miss Trent (for men, you know, are foolishly susceptible to the superficial charms of a pretty face and insinuating manners!) and purposes to save me from all such designing females. In truth, I never did have any serious interest in Miss Trent—and certainly I have none *now*—but during her previous stay was merely entertaining her, and myself, with a little harmless flirtation. When we heard of Miss Trent's coming visit, however, I took care to give the impression of being transported to a state of no common delight in the prospect; and I have every reason to congratulate myself that I did—for it has proved to be my passage to Highbury!"

Jane could not like this story; but she set aside her misgivings, and fixed her thoughts on the happy knowledge that Frank would be with her soon. Indeed, almost from the moment of receiving this second letter, and before there could be any possibility of his arrival, she began to watch for him: whatever she was doing, she tried to place herself near a window, that she might sometimes peer out and look down the road in hopes of catching a glimpse of him, without arousing her aunt's suspicions. On the very day after his second letter came, she had gone into the bedroom to fetch her housewife, and stopped a moment to glance out of the window before returning to the parlour. The clock struck one just as she perceived two gentlemen at some distance, walking along on the opposite side of the street, and coming from the direction of Hartfield. The gentleman on the left, she thought, looked very much like Mr. Weston. The other—but it could not be Frank, of course. She knew it was not Frank. He could not possibly reach Highbury before four o'clock. Still, she could not take her eyes from the two figures as they progressed up the street. When they came closer, she saw that the first man certainly was Mr. Weston—and that the young man walking beside him was indeed Frank. They stopped in front of the Crown, and she thought they would both go in; but Mr. Weston, after pointing out Mrs. Bates's house to his son, went in alone, and Frank proceeded briskly up the street, and crossed to her door.

A minute later, she heard his voice in the parlour—heard

Mrs. Bates welcoming him civilly, and Miss Bates offering him a chair, assuring him that her niece was just gone into the other room and would be out directly. Jane could not come out just yet, however; she was trembling too violently from head to foot. It would not do to let her aunt and grandmother see her agitation. She paused, endeavouring to calm herself; then she took a deep breath, opened the door, and stepped out.

Frank stood as she entered. "Miss Fairfax," he said warmly, coming toward her, "I am very happy to see you again."

She did not feel quite calm enough to meet his eyes, but she gave him her hand, saying rather shakily, "How do you do, Mr. Churchill?" Then she sat down and found she had nothing to say—nothing, at least, that might be said in the presence of aunt Hetty and grandmama. Luckily, she was not required to speak; Miss Bates was talking. She was besieging Frank with a host of questions, and occasionally allowing him to reply. Jane, meanwhile, tried to steel herself to look at him. When at last she did, he was not looking at her. He was telling her aunt that he had reached Randalls the night before.

"I wrote to my father that he should expect me today," he said, "but I have been looking forward to this visit such a long time," (here he glanced at Jane, with a quick, meaningful smile; and she saw that his eyes, too, were bright with excitement) "—I was so impatient to arrive, that I found myself leaving earlier, and travelling later and faster than I had intended. I was a little uneasy, lest Mrs. Weston should be put to any extra trouble by my early appearance. I did not wish her to think I meant any disrespect in taking such a liberty. However, nothing could be kinder than the reception I met with when I got home, from both my parents."

"You were favourably impressed, then," asked Mrs. Bates, "with your new mother-in-law?"

"Very much so, ma'am. I had heard a good deal in her praise before—which, I confess, I thought must be at least a little exaggerated. In this instance, however, truth exceeded report. A somewhat elegant person, and a pleasing manner I did expect; but that Mrs. Weston should be so young and pretty I had not any idea. And then, she was so obliging, so solicitous of my comfort! I really cannot do justice to her kindness."

"When you know her better, Mr. Churchill," Jane ventured to interject (managing to express herself, she thought, in a tolerably ordinary tone), "I think you will esteem her still more."

He turned to her. "I have not a doubt of it. Her goodness to me aside, the woman who has brought such happiness to my father should always have a strong claim to my regard. Mr. Weston has, I think you will agree, ma'am," (to Miss Bates), "a temper which must always guard him against real discontent; but I find him now more thoroughly happy than I have ever seen him," (turning back again to Jane, with a keen look that kindled a brilliant glow in her cheeks) "—as any man not insensible must be, to know himself loved by so superior a woman."

Miss Bates, all unawares, chimed in, "Well, now your father has set you such a good example, Mr. Churchill, perhaps you may soon resolve to take a leaf from his book. And who can say," she added cheerfully, and certainly not aiming at any allusion to her niece in the remark, "but that it may be some young lady hereabouts, who will catch your fancy?"

"Indeed," said he with a mirthful eye, "who can say?" The exchange did nothing to quiet Jane's agitation.

"And so you have already been to Hartfield this morning?" Miss Bates went on. "How did you find our good friends the Woodhouses? Is not Miss Emma Woodhouse a very beautiful and charming young lady?"

Frank gave his ready assent, and she continued, "Miss Woodhouse has always been such a kind neighbour to us—and such a good friend to my niece, too. She called almost immediately after Jane came to us, you know, which really was more than civil of her; and during that very same visit, she invited us all to spend an evening at Hartfield!"

She then proceeded to give him a very minute account of the little party at Hartfield: the various refreshments served, the subjects discussed, the pieces played by both young ladies—stopping at this juncture to ask him, whether he had ever happened to hear her niece play when they were at Weymouth together?

"Oh! yes, ma'am," he answered, "several times—with very great pleasure. And I hope," he added with a twinkle at Jane, "I may look forward to the happiness of hearing Miss Fairfax play again while I am in Highbury."

Miss Bates assured him that he would. "There will be the Coles' party on Tuesday; we received Mrs. Cole's kind invitation just yesterday. I don't suppose you can have met either of the Coles yet, but I make no doubt Mrs. Cole will include you, as soon as she knows of your coming. Mr. and Mrs. Cole are such excellent people—very good friends of your father and Mrs. Weston. They have quite recently acquired a new grand pianoforte, so it is certain all the young ladies will be called on to play. And perhaps we may be invited again to Hartfield as well, one evening. Miss Woodhouse was so good as to entreat Jane to play when we were there last; and would do so again, I daresay. Jane is always happy to oblige her friends by playing, whenever she is asked. Indeed, Mr. Churchill, I am sure she would be delighted to play for you now—would not you, dear?—only of course, we have not got any pianoforte here."

Frank appeared a little startled by this intelligence, given out so carelessly, and for the first time made a quick survey of his surroundings. He said nothing, however, and Miss Bates continued uninterrupted, until she was called out of the room by Patty's requiring her assistance about some minor problem in the kitchen.

As soon as she was gone, he glanced over at Mrs. Bates, who had fallen into a light doze. He rose from his seat, saying meaningfully to Jane, "I wonder, Miss Fairfax, if you would be so good as to come over to the window, and point out to me which of those establishments across the way is Ford's?"

When she joined him in the window recess, where they were screened from the view of the sleeping Mrs. Bates, he took up her hands in both of his own. Could he feel how she trembled?

"Dearest Jane!" he said in a low voice, "I am so glad to see you at last! But how are you? You look pale; I fear you have been ill."

"Oh! no—I am perfectly well."

He inclined his head to one side, and eyed her archly. "So much for the flattering notion that you have been languishing for the want of me. Did not you miss me at all?"

She could not help smiling. "Hush! For shame," (lowering her eyes) "—you know very well that I did."

He attempted then to raise her hand to his lips, but she withdrew it hastily. "Frank, you mustn't—my aunt may return at any moment!"

And indeed, she had no sooner given the warning, than Miss Bates's tread was heard on the stair, and an instant later, she stepped into the parlour.

"So that is Ford's!" Frank exclaimed a little too loudly, peering out the window as she entered. "Thank you, Miss Fairfax. My father has mentioned the place to me so often, I have a great curiosity to see it. Ah, Miss Bates; you are come back. Your niece was just indulging me by showing me where Ford's is. Now, I think I must buy something there as soon as possible, that I may be properly launched in Highbury society."

# Chapter Twenty-Nine

**THOUGH HOPING THE** following day would bring some opportunity of seeing Jane again, Frank spent the better part of the next morning sitting companionably with Mrs. Weston at home. His father had gone out early to Donwell; but Frank felt no disinclination to a *tête-à-tête* with his mother-in-law—indeed, he had taken to her quite cordially. Already he was discovering, in this belated visit, what an uncommon degree of easy comfort, rational enjoyment, and harmonious society were to be met with at Randalls, in comparison of Enscombe.

Despite Jane's flattering portrait of her, Frank had been perfectly candid in telling Miss Bates how surprised he was to find his father's bride so agreeable, and so young a woman. Jane, after all, had seen the lady in question only during infrequent visits to Highbury, and could not be supposed to have a thorough knowledge of her character; nor was she very inclined to judge anyone severely, he knew. Thus he had expected to find in Mrs. Weston a matronly, middle-aged, good sort of woman, who had been induced to marry chiefly from the desire of an establishment. On meeting her, however, he saw at once how greatly he had erred. She was in fact very pretty: she could hardly have been many years beyond five and thirty, and in her person appeared even more youthful; and she was, moreover, most sincerely attached to her husband.

As has been previously noted, Frank held his guardians in considerable respect; and for his uncle in particular he felt the strongest affection and gratitude. But to be continually in the company of an active, sociable man like his father, and a warm, sensible woman like Mrs. Weston, to be witness to the mutual attachment and quiet amity of their daily intercourse, was a lesson in domestic felicity he could never have learned—could scarcely have imagined, within the walls of Enscombe. And observing the happiness of Mr. and Mrs. Weston only increased his impatience for the day when he and Jane would finally be united. He was wild to see her again!

When, therefore, at her usual hour of exercise, Mrs. Weston asked Frank to choose their walk, he immediately fixed on Highbury. "I do not doubt," said he, "that there are very pleasant walks in every direction. But if it were left to me, I should always choose the same. Highbury—that airy, cheerful, happy-looking Highbury—would be my constant attraction."

Though Highbury, to Frank, meant Mrs. Bates's house and Jane, to Mrs. Weston it stood for Hartfield; and she trusted to its bearing the same construction with him. With no suspicion of any prior attachment, she and her husband entertained some hopes of a match between Frank and Miss Woodhouse. Mr. Weston had even given his son a little hint of it the day before; and Frank had determined on seeming well-disposed to fall in with their design, as a blind to his real situation. Miss Woodhouse was another young lady, he felt sure, who would enjoy a little light-hearted flirtation for its own sake, and would not be apt to misunderstand him. Thus he offered no objection to calling at Hartfield, and walked there arm in arm with Mrs. Weston—confident that in the course of their rambles he would sooner or later lead her to the desired destination.

Miss Woodhouse welcomed them with some surprise, and with evident pleasure. After a sufficient interval had been given to walking about and admiring the shrubberies of Hartfield, Frank ventured to suggest their going farther; confessing his wish to be made acquainted with the whole village. The ladies were quite willing, and the three of them proceeded to make a thorough exploration of the streets and lanes of Highbury proper.

At one point they stopped outside the Crown Inn, where Frank noticed the spacious wing, visibly added, which had in bygone times been used as a ballroom.

"But Miss Woodhouse," he exclaimed as he looked in at the large, open windows, "Why have not you revived the former good old days of the room? You, who might do anything in Highbury! Why, you ought to have balls here at least every fortnight through the winter. I could not have believed you would allow such a delightful custom to fade away."

"I am afraid the neighbourhood holds far too few families of the sort required for such a purpose, Mr. Churchill," she replied. "And fewer still would be tempted to attend from any distance."

"What! So many good-looking houses as I see around me, not furnish numbers enough for such a meeting? Impossible!"

Particulars were given and families described; but he was unwilling to admit that the inconvenience of such a mixture would be anything, or that there would be the smallest difficulty in everybody's returning into their proper place the next morning. He argued the point for some time, not able immediately to give up the prospect of dancing again with Jane, as he had often done at Weymouth; but at last he was persuaded to move on.

On their coming up almost to the front of the Bates's house, he was gratified by Miss Woodhouse's recollecting his intended visit there the day before, and asking him if he had paid it.

"Oh! yes," he replied. "I was just going to mention it. A very successful visit. I saw all the three ladies, and felt very much obliged to you for your preparatory hint. If the talking aunt had taken me quite by surprise, it must have been the death of me. As it was, I was only betrayed into paying a most unreasonable visit. Ten minutes would have been all that was necessary, perhaps all that was proper; and I had told my father I should certainly be at home before him— but there was no getting away, no pause; and when he (finding me nowhere else) joined me there at last, I found to my utter astonishment that I had been actually sitting with them very nearly three-quarters of an hour. The good lady had not given me the possibility of escape before."

"And how did you think Miss Fairfax looking?"

"Ill, very ill," said he with a frown. Then, shaking off what he feared might be a too-eloquent gravity, he continued more lightly, "That is, if a young lady can ever be allowed to look ill. But the expression is hardly admissible, Mrs. Weston, is it? Ladies can never look ill. And seriously, Miss Fairfax is naturally so pale, as almost always to give the appearance of ill health." Recalling an ill-natured remark of his aunt's, made after meeting Jane at Weymouth, he added with a private smile of amusement, "A most deplorable want of complexion."

Emma would not agree to this and, to Frank's delight, began a warm defence of Miss Fairfax's complexion. He listened with an appearance of deference; acknowledged that he had heard many people say the same; but yet he must confess that, to him, nothing could make amends for the want of the fine glow of health.

"Well," said Emma, "there is no disputing about taste. At least you admire her except her complexion."

He shook his head and laughed. "I cannot separate Miss Fairfax and her complexion," he said.

She inquired if he had met Jane often at Weymouth; and then he began to doubt—to wonder what she meant by all these questions. Her perseverance was puzzling. Was it simple curiosity? Or did she, in fact, suspect something? They were just then approaching Ford's, and, uncertain of what he might with security divulge, he hastily exclaimed,

"Ha! This must be the very shop that everybody attends every day of their lives, as my father informs me. If it be not inconvenient to you, pray let us go in, that I may prove myself to belong to the place, to be a true citizen of Highbury. I must buy something at Ford's."

They went in; and having gained, while the parcels of 'Men's Beavers' and 'York Tan' were bringing down and displaying on the counter, a little time in which to determine his best course, he begged Miss Woodhouse to repeat her question.

"I merely asked, whether you had known much of Miss Fairfax and her party at Weymouth."

With a sportive air, he pronounced the question to be a very unfair one. It was always the lady's right to decide on the degree of acquaintance. Miss Fairfax must already have given her account; he would not commit himself by claiming more than she might choose to allow.

"Upon my word!" she said, "you answer as discreetly as she could do herself. But her account of everything leaves so much to be guessed, she is so very reserved, so very unwilling to give the least information about anybody, that I really think you may say what you like of your acquaintance with her."

Reserve from them both, he considered, might only serve to confirm Miss Woodhouse's suspicions, if she had them, or to awaken them if she had not. He decided therefore to speak openly—as openly, at least, as was compatible with the concealment of his secret. "Then I will speak the truth, and nothing suits me so well. I met her frequently at Weymouth. I had known the Campbells a little in town; and at Weymouth we were very much in the same set. Colonel

Campbell is a very agreeable man, and Mrs. Campbell a friendly, warm-hearted woman. I like them all."

When the gloves were bought, and they had quitted the shop again, Frank, reluctant to abandon the pleasure of talking about Jane (and hoping for a clearer understanding of Miss Woodhouse's views), resumed, "Did you ever hear the young lady we were speaking of, play?"

"Ever hear her!" repeated Emma. "You forget how much she belongs to Highbury. I have heard her every year of our lives since we both began. She plays charmingly."

He thought so himself, he told her, but had wanted the opinion of some one who could really judge. He had been used to hear her performance admired, and particularly remembered one proof of her being thought to play well: a man, a very musical man, and in love with another woman—engaged to her—on the point of marriage—would yet never ask that other woman to sit down to the instrument, if Miss Fairfax could sit down instead. That, he thought, in a man of known musical talent, was some proof. Miss Woodhouse guessed at once that Mr. Dixon and Miss Campbell were the persons referred to—and agreed it was a very strong proof indeed.

"To own the truth," said she, "a great deal stronger than, if *I* had been Miss Campbell, would have been at all agreeable to me. I could not excuse a man's having more music than love—more ear than eye—a more acute sensibility to fine sounds than to my feelings. How did Miss Campbell appear to like it?"

"It was her very particular friend, you know."

"Poor comfort!" said Emma, laughing. "One would rather have a stranger preferred than one's very particular friend—with a stranger it might not recur again—but the misery of having a very particular friend always at hand, to do everything better than one does oneself! Poor Mrs. Dixon! Well, I am glad she is gone to settle in Ireland."

"You are right. It was not very flattering to her; but she really did not seem to feel it."

"So much the better—or so much the worse—I do not know which. But be it sweetness or stupidity in her—quickness of friendship, or dullness of feeling—there was one person, I think, who must have felt it: Miss Fairfax herself. *She* must have felt the improper and dangerous distinction."

"As to that—I do not—"

"Oh! do not imagine that I expect an account of Miss Fairfax's sensations from you, or from anybody else. They are known to no human being, I guess, but herself. But if she continued to play whenever she was asked by Mr. Dixon, one may guess what one chooses."

"There appeared such a perfectly good understanding among them all," he began rather quickly; but it struck him suddenly, that she seemed almost to be suggesting the idea of some secret attachment between Jane and Mr. Dixon! Highly diverted by the notion himself, and judging it politic not to disabuse her of it at once, he checked himself; adding, "However, it is impossible for me to say on what terms they really were—how it might all be behind the scenes. But you, who have known Miss Fairfax from a child, must be a better judge of her character than I can be."

"I have known her from a child, undoubtedly; and it is natural to suppose that we should be intimate friends. But we never were. I hardly know how it has happened. A little, perhaps, from that wickedness on my side which was prone to take disgust towards a girl so idolised and so cried up as she always was, by her aunt and grandmother, and all their set. And then, her reserve—I never could attach myself to anyone so completely reserved."

"It is a most repulsive quality, indeed," said he, with increasing complacency. If Miss Woodhouse perceived even a glimmer of his secret, surely she would not be half so candid. "There is safety in reserve, but no attraction. One cannot love a reserved person."

"Not till the reserve ceases towards oneself," she said; "and then the attraction may be the greater."

He eyed her speculatively. That remark did seem to touch directly upon the truth! "But," she continued smoothly, "I must be more in want of a friend, or an agreeable companion, than I have yet been, to take the trouble of conquering anybody's reserve to procure one. I have no reason to think ill of her—not the least—except that such extreme and perpetual cautiousness of word and manner, such a dread of giving a distinct idea about anybody, is apt to suggest suspicions of there being something to conceal."

His eyes shone with silent merriment. Something to conceal, indeed! Yet as he expressed his perfect agreement, he gave her another appraising glance. His father had often told him that Miss Woodhouse was clever—very clever; and there did seem a double meaning to some of her utterances.

Could it be she had begun already to unravel the mystery? Was she beginning, already, to understand him?

# Chapter Thirty

**THAT SAME MORNING,** Jane was sitting at home, waiting for Frank to come. He had not said he would come; indeed, he could have no excuse for coming again so soon. Still, she thought he *would* come, if he could contrive it. Miss Bates was out, calling at Mrs. Goddard's, and Jane and her grandmother were sitting together quietly, Mrs. Bates mending stockings, and Jane hemming handkerchiefs for her aunt.

Occupied though she was, she could not help listening for the sound of voices below, the tread of footsteps on the stair, which might announce the arrival of a visitor. At length she did hear a voice—but it was only aunt Hetty, returned from her outing. Frank did not come; and she later learned from Mrs. Ford that he had spent the entire morning walking about Highbury with Mrs. Weston and Miss Woodhouse.

It was perfectly right that he should do so. To call too often at Mrs. Bates's could only excite dangerous suspicions; and Mrs. Weston's connection to Hartfield, she reminded herself, would inevitably give rise to a certain degree of intimacy *there*. Nonetheless, in contemplating the subject she felt unreasonably discontented and, perhaps equally unreasonably, jealous. She imagined Frank strolling down the sunny lanes and tree-shaded byways of Highbury with Miss Woodhouse—handsome, charming Miss Woodhouse—wealthy Miss Woodhouse, whom his rich relations would no doubt think a fitting match for their nephew and heir—and he wondering all the while whether Jane would be so contemptible as to hold him to an ill-advised engagement, if he wished to be released from it.

Her discontent was heightened on the following morning, when, meeting Mr. Weston by chance outside the post-office, she learned that Frank had gone off to London for the day.

With a hearty laugh, he said, "My jackanapes of a son,

Miss Fairfax, was seized by a sudden freak at breakfast this morning, and nothing would do but he must race off to town at once. Why, you may wonder? Why, only to have his hair cut! Is not that an excellent story?"

Jane was so dismayed by this intelligence she could hardly conceal her astonishment. Gone sixteen miles to London and back, to have his hair cut! Having waited so long to come to Highbury, and with so short an interval granted for his stay—to squander an entire day, for such a purpose!

"Well," Mr. Weston went on, still chuckling, and oblivious to her distress, "He promised us he would be home again before dinner. As my good wife remarked, 'all young people will have their little whims.' But is not it a capital joke, Miss Fairfax? Do not you think my son the most thorough coxcomb from here to Timbuctoo?"

This encounter left Jane in a dismal mood, and even the letters she received that day (one from Miss Devere, and another from Mrs. Campbell) could do little to lighten it. They were only short letters, anyway; written, she supposed morosely, just to send the news that there was no news to send. Her ill humour continued into the next day. A small indiscretion of Miss Bates's—her unthinkingly admitting to Mr. Knightley that the apples he had sent over from Donwell last autumn were nearly gone—vexed Jane; and she scolded her poor aunt, as she thought, beyond justification. In truth she delivered the mildest of reproofs, which troubled Miss Bates not in the least. But unaccustomed as she was to any manner of contention with those she loved, Jane could scarcely forgive herself for this display of temper.

She saw nothing of Frank until Sunday, when they met outside after church. He was with the Westons and Miss Woodhouse, of course. Miss Woodhouse, Jane could not fail to perceive, appeared quite delighted with him, and his admiration for her was but too evident. Emma rallied him on the vanity of driving all the way to London just to have his hair cut. He laughed at himself with a very good grace, but without seeming at all ashamed of what he had done; indeed, he seemed to find an uncommon pleasure in talking of it. He, like his father, seemed to think it a capital joke. He was in very high spirits, quite as lively and engaging as ever; but now it was Miss Woodhouse for whom all his powers of pleasing were exerted. Jane was shocked to find the two of them already on terms of such easy familiarity.

How overjoyed she had been, when he had written that he was finally coming to Highbury!—and it cannot be supposed that she was yet quite ready to wish he had remained in Yorkshire. Still, she asked herself, why had he bothered to come, if they were never to see each other? And why should she have wished him to come, if he came but to keep company with Emma Woodhouse? Such reflections plunged her into a melancholy, and she went to bed Sunday night with a weary heart and an aching head.

But the next day brought a startling *eclaircissement.* She was down in the kitchen helping her aunt go through the stores of preserves, to ascertain how many jars they had left, and of what kind—which no longer fit for use—and how many quarts must be put up this summer for the following winter. As they worked, they talked of Mr. Knightley. Having been apprised by Miss Bates on Saturday morning that they were short of apples, their generous friend had sent over a bushel on Saturday night; and Patty was gone out now, to deliver this bounty to Mrs. Wallis to be baked.

"How kind of Mr. Knightley to send us another basket of apples!" said Miss Bates. "But then, he is always kind, is not he?"

"Extremely kind; only I still cannot help but wish, my dear aunt, that you had not let him know our stock of apples was so low."

"Well, my dear, and so I should not have, but that he happened to come in when you were eating one—and when I said how much you enjoyed them, he asked whether we were not got to the end of our supply. 'I am sure you must be,' said he, 'and I have a great many more than I can ever use. I will send you another bushel, before they get good for nothing.' And I really did say as much as I could, you know. I begged he would not send any others—though as to ours being gone, I could not truthfully say that we had a great many left, since it was but half a dozen; but I did assure him, you remember, that they should be all kept for you, as you like them so well; and I told him I could not bear that he should be sending us more, so liberal as he had been already; and you said much the same."

"Yes—I recollect it, aunt."

"But Mr. Knightley has always been so fond of you, Jane—it pleases him to do anything for you. And the apples from Donwell are the very finest sort for baking, you know; and there never was such a keeping apple anywhere. But I was really quite shocked after William Larkins brought them to us. Patty said he told her it was all the apples of that sort his master had; he had brought them all, and now his master had not one left to bake or boil."

"Aunt Hetty!"

"Oh, dear me—I did mean to keep that from you; but now I have let it slip out before I was aware! I sometimes do let a thing slip out without meaning to, you know. However, William did not seem to mind about it himself. He was only pleased his master had sold so many; but he said Mrs. Hodges was very vexed that her master should not be able to have another apple-tart this spring. He told Patty, though, to be sure not to say anything to us about it, for Mrs. Hodges would be cross sometimes, and as long as so many sacks were sold, it did not signify who ate the remainder. So Patty told me, and I was excessively shocked indeed!"

"I am grieved to hear it, aunt. To think of Mr. Knightley sending us all his apples, and keeping none for himself! I am very, very sorry for it."

There was at that instant a loud rapping at the front door. Patty being out, Miss Bates ran off herself to answer it, while Jane remained in the kitchen, gazing at the shelves of preserves in dismay. She was greatly distressed to think of Mr. Knightley's being without any more apples to eat, and was even trying to consider whether there were any way they might return some of the apples to him without affront, when she heard her aunt calling her to come up. She hastened up the stairs, and Miss Bates exclaimed,

"Jane! This man is come all the way from Broadwood's, in London, and he says he has a pianoforte to deliver—to you!"

"A pianoforte, for me? But that is impossible—it cannot be. There must be some mistake."

"So I told him, my dear—but he insists there is none."

"But who ordered it?"

"As to that, ma'am," said the carter, "I couldn't say. I was only told where to bring it."

"I am sure, sir," said Jane, "there must be some error. Perhaps you were given the wrong address, or you have misread the name. It is quite impossible that a pianoforte should be sent to me. I am very sorry you have had so much trouble for nothing—but indeed, you must have been misdirected, or—"

The carter, growing a little impatient with being told he

did not know his own business, interrupted her, declaring quite firmly, "Begging your pardon, ma'am—but if you be Miss Jane Fairfax, at Number Twelve, High Street, in the village of Highbury, in the county of Surrey, then there is no mistake about it, ma'am—the instrument is for you. So, if you please, ma'am, I wish you would be about deciding where you want to put it, so me and the lads can bring it in, and be on our way."

Jane, looking out at the carter's wagon, could no longer doubt, though her perplexity was great; so she and Miss Bates walked up at once to relate the circumstance to Mrs. Bates, who was quite as surprised as her daughter and granddaughter could be—and to determine where in the little parlour they could find sufficient space for the unexpected delivery.

"Jane," said Mrs. Bates after a little thought, "I believe there can be only one explanation. Colonel and Mrs. Campbell must have sent the pianoforte to you. They are aware you have no instrument here, and would know how welcome such a gift must be."

"But I had a letter from Mrs. Campbell on Friday," Jane protested, "and she made no mention of it."

"Perhaps, then," Miss Bates suggested, "they meant it for a surprise—a delightful surprise, to be sure. Such a generous gift! But really, Jane, now I think on it, I must agree with your grandmama. The pianoforte certainly can be from no one else but the Campbells."

It *was* the only logical explanation; and to her aunt and grandmother, Jane could tender no other. But she knew Colonel Campbell would never send her such a gift without advising her of it first. No—her own thoughts, it must be admitted, had begun to fix on a very different benefactor: she was convinced the instrument could have come only from Frank. He had been plainly struck, when he called on Wednesday, by there being no pianoforte in the house. His sudden trip to town, ostensibly to have his hair cut, must in fact have been for the purpose of buying it!

She felt a thrill of delight at the very idea of the pianoforte's being from Frank. To send her such a present was, without question, extravagant, impulsive, even reckless; but though she could by no means approve the imprudence of such a deed, the generosity of the gift—the warmth of heart which prompted it—the affection it implied, must give her considerable pleasure.

Her conjecture was soon confirmed beyond a doubt. The carter and his two helpers managed, with a great deal of trouble, to maneuver the pianoforte up into Mrs. Bates's parlour; and while the elder ladies were admiring it (for it was a very handsome, elegant-looking instrument; not a grand but a large-sized square pianoforte) the carter handed Jane a small parcel covered in brown paper. She unwrapped it, and found within a selection of music, including three nocturnes by Field, a new set of Irish melodies, and a sonata by Cramer—the latter unmistakably a playful reference to the alias under which Frank received her letters. Conspicuously placed at the top of the pile lay the very first duet they had ever sung together. Folded within this was a brief note, which she furtively read and, with a deep flush upon her cheek, hastily thrust into her pocket—in all likelihood to peruse again more closely when she should be safely alone.

Dearest, (it said)

What think you of Mr. Broadwood's handiwork—is not he an excellent barber? I shall find it hard going indeed, to wait until Tuesday to know your opinion of my *haircut*; but I trust that in its sweet strains you will not fail to perceive all the ardent love and attachment with which it was sent, from one whose heart is ever your own—

F.

# Chapter Thirty-One

**THE COLES HAD** been settled some years in Highbury, and were very good sort of people: friendly, liberal, and unpretending, though of low origin, in trade, and only moderately genteel. The last year or two had brought them a considerable increase of means; and by this time they were, in fortune and style of living, second only to the family at Hartfield. Money, love of society, and a new dining-room, combined to give them a wish of keeping dinner company; and the party Miss Bates had earlier mentioned to Frank Churchill would be the first to assemble all the principal families of the neighbourhood around their table: invitations to dinner had been received, and accepted, at Donwell, Hartfield, and Randalls. The less worthy females, like Jane and her aunt, were to come after dinner.

Old Mrs. Bates was already gone to Hartfield, to spend the evening with Mrs. Goddard and Mr. Woodhouse, when Mr. Knightley's carriage arrived to carry Jane and Miss Bates to the party. Miss Bates talked through their short journey in her usual fashion, making remarks on Mr. Knightley's thoughtfulness, the Coles' hospitality, Jane's good looks, Colonel Campbell's generosity, and any other topic that chanced to pop into her head. Jane, however, hardly heard what her aunt said; the occasion found her in a state of anxious expectancy. There was the certainty of seeing Frank again—perhaps even, in such a large party, the chance of speaking to him privately for a few moments. But there was also the awful prospect of the many questions and comments which were sure to be offered respecting her new pianoforte. She had been out to Ford's earlier in the day to buy some ribbons; and, on returning home, learned that Mrs. Cole had called during her absence, and been much astonished by, and much impressed with, the new instrument. Knowledge of the gift must by now have been communicated to all their acquaintance.

When she entered the Cole's drawing-room, therefore, it could not surprise her that the subject of the pianoforte was almost immediately introduced. The gentlemen had not yet

come in from the dining-room, and Frank, as she quickly
perceived, was nowhere to be seen. Her courage flagged.
With a deep blush of consciousness, the congratulations of
her neighbours were received, and with painful sensations,
"my excellent friend Colonel Campbell" was named. Mrs.
Weston, kind-hearted and musical, was particularly interested by the circumstance, and had much to ask and to say
as to tone, touch, and pedal—totally unsuspicious of that
wish of saying as little about it as possible, which Jane
feared must be plainly stamped on her countenance. She
was relieved to find Miss Woodhouse at a distance while the
pianoforte was under discussion, sparing her the scrutiny
at least of one acute observer.

After what seemed a long interval, they were joined by
some of the gentlemen; and the sight of Frank among the
very first revived her directly. He walked in smiling, and
came at once to pay his compliments to her and her aunt.

"May I congratulate you on your recent acquisition, Miss
Fairfax?" said he, twinkling down at her. "It gratifies me to
know that someone who plays so well as you do, should
have an instrument worthy of her talents. A very fortunate
thought of Colonel Campbell's, to send the instrument. Do
not you agree, ma'am?"

This last question was addressed to Miss Bates, who expressed her agreement quite volubly. While aunt Hetty
talked, Frank caught Jane's eye, and provoked her to smile
in spite of herself; and with a little prick of conscience, she
found herself fervently wishing her dear aunt would but go
and talk to Mrs. Cox for five minutes! Miss Bates, however,
was perfectly comfortable where she was, and Frank soon
made his excuses, bowed, and left them. He crossed directly
to the opposite side of the room, where Miss Woodhouse
sat; and Jane watched with a sinking heart, as he found a
seat by her. She saw then how it would be—how it must be;
and all her pleasure, all her foolish hopes of spending the
evening in Frank's company, vanished in an instant.

A moment later, Mrs. Cole came up and began talking to
her about the pianoforte. "I was telling your aunt when I
called yesterday, Miss Fairfax," she said, "of the great satisfaction this present of Colonel Campbell's has given me. I
have always thought it such a shame that you, who play so
delightfully, should not have any kind of instrument—
especially considering how many houses there are where
fine instruments are absolutely thrown away. I really was

ashamed to look at our own new grand pianoforte, when I do not know one note from another, and our little girls perhaps may never make anything of it at all—and there you were, mistress of music, without even the pitifullest old spinet in the world to amuse yourself with. I was saying this to Mr. Cole but yesterday, and he quite agreed with me; only he is so very fond of music that he could not help indulging himself in the purchase, hoping that some of our neighbours might be so obliging as occasionally to put it to a better use than we can; and we are in great hopes that you and Miss Woodhouse may be prevailed with to play for us this evening."

Jane said what was required—was very grateful for such kind wishes, should be very happy to play, &c.—and though given with somewhat of an absent mind, the response seemed perfectly to satisfy their hostess. Mrs. Cole and Miss Bates then pursued the subject further between themselves, leaving Jane at liberty to work herself into a most promising state of misery by looking over at Frank and Miss Woodhouse as often as she dared.

After a time, the other gentlemen came in, and Mrs. Cole went away to say something to Mr. Weston. Soon afterwards, Miss Bates left her niece, to assail Mr. Knightley with more thanks for the use of his carriage—which, had she consulted his feelings in the matter instead of her own, she would have refrained from offering at all.

Jane was left quite alone for the moment, and her eyes were instinctively drawn again towards that division of the room where Frank and Miss Woodhouse were sitting. To her confusion, she discovered that Frank was just then gazing intently at herself—his companion's attention being claimed, at least temporarily, by Mr. Cole. She had begun to think he must be making up his mind to come and talk to her, when Emma turned back to address him, and caught him staring. Jane quickly averted her eyes. When she felt it safe to look again, the two were engaged in a very animated dialogue. It appeared he had explained away his behaviour to Emma's satisfaction—and had also lost his best chance of slipping away from her; but a minute later he rose from his seat (laughing, as if at some witty remark of Miss Woodhouse's) and came to stand, smiling, before Jane. Happily, the noise of so many conversations going on at once was sufficient to cloak the sounds of any particular one. They could speak freely.

"I hope, Jane," he began, "you were pleased with my present."

"The pianoforte! How can I ever thank you? But—it was so extravagant! You ought not to have done it."

"Why not? I cannot think of any purchase that has given me greater pleasure."

"But the expense, Frank—and the risk! Suppose it should be discovered that you were the one who sent it?"

"How should it be discovered? Everyone is convinced that the instrument came from Colonel Campbell—everyone, that is, except Miss Woodhouse; and *her* suspicions," he added with an amused grin, "fall in another quarter entirely."

"Another quarter—? What do you mean?"

After a quick glance back at Emma, who was safely occupied with Mrs. Weston, he sat down beside Jane and said in a lowered voice, "What do you think, Jane—Miss Woodhouse has been conjuring up an intrigue, between you and... Mr. Dixon!"

"What—! Mr. Dixon! No. You must be joking. Please, do not tease me about such a thing."

"I am perfectly serious, I assure you. Though I own I am more than a little diverted by her conjectures."

"Mr. Dixon!" she repeated again. She was appalled by what Frank, apparently, could view so lightly. "The husband of my dearest friend! I know I have never been a great favourite with Miss Woodhouse; but still, I cannot think she would really believe that I—"

"She most certainly does believe. She imparted her suspicions to me before you came. She thinks Mr. Dixon is in love with you, and married your friend only for the sake of her fortune. She is entirely persuaded the instrument comes from him."

"But how—? On what grounds can she have formed such a shocking notion?"

"As to that, I can hardly explain it. She began with a slender thread or two—Mr. Dixon's preferring your playing to Miss Campbell's, and his having saved your life, when you were nearly swept off the boat at Weymouth—and she embellished, and embroidered, until she had fashioned quite a magnificent piece of fancy-work. And," he concluded with a chuckle, "I think you and I must do all we can to encourage her in her mistake."

She looked at him in disbelief. "Encourage her! Frank,

you cannot mean it—you would not think of doing such a thing!"

"What better way to conceal our secret? Miss Woodhouse is in general very acute, I think. She has already penetrated so far as to be sure that something very particular must bring you to Highbury just now, when you might be in Ireland with your friends. If we are not careful to confound her, she may soon hit on the truth. But so long as she suspects Mr. Dixon, she will never think of *me*."

Jane was aghast. "Oh, this is too horrible! I knew some trouble must come of your sending that pianoforte. I wish you had not!"

Now it was his turn to frown. "I regret to have caused you any uneasiness," he said coldly. "I did think the gift would please you. I am very sorry if you do not like it."

"Frank—of course I like it. I love it. It is a beautiful instrument; I have never played a better. It was terribly generous of you, and I am very grateful—truly."

A look of entreaty accompanied her words, and in an instant his resentment was forgotten. "In one suspicion, at least," he said with renewed warmth, "Miss Woodhouse is not deceived. The pianoforte was indeed an offering of love."

A little bustle in the room just then proclaimed that tea was over, and the instrument in preparation. Mr. Cole was appealing to Miss Woodhouse to do them the honour of being the first to try it, and Frank hastened to add his own pleas, offering his services as page-turner. As Emma graciously gave her assent, he rose and escorted her to the pianoforte.

Her performance Jane found agreeable as always, despite a somewhat dubious addition in Frank's taking the second part; for to watch the two performing together so pleasantly raised a contrariety of uncomfortable feelings within her breast. She was disturbed not only by her own jealousy, and by Emma's suspicions, and Frank's jesting talk of encouraging them; but for the first time she began also to fear some danger to Miss Woodhouse from his gallantry. Her gratification in his attentions was plain; and though their acquaintance was of short duration, it could not be doubted that she liked him very much already. And indeed, as Jane knew too well, it did not need a long acquaintance for Frank to capture a woman's heart.

They sang together twice. Miss Woodhouse was then compelled to resign her place to Miss Fairfax. Frank, however, remained where he was to turn the pages for Jane, and to sing in harmony with her as he had done with Emma. Her misgivings were soon forgotten in the enjoyment of singing with him again; and she began at last to feel a real pleasure in the evening.

Towards the end of their second song, her voice grew a little thick. The audience begged another: "One more; they would not fatigue Miss Fairfax on any account, and would only ask for one more."

Frank, knowing Jane would likely go on singing as long as her friends wished for it, recommended a piece that at least would not strain her voice too far. "I think you could manage this without effort," he said, opening the music and placing it before her. "The first part is very trifling. The strength of the song falls on the second."

Jane acquiesced in his choice, and they had just performed the opening measures when Miss Bates, concerned for her niece's throat, stepped forward and put an end to all further singing. Here ceased the concert part of the evening, for Miss Fairfax and Miss Woodhouse were the only young lady performers; but within five minutes, Frank had tossed out a hint of dancing, which was so effectually promoted by Mr. and Mrs. Cole that everything was rapidly clearing away to give proper space. Mrs. Weston, capital in her country dances, was promptly seated, and beginning an irresistible waltz; but Jane's momentary delight quickly turned to disappointment, as Frank eagerly secured Miss Woodhouse's hand and led her up to the top.

Unhappy though she was, she was presently asked by William Cox to join the dance, and must needs go through it with some semblance of attention to the steps, and some effort at civility towards her partner. She was cheered by the thought that Frank could dance only the first two dances with Miss Woodhouse, and would surely claim her own hand for the second two. They were, after all, but five couple altogether. The idea received strength from a certain look and a smile from Frank, when he passed near her in the dance; and once again she was aglow with happy anticipation.

Two dances, unfortunately, were all that could be allowed. It was growing late, and Miss Bates became anxious to get home on her mother's account. Jane could not oppose her wish of leaving, but stood by hopefully as Frank and Miss Woodhouse, and some of the others, pleaded with her to stay just another half-hour. Miss Bates, however, was not to be persuaded. She and Jane gave their thanks and made their farewells. The other guests began to do the same; and the very last sight Jane saw, as she and her aunt drove off in Mr. Knightley's carriage, was Mr. Frank Churchill gallantly handing Miss Emma Woodhouse into hers.

# Chapter Thirty-Two

A CALAMITY BEFELL the Bates household on the following morning: a rivet came out of Mrs. Bates's spectacles. Jane's only comment was, that it certainly was unlucky, "for now grandmama could not see to do her needlework,"— and suggested that she ought to keep two pair, as Colonel Campbell did; but Miss Bates's grief was not so reticent. She had meant, of course, to take the traitorous spectacles to John Saunders to be mended, almost as soon as the trouble was discovered; but she had first to determine that Jane had caught no cold last night, and to see that she had enough to eat this morning; then Patty came up to tell her that the kitchen chimney wanted sweeping, and presently the baked apples came back from Mrs. Wallis, so there was the boy to be thanked, and the apples to be put away. Thus, with one thing and another, it transpired that she was still lamenting the accident, when Mrs. Weston and her son were announced. Having overheard his mother-in-law, the night before, telling Miss Bates that she would come soon to hear the new pianoforte, Frank afterwards persuaded her to think she had promised to call this very morning. She was not aware of it, she told him—did not know she had fixed a day—but as he assured her she did, she could not but believe him, and go; only begging the favour, which he did not hesitate to grant, of his escorting her thither.

Jane was very happily surprised to see him again so soon, in spite of the previous evening's irritations. He took a seat beside her, though not a word, except of the most commonplace kind, could be said. Miss Bates, anxious as she was to know Mrs. Weston's opinion of the pianoforte, could not be satisfied without offering, while she helped them to the baked apple, very frequent interjections concerning the broken spectacles; interrupting herself at intervals with the shocking story of Mr. Knightley's having sent them all his best fruit,  an occasional remark on the civility of the Wallises, and a few exclamations on Jane's want of appetite for anything but baked apples.

Nevertheless, there was sufficient opportunity for discussion of the pianoforte, requiring many further references to and questions about Colonel Campbell's supposed generosity; so it was with great relief that Jane heard Frank declare they had talked enough about the instrument. It was time now to listen, he said, and to judge for themselves.

"And if Miss Fairfax will oblige us," he proposed, "I shall try to make myself useful, by attempting to repair Mrs. Bates's broken spectacles."

Miss Bates protested against such an imposition. "Oh!" said he, "I do think I can fasten the rivet. I like a job of this kind excessively."

"Well, really," said she, "it is so obliging of you, Mr. Churchill—so very obliging to offer! And my mother I am sure would thank you herself, but, as you see," (lowering her voice a little) "she is gone to sleep. However, I am sure you will excuse her; for without the use of her spectacles, she cannot see to do her sewing, plain or fancy—nor any knitting either; and with no work to apply herself to, she is inclined to nod off, I am afraid. Her eyes are not so good as they were; however, she can still see amazingly well, thank God! with the help of her spectacles. Jane often remarks on how strong her grandmama's eyes are—do not you, my dear? And it really is an excellent pair of spectacles, you know, but for this misfortune of the rivet falling out. Indeed, Mr. Churchill, I would not put you to so much trouble for the world—but that my poor Mama is quite at a loss without them."

Frank assured her it would give him the greatest pleasure to do the job. "Ladies have a material advantage in having always some odd bit of stitching or carpet-work at hand, to employ them during any idle moment; while we men must sit by, like the great useless louts we are, looking foolish and awkward, and quite good-for-nothing. I should be very glad indeed to be of service."

There was a mighty outcry against his being thought in any way foolish, loutish, or anything of the sort. He then seated himself at a table near Mrs. Bates, and diligently set about his task; while Jane, in no unhappy state, began to play and sing a Scottish air, 'O My Love Is Like a Red, Red Rose', with Frank humming a soft harmony along with her as he worked, and joining in full voice on the last lines.

At the song's close, Mrs. Weston pronounced herself delighted with the instrument. "I should think," said she, "it is very nearly as good as the pianoforte at Hartfield—only taking into account the usual difference between a grand and a square pianoforte."

"Well, you are very kind to say so!" said Miss Bates, "Did you hear that, Jane? Mrs. Weston thinks the pianoforte nearly as good as Miss Woodhouse's!"

"I did indeed," said Jane, smiling, and trying hard not to look at Frank. "I am very glad you approve, Mrs. Weston."

"And I have no doubt Miss Woodhouse will agree with my opinion, whenever she shall have an opportunity of hearing the pianoforte herself. Frank and I met her at Ford's with Miss Smith, just as we were on our way here; and when I told her we were coming to hear the new instrument, she said she had every expectation of its being a superior one."

"Now, I must say," said the delighted Miss Bates, "that really is so very—! And she is used to quite the finest instrument, you know, and a very accomplished musician herself. But do you think Miss Woodhouse is still at Ford's, Mrs. Weston?"

"Very likely, I should think. It did not appear to me Miss Smith would be at all quick in making up her mind."

"Oh! then I must run across; I am sure Miss Woodhouse will allow me just to run across and entreat her to come in. My mother will be so very happy to see her—and now we are such a nice party, she cannot refuse."

"Aye, pray do," said Frank. "Miss Woodhouse's opinion of the instrument will be worth having.'

"But, I shall be more sure of succeeding if one of you will go with me."

"Wait half a minute, ma'am," said he, "till I have finished my job, and I shall be very happy to accompany you. But I should not like to leave off in the middle, for fear of losing what little progress I have made thus far."

"Oh," she exclaimed, "I would not on any account interrupt your labour, Mr. Churchill, as Mama will be so very glad to have the use of her spectacles again. So very kind of you, indeed!" So she begged Mrs. Weston would have the goodness to come along instead, to induce Miss Woodhouse to do them the honour, &c., &c. Mrs. Weston complied readily, and they departed together, leaving Jane and Frank with only the slumbering Mrs. Bates for a chaperone.

Putting aside the spectacles as soon as they had gone, Frank gave Jane a meaningful look and rose, saying in distinct accents (lest the old woman were not quite soundly asleep), "I think, Miss Fairfax, there is a little unevenness there in the floor beneath your pianoforte. Have you a sheet of paper we might wedge underneath the leg, to make it firm?"

"Oh!—yes."

She turned to the little desk in the corner behind her, and retrieved some old laundry bills from the drawer. "Will these do?" she asked, holding them out to him.

"Perfectly," said he, grinning. "Now, I think between us we may contrive to stabilize the instrument."

Then they knelt down at the base of the piano, their two heads very close together. By this expedient, they might carry on a hushed conversation—all the while appearing (if Mrs. Bates should awaken, or the others walk in suddenly) to be quite innocently occupied in steadying the pianoforte.

"Jane," he began, careful to keep his voice as low as possible, "we may have only a few minutes—and there is so much I wish to say to you. I scarcely thought, before I came to Highbury, how seldom I should have any chance of talking to you alone. And now my time here is already half gone—and I have hardly seen you!"

"You do not regret having come?"

"Of course not! It is vastly better to be with you, even" (grinning again) "amidst an army of spies, than to be apart from you. Only—is there not any time I might safely call, when I would be likely to find you by yourself? Think, Jane!"

After a short pause, she said, "Grandmama and aunt Hetty often take a little exercise together after breakfast, when the weather is fine—about eleven o'clock. But they are seldom out much beyond a quarter of an hour."

"A quarter of an hour! As matters stand, I should be glad even of that; any more, I suppose, would lay us open to suspicion. But eleven o'clock—it will be difficult to get away. I will try. If you do not see me tomorrow, look for me the day after."

And though still they had much to say to each other, and scant time to say it, they forgot themselves so far as to waste several precious moments foolishly smiling at one another.

"Frank," she said finally, "I did wish to speak to you seriously, about—Miss Woodhouse. I cannot think it quite prudent that you should be so—so very particular in your attentions towards her."

"Ah," said he, not taking the point quite as seriously as she had intended—for her question, in fact, brought another broad grin to his handsome face. "You are jealous!"

"It is not that," she protested; then, with a half-smile of acknowledgement, "Well, I suppose I am, a little," she admitted. "But truly, it is not only that. You cannot know what mischief you may cause by your conduct. Remember that, for all Miss Woodhouse knows, you are entirely disengaged; and if you continue to pay her such marked attentions, you may give rise to expectations—"

"I have no reason whatever to suppose Miss Woodhouse thinks any more of me than I do of her. I find her society very agreeable, and I hope she finds mine the same. Since Mrs. Weston, who was in the place of a mother to her, is married to my father, she and I are very nearly brother and sister, you know."

"That may be your view; but I cannot believe it to be Miss Woodhouse's."

"Come, Jane—my father may call me a coxcomb, but I am not so vain as to imagine every woman who finds me amusing must be dying of love for me; though I should not be very sorry to have you imagine it, considering I must bear with the knowledge that every gentleman who sees *you* is certain to fall in love with you. How I hated Mr. William Cox last night—that he should have the happiness of dancing with you, when I could not."

She had not the heart to admonish him further after such a statement; and would gladly have assured him of her unfailing love, in return for such gratifying avowals of indifference to Miss Woodhouse, and unvarying devotion to herself, as he might care to offer; but there was time neither for admonitions nor avowals. aunt Hetty's voice drifted up from the stairwell. He hastily retreated to the table, and Jane turned away to her pianoforte as the ladies entered.

In defiance of the caution she had just given him, Frank greeted Emma most warmly. Mrs. Weston, observing how little progress he had made on the spectacles during their absence, exclaimed, "What! have not you finished it yet? You would not earn a very good livelihood as a working silversmith at this rate."

"I have not been working uninterruptedly," he replied. "I have been assisting Miss Fairfax in trying to make her instrument stand steadily; it was not quite firm—an unevenness in the floor, I believe. You see we have been wedging one leg with paper." To Miss Woodhouse, he said, "This was very kind of you to be persuaded to come. I was almost afraid you would be hurrying home."

He then contrived that Emma should be seated by him, and made such a display of looking out the best baked apple for her, and trying to make her help or advise him in his work, as set Jane's nerves quite on edge; and she was unable immediately to sit down to her pianoforte again. At last, however, she was ready to begin. Though the first bars were feebly given, the pleasure of playing so fine an instrument, and the remembrance that *he* had given it, quieted her apprehensions; and the powers of the pianoforte were gradually done full justice to. Mrs. Weston and Miss Woodhouse were united in their praise, and the pianoforte, with every proper discrimination, was pronounced to be altogether of the highest promise. Miss Smith said nothing, but joined in the admiration with nods and smiles.

"Whoever Colonel Campbell might employ," said Frank with a smile at Emma, "the person has not chosen ill—"

Jane, as she listened politely to some remarks of Mrs. Weston's, strained to hear what else he was saying to Miss Woodhouse, but could catch only the words 'Colonel Campbell' and 'Weymouth'. Soon afterwards, however, he addressed her directly.

"How much your friends in Ireland must be enjoying your pleasure on this occasion, Miss Fairfax. I dare say they often think of you, and wonder which will be the day, the precise day of the instrument's coming to hand. Do you imagine Colonel Campbell knows the business to be going forward just at this time? Do you imagine it to be the consequence of an immediate commission from him, or that he may have sent only a general direction, an order indefinite as to time, to depend upon contingencies and conveniences?"

He paused, waiting for her answer. *How can he be so brazen?* she thought.

"Till I have a letter from Colonel Campbell," said she, trying for an appearance of calmness, "I can imagine nothing with any confidence. It must be all conjecture."

"Conjecture—aye, sometimes one conjectures right, and sometimes one conjectures wrong. I wish I could conjecture how soon I shall make this rivet quite firm. What nonsense one talks, Miss Woodhouse, when hard at work, if one talks at all. Your real workmen, I suppose, hold their tongues; but we gentlemen labourers, if we get hold of a word—Miss Fairfax said something about conjecturing. There, it is done. I have the pleasure, madam," (to Mrs. Bates, now awake) "of restoring your spectacles, healed for the present."

He was very warmly thanked both by mother and daughter. Escaping after a little while from the latter, he went to the pianoforte, and begged Jane, who was still sitting at it, to play something more.

"If you are very kind," said he, "it will be one of the waltzes we danced last night; let me live them over again. You did not enjoy them as I did; you appeared tired the whole time. I believe you were glad we danced no longer; but I would have given worlds—all the worlds one ever has to give—for another half-hour."

She played.

"What felicity it is to hear a tune again which has made one happy! If I mistake not," he said with a particular emphasis when the piece was ended, "that was danced at Weymouth."

It was, indeed, a waltz they had once danced together. She looked up at him for a moment, colouring deeply at the recollection; and, glad of an occupation to cover her emotion, played something else. He took some music from a chair near the pianoforte, and said to Miss Woodhouse, in a voice perfectly audible to Jane,

"Here is something quite new to me. Do you know it?— *Cramer*. And here are a new set of Irish melodies. That, from such a quarter, one might expect. This was all sent with the instrument. Very thoughtful of Colonel Campbell, was not it? He knew Miss Fairfax could have no music here. I honour that part of the attention particularly," (speaking still more emphatically) "—it shows it to have been so thoroughly from the heart. Nothing hastily done; nothing incomplete. True affection only could have prompted it."

It was impossible entirely to suppress the deep blush of consciousness, the smile of secret delight, which his words provoked. At the same time, she wished he would not speak so plain! That he might intend by his remarks to further mislead Miss Woodhouse, however—that he might be proceeding with his plan of encouraging her suspicions of Mr. Dixon—did not occur to her. He had talked of it the night before in jest; she did not, upon reflection, believe him really capable of carrying it out. It was but an effusion of lively spirits. His playful temper, though it had lately caused her some pain, was enchanting to her still, as it had been from the first. She did love him dearly!

He brought all the music to Miss Woodhouse, and they looked it over together. Emma whispered something to him, and the two spoke together in confidential tones that, again, did not reach Jane's ear, for all she wished to hear them. Realizing with another blush that she ought not to be *trying* to listen to a private conversation, she began playing 'Robin Adair.' As the piece was concluding, Miss Bates, passing near the window, exclaimed,

"Mr. Knightley, I declare! I must speak to him, just to thank him. I will not open the window here; it would give you all cold; but I can go into my mother's room, you know. I dare say he will come in when he knows who is here. Quite delightful to have you all meet so! Our little room so honoured!"

She was hastening into the adjoining chamber as she spoke, and, opening the casement there, immediately called out to Mr. Knightley. Every syllable of their conversation was clearly heard by the others. She began by thanking him for the use of his carriage the night before, and begging him to come up and join their party. Mr. Knightley seemed determined to be heard in his turn; for most resolutely and commandingly did he say,

"How is your niece, Miss Bates? I want to inquire after you all, but particularly your niece. How is Miss Fairfax? I hope she caught no cold last night. How is she today? Tell me how Miss Fairfax is."

So persevering was he, that Miss Bates was obliged to give a direct answer before he would hear her say anything else. His inquiries perhaps provided Frank a little taste of that jealousy he had lately been inflicting on Jane, for he gave a sharp look in her direction, to see how she received these proofs of Mr. Knightley's regard. He found nothing in her countenance, however, to alarm him, and heard the rest of the conversation without anxiety.

"I am going to Kingston," said Mr. Knightley. "Can I do anything for you?"

"Oh! dear, Kingston—are you?" said she. "Mrs. Cole was saying the other day she wanted something from Kingston."

"Mrs. Cole has servants to send. Can I do anything for you?"

"No, I thank you. But do come in. Who do you think is here? Miss Woodhouse and Miss Smith; so kind as to call to hear the new pianoforte. Do put up your horse at the Crown, and come in."

"Well," said he in a deliberating manner, "for five minutes, perhaps."

"And here is Mrs. Weston and Mr. Frank Churchill too! Quite delightful; so many friends!"

"No, not now, I thank you. I could not stay two minutes. I must get on to Kingston as fast as I can."

"Oh! do come in. They will be so very happy to see you."

"No, no, your room is full enough. I will call another day, and hear the pianoforte."

"Well, I am so sorry! Oh! Mr. Knightley, what a delightful party last night; did you ever see such dancing? Was not it delightful? Miss Woodhouse and Mr. Frank Churchill; I never saw anything equal to it."

"Oh! very delightful indeed; I can say nothing less, for I suppose Miss Woodhouse and Mr. Frank Churchill are hearing everything that passes. And," (raising his voice) "I do not see why Miss Fairfax should not be mentioned too. I think Miss Fairfax dances very well; and Mrs. Weston is the very best country-dance player, without exception, in England. Now, if your friends have any gratitude, they will say something pretty loud about you and me in return; but I cannot stay to hear it."

"Oh! Mr. Knightley, one moment more; something of consequence—so shocked! Jane and I are both so shocked about the apples!"

"What is the matter now?"

"To think of your sending us all your store of apples. You said you had a great many, and now you have not one left. We really are so shocked! Mrs. Hodges may well be angry. William Larkins mentioned it here. You should not have done it, indeed you should not. Ah! he is off. He never can bear to be thanked. But I thought he would have staid now, and it would have been a pity not to have mentioned... Well," (returning to the room) "I have not been able to succeed. Mr. Knightley cannot stop. He is going to Kingston. He asked me if he could do anything—"

"Yes," said Jane, "we heard his kind offers; we heard everything."

"Oh! yes, my dear, I dare say you might, because you know, the door was open, and the window was open, and

Mr. Knightley spoke loud. You must have heard everything to be sure. Can I do anything for you at Kingston?' said he; so I just mentioned—Oh! Miss Woodhouse, must you be going? You seem but just come—so very obliging of you."

"My goodness," said Mrs. Weston, with a glance at the mantel clock, "I had no idea it was grown so late! I think we have just time, Frank, to see Emma and Harriet back to Hartfield—and then we really must be getting home."

# Chapter Thirty-Three

**THE NEXT DAY** it rained. Miss Bates and her mother took no morning walk, and Frank did not come. Nor did he come the following morning, though the weather was fine, and the opportunity fair—the elder ladies out, and the young lady waiting. Jane tried to check her disappointment. He had told her, after all, that it would be difficult for him to get away at the appointed hour. It was for the best, she was sure; he really ought not to come. But the thought would recur (try as she might to extinguish it) that he likely found no difficulties in calling on Emma Woodhouse, at whatever hour he chose.

Jealousy, she had often read, was a hurtful emotion, and poisonous to love. It "not only affects the mind, but every fibre of the frame is a victim to it." And she did not believe she should be naturally inclined to jealousy, in ordinary circumstances. She had no reason to doubt Frank's constancy; indeed, when she was with him, she never did doubt it, for in his presence the warmth of his affection was almost palpable to her. Unfortunately, she was in his presence all too infrequently; and under *these* circumstances, unhappily, she found herself at times falling prey to jealous fancies.

With such musings as these running through her head, she sat at the new pianoforte that afternoon, playing some rather mournful ballads as her aunt and grandmother worked at their stitching; and the instrument itself seemed almost to reproach her for her want of trust. Was not the proof of Frank's love, the evidence that he was always thinking of her even in his absence, at that very moment singing beneath her fingertips; responding with the most ready pliancy, the most beautiful sympathy, to her every touch?

While Jane was absorbed in brooding about Frank, his own thoughts were, in fact, pretty completely occupied with her. The idea which had occurred to him on seeing the

Crown Inn, of having a ball, and dancing with her again, had not been forgotten. He had broached the subject to Miss Woodhouse, and they had discussed, and ultimately dismissed as impracticable, his first scheme of giving a ball at Randalls. But this morning Mr. Weston had proposed a new plan, of having the ball at the Crown itself. Mrs. Weston having granted her tentative approbation, she and her husband had repaired at once to the inn to inspect the premises, while Frank hastened to Hartfield to bring Miss Woodhouse into the project.

When they all met at the Crown, there was initially some disagreement between the ladies and the gentlemen.

"Emma," said Mrs. Weston, "this paper is worse than I expected. Look! in places you see it is dreadfully dirty; and the wainscot is more yellow and forlorn than anything I could have imagined."

"My dear, you are too particular," said her husband. "What does all that signify? You will see nothing of it by candlelight. It will be as clean as Randalls by candlelight. We never see anything of it on our club-nights."

The ladies here probably exchanged looks which meant, "Men never know when things are dirty or not;" and the gentlemen perhaps thought each to himself, "Women will have their little nonsenses and needless cares."

They were united, however, in their concern for the lack of a supper-room adjoining the ballroom. There was a small card-room which might serve the purpose, if card-playing were conveniently voted unnecessary by their four selves; but it seemed too small for any comfortable supper. The only other room of adequate size was at the other end of the house, and a long awkward passage must be gone through to get at it. Mrs. Weston was afraid of draughts for the young people in that passage, and neither Emma nor the gentlemen could tolerate the prospect of being miserably crowded at supper.

Mrs. Weston proposed having no regular supper—merely sandwiches, &c., set out in the little card-room; but a private dance, without sitting down to supper, was denounced by the rest as an infamous fraud upon the rights of men and women, and Mrs. Weston was bid not to speak of it again.

"I wish one could know," said she, after some further discussion, "which arrangement our guests in general would like best. To do what would be most generally pleasing must be our object—if one could but tell what that would be."

We have previously seen that Frank Churchill had not lived so long with a willful and capricious relation, without discovering certain means for achieving his own ends while seeming to cater to the wishes of others. Though such devices were probably unnecessary with the present company, and in the present situation, he was perhaps too accustomed to employing them to abandon them all at once.

"Yes," he now cried. "Very true. You want your neighbours' opinions. If one could ascertain what the chief of them—the Coles, for instance. They are not far off. Shall I call upon them? Or Miss Bates? She is still nearer—and I do not know whether Miss Bates is not as likely to understand the inclinations of the rest of the people as anybody. I think we do want a larger council. Suppose I go and invite Miss Bates to join us?"

"Well—if you please," said Mrs. Weston, rather hesitating, "if you think she will be of any use."

Emma protested they would get nothing to the purpose from Miss Bates.

"But," said he, "she is so amusing, so extremely amusing! I am very fond of hearing Miss Bates talk."

"Aye, do, Frank," said his father. "Go and fetch Miss Bates, and let us end the matter at once. She will enjoy the scheme, I am sure; and I do not know a properer person for showing us how to do away difficulties. We are growing a little too nice. She is a standing lesson of how to be happy. But fetch them both. Invite them both."

Frank, feigning great stupidity, replied, "Both, sir! Can the old lady—?"

"The old lady! No, the young lady, to be sure. I shall think you a great blockhead, Frank, if you bring the aunt without the niece."

"Oh! I beg your pardon, sir. I did not immediately recollect. Undoubtedly if you wish it, I will endeavour to persuade them both." And away he ran.

Jane was still at the piano, where she had been fixed almost since her aunt and grandmother returned from their walk, when Patty came up to announce "Mr. Frank Churchill." She had but a moment to prepare for happiness; he was shown in directly. He came in all smiles, asking how they were; and after listening to some extended replies by Miss Bates—with abundant thanks for his civility in calling on them, and repeated compliments on the capital job he had done the day before, of replacing the rivet in Mrs. Bates's spectacles—he explained his errand; concluding,

"Mrs. Weston and Miss Woodhouse are at the Crown with my father at this moment, examining the rooms, and determining how they may best be made to suit our purpose; and they desired me to step across and see if I could persuade you, ma'am, and Miss Fairfax," (with a smile at Jane) "to come and give us your advice. We all felt what an advantage your opinions would be in such an undertaking—if you would allow me the pleasure of attending you both there."

Miss Bates made no difficulties, only thanked him again, and expressed a sense of wonder, as she and Jane donned their coats and bonnets, that anyone should place any value on her poor opinion; and spoke at length of their good fortune in having such attentive and obliging friends. Chattering on, she led the way down the dark, narrow stairs, allowing Frank to say softly in Jane's ear as they descended,

"I have written to Enscombe for permission to extend my visit. I am determined I shall not lose another chance of dancing with you!"

By the time they entered the Crown, Mrs. Weston, like a sweet-tempered woman and a good wife, had examined the passage again, and found the evils of it much less than she had supposed before—indeed very trifling; and here ended the difficulties of decision. All the rest, in speculation at least, was perfectly smooth. All the minor arrangements of table and chair, lights and music, tea and supper, made themselves; or were left as mere trifles to be settled at any time between Mrs. Weston and Mrs. Stokes, the woman who kept the inn.

Most cordially did Miss Bates agree to it all. As a counsellor she was not wanted; but as an approver (a much safer character), she was truly welcome. Her approbation, at once general and minute, warm and incessant, could not but please; and for another half-hour they were all walking to and fro, between the different rooms, some suggesting, some attending, and all in happy enjoyment of the future. The prospect of the ball, and the hope of Frank's remaining longer in Highbury, made Jane animated and cheerful to so extraordinary a degree that, in a burst of open-hearted enthusiasm, she exclaimed to Emma, "Oh! Miss Woodhouse, I hope nothing may happen to prevent the ball. What a disappointment it would be! I do look forward to it, I own, with very great pleasure."

Thus, in eager anticipation of an evening of music, dancing and agreeable society, did Jane Fairfax and Emma Woodhouse fleetingly share that fellowship of youth and spirits, which any two young ladies not absolutely detesting each other might. Even the disgraceful spectacle of Frank soliciting Emma's hand for the first two dances could scarcely blunt Jane's pleasure. Jealousy was banished now; henceforth she would entertain no doubts of his love and devotion. It was as well, perhaps, that she had not the misfortune to overhear Mr. Weston whisper to his wife just then, "He has asked her, my dear. That's right. I knew he would!"—for though her jealousy might be quieted, her sense of wrongdoing could never be altogether reasoned or beguiled away; and she still could help feeling that Frank's showing such great attentions to Miss Woodhouse in order to conceal his true situation, was a deception too likely to cause real injury to be willingly countenanced.

Alas! there was soon no occasion for these scruples. Though her nephew's wish of staying longer evidently did not please Mrs. Churchill, it was not at first opposed. But two days of joyful security were immediately followed by the overthrow of everything. A letter arrived from Mr. Churchill to urge Frank's instant return. Mrs. Churchill was unwell— far too unwell to do without him; she had been in a very suffering state (so said her husband) when writing to her nephew two days before, though from her usual unwillingness to give pain, and constant habit of never thinking of herself, she had not mentioned it; but now she was too ill to trifle, and must entreat him to set off for Enscombe without delay. He must be gone within a few hours; though without feeling any real alarm for his aunt to lessen his repugnance. He could only allow himself time to hurry to Highbury after breakfast to say goodbye to Jane, and to take his leave of Miss Woodhouse and her father, before departing in great haste for Yorkshire.

Jane's pleasure at his unexpected appearance that morning—and just a few minutes after Miss Bates and her mother had gone out—was promptly driven off by his gloomy aspect.

"Frank!" she exclaimed when Patty left them alone, "Whatever is the matter?!"

"I am called back to Enscombe at once," he told her. "I must leave this morning!"

"This morning!"

She sank down onto the sofa, unable for a time to speak another word. He sat down beside her, equally mute. After a long interval, she broke the silence by saying,

"But—you will come back again. Surely you will be able to come again soon."

He shook his head grimly. "God knows when that may be. Indeed, if we should go to town this spring—but I fear there is little hope of it. I shall try, Jane," (taking up her hand), "with all my heart. It will be my first, my dearest object!— And whatever may happen, I shall have at least a few very sweet memories to console me, when I am returned to Yorkshire."

Jane was growing frightened at his way of talking. 'Whatever may happen,' and 'God knows when!' It really sounded as if he did not expect to be in Highbury again for a very long time; as if, perhaps, he did not think to come back at all!

"When I recollect," he went on in a sorrowful tone, "how much of my time here has been taken up with others—how little I have been able to be with you! But it could not have been otherwise, I suppose."

"Surely you do not regret your friendship with Mrs. Weston," she said; adding, a little apprehensively, "Or Miss Woodhouse?"

He gave her a faint smile. "I like them both very much indeed—and the rest as well. I am truly sorry to leave them all."

She wished she could say plainly: "Do you repent of our engagement? Do you wish to give it up?"—but she had not the courage. Instead, she asked, "Then you still do not regret—coming to Highbury?"

"I regret nothing, my dearest girl," (with a look and tone of the fondest affection) "except having seen so little of you, and having to leave you so soon. I have lived these few days past upon the expectation of dancing with you again!"

This was a little reassuring; and more reassuring still was the promise, which followed next, that some way or other he would find a way to come back before long; and in the meantime he would be writing to her constantly, and hoping to hear from her very often.

The entrance of her aunt and grandmother soon put an end to this dialogue. Frank greeted them with the sad news.

"Miss Fairfax was so good as to allow me to stay until

your return," he said. "I could not leave without bidding you all goodbye."

Mrs. Bates said she was sorry he should have to go before time. She wished him a safe journey, and hoped he should find his aunt recovering when he reached Enscombe. Miss Bates had a great deal more to say, and to recollect; a great many thanks to offer, and circumstances to lament: disappointment of the Westons—loss of the ball—the Crown—Miss Woodhouse—Mr.Knightley—baked apples—spectacles—Coles—pianoforte—Campbells—Weymouth—Dixons—Ireland—Yorkshire—Mrs.Churchill—invalids—Bath—Mr.Elton—Mrs. Elton—and—

"And you are really to go so soon, Mr. Churchill!" she exclaimed, at the end of these reflections.

"Yes. I am on my way now to take leave of my friends at Hartfield. My father is to join me there, and we shall walk back together; then I must be off immediately. But Mrs. Weston has been so kind as to promise to correspond with me; and I know I may rely on her to give me all the particulars of everything that happens in dear Highbury. *She* will know," he said, with an inflection Jane alone understood—he spoke of Mrs. Weston, but he meant the words for her—"that she cannot write too much, or too often, were she to send me ten sheets a day. Through her letters I shall almost be with you again."

He could tarry no longer. He bowed over each lady's hand, Jane's the last. He gave her one last look, one last smile—and, once again, was gone!

# Chapter Thirty-Four

FOLLOWING FRANK'S departure, Jane suffered from headache to a degree which so worried Miss Bates, that she very nearly forbade her to take her daily walk to the post-office. This prohibition, of course, Jane could not consent to; but the letter she was watching for came with comforting despatch—and the arrival of the letter was succeeded by the retreat of the headache.

Frank had reached Enscombe to find his aunt much as he expected: not dangerously ill, but more querulous and demanding than ever—or perhaps only seeming so, he said, in contrast to the companions he had left behind in Highbury. Of the joy he had felt in seeing Jane again, and the pain he had felt on parting from her, he had a good deal to say—though not so much as to weary her of reading. He wrote also in the warmest terms of his father and Mrs. Weston, and with many expressions of gratitude for the kindness he had met with in every quarter. Miss Woodhouse he could not avoid naming, but his pen wisely did not linger on her. It was, of course, too early to predict how soon he might venture to propose leaving Mrs. Churchill again; but he vowed he would be watchful for any opening which might present itself.

In the usual course of things, young ladies, when they fall in love, will take every opportunity of introducing their lover's name into conversation, even by the most commonplace of remarks: "Mr. So-and-So says there has been more rain than usual this year,"—"Mr. So-and-So prefers blackberry preserves to strawberry,"—"Mr. So-and-So thinks Byron a better poet than Scott." Jane Fairfax could take no such liberties with the name of her lover—could allow herself no such pleasure. It was therefore a gratification to her (albeit one not unmixed with agitation) when Frank Churchill was talked of by others; and for this reason, she was quite willing to accede to her aunt's proposal one morning, that they should walk to Randalls to call on Mrs. Weston.

As Frank's chief *acknowledged* correspondent, Mrs. Weston would perhaps have a letter herself to show them. At the very least, she was sure to have many thoughts and observations to offer on the subject of her son-in-law.

On entering the drawing-room at Randalls, Jane was a little irritated to find Miss Woodhouse sitting with her friend. Anticipating nothing but pleasure from anything Mrs. Weston might choose to say about Frank, she could expect little but pain from a discussion of the same subject with Emma Woodhouse. The two ladies greeted them very cordially, however; and they had not been seated together five minutes, before Miss Woodhouse began lamenting the young man's departure, and the loss of the ball which was to have brought such great enjoyment to all.

"But I feared it would be so," she concluded with a sigh. "I felt from the first there was a danger in any plan which must depend for its fulfillment upon the goodwill of such a woman as Mrs. Churchill."

"Ah, Miss Woodhouse," said Miss Bates, "you are always so quick to see all the ins and outs, and ups and downs of a thing! I am sure I never did foresee the least reason why we should not be able to have our ball—why Mr. Frank Churchill should not be permitted to stay a few days longer in Highbury. But you knew better, Miss Woodhouse; you are always right."

"In this instance, as I told Mr. Churchill before he left, I am very sorry to be right; I would much rather be merry. But you, Miss Fairfax, must be feeling the loss of our ball quite as keenly as I do. I have not forgotten how delighted you were in the prospect of it, that day we all met at the Crown."

"I regret it very much," said Jane quietly, and her aunt at once chimed in,

"Indeed we are all quite shockingly disappointed! But really, Miss Woodhouse, I must tell you that poor Jane has been so very unwell these few days past, that even had the ball taken place, I do believe she could not have gone. However, she is rather better today, I think—are not you, my dear?"

"Oh! yes," she replied, though in truth her head was beginning to throb again. "Much better."

"Mr. Frank Churchill," said Miss Bates, "is such a charming young man, Mrs. Weston. What a comfort he must be to you, and to his good father. So very obliging! Do you know,

Miss Woodhouse, he fixed the rivet in my mother's spectacles when he was here, and it has not come out again since. And—"

"Yes, ma'am," Miss Woodhouse broke in. "Miss Smith and I had the pleasure of calling on you that day, and witnessed his work ourselves."

"Ah, yes, so you did; I recollect it now. You came to hear Jane's new pianoforte, I believe; and—"

"But as you have taken such a liking to Mr. Churchill, ma'am," Emma cried, "perhaps you will be interested to hear what he wrote in his letter to Mrs. Weston. She received one from him just this morning, you know."

"Have you indeed, Mrs. Weston!" said Miss Bates. "And so soon, too! How very thoughtful of him, I do declare. Do not you think so, Jane?"

She ventured a bland affirmative. After some further commentary, Miss Bates begged to hear the letter, and Mrs. Weston complied without hesitation. Jane listened attentively. In his letter to his mother-in-law, Frank repeated much of what he had already related in his letter to Jane— though in rather a different tone, and excluding, of course, all that pertained to his feelings for herself. Indeed, her own name was touched on but once, *en passant*; but "Miss Woodhouse" was referred to several times, with various compliments to her taste, her wit, her understanding, and her amiability. Even for Harriet Smith ('Miss Woodhouse's beautiful little friend,' as he called her) he could spare two full sentences out of a long letter. It was irrational to resent—to be vexed by what she knew was merely a device on his part, employed for the purpose of protecting their secret; but Jane felt vexed all the same, as the letter was talked over at length among them. Mrs. Weston and Miss Bates were delighted with it, and Miss Woodhouse obviously pleased with the many tributes to herself which it contained. Between an unreasonable jealousy, a fear of giving anything away, and fresh anxieties for Miss Woodhouse's feelings, Jane said as little as possible on the subject; hoping her reticence would be attributed to the languor of ill-health, and its true cause continue unsuspected.

Miss Bates had just begun to talk of going home, when Mrs. Cole came in. She brought word that Mr. Elton, the vicar, was to be married in Bath on Saturday next. Both bride and bride-groom, she said, were expected to travel to Highbury, after a short wedding trip, on the following Friday.

Recollecting the mystery which seemed to surround the relationship of Miss Woodhouse and Mr. Elton, Jane did not fail to remark the shadow which again crossed Emma's face at the mention of the absent clergyman. But in a moment it was gone, and no conclusions could be drawn from it, regarding the nature of their connection. As for any unprofitable attachment on the lady's side, however, *that* now appeared to Jane more unlikely than ever. Had she not often observed, in Emma's manner to Frank, but too plain a confirmation that her heart was not bestowed elsewhere? And though Emma might have withstood all Mr. Elton's reputed charms, was it likely she could resist Frank's?

As they walked back together through the village, Miss Bates had much to say, both about Frank Churchill, and about Mr. Elton's approaching marriage.

"Aunt Hetty," Jane said suddenly, "when you were younger, was there never anyone—that is—did you never think to be married yourself?" Oddly, it was a question she had never asked her aunt in all these years.

"I, married? Well, yes. In truth, my dear, there *was* a young man once, when I was a little younger than yourself—when I was sixteen, to be precise—Mr. Bradley, who was your grandpapa's curate for a few years. I did quite like him. I liked him very much. He was, indeed, a little like our own dear Mr. Elton—in manner, I mean, not in look. Not quite so polished, but very amiable. And not handsome; certainly not handsome. Still, I found myself becoming quite attached to him. And at one time I did hope—I did think that he was growing a little attached to me, too."

"But he never made you an offer?"

"Oh! no. Perhaps he thought me too young. And then his elder brother, you see, died of a fever; and so Mr. Bradley came into his father's property (a considerable property, as I understood)—and of course, he gave up his curacy, and returned to his home in Kent. And that was that."

"You never saw him again?"

"No. I never did."

"You never told me before. How sad!"

"Well," said Miss Bates, smiling, though her eyes shone with unshed tears, "such matters are pleasant to think on now and again, but it does not do to dwell on them. And indeed, I have no cause to repine. I am very well off as I am."

At home, they communicated to Mrs. Bates the news of

Mr. Elton's impending nuptials. Mrs. Bates had her own bit of news to share with them as well: Mrs. Perry had called in their absence, and confided that Mr. Perry was very nearly resolved on setting up his carriage. It was a matter of great satisfaction to Mrs. Perry. She was sure her husband's being out in bad weather did him a great deal of harm, and was happy indeed to think she had at last persuaded him. His plans, as Mrs. Bates told them, were to be kept a secret for the moment; but Jane, writing to Frank that night about her visit to Randalls, could see no harm in including in her letter word both of Mr. Perry's carriage, and Mr. Elton's marriage; along with all the other little bits of Highbury news in which she imagined he might feel any interest.

Soon there was a second letter from Frank. He wrote entertainingly of how he spent his days, and talked reassuringly of missing her, and longing to see her again; still, he confessed with some mortification, he could as yet name no definite time for his return.

The same post which conveyed his letter also brought a packet from Margaret Devere, which promised, by its thickness, to communicate news of some consequence. Frank's letter having been read three times over, Jane found herself able to give Miss Devere's her full attention.

My dear Miss Fairfax, (it read)

My last letter to you was unpardonably brief; but I hope you will consider this one fair recompense, for I intend to fill the paper so full, and cross it so thoroughly, that you are sure to find it wholly illegible.—J. is at last come back to Weymouth. I had not heard of his return; but I was reading in the parlour yesterday (my brother was not at home) when I saw him entering the yard. Supposing he must be on his way to the carriage house, I thought to go out and speak to him; I wished to express my sympathy for his loss—yet was uncertain such an overture would be welcome. Before I could make up my mind, however, I found he was knocking at the rectory door! He walked in, looking very tired and drawn. His manner, too, as he asked me how I did, was quite subdued.

'I was so very sorry,' I said, 'to hear of your father's death. And your poor mother!—I hope she is not entirely overcome by such a grievous loss.'

'Thank you,' he replied. Then, clearing his throat after a moment, he said, 'Indeed, it is about my mother that I

wished to speak to you, Miss Devere. This is rather awkward, but—I am come to ask a favour of you; if I do not
presume too much on our—' friendship, I thought he would
say; but after a slight hesitation, he concluded with 'acquaintance.'

'Not at all,' I murmured, and entreated him to continue.

'After I had taken care,' he resumed, 'of the necessary
business entailed in settling my father's estate, I felt I could
no longer neglect my work. Yet (as no doubt you may imagine) I was unhappy at the idea of leaving my mother alone.
She is naturally much affected by my father's death, and
her health has suffered in consequence. After some deliberation, I determined to bring her back here with me, where
I might keep an eye on her.'

'Mrs. Hammond is at Weymouth?' I asked in some surprise.

'I thought it best. But as I must spend the better part of
each day at my painting—indeed, she will not hear of my
doing otherwise—I am afraid she will be left a good deal by
herself. So I thought, perhaps, if you would be so good—it
would oblige me very greatly, if you would be so good as to
call on her. I believe she would find your society—
agreeable.'

As you may suppose, Miss Fairfax, this was an application from which I received no small gratification. I gave him
my consent most happily; and the smile of gratitude and
pleasure which brightened his countenance was all the reply I could have desired. The afternoon being already half
gone, it was soon settled between us that I should call on
Mrs. H. the following morning.

Accordingly, the next day I put on my bonnet and pelisse, and walked the little distance to their lodgings. He
himself opened the door to their apartments; and, thanking
me for coming, led me directly into the sitting room. His
mother had been reclining on a sofa, but rose at once when
we entered, though I begged she would not disturb herself
on my account. She was neither so elderly nor so frail as I
had imagined, but was in a temporary state of weakness
brought on by her late afflictions. There was, however, a
certain animation in her eye, which hinted at an active
mind, and a lively spirit.

He performed the introduction, and sat with us a for a
little while; until, satisfied that we should shift well enough
for ourselves, he made his excuses—kissed her—bowed to

me—and left.

I found her very well-disposed to talk; and it needed but little urging to induce her, after a few preliminaries, to tell me a good deal of her history. Her father had been a gentleman, she said, and ought to have had an independent fortune of his father: 'He was brought up to expect it, and not educated for any profession. One season in London, however, he fell in love with my mother, who was an actress on the stage—and for marrying her he was promptly disinherited. Luckily, he was a resourceful man, and not afraid of work. He had always taken an interest in the home farm on my grandfather's estate, and was knowledgable about cattle and sheep; so he was able, eventually, to obtain a position managing stock in a neighbouring county; and my mother gladly gave up her career, though it had been a promising one. They had a good life together, if a humble one, and were respected, for their industry and their benevolence, by all who knew them.'

I asked her—for I guessed she would feel it an indulgence to speak of him, and I had no small curiosity on the subject myself—how she had met her own husband?

'I'd known Isaac all my life,' said she. 'We grew up in the same village; he was my best friend, from childhood on. When I was eight years old, and he was ten, he said he wanted to marry me when we were grown. He even gave me a wooden ring he had made in his father's workshop— Isaac's father was a carpenter, and Isaac learned the trade of him.'

I asked her what sort of man her husband had been— whether he was very handsome or clever?

She smiled. 'Handsome? Nobody seemed to think so but me; but I thought him quite handsome enough. He had not much education, but he *was* clever—he read every book he could get hold of. And he was the finest cabinet-maker in the county. His pieces were not merely well-made; they were beautiful. I have often thought Jemmy must come by his artistic talents through his father. But what was I speaking of? Oh, yes. Isaac "came a-courting" in due form when I was sixteen; and we were married two years later. My parents thought I could do better. I mean no boast in saying it, Miss Devere, but I was rather pretty in my youth; and of course, my father having come of such a good family, it was expected—. But they knew Isaac was a good man, and devoted to me; and I loved and esteemed him above all others. So in the end they gave their permission for us to marry.'

'And is Mr. James Hammond your only child?' said I. (Do not condemn me, Miss Fairfax, for introducing his name into the conversation—how could I resist?)

She nodded, saying, 'At first, we feared we should not be blessed with children at all, for we were married four years before he came. Then for some time afterwards, we did think there would be others; but it was not to be. Jemmy was enough, though. Blessed as I have been, with such a husband and such a son, I can have no quarrel with the wisdom of Providence.'

'But little boys can be troublesome, cannot they?'

'Not my Jemmy. He was always a great help to me, and to Isaac. He was independent, like his papa, but not the least bit wild. He loved to bide in Isaac's workshop, and look on as he worked; he was just as proud as could be when Isaac gave him anything to do. He always applied himself, whatever the task, with an energy and diligence quite extraordinary in a boy his age. We thought he would be a cabinet-maker, like his father, and his grandfather. But then he began to make up sketches and drawings on any little scraps of paper he could find; and one day he told us he wanted to be a painter! How he even knew there was such a profession in the world, I cannot conceive—but he was decided; and Isaac and I felt it our duty to do what we could to assist him into the life he had chosen.'

'Mr. Hammond has spoken to me,' said I, 'of the many sacrifices his parents made towards his education.'

'If we made any, Miss Devere,' said she, 'we were repaid a thousandfold.'

'But it must be gratifying, indeed, to know you have contributed so much to make your son what he is. You have every reason to be proud of his success.'

'Success or no, I should always have been proud of him.—But,' said she after a moment's pause, 'I am selfish to go on talking so long about myself.' And she began asking me some questions about my own family, &c., &c. But oh! Miss Fairfax—had she but known with what sincere interest I heard all she had been saying on *one* subject—she would not have thought it necessary to talk on any other!

After a time, I saw she was growing tired; so I took my leave, with a promise to call on her again very soon, and an assurance that I would be delighted to see her at the rectory, whenever she was well enough to come. And I own to you with perfect candour, Miss Fairfax, that I look forward with pleasure to improving my acquaintance with Mrs. H.—for her own sake, as well as for her son's.

Her good example reminds me that I have been trying your patience with an endless recounting of my own affairs, without the smallest inquiry into yours. So, Mr. Frank Churchill, you told me in your last, has been visiting his father at Highbury! I had quite forgot that you and he did, once upon a time, come from the same place. Did you see much of him during his visit? And did the two of you talk over your absent friends from Weymouth? I hope you had leisure enough to abuse us all quite thoroughly. Pray remember me to him, if he is not gone away by the time you receive this.

Of my brother and Miss L., I have nothing new to report; and my paper contrives to spare you any further trial, by leaving me only a little space in which to conclude. My best regards to your aunt and grandmother—and thanking you again and again for your indulgence, in bearing with my too long-winded account, I am,

> Yours most aff'ly,
> Margaret Devere

# Chapter Thirty-Five

**AS THE WIFE** and daughter of Highbury's former clergyman, Mrs. and Miss Bates had for many years occupied
the vicarage pew at the Highbury church. When Mr. Elton
(then a single gentleman) succeeded to the living, he had
entreated the two ladies to do him the honour of occupying
it once more. Both had been exceedingly grateful for the attention; and *his* kindness, and *their* goodwill, being
thereafter communicated throughout the village by Miss
Bates, had done much to establish a reputation for Mr.
Elton in Highbury as a pattern-card of delicacy, courtesy,
and affability.

The advent of a *Mrs.* Elton was therefore a matter of no
small consequence to the elderly widow and her daughter,
and how best to show their respect the subject of no little
discussion between them. The question of what to do about
the pew—whether they might take the liberty of continuing
there without an express invitation to do so, now that Mr.
Elton was married—was extremely troubling. To occupy the
pew, or to vacate it: either might be viewed as an affront,
depending upon the humour of the bride. To avoid any dis-
turbance at church was of the first importance; yet to call
upon the young lady before she had been given time even to
unpack her trunks, seemed unfeeling. Still, as the happy
couple were due to arrive in Highbury on Friday night (leaving but one day before a certain encounter on Sunday),
Mrs. Bates at last settled it that her daughter and granddaughter should make a brief visit to the vicarage on
Saturday afternoon.

Jane was not averse to accompanying her aunt on this
errand. With Frank gone there was little, save what arrived
by post, to enliven her days, and she found herself looking
forward to the arrival of the newlyweds with some interest—
hoping to find in Mrs. Elton a young woman with whom,
perhaps, she might enjoy that sympathy of taste and sentiment, which she had been sorely feeling the want of.

Indeed, if Mrs. Elton should prove even moderately accomplished, or tolerably well-informed, she would be a very valuable addition to their limited circle.

The vicar was not at home when Miss Bates and her niece, at about three o'clock on Saturday, called at the vicarage; but his wife received them most graciously, and with a degree of assurance quite astonishing in a new bride, and one moreover residing among strangers. She was something between pretty and plain, and elegantly dressed. Her manner was very civil, and in loquacity she rivalled Miss Bates. Much to the relief of the latter, Mrs. Elton herself brought up the subject of the vicarage pew, telling them her husband had already apprised her of the situation, and of his particular wish that Mrs. Bates and her daughter should retain their seats.

"And though Mr. E., as my lord and master, has every right to dictate his will to me in all such matters (and of course I should deem it my solemn duty to obey), I assure you, my dear Miss Bates, that my *caro sposo* and I are in perfect agreement on this, as on every other subject. There is more than enough room to accomodate us all, you and your mother and I, as well as your sweet niece, quite comfortably; unless—or until—Providence sees fit to bless us," (lowering her eyes demurely for a moment), "with a considerable brood."

Miss Bates waxed eloquent for some minutes on the theme of Mr. and Mrs. Elton's goodness, and her own sense of gratitude. Mrs. Elton was receiving her compliments with a complacent smile when a tall, well-favoured gentleman entered the room.

"Ah!" said Mrs. Elton, "Here is my *caro sposo* now. My dear Mr. E.—here are Miss Bates and her charming niece, Jane Fairfax, come on purpose to pay their respects to your blushing bride! Is not that neighbourly of them?"

Miss Bates introduced him to Jane, and he greeted them both with an excess of courtesy. He was handsome, certainly; but Jane could not help thinking, as he spoke, that he had not Frank's charm. Neither did he appear to possess Mr. Knightley's forthright kindness—Mr. Dixon's well-bred good humour—Colonel Campbell's fatherly mildness—or even Mr. Devere's sober dignity. There was a sort of studied gallantry in his address which, in truth, was not much to her liking. She did not wish to jump to a too-hasty conclusion, however; and considering the awkwardness intrinsic to these visits of ceremony, she was not inclined to judge either husband or wife very severely. It was charitable to attribute both the gentleman's overblown flatteries, and the lady's presuming familiarity, to that embarrassment which Jane was sure she herself should feel under a similar circumstance.

"I was telling Mr. E. before he left this morning," said Mrs. Elton, "how charmed I am with my first view of Highbury. Oh, I do assure you, Miss Bates, I find our little village quite delightful—so very placid and homely! After all the ostentation of Bath, and the busy-ness of Bristol, this rural retirement will be quite a pleasure to me. Of course, one has not the advantages of the shops, and theatres, and assemblies, in the country—nor the stimulation of a large and diverse society. This house, too—Mr. E. feared I should find it too plain and small, after what I had been used to at Maple Grove—the seat of my brother, Mr. Suckling, where I have been used to spend a great deal of my time. Indeed, poor Mr. E. was in quite a state of apprehension about it all—were not you, my love? But I was quick to assure him I had not the smallest misgiving on that head, or on any other. Indeed, blessed as I am with so many resources within myself, I am really quite indifferent to such things. The world and its distractions I do not require. Those without resources might find themselves at a loss; but as for myself—my own resources are more than sufficient to keep me happily occupied anywhere. And as to smaller-sized rooms than I had been used to—I hoped I was perfectly equal to any sacrifice of *that* kind. Certainly I have been accustomed to every luxury at Maple Grove; but I did assure Mr. E. that two carriages were not necessary to my happiness; nor were spacious apartments. I only ventured so far as to hope I would be coming into a musical society. I conditioned for nothing else; but without music, Miss Bates, I confess, life would be blank to me. I cannot pretend to any extraordinary talent in that way (though my friends say I am not entirely devoid of taste); but I am fond, passionately fond of music. And I trust my *caro sposo* did not impose upon me, when he promised I would find many enthusiasts, and some very good performers, among my new neighbours."

"Oh! yes, indeed," said Miss Bates. "I do not play a note myself; but there is Miss Woodhouse, and Mrs. Weston, who both play charmingly; and the Coles' little girls just learning. And then Jane, you know, is quite an accomplished musician—though I ought not to say so myself."

Mrs. Elton turned to Jane. "Are you! Then, my dear Miss Fairfax, you must give us a little concert this morning."

"I thank you for the kindness of wishing it, ma'am," said Jane, "and I should be very happy to oblige you another time; but—"

"Now, now, my dear, no bashfulness with *me*, if you please. I have a reputation among my friends—whether deserved or not, I do not say—as an excellent judge of people; and I think I may say, that you are quite transparent to me already. With other young women, I should take this refusal as a *charade*—a mere affectation of modesty. But I have so far penetrated *your* character, as to be quite confident that your timidity is altogether unaffected—that you are quite in the habit of keeping yourself back from notice. But it will not do, my dear Miss Fairfax—it will not do. We shall not allow you to go on hiding your light under a bushel—shall we, Mr. E.?"

"Certainly not," said he, "But my dear Augusta, perhaps you are forgetting—"

"I will appeal to your good nature, Miss Fairfax, if I must," she went on, "for I declare, you would be giving us both the greatest pleasure, if you would play for us now. Is it not so, Mr. E.?"

"Most assuredly, Augusta," he replied, "Only—"

"Oh, I am a great advocate for timidity, genuine timidity, I assure you. I think it a most charming quality, and only too rare; for I am sure I have met with very little of it. But my dear Jane—you must allow me to call you Jane—it can be carried too far. I cannot allow you to let timidity consign you to obscurity—or to prevent you from giving enjoyment to your companions. I speak to you as a friend, who (though not much older than yourself) has seen a good deal of the world, and associated, I think I may say, with those in the first circles. Now, you must play for us. I shall not allow you to refuse."

"But, my dear—" said Mr. Elton.

"Your aunt," she continued, "I am sure, will agree with me. Am I not right, Miss Bates?"

Miss Bates, quite overpowered by Mrs. Elton's condescension, gave forth many disconnected utterances on the subject. Jane hardly knew what to say herself, for she had never before encountered such a mixture of beneficence and audacity in her life. Mrs. Elton's goodwill seemed genuine, but the pert overfamiliarity of her manner was repugnant.

"Augusta, my dear," Mr. Elton began again when there was a little pause in Miss Bates's speech, "You have forgotten, I think, that your pianoforte is not yet come from Bristol. So," (turning to Jane) "Though my wife and I should both have been delighted to hear you play, Miss Fairfax, I very much regret that we have, at present, no instrument for you to play upon."

Mrs. Elton had now nothing to do but to look rather foolish; and Jane perceived in an instant that beneath all her superficial ease, lay a deeply-rooted consciousness of her own insignificance.

"It is no matter," Jane said gently. "As I had been about to say, we really must be going away. We have had such a pleasant visit, I am afraid we have already stayed much longer than we intended. Aunt Hetty, I am sure grandmama will be growing anxious about us, if we do not go home directly."

As they walked back, Miss Bates could talk of nothing but Mrs. Elton's friendliness, and Mr. Elton's civility, and how delightful it was that two such amiable young persons should be united as one. She was sure Mrs. Elton would be a most enchanting neighbour, and that the pair would be blissfully happy together. Jane could not but agree that they seemed very well suited to one another. She felt somehow rather sorry for Mrs. Elton; but she could not like her. She wondered idly what Frank would think of her, whenever they should meet. She would write to him tonight, and tell him all about the visit.

They saw the newlyweds again at church on Sunday; and Mrs. Elton returned their call soon afterwards. By that time, she had learned the whole of Jane's history from Mrs. Cole, and (with motives perhaps not altogether unlike those which had prompted Miss Woodhouse to take Harriet Smith under her wing) had resolved on becoming her patroness. Jane might have been justified in considering her interference officious—or in taking offence at Mrs. Elton's calling her, from their very first meeting, by her Christian name. But after observing how little inclined that lady was to address anyone with due deference (she had even taken to referring to the master of Donwell Abbey by the irreverent designation of *Knightley!*), Jane was forced to conclude that such informality must be the established mode in Bristol.

At all events, Mrs. Elton was as delighted with Jane's command of music as with her fancied timidity, and quickly determined on doing everything in her power to encourage her, draw out her talents, and 'bring her forward'; and over the next few weeks, Miss Bates's gratitude and good nature hurried Jane into an intimacy with the Eltons which was far from agreeable to her. Nevertheless, as the Eltons, however presumptuous, were in their own way kind to her—and as aunt Hetty was quick to accept on Jane's behalf every invitation which was offered—she must make the best of the situation. Around Highbury it was soon a matter of general report that Miss Fairfax had been to dinner with the Eltons, gone out walking with the Eltons, spent a day with the Eltons. And except among some few within the precincts of Hartfield and Randalls, and, perhaps, Donwell, the reports inspired little wonder.

Jane's acquaintance with Mrs. Elton at least furnished her with a distraction of sorts; for she missed Frank intensely, and was filled with an unceasing anxiety about the future. But no matter how she occupied herself by day, at night she was invariably wakeful, wondering when she would see Frank again—whether their marriage would ever take place—how Mrs. Churchill's sanction was ever to be obtained—how her friends would react when they learned of her duplicity—whether any good end could ever come of such a bad beginning. The strain of endeavouring to appear tolerably cheerful in the face of these cares soon began to take its toll, and "concealment fed on her damask cheek,"—rendering her paler, thinner, and more reserved than ever.

Letters became her sustenance. Frank, true to his promise, wrote often, and a packet came from Yorkshire every two or three days. But Frank's letters, though delightful, were a poor substitute for his presence; and as the time dragged on without any date fixed for his return, she began to feel there must sooner or later be some terrible crisis, which would rapidly bring all to a happy conclusion—or to utter wretchedness.

# Chapter Thirty-Six

**FRANK, OF COURSE,** was not Jane's sole correspondent, nor the only one whose letters she read with pleasure. Along with those regularly received from the Campbells, Helen Dixon, and Miss Devere, one other letter, from an unexpected quarter, gave her considerable satisfaction: it came from Mrs. Nesbit, whom (she was ashamed to recollect) she had scarcely thought of since leaving Weymouth. The elderly lady had been wanting to write for some months; but, she said, "not wishing to impose on you an expensive correspondence, which your goodness would too willingly engage you in, however much your purse might object," she had put it off till now. She wrote in improved health and excellent spirits, and was particularly happy in the prospect of a visit from her sister, "whom Miss Fairfax had been so kind to in London." The projected visit, she explained, had been arranged through the thoughtfulness of Frank Churchill.

"How few young gentleman would take so much trouble over a tiresome old woman like myself! But my dearest boy is as steady as the Pole Star. He has written me several times since he left Weymouth; and despite my repeated assurances that I do not want for anything (for I cannot think it right he should pay for my bread), he always encloses 'a little something to cover the postage,' as he puts it—though his 'little somethings' cover a good deal more. And I will confess to *you*, Miss Fairfax, that were it not for his generosity, my situation would be poor indeed. (I beg you will not mention anything about it, however, if you should chance to see him again; for now I recall his writing, in his last letter, that he had the pleasure of seeing you last month when he visited his father in Surrey.)"

Frank was much admired, of course, among Jane's Highbury neighbours; but their estimation of him was founded chiefly on superficialities—on looks and manner. Mrs. Nesbit spoke of what was deeper, and therefore, of greater value: Frank's kindness, generosity, and constancy. The old woman's praise provided a seasonable cordial to Jane, at a time when she stood most in need of it; and prompted some agreeable reflections in the days that followed.

In April she received word from the Campbells that, instead of returning to London as originally planned, they had promised to stay on with the Dixons at least till Midsummer. Fresh appeals and entreaties arrived from Helen for Jane to join them at Baly-craig: would she but come, means would be found, servants sent, friends contrived—no travelling difficulty allowed to exist.

"Your excellent grandmama and aunt," wrote Mrs. Dixon, "have enjoyed your company quite long enough, dear Jane, and I hope they are ready now to resign you to other friends—friends who, though having no rightful claim to your society (save what a very sincere and long-standing affection might authorise) are nonetheless impatient to enjoy it once again."

With many feelings of regret did Jane write to decline her friend's kind invitation. It was rather hard, after all, that she should have to forgo the treasured companionship of the Dixons and Campbells, and suffer instead the impertinent patronage of Mrs. Elton; though it was, perhaps, a fitting penance for her sins. Yet these privations would be trifling, if she could but see Frank again! Her life now seemed made up of waiting. She had once read that genius was nothing but a great aptitude for patience; if so, she reflected wryly, there can be no genius in the world superior to a woman in love. She thought of Miss Devere, waiting for an old passion to re-kindle; and of Miss Lodge, waiting for a new one to begin. Oh! how many hours—weeks—years of a woman's life, may be expended in waiting!

One diversion, in the midst of all her waiting, came in the form of a dinner for the Eltons at Hartfield, to which she was invited. The arrival of the invitation roused Miss Bates to her usual raptures, though she herself was not to be one of the guests. She knew their old friend and his ways too well to resent the omission, however, and thought only of the distinction of Jane's being included among the favoured few.

"Poor Mr. Woodhouse's health, you know," she told Jane, "is so very delicate! How often we have heard him say—have not we, Mama?—that his nerves can never bear to have more than eight to dinner, at the very utmost! And of course, besides Mr. and Mrs. Elton, it is only natural they should want Mr. Knightley, and the Westons—which would make them just seven, altogether. And considering Miss Woodhouse's great intimacy with Miss Smith, I own I am surprised at her not being the eighth. But perhaps she might not choose to go, for some reason or other; though I really cannot imagine what. At any rate, Jane, it is quite an honour for you to be asked. Not that I should ever be surprised by anyone's taking notice of you. Everyone that knows you must esteem you. But such attentions as you always receive from the Woodhouses and Mr. Knightley— the Coles and the Eltons—and of course, the Campbells, and the Dixons. Only think of Mrs. Dixon's last letter, pressing you so urgently to come to Ireland! It really is quite out of the common way—though no more than you deserve, to be sure."

The sky on the morning of the Hartfield party was sullen and gray, and promising rain at any moment; but Jane went out before breakfast, as usual, on her daily walk to the post-office. There had been no letter from Frank since Monday, so she felt sure there would be something from him in today's post. She had not gone twenty steps from her own door, and had already seen several raindrops, when she met Mr. John Knightley with two of his sons. The boys, he told her, were engaged to pay their grandpapa and aunt a visit of some weeks, and he had brought them down from London the day before.

John Knightley, like his elder brother, was an old acquaintance, and one she was always happy to meet. He was a tall, gentleman-like, and very clever man, rising in his profession, and respectable in his private character. On his telling her now, that he looked forward to the pleasure of seeing her at dinner that evening, she recollected 'poor old Mr. Woodhouse's nerves,' and wondered how they would bear the addition of a ninth at table. As if reading her thoughts, he said, in a confidential tone,

"I think my fair sister-in-law, Miss Fairfax, was a little annoyed by my proposing to come just now. My presence, you see, might have made a muddle of her dinner arrangements, and threatened Mr. Woodhouse with the noise of one extra guest at table—though how *I* should add so great a quantity of noise, as could make any material difference to him, I cannot conceive; for I am hardly in the habit of bellowing or chattering, or clanking my silver. But as luck would have it, Mr. Weston is summoned to town without warning, and cannot be back in time for dinner. So my sin is forgiven, and peace reigns once more at Hartfield."

Jane smiled. She knew John Knightley was really very fond of his sister- and father-in-law—if not always quite so respectfully forbearing toward Mr. Woodhouse, nor so blindly admiring of Emma, as the latter would have liked.

Presently, her attention was claimed by the two boys, who wished to show off what they had learned since she last saw them; and she might have been detained a good while by Henry Knightley reciting his 'times tables', and young John saying his alphabet, had not the weather and their father intervened. The drops were beginning to fall more thickly; and, as he and his sons set off toward Hartfield, John Knightley urged her to return home directly. She hastened on to the post-office, however, and was not disappointed in her errand: the wished-for letter from Yorkshire had arrived. After paying out the postage and thrusting the letter hastily into her reticule, she dashed back out into the shower, arriving home with eyes and cheeks glowing, and gown, shoes, and stockings damp with spring rain.

Miss Bates was helping Patty down in the kitchen when she came in; but her grandmother was quick to observe the state of her clothing, and exhorted her to change at once. "You look quite flushed from your walk, dear!" said she.

Dutifully, if hurriedly, Jane put on a dry gown and stockings before allowing herself the happiness of opening her letter. Frank sent a few lines only, but those few conveyed very cheering news:

"My dear aunt," he wrote, "has taken it into her head—with a good bit of skillful management, I own, on the part of your disreputable correspondent—that Yorkshire is too cold for her; and we are all to come up to town on her account. I hope you admire how well I have contrived it! Indeed, my aunt is now so impatient to be gone, that she means to sleep only two nights on the road. So I think it likely we will be in Manchester Street by Thursday next, at the latest—and from there I shall ride out to Highbury at the very earliest opportunity."

Jane was therefore in a most happy mood when she stepped into the Eltons' well-sprung carriage later that evening. The vicar had gone to Donwell earlier on business, and was to walk over to Hartfield with Mr. Knightley; so

Jane and Mrs. Elton had the carriage to themselves. After making some compliments on Jane's dress, and accepting some on her own, Mrs. Elton introduced a new subject, saying,

"I was certainly pleased to hear that we will not be required to put up with that odious Harriet Smith tonight."

"Miss Smith—odious?" said Jane, wondering if she had missed something; for she had, in truth, been giving her companion only a divided attention.

"I never will understand what Emma Woodhouse sees in that girl. But perhaps she is at last come to her senses—or has at least realised how unacceptable it would be to *some* of her acquaintance, to have to endure the society of that irksome *parvenu.*"

"I have met Miss Smith only a few times myself; but I confess, to me she seemed quiet and unassuming."

"My dear Jane, it is an act—all an act, I assure you. In truth she is as scheming and grasping a little creature as ever lived."

"Miss Smith!"

"It is true, absolutely true. Why, my *caro sposo* told me such a story the other day, as you would hardly suppose possible. Indeed, perhaps I ought not to repeat it, it is really so very—and I would not tell another soul, of course—but I know I may trust to *your* discretion."

"If it is a matter of confidence, Mrs. Elton, I beg you will not—"

"Oh! it is nothing which reflects discredit on anyone but Harriet Smith. Though indeed our Miss Emma has much to answer for in the affair as well; for I cannot imagine the girl would have presumed so far, had she not received a great deal of encouragement from her friend."

"I should be very surprised," said Jane, "to hear of Miss Woodhouse encouraging presumption in anyone. She places rather a high value on the distinctions of rank, I believe."

"Be that as it may, Jane, it is a fact that Harriet Smith once actually attempted—apparently with the full knowledge and sanction of Emma Woodhouse—to ensnare poor Mr. E. into marrying her! As soon as he discovered their plot, however, he quite prudently removed himself to Bath, and circumvented it—else who knows what might have become of him!"

Jane felt some curiosity to know more; but as she had a strong distaste for this sort of gossipping confidence, she said nothing. Her companion, however, needed no encouragement to continue.

"Mr. E., as you know," said Mrs. Elton, "has the most affable manners!—for he considers it his duty, as a clergyman, to be on friendly terms with all his neighbours; and he is especially obliging to the female sex, as I'm sure you must have observed. As a bachelor, though, he was always exceedingly careful not to be too particular in his attentions to any one lady—and was, I believe, quite as gallant to your good old grandmama, as to any of the *young* ladies in the parish. He paid such attentions to Emma Woodhouse as he felt to be her due, as the daughter of one of the principal families in Highbury; and she was always very cordial to him. But all of a sudden, some months ago, her manner grew positively forward; so forward, indeed, that even a man as extremely modest as Mr. E. is, could interpret her conduct in no other light, than that she had set her cap at him!"

Mrs. Elton waited a moment for Jane to offer the sprightly little compliment she herself would have offered, were their positions reversed: declaring with a knowing smile that the vicar's perfections had no doubt produced a similar effect on many ladies, but his heart and hand had been reserved for the *one* lady most worthy of them. Receiving no such response, however (she could not, perhaps, expect everyone to equal *her* in wit and vivacity), she went on,

"Now dear Mr. E., I do assure you, never had any idea of the kind about *her*, but after all, it was quite impossible he should not feel in some degree flattered by such a marked preference. Whatever her faults, you know, she *can* be agreeable, where she wishes it; and some would even call her pretty—or nearly so. And though I think I may say that my *caro sposo* is as unmercenary a gentleman as ever lived—well, a fortune of thirty-thousand pounds is not to be dismissed out of hand by any man.

"Mr. E., however, was not at all certain he could summon up any feelings for her, such as would justify him in making her an offer (his sense of honour is very strict); so he thought it best to go on as he had done before, making himself agreeable, and allow matters to take their course in due time.

"Well, one evening, after a dinner party at Randalls, it seems, there was some sort of mix-up about the carriages, and poor Mr. E. found himself being driven home *tête-à-tête* with Miss Emma. To relieve the awkwardness of the circumstance (as he felt called on to do), he was paying her such inoffensive compliments as he believed she would be expecting, when she began all at once speaking in the most particular way, of Harriet Smith; talking as if she thought Mr. E. wanted to marry Harriet, and claiming that her own complaisance to him had been for her friend's sake only—that Harriet was desperately in love with him, and that she, Emma Woodhouse, actually believed *him* to be in love with Harriet! Can you conceive of it? Actually to think that Mr. E. would lower himself—that he would be so blind to what he is entitled to, as to degrade himself by an alliance with—"

"But do you think," Jane interposed, "that Miss Smith was really in love with Mr. Elton?"

"Oh, certainly not! She was only out for what she could get, I assure you. The one thing I cannot quite decide on, is whether or not Emma really did wish to make up the match for Harriet. Marriage to a *gentleman* such as Mr. E., would indeed have accorded her friend a measure of respectability, which she very sorely needs—you know what she is. But for my part, I am inclined to think Miss Emma at first meant to catch him for herself, but then changed her mind (intending, perhaps, to hold out for a title, or a larger fortune)— and, being aware of Harriet's ambitions, chose to pretend *that* had been her object all along."

So this, Jane thought, was the solution to the mystery of Miss Woodhouse and Mr. Elton—or at least a clue to it; for Miss Woodhouse's account of the affair, she supposed, might differ considerably from Mr. Elton's. Her own surmises, it seemed, had not been far off from the truth. She was not at all convinced by Mrs. Elton's assurances, however, of Miss Smith's not being in love with Mr. Elton. She could in no way credit that a simple, artless girl, such as Miss Smith appeared to be, was capable of behaviour so calculated; she seemed a creature much more likely to be governed by sentiment than by avarice. Moreover, Jane could easily imagine how Miss Smith, if she really were in love with Mr. Elton, must be feeling now—now that he had wed another. For if her own attachment to Frank had been unrequited; if they had not come to an understanding before he left Weymouth; if he had come to Highbury, and fallen in love with Miss Woodhouse—what torment would it have been to Jane to see them together! It was no wonder, then, if Miss Smith chose to stay at home today, rather than suffer the sight of the happy couple.

Yes, she knew exactly how Harriet Smith must feel; and oh!—she pitied her from the bottom of her heart!

# Chapter Thirty-Seven

**MISS WOODHOUSE WAS** gracious as ever in welcoming them to Hartfield. Mr. John Knightley spoke to Jane shortly after their arrival, expressing a hope that she had avoided being soaked by the morning's rain.

"The post-office," said he, "has a great charm at one period of our lives; but when you have lived to my age, you will begin to think letters are never worth going through the rain for."

*Oh! but this one was,* she thought with a little blush. "I must not hope, sir," she told him, "to be ever situated as you are, in the midst of every dearest connection; and therefore I cannot expect that simply growing older should make me indifferent about letters."

"Indifferent—oh, no! I never conceived you could become indifferent. Letters are no matter of indifference; they are generally a very positive curse."

"You are speaking of letters of business; mine are letters of friendship."

"I have often thought them the worst of the two," he replied coolly. "Business, you know, may bring money—but friendship hardly ever does."

"Ah! you are not serious now. I know Mr. John Knightley too well—I am very sure he understands the value of friendship as well as anybody. I can easily believe that letters are very little to you, much less than to me; however, it is not age which makes the difference, but situation. You have everybody dearest to you always at hand, I probably never shall again; and therefore, till I have outlived all my affections, a post-office, I think, must always have power to draw me out, in worse weather than today."

"When I talked of your being altered by time," said he, "I meant to imply the change of situation which time usually brings. As an old friend, Miss Fairfax, you will allow me to hope that ten years hence you may have as many concentrated objects as I have."

She tried to acknowledge his good wishes with an easy smile and a simple "thank you;" but, perversely, the very kindness with which he expressed them made her eyes well up. Would she indeed be more happily circumstanced ten years hence—or less so?

Mr. Woodhouse, who was making the circle of his guests, and paying his particular compliments to the ladies, now approached her. He, too, had something to say on the subject of her having been out in the rain.

"Young ladies," he declared, "should take care of themselves. Young ladies are delicate plants. They should take care of their health and their complexion. My dear, did you change your stockings?"

Eventually, the walk in the rain reached Mrs. Elton, and her remonstrances opened upon Jane.

"My dear Jane, what is this I hear? Going to the post-office in the rain! This must not be, I assure you. You sad girl, how could you do such a thing? It is a sign I was not there to take care of you."

Though Jane assured her as steadily as she could that she had not caught any cold, Mrs. Elton persisted, and even solicited the intervention of Mrs. Weston, who was standing near them.

"My advice," said Mrs. Weston kindly and persuasively, "I certainly do feel tempted to give. Liable as you have been to severe colds, Miss Fairfax, indeed you ought to be particularly careful, especially at this time of year. Better wait an hour or two, or even half a day for your letters, than run the risk of bringing on your cough again. Now do not you feel that you had? Yes, I am sure you are much too reasonable. You look as if you would not do such a thing again."

Jane looked at Mrs. Weston gratefully—certainly Mrs. Elton must now be satisfied. She was not, however.

"Oh!" said the vicar's wife, "she *shall* not do such a thing again—we will not allow it. I shall speak to Mr. E. The man who fetches our letters every morning (one of our men, I forget his name) shall inquire for yours, too, and bring them to you. That will obviate all difficulties, you know; and from us I really think, my dear Jane, you can have no scruple to accept such an accommodation."

"You are extremely kind," said Jane in dismay, "but I cannot give up my early walk. I am advised to be out of doors as much as I can, I must walk somewhere, and the post-office is an object; and upon my word, I have scarcely ever had a bad morning before."

"My dear Jane, say no more about it. The thing is determined, that is," (laughing affectedly) "as far as I can presume to determine anything without the concurrence of my lord and master. You know, Mrs. Weston, you and I must be cautious how we express ourselves. But I do flatter myself, my dear Jane, that my influence is not entirely worn out. If I meet with no insuperable difficulties therefore, consider that point as settled."

"Excuse me," said Jane earnestly, "I cannot by any means consent to such an arrangement, so needlessly troublesome to your servant. If the errand were not a pleasure to me, it could be done, as it is when I am not here, by my grandmama's—"

"Oh! my dear; but so much as Patty has to do! And it is a kindness to employ our men."

Jane was vexed. She turned again to Mr. John Knightley, and began chattering nervously about the merits of the post-office: the regularity and despatch of it—the variety of hands to be deciphered—how seldom any letter was carried wrong—how rarely actually lost! Other members of the party soon came into the conversation, allowing Jane a little interval to breathe freely. The varieties of handwriting were further talked of, and observations and comparisons made. Then Jane's composure was once more a little shaken, when Miss Woodhouse suddenly observed,

"Mr. Frank Churchill writes one of the best gentleman's hands I ever saw."

"I do not admire it," said Mr. Knightley. "It is too small—wants strength. It is like a woman's writing."

If Jane resented this accusation on her lover's behalf, she was required to leave his vindication to others. Miss Woodhouse and Mrs. Weston, however, were prompt in their response: Mr. Frank Churchill's writing by no means wanted strength—it was not a large hand, but very clear and certainly strong. Had not Mrs. Weston any letter about her to produce? No, she had heard from him very lately, but having answered the letter, had put it away.

"If I had my writing-desk," said Emma, "I am sure I could produce a specimen. I have a note of his. Do not you remember, Mrs. Weston, employing him to write for you one day?"

"He chose to say he was employed—"

"Well, well, I have that note; and can show it after dinner

to convince Mr. Knightley."

"Oh! when a gallant young man like Mr. Frank Churchill," said Mr. Knightley dryly, "writes to a fair lady like Miss Woodhouse, he will, of course, put forth his best."

Though Jane might appreciate Emma's able defence of Frank's handwriting, she could hardly be made more comfortable by its warmth. She was surprised, too, by Mr. Knightley's cutting tone. There was little time to reflect on its meaning, however—dinner was on table. Mrs. Elton, before she could be spoken to, was ready; before Mr. Woodhouse had reached her with his request to be allowed to hand her into the dining-parlour, she was saying, "Must I go first? I really am ashamed of always leading the way." And Miss Fairfax and Miss Woodhouse followed the others out arm in arm, with every appearance of good-will.

The dinner itself was in the usual Hartfield style of elegance and abundance, and passed pleasantly for Jane, with Mr. John Knightley at her left, making his usual quiet, rational, and often sardonic observations; and Mrs. Weston at her right—whose conversation, always agreeable, was rendered still more so by the occasional mention of Frank. It was a welcome if brief respite from Mrs. Elton's oppressive benevolence.

A particularly wearing aspect of Mrs. Elton's patronage was her insistence on looking out for an eligible situation for Jane. Seeing her placed as governess in a home where all her abilities would be properly valued had become a favourite project, and Jane's steadfast opposition in no way discouraged her. The matter had been the subject of considerable debate between them; and this evening, when the ladies retired to the drawing-room, it was not long before Mrs. Elton returned to it—engrossing Jane's attention almost entirely, and all but ignoring Miss Woodhouse and Mrs. Weston. Jane felt the rudeness of her behaviour; but her gentle efforts to bring the other two ladies into their conversation were no match for Mrs. Elton's stubborn ill-breeding. If Jane repressed her for a little time, she soon began again.

"Here is April come!" said Mrs. Elton. "I get quite anxious about you. June will soon be here."

"But I have never fixed on June or any other month— merely looked forward to the summer in general."

"But have you really heard of nothing?"

"I have not even made any inquiry; I do not wish to make

any yet."

"Oh! my dear, we cannot begin too early; you are not aware of the difficulty of procuring exactly the desirable thing."

"I not aware!" Jane exclaimed. "Dear Mrs. Elton, who can have thought of it as I have done?"

"But you have not seen so much of the world as I have. You do not know how many candidates there always are for the first situations. I saw a vast deal of that in the neighbourhood round Maple Grove. A cousin of Mr. Suckling, Mrs. Bragge, had such an infinity of applications; everybody was anxious to be in her family, for she moves in the first circle. Wax candles in the schoolroom! You may imagine how desirable! Of all houses in the kingdom, Mrs. Bragge's is the one I would most wish to see you in."

"Colonel and Mrs. Campbell are to be in town again by midsummer," said Jane. "I must spend some time with them; I am sure they will want it. Afterwards I may probably be glad to dispose of myself. But I would not wish you to take the trouble of making any inquiries at present."

"Trouble! aye, I know your scruples. You are afraid of giving me trouble; but I assure you, my dear Jane, the Campbells can hardly be more interested about you than I am."

Jane's eyes widened at this assertion; but the absurdity of assigning to herself, after a few weeks' acquaintance, an interest in her companion's welfare equal to that of the dear friends with whom she had lived as one of the family for a dozen years, was quite lost upon Mrs. Elton.

"I shall write to Mrs. Partridge in a day or two," she continued, "and shall give her a strict charge to be on the look-out for anything eligible."

"Thank you, but I would rather you did not mention the subject to her; till the time draws nearer, I do not wish to be giving anybody trouble."

"But, my dear child, the time is drawing near. Here is April; and June, or say even July, is very near, with such business to accomplish before us. Your inexperience really amuses me! A situation such as you deserve, and your friends would require for you, is no everyday occurrence, is not obtained at a moment's notice; indeed, indeed, we must begin inquiring directly."

Jane took a deep breath to steady herself. "Excuse me, ma'am, but this is by no means my intention; I make no inquiry myself, and should be sorry to have any made by my friends. When I am quite determined as to the time, I am not at all afraid of being long unemployed. There are places in town, offices, where inquiry would soon produce something—offices for the sale—not quite of human flesh—but of human intellect."

"Oh! my dear, human flesh! You quite shock me; if you mean a fling at the slave-trade, I assure you Mr. Suckling was always rather a friend to the abolition."

"I did not mean, I was not thinking of the slave-trade," replied Jane. "Governess-trade, I assure you, was all that I had in view; widely different certainly as to the guilt of those who carry it on; but as to the greater misery of the victims, I do not know where it lies. But I only mean to say that there are advertising offices, and that by applying to them I should have no doubt of very soon meeting with something that would do."

"Something that would do!" repeated Mrs. Elton. "Aye, that may suit your humble ideas of yourself—I know what a modest creature you are; but it will not satisfy your friends to have you taking up with anything that may offer, any inferior, commonplace situation, in a family not moving in a certain circle, or able to command the elegancies of life."

"You are very obliging; but as to all that, I am very indifferent. It would be no object to me to be with the rich. My mortifications, I think, would only be the greater; I should suffer more from comparison. A gentleman's family is all that I should condition for."

"I know you, I know you; you would take up with anything; but I shall be a little more nice, and I am sure the good Campbells will be quite on my side. With your superior talents, you have a right to move in the first circle. Your musical knowledge alone would entitle you to name your own terms, have as many rooms as you like, and mix in the family as much as you chose; that is—I do not know—if you knew the harp, you might do all that, I am very sure; but you sing as well as play—yes, I really believe you might, even without the harp, stipulate for what you chose—and you must and shall be delightfully, honourably and comfortably settled before the Campbells or I have any rest."

"You may well class the delight, the honour, and the comfort of such a situation together," said Jane, unable to keep a shade of irony from colouring her reply, "they are pretty sure to be equal; however," she added as firmly as she could, "I am very serious in not wishing anything to be attempted at present for me. I am exceedingly obliged to you, Mrs. Elton, I am obliged to anybody who feels for me, but I am quite serious in wishing nothing to be done till the summer. For two or three months longer I shall remain where I am, and as I am."

"And I am quite serious too, I assure you," replied Mrs. Elton gaily, "in resolving to be always on the watch, and employing my friends to watch also, that nothing really unexceptionable may pass us."

It may seem to some of my readers rather wonderful—perhaps hardly credible—that anyone could remain altogether civil in the face of so much benevolent impertinence; and there can be no doubt that Mrs. Elton's unremitting endeavours to hurry her into a delightful situation against her will were to Jane a trial of no small proportions. Yet it was impossible for her to forget that she was concealing from Mrs. Elton her true circumstances; and so long as she was kept in ignorance, Jane felt it would be too great an injustice, too mean an ingratitude, to blame her for efforts which, however objectionable, were at least in part—perhaps in the greatest part—kindly meant.

Mrs. Elton ran on in the same style till Mr. Woodhouse came into the room. Her vanity then had at last a change of object.

"Here comes this dear old beau of mine, I protest!" she said in a half-whisper to Jane. "Only think of his gallantry in coming away before the other men! What a dear creature he is; I assure you I like him excessively. I admire all that quaint, old-fashioned politeness; it is much more to my taste than modern ease. Modern ease often disgusts me. But this good old Mr. Woodhouse, I wish you had heard his gallant speeches to me at dinner. Oh! I assure you I began to think my *caro sposo* would be absolutely jealous. I fancy I am rather a favourite; he took notice of my gown. How do you like it? Selina's choice—handsome, I think, but I do not know whether it is not over-trimmed. I have the greatest dislike to the idea of being over-trimmed—quite a horror of finery. I must put on a few ornaments now, because it is expected of me, but my natural taste is all for simplicity; a simple style of dress is so infinitely preferable to finery. But I am quite in the minority, I believe. Few people seem to value simplicity of dress; show and finery are everything. I have some notion of putting such a trimming as this to my white and silver poplin. Do you think it will look well?"

The whole party were but just reassembled in the draw-ing-room when Mr. Weston made his appearance; he had returned to a late dinner, and walked to Hartfield as soon as it was over. He had been too much expected for sur-prise—but there was great joy. Mr. Woodhouse was almost as glad to see him now, as he would have been sorry to see him before. John Knightley only was in astonishment.

"That a man," he said aside to Jane, "who might have spent his evening quietly at home after a day of business in London, should set off again, and walk half a mile to an-other man's house, for the sake of being in mixed company till bedtime—of finishing his day in the efforts of civility and the noise of numbers—is to me quite incomprehensible! A man who has been in motion since eight o'clock in the morning, and might now be still—who has been long talk-ing, and might now be silent—who has been in more than one crowd, and might now be alone! To quit the tranquillity and independence of his own fireside, and on the evening of a cold sleety April day rush out again into the world—unfathomable! Could he, by a touch of his finger, instantly take back his wife, there would be a motive. But his coming now will probably prolong rather than break up the party."

He gazed incredulously at the offender for several mo-ments; then with a shrug, and a sigh, and a shake of his head, concluded, "I could not have believed it even of him."

# Chapter Thirty-Eight

**MR. WESTON,** meanwhile, perfectly unsuspicious of the indignation he was exciting, happy and cheerful as usual, and with all the right of being principal talker, which a day spent anywhere from home confers, was soon making himself agreeable among the rest. Jane was then still engaged in conversing with Mr. John Knightley; but glancing across the room at Mr. Weston, she saw him hand his wife a letter, and heard him say in a hearty voice,

"Read it, read it—it will give you pleasure. Only a few lines—will not take you long; read it to Emma."

By the expression of happiness on his face, and of pleasure on the two ladies', she could not doubt of the letter being Frank's, and announcing his expected return to Highbury. She would have liked to hear all that they were saying on the subject, and more particularly, would have liked to see how Miss Woodhouse bore the news. Mr. John Knightley, however, was relating to her some details of a legal case with which he had been much occupied of late, and it was necessary to give him her attention.

After a while, they were all interrupted by the appearance of the tea. While it was carrying round, her companion excused himself, going off to speak to his brother. Mr. Weston soon afterwards approached Jane with a broad smile.

"Miss Fairfax, how d'ye do—how d'ye do?" he said. "Well now, I have some news I think you will like to hear. I have just been talking of it to the others. My son is coming— Frank is coming to London, and we will have him here soon. Mrs. Weston had a letter from him today. Good news, I think—eh?"

She had no difficulty in matching his enthusiasm, if not his eloquence; but she said enough to satisfy him, and he continued,

"They are all coming up to town on Mrs. Churchill's account, you see. She has not been well the whole winter, and fancies Yorkshire is too cold for her. It will be an excellent thing, will not it, to have Frank among us again, so near as town? They will stay a good while when they do come, and I daresay we shall see him often all through the spring—and just the season for it, too. When he was here before, we could not do half that we intended; there is always such a deal of damp, dreary weather, in February! But now it will be complete enjoyment. And are you not of my mind, Miss Fairfax, that the uncertainty—the sort of constant expectation there will be of his coming in today or tomorrow, at any hour—may not be more conducive of happiness than having him actually here? I own, I think it is the state of mind which gives most spirit and delight."

Jane, feeling she should much prefer the certainty of knowing when she would see Frank, did not answer the question directly, but instead inquired, whether Mrs. Weston and the others were pleased by the news?

"Oh! indeed," he replied. "My wife's partiality for him is very great, as you know—she thinks nobody equal to him. Our friends, too, are all very warm in their congratulations, which gratifies me a great deal. Mrs. Elton was so good as to say they would be delighted to see Frank at the vicarage—which I thought very handsome of her, considering they have neither of them ever clapped eyes on him."

Jane having agreed to the handsomeness of Mrs. Elton's declaration, he went on, "They shall be in town next week at the latest, I daresay; for Mrs. Churchill is impatient as the devil when anything is to be done. To you, Miss Fairfax, I will confess I do not put much store in Mrs. Churchill's illnesses. Yorkshire, I suppose, is no colder this year than it has been for the last twenty. But the truth is, it is her temper to be dissatisfied, and to be always complaining of this or that, and to find fault with whatever is before her; so she can never long be happy in any place. No doubt she is tired of Enscombe, and wants a change. But she has been good to Frank, and is very fond of him in her way; and so I do not like to speak ill of her.

"And her illness may not be entirely imaginary," he continued. "In his last letter, Frank said she had been unable to leave the sofa for a week together, and complained of being too weak to get into her conservatory without having both his arm and his uncle's! Yet now she is so impatient to be in town, that she means to sleep only two nights on the road—which does make it seem as if is not nearly so sick as she pretends to be. I should be sorry to do anyone injustice,

Miss Fairfax; but it is difficult for me to speak of her with perfect charity. You are an old friend, I know you will make allowances. I think you are aware of my connection with the family, and the treatment I have met with; and, between ourselves, the whole blame of it is to be laid to her. She is all arrogance and insolence! And what is the more provoking, she has no fair claim herself to family or blood. She was barely a gentleman's daughter, by birth; but ever since she became a Churchill, she has out-Churchill'd them all with her high and mighty airs.—But I had forgotten—you met her yourself, did not you, Miss Fairfax? You met them both, I believe, at Weymouth. How did they seem to you?"

Surprised by the application, Jane chose her words carefully. "I really was so little acquainted with either, Mr. Weston, I can scarcely tell you; I met them but once or twice. I did find Mr. Churchill—Mr. Frank Churchill's uncle, I mean—a pleasing, gentlemanlike sort of man. Mrs. Churchill was not—did not seem altogether in a good humour—but that might be attributed to her ill-health, of course. From something your son once said, however, I did receive an impression that—that she prides herself particularly on the consequence of the Churchill name and fortune;—and," she ventured with some hesitation, "that she expects her nephew to add to it—by making a very great marriage."

Luckily Mr. Weston was not of a suspicious turn, or he might have wondered at her introducing this subject. "Oh," said he, laughing, "without a doubt, without a doubt! There is no telling how high she might set her sights. An Earl's daughter with a hundred thousand or so would do, I suppose," he suggested gaily. "But if Frank should not happen to meet with such a *nonpareil*—or if his inclination should be in favour of a young lady of more modest claims," (with a glance at Miss Woodhouse, which stung Jane to the quick) "then she may be forced to settle for a daughter-in-law a *little* less exalted."

A response of some sort was called for, and Jane, with a feeling of bitterness at her heart, asked, "But is it likely your son would marry anyone, without the Churchills' approval? And is it likely his aunt would approve his choice, if it did not answer all her ideas of a suitable match?"

Mr. Weston again perceived nothing odd in her remarks, for it was a topic he had himself considered at some length, and one which he could not doubt to be of interest to all Frank's friends. "It really is impossible to know," he replied seriously, "what might satisfy Mrs. Churchill—or how much she might attempt to impose her will upon poor Frank, if it should come to that. I am afraid there is too much reason to believe she would go to great lengths, to keep him from marrying without her consent. However," he said more cheerfully, "there is no reason to suppose she would reject a young lady of excellent family, and a very good, if not a grand fortune. After all, there are only so many earl's daughters with vast riches to be had, eh?"

Jane could not at that moment give the hearty laugh he looked for, and only smiled weakly.

"As for Mrs. Weston and myself," he added, "we should welcome any bride he chose, so long as she were sincerely attached to him. If she were as poor as a churchmouse, *we* would make no difficulties, I assure you."

At this, Jane's smile grew a little brighter. "I am sure you have only your son's happiness at heart," she said.

"Indeed I have. And from my own experience, Miss Fairfax, I believe I can state with confidence that a man is no less likely to find happiness in marriage, if he wed a truly amiable woman of no fortune at all," (looking fondly across at Mrs. Weston) "than if he should wed the greatest heiress in the county."

# Chapter Thirty-Nine

**IT WAS NOT** very long, though rather longer than Mr. Weston had foreseen, before the Enscombe family were in London; and Frank was at Highbury very soon afterwards. He sent Jane no word of his coming; but she and Miss Bates, having been out at Ford's to look over some figured muslins just arrived, were on their way home when they met him in High Street. Discomposed at seeing him so unexpectedly, she could scarcely disguise her confusion. Neither was he very calm; his spirits were quite evidently fluttered. He hardly looked at her, and responded to Miss Bates's friendly questions with an air of abstraction. He had reached Manchester Street with his aunt and uncle the day before yesterday, he told them, and had ridden down this morning for a couple of hours only. He could not yet do more; Mrs. Churchill was too ill for him to make any prolonged absence. He had been to Randalls already, and was now on his way to Hartfield, to pay his respects to Miss Woodhouse and her father.

"I do hope," said Miss Bates, "you will have time to call on us before you go back to town, Mr. Churchill. My mother will be so delighted to see you. We often talk of your goodness in fixing her spectacles for her, when you were here before. And upon my word, the rivet is just as firm as ever—such a neat job you made of it, I declare! She will indeed be happy to see you again—"

"You are very good, ma'am," he interrupted her, "and I should be sorry to miss the pleasure of seeing Mrs. Bates; but I am afraid—that is, my time is so limited today," (glancing at Jane with an expression she could not understand) "—but I shall try to stop for a moment, before I go." Then bowing to them both, he hurried off.

His manner so altered! What could it mean? Jane asked herself, while Miss Bates chatted away cheerfully as they continued in their way home. But in half an hour he was seated in their own little parlour, seeming much more like himself, though still restless and agitated. His visit was short; and, as the two elder ladies never left the room, they could say nothing to each other that anyone might not hear.

This was her only glimpse of him in the course of ten days. His letters came more frequently than ever; and the first she received accounted for his strange behaviour that day, as being provoked by a perception of *her* agitation, and by his vexation and disappointment at having so short a time for his visit. His fear that he might be required to spend the whole of it at Hartfield had got the better of him, he wrote, and in consequence, he had been out of humour the whole day.

Jane could have pointed out, in her reply, that this latter vexation might have been avoided had he but shown from the outset more precaution in his attentions to Miss Woodhouse. She endeavoured instead to be satisfied with his explanation, which was, after all, perfectly reasonable. But the awkwardness of her situation, and the little hope she had of its being amended very soon, had an unfortunate if natural tendency to make her irritable, anxious and mistrustful. She reproached herself for being so; but she could not help it.

As the days wore on, Frank was often hoping, often intending to come again to Highbury—but was always prevented. His aunt could not bear to have him leave her. Mrs. Churchill's removal to London had been of no service, it seemed, to the willful or nervous part of her disorder. That she was really ill was very certain; he declared himself convinced of it. Though much might be fancy, he could not doubt, when he looked back, that she was in a weaker state of health than she had been half a year ago. He did not believe it to proceed from anything that care and medicine might not remove, or at least that she might not have many years of existence before her; but he certainly could not say that her complaints were merely imaginary, or that she was as strong as ever.

Jane read over this part of Frank's letter several times, with a vague sense of disquiet. It was horrible to suspect him of coldly calculating his aunt's chances of recuperation; of casting up how many months or years she might yet have to live; of weighing how much longer her existence might continue an obstacle to their happiness. There was nothing in his statements, really, to warrant these suspicions; but perhaps, she thought with even greater horror, they were merely the reflection of ideas lurking darkly at the back of her own mind; and she offered up many a prayer that Heaven would preserve Mrs. Churchill from an untimely death—and Frank and herself from arrant wickedness.

It soon appeared that London was not the place for Mrs. Churchill. She could not endure its noise. Her nerves were under continual irritation and suffering; and by ten days' end, Frank wrote joyfully of a change of plan: they were to remove immediately to Richmond. Mrs. Churchill had been recommended to the medical skill of an eminent person there, and had otherwise a fancy for the place. A ready-furnished house was engaged, and much benefit expected from the change. The house was taken for May and June, and he wrote with the greatest confidence of being often in Highbury—almost as often as he could even wish.

Jane was elated; and earnestly wished Mrs. Churchill so great a restoration of health, as might induce her to settle at Richmond indefinitely. Miss Bates was quick to remark her improved spirits, and Mrs. Ford, when Jane ran across the street to buy some thread, commented on the renewed bloom of her complexion. Calling at Randalls one morning, she learned that preparations were once again underway for the ball at the Crown. A few lines from Frank, to say that his aunt felt already much better for the change, and that he had no doubt of being able to join them for twenty-four hours at any given time, had prompted the Westons to name as early a day as possible.

No misfortune occurred, again to prevent the ball. The day approached, the day arrived—and happiness was at hand. Frank came in good time, reaching Randalls before dinner; and on their way to the Crown that evening, the Westons stopped at Mrs. Bates's door so he might run up to offer the use of their carriage. The aunt and niece, however, (as he was informed by Miss Bates), were to be brought by the Eltons.

"But how very thoughtful of Mr. and Mrs. Weston," cried she, "to remember us—and with so much as they have had to do, too, to get everything ready for tonight! Pray do convey my warmest thanks to them both. We are indeed fortunate to have so many kind friends. You have not yet met our dear Mrs. Elton, of course; but she is just such another. So very pleasant and amiable! You will be perfectly delighted with her, I am sure. Her attentiveness to us is wonderful indeed. She insisted that my mother and I should continue to sit in the vicarage pew—which really was almost too obliging of her—and she has been so exceedingly kind to Jane. She seems to have taken quite a fancy to her—which does not surprise me at all, for Jane is so very—; and indeed, everyone is always kind to Jane. The Campbells and the Dixons, and Mr. Knightley, and Miss Woodhouse, and of course, your dear father and mother, and—; but still it is quite remarkable the attentions Mrs. Elton has shown her—and on such a short acquaintance! Jane has been to dinner at the vicarage three—no, four times already, and has gone out walking twice with Mr. and Mrs. Elton—has even spent an entire day with them, once. Mrs. Elton is a great admirer of Jane's musical accomplishments; and has interested herself most kindly in Jane's affairs. But I daresay you have heard all about it from Mrs. Weston—"

As her aunt made this speech, Jane stood by in silence, colouring faintly. Her colour deepened at Frank's grinning reply: "Yes, ma'am; I have heard it all—from Mrs. Weston, as you say."

Miss Bates probably had more gratitude to express, and more to say of Mrs. Elton, and of other matters; but Frank could not stay to listen; his father's carriage awaited him below. So, with a bow to all three ladies, saying that he looked forward to seeing Miss Bates and Miss Fairfax again shortly, he departed.

Mrs. Bates was soon afterwards driven off in the Hartfield coach to spend the evening with Mr. Woodhouse, and Jane and her aunt had been ready nearly half an hour when the Eltons' empty carriage at last arrived to convey them the short distance to the ball. A gentle rain was falling, and as they alighted from the coach, two gentlemen with umbrellas came forward from the Crown's entrance to assist them: Mr. Weston and his son. Miss Bates, who had been talking steadily on the way over, now addressed her remarks to Mr. Weston as she took his arm and stepped across the yard to the inn. Frank claimed Jane's hand, tucking it snugly into the crook of his arm with a look of exultation. He led her to the door; and as they traversed the dim passageway toward the ballroom, lagging a trifle behind the other two, he bent his head to hers and whispered, "Save the second two dances for me, Jane!" A moment later they stepped into the well-lit ballroom, and joined the company assembled round the fire.

Miss Bates continued talking, in her usual desultory

fashion, of the weather, and the ballroom, and her mother—
inquiring after the state of Mrs. Weston's health, and the
dryness of Jane's feet—thanking Mrs. Elton for having sent
her carriage, and Mrs. Weston for having offered hers—and
cordially greeting all her neighbours. With a smile, Frank
bowed to Jane, and went off to stand by Miss Woodhouse.
Jane would not be provoked however; it was only what she
had expected, after all, and there was a great deal too much
happiness in view, to let jealousy or anxiety oppress her.

Mrs. Elton soon replaced Frank at her side—a most inferior substitute. Her presence, however, was a useful check
on Jane's excitement; for she must not appear *too* happy.
She said as little as possible in response to Mrs. Elton's
many compliments on her dress and looks. Then Mrs. Elton
was evidently wanting to be complimented herself; and it
was, "How do you like my gown?—How do you like my
trimming?—How has Wright done my hair?"—with many
other relative questions, which Jane endeavoured to answer
with patient politeness.

"Nobody," Mrs. Elton then said, "can think less of dress in
general than I do—but upon such an occasion as this, when
everybody's eyes are so much upon me, and in compliment
to the Westons—who I have no doubt are giving this ball
chiefly to do me honour—I would not wish to be inferior to
others—and," (looking about her) "I see very few pearls in
the room except mine.—So, Frank Churchill is a capital
dancer, I understand. We shall see if our styles suit. A fine
young man certainly is Frank Churchill. I like him very
well.—Miss Emma is looking rather well this evening.
Though," she continued in a lower voice, after another
glance around her to be sure she should not be overheard,
"I own I am surprised she is wearing so little jewellery! And
her hair—that style is not at all flattering on her. I declare,
it makes her features look so sharp! Do not you think so,
Jane?"

Jane murmured that she thought Miss Woodhouse in
very good looks. Mr. Elton joined them presently, and soon
afterwards, Mr. Weston advanced toward them, requesting
Mrs. Elton to open the ball as his partner in the first dance.
Her vanity was wholly gratified by the distinction, and she
led the way with a complacent smile. Frank and Emma
soon followed. Mr. Elton turned to Jane and, with his usual
air of affected gallantry, offered himself as her partner.

"No doubt, Miss Fairfax," said he, "you will have numerous beaux this evening—all, I am sure, more engaging companions, and more adept at dancing, than an old married man like myself; but none, I trust," (with a low bow) "who could be happier than I, at being so honoured."

The vicar proved a competent dancer; and when their two dances were over, Jane thanked him civilly, and returned him into the custody of his wife. She had not long to wait then, for the moment of joy to arrive: after a short interval, Frank came to claim her hand for the next two dances.

Standing opposite each other in the set, they hardly spoke. What, after all, could they say to one another, in the midst of such a crowd? But hands could touch—eyes meet—smiles be exchanged; it was no more than the dance required, and could rouse no suspicion. How blissful, just to be near one another—to be dancing together once again! All the difficulties of their situation, the shame of concealment, the anxieties for the future, were forgotten; and Jane, always light and graceful, floated through the dance like a radiant and delicate fairy.

But joy is fleeting. Two dances, no matter how delightful, cannot last forever. Too soon the music ceased. Frank retained her hand for just a moment, before taking her back to that end of the room where Miss Bates was seated.

Jane had the next two dances with Mr. George Otway, a pleasant young man of florid face, stout build, and rather heavy step. He was not a great talker, which suited her very well; for she was still in a haze of happiness, and did not wish the spell to be broken, the mood dissipated in idle conversation. Two dances followed with Mr. Richard Hughes. He was a bit of a rattle, just down from Cambridge, and regaled Jane with tales of his roguish friends and prankish exploits at University—with some fanciful embellishments; for in fact he was a generally dutiful, and only occasionally mischievous young man; and his friends were mostly a sober, studious set, the sons of circumspect parsons, prosperous lawyers, and gentleman-farmers.

As their dance began, however, something rather extraordinary occurred. They were taking their places in the set, when she noticed Mr. Elton—who had danced all the previous dances—strolling about at leisure; and Harriet Smith sitting down nearby, in want of a partner. After the story she had heard from Mrs. Elton, Jane was persuaded the vicar would feel a strong dislike to dancing with Miss Smith; yet, under the circumstances, *not* to ask her would be more than uncivil. But poor Miss Smith! It really looked very much as if he did not mean to ask her. As if, indeed, he was making a pointed *show* of not asking her. Jane was turned away from the scene for a minute by the movements of the dance; but when next she had leisure to look about, she saw a beaming Miss Smith being led to the set—by Mr. Knightley!

Jane was very much struck by it. Mr. Knightley had never asked *her* to dance. He never did dance, so far as she knew, though she could hardly imagine why; surely a man so youthful and active as he, could not be ungraceful on the dance floor. She had always supposed he simply had no pleasure in dancing. However, she knew of no one more naturally kind than Mr. Knightley—no one more likely to feel compassion for a slighted, mortified girl—no one more disposed to do even what he did not like, if in the doing he might give relief to another.

And what happiness for Miss Smith, to be so honoured! It must do her good in getting the better of her unlucky passion (if such it was) for Mr. Elton—not only by his having shown himself, by his ill-breeding, to be unworthy of her esteem; but by the inevitable comparison of the two men which must certainly offer itself to her mind. The cure might be worse than the disease, however. If she were now to fall in love with Mr. Knightley (and a sweet, tender-hearted girl like Miss Smith would always be in love with somebody)—she could hardly allow herself even the hope of a return. Mr. Knightley was infinitely her superior, not merely in fortune and consequence—which inequality Jane, given her own inferiority of station relative to Frank's, could not consider so *very* great an impediment—but in abilities and understanding. Indeed, for Harriet Smith, even Mr. Elton, an 'old married man,' could scarcely be more unattainable than Mr. Knightley, though a bachelor. But unlike Mr. Elton, Mr. Knightley would do nothing to injure Harriet's good opinion of him. No; if she *were* to fall in love with him, it must be long, very long, before she might learn to think of him no more.

Jane found she was not the only one to remark this singular occurrence. The smile which lit Miss Woodhouse's countenance on the occasion plainly expressed her pleasure, approbation, and gratitude for Mr. Knightley's kindness to her friend. Mrs. Elton spoke some of *her* feelings, by observing audibly to her partner (with a peevish simper),

"Knightley has taken pity on poor little Miss Smith!—Very good-natured, I declare." Mr. Elton, having publicly betrayed himself by his ungentlemanly conduct, had retreated to the card-room, and was nowhere to be seen.

At the close of these two dances, supper was announced. The move began; and from that moment Miss Bates spoke almost without interruption, till her being seated at table and taking up her spoon:

"Jane, Jane—my dear Jane, where are you? Here is your tippet. Mrs. Weston begs you to put on your tippet. She says she is afraid there will be draughts in the passage, though everything has been done—one door nailed up— quantities of matting—my dear Jane, indeed you must—"

Frank, who was standing nearby, quickly stepped up behind them, taking the tippet from Miss Bates; and Jane felt him gently place it across her shoulders with his own hands. She looked back at him as he was carefully arranging it, but immediately turned away with a blush on seeing the tender expression in his eyes. He ought to be more guarded—what if aunt Hetty should notice? By way of a distraction, she asked Miss Bates (who was herself still talking),

"Have you looked in on grandmama yet, aunt Hetty? Is she returned safely from Hartfield?"

"Mr. Churchill," said Miss Bates, "Oh! you are too obliging! How well you put it on!—so gratified! Excellent dancing indeed! Yes, my dear," (to Jane) "I ran home, as I said I should, to help grandmama to bed, and got back again, and nobody missed me. I set off without saying a word, just as I told you. Grandmama was quite well, had a charming evening with Mr. Woodhouse, a vast deal of chat, and backgammon. Tea was made downstairs, biscuits and baked apples and wine before she came away; amazing luck in some of her throws; and she inquired a great deal about you, how you were amused, and who were your partners. 'Oh!' said I, 'I shall not forestall Jane; I left her dancing with Mr. George Otway; she will love to tell you all about it herself tomorrow. Her first partner was Mr. Elton, I do not know who will ask her next—perhaps Mr. William Cox.'"

Frank offered an arm to lead Miss Bates in to dinner. "My dear sir, you are too obliging. Is there nobody you would not rather?—I am not helpless."

Helpless or no, she gratefully took his arm, and he turned with satisfaction to offer the other to Jane. She took it happily as her aunt continued,

"Sir, you are most kind. Upon my word, Jane on one arm, and me on the other!—Stop, stop, let us stand a little back, Mrs. Elton is going. Dear Mrs. Elton, how elegant she looks!—Beautiful lace! Now we all follow in her train. Quite the queen of the evening! Well, here we are at the passage. Two steps, Jane, take care of the two steps. Oh! no, there is but one. Well, I was persuaded there were two. How very odd! I was convinced there were two, and there is but one. I never saw anything equal to the comfort and style—candles everywhere. I was telling you of your grandmama, Jane—"

Miss Bates then related, in the shadowy passageway, the sad tale of her mother's disappointment over a fricassee of sweetbread and some asparagus at Hartfield. Jane stole a glance at Frank, who grinned down at her, brimming with mirth, just before they entered the bright parlour where the supper had been laid out.

"Well, this is brilliant," said Miss Bates. "I am all amazement!—could not have supposed anything! Such elegance and profusion! I have seen nothing like it since—Well, where shall we sit? Where shall we sit? Anywhere, so that Jane is not in a draught. Where I sit is of no consequence—"

Frank pulled out a chair for Jane, and another for Miss Bates. "Oh!" she exclaimed, "do you recommend this side?—Well, I am sure, Mr. Churchill—only it seems too good—but just as you please. What you direct in this house cannot be wrong. Dear Jane, how shall we ever recollect half the dishes for grandmama? Soup too! Bless me! I should not be helped so soon, but it smells most excellent, and I cannot help beginning."

To Jane's delight, Frank took the vacant chair beside herself. And Miss Woodhouse, she observed with a little glow of exhilaration, was seated between Mr. Weston and William Cox—quite at the other end of the room.

# Chapter Forty

**WHILE THEIR NEAREST** neighbours were occupied in other conversations and the general din made it safe to talk, Frank turned to her and asked in a low voice, "Will it be possible for you to go out for a walk tomorrow morning, after breakfast?"

"I suppose so," she replied in some surprise. "Why?"

"If the day is fair, I shall take my way out on foot—say about eleven o'clock?—and send my horses ahead to meet me by another road, a mile or two beyond Highbury. And if you will just come across the field that lies between Hartfield and the Richmond road, out to where the road turns, about a half-mile outside of town—do you know the spot? It is quite retired; shaded on both sides, by elms, I believe."

"Where there is a grassy patch a bit farther up," she said tentatively, "and a bank opposite? A rather steep one, with a little hedge at the top?"

He nodded. "Yes, that's the place. Now, if you should happen to be walking there, as I happen to be passing by, we might meet—quite by accident—and walk on a little way together without exciting suspicion, if anyone should chance to see us; which, however, in such an unfrequented quarter, I think perfectly unlikely."

Jane could not make him any reply at once, as a question from her aunt just at that instant, which a little startled her, required that her attention be directed for a time to Miss Bates. When the danger was past, she turned back to Frank.

"I do not think," she began, "it would be wise for us to meet. Though the place you speak of is comparatively secluded, it is really far from unfrequented. Farmer Mitchell's wagon often travels back and forth along the Richmond road, I know, and the pupils from Mrs. Goddard's sometimes walk there, too. Indeed, I have walked there myself, on occasion.

"All the better—then your walking there again can give no

cause for comment."

"But it certainly would be remarked, if you and I were to be seen walking there together."

He frowned a little. "Then you do not wish to meet me?"

"It is not a question of my wishes, Frank. The risk is too great."

"You are too cautious," he said, and turned a moment later to address a remark to his other neighbour, Mrs. Hughes. Jane saw that he was displeased—unreasonably so, in her view. But she was determined to remain firm, even in the face of his displeasure. She felt herself to be in the right, and she *would* act prudently.

They were engaged for two more dances later in the evening; and though he was, during the first dance, rather silent and sullen, by the end of it he had begun to relent. During the second his ill-humour cleared off entirely, and when it was over he appeared quite unwilling to relinquish her hand and return her to Miss Bates. However, he went off cheerfully, to devote himself to Miss Woodhouse for the rest of the evening—by which action, however, Jane was still resolved not to be annoyed; and she ended the ball in a state, if not of unalloyed happiness, at least of tolerable contentment.

The morrow brought Frank to Mrs. Bates's house just after the three ladies had finished their breakfast. He had, it seemed, borrowed a small pair of scissors from Miss Bates during the course of the previous evening, and conveniently neglected to return it to her—by that means furnishing himself an excuse to see Jane once more before leaving for Richmond.

Miss Bates was all gratitude at this unlooked-for civility—such excessive goodness, putting himself to so much trouble just to bring back her scissor! It was but an old one which she always kept in her reticule—for one never knew when such a thing might be wanted—and this was not the first time it had come in handy in some little crisis or other. She hoped it had performed its office well—hoped Mrs. Weston had been able to trim the thread hanging from the back of his collar without any unravelling—only wished he had asked some greater favour, that she might repay the wonderful service he had done them, in fixing her mother's spectacles, as well as his being always so kind as to call on them, and all the many attentions he had shown Jane and herself last night. How well he danced! She really had never seen anything to exceed the dancing of Mr. Frank Churchill and Miss Woodhouse; and his dances with Jane, too, had given her such enjoyment!

"Jane is an excellent dancer, is not she?—though perhaps I ought not to say so. But we take no credit for it, indeed. It is all thanks to the Campbells, who have been so very kind to her. I suppose, of course, there is something due to Jane's natural grace, which, I believe, is rather beyond the common. But one must be taught to dance—one must have instruction, certainly; and our dear good Colonel Campbell has neglected nothing in Jane's education. Yes, ma'am," (to Mrs. Bates) "we will take our walk presently; I think you may go now and put your bonnet on—" (more loudly) "—go and put your bonnet on! My mother is a little deaf, you know, sir; sometimes I must raise my voice just a little, or she will not hear me. We always take a walk after breakfast, Mama and I, if the weather is fair. Perhaps, Mr. Churchill, if you are going now, you will give us the pleasure of walking a little way with us?"

He acceded to her proposal most readily, and Miss Bates continued,

"You are too good, sir. We can go in whatever direction you are taking. We never walk very far—it is just for my mother to take her daily exercise, and get a bit of fresh air. Jane, if you will stay with Mr. Churchill for a moment, I shall just go and get my bonnet and shawl too, and then we three can be off directly. I shall not detain you a minute, Mr. Churchill."

True to her word, Miss Bates was scarcely out of the room ere she returned; but the interval was long enough for Frank to slip into Jane's hand a note, folded up small, which he had kept concealed within his palm all the while Miss Bates had been talking to him. The note, which Jane unfolded and read as soon as they had departed, was as follows:

Dearest,

I hope you will forgive me for being such a brute as to quarrel with you last night. Indeed, I am certain you have forgiven me already, however little I may deserve your forbearance; and trusting to that forbearance, I mean to try it a little further—by again entreating you to meet me before I go, at the place I mentioned to you yesterday. Do not doubt that I do full justice to your wish to be circumspect, knowing that wish to proceed as much from an anxiety for my welfare as your own—nay, more. But I cannot give up the hope of seeing you alone this morning, without attempting to persuade you such a meeting might take place with perfect safety.

Consider first the retirement of the spot: though it may indeed be the chosen route of Farmer Mitchell's wagon, and the occasional walk of Mrs. Goddard's scholars, certainly there can be nothing like a steady rush of travelers along such a road; and the likelihood of anyone observing our meeting must, I think, be very small. Moreover, if anyone *should* chance to see us together—which, as I have said, is quite improbable—I am persuaded they would see nothing strange in it. The Westons are good friends of Mrs. Bates and all her family, and you and I are known to have been acquainted at Weymouth. In Highbury we have met often among our mutual friends. What could be more natural than that, walking out separately, and meeting by accident, we should walk on a little way together—as any two friendly acquaintances might?

This is my argument. I can offer no better—save to tell you that such a meeting would mean all the world to me. I will wait near the appointed spot until eleven o'clock; longer than that I must not delay. But you have granted me such indulgence already, I know you will not fail to grant but a little more, to your own—

F.

Tears stung at her eyes as she read. He could not desire the meeting more than she did herself; but the dangers of such a meeting appeared to her no less this morning than they had appeared last night; and cost her what it would, she would not run such a risk. Let him be ever so angry, *she* at least would be sensible.

Mrs. and Miss Bates returned shortly, and all three ladies settled down quietly to their work—or rather, two of them were quiet: Miss Bates talked at random about the ball, and Mr. Frank Churchill, and sundry other matters. After they had been thus occupied for about an hour, their solitude was interrupted by a call from Miss Nash. Miss Nash was head teacher at Mrs. Goddard's school, and a good friend of Miss Bates; an energetic, upright little woman, not young, but not very far beyond youth; plain, but with a keen and lively eye. Like Miss Bates, her mind was much occupied with all the ordinary and extraordinary business of the neighbourhood; and today she had a tale to tell which proved of unexpected interest to Jane.

It seemed that Harriet Smith and Maria Bickerton (another parlour boarder at Mrs. Goddard's) had walked out together earlier that morning along the Richmond road; and about half a mile beyond Highbury, they had suddenly perceived at a small distance before them, on a patch of greensward by the side of the road, a party of gypsies! A child on the watch came towards them to beg; and Miss Bickerton, excessively frightened, gave a great scream, and calling on Harriet to follow her, ran up a steep bank, cleared the slight hedge at the top, and made the best of her way by a short cut back to Highbury. But Harriet could not follow. The poor girl had suffered very much from cramp after dancing at the ball last night, and her first attempt to mount the bank brought on such a return of it as made her absolutely powerless—and in this state, and exceedingly terrified, she had been obliged to remain.

How the trampers might have behaved, had the young ladies been more courageous, must be doubtful; but such an invitation for attack could not be resisted; and Harriet was soon assailed by half a dozen children, headed by a stout woman and a great boy, all clamorous, and impertinent in look, though not absolutely in word. More and more frightened, she promised them money, giving them a shilling, and begging them not to want more, or to use her ill. She was then able to walk, though but slowly, and was moving away—but her terror and her purse were too tempting, and she was followed, or rather surrounded, by the whole gang, demanding more.

From this perilous situation she had been rescued, by none other than Mr. Weston's son—in short, by Mr. Frank Churchill! By a most fortunate chance, his leaving Highbury had been delayed so as to bring him to her assistance at this critical moment; and being on foot, he was unseen by the whole party till almost upon them. He had left the gypsies completely frightened; and Harriet, hardly able to speak, and eagerly clinging to him the whole way, had had just strength enough to reach Hartfield, before her spirits were quite overcome, and she fainted away.

Here Miss Bates could not refrain from breaking in. "How dreadful for those two poor girls! Had it been me, I declare I should have been frightened out of my wits. Gypsies in

Highbury—I could never have supposed. What will Mr. Knightley say when he hears of it? And poor Mr. Woodhouse—what a shock to his nerves, to see poor Miss Smith brought to Hartfield in such a state—and from such a cause! I hope he was not too much overcome by it—I must go and call on him today, indeed I must. But what good fortune for Miss Smith, that Mr. Churchill should have been at hand so directly to rescue her! And how good-natured of him, to see her safely all the way back to Hartfield! But he is indeed a very good young man. He was so kind this morning as to call here, for no reason but just to return an old pair of scissors of mine, which he had borrowed of me last night at the Crown—(you would not have known Mrs. Stokes's old rooms, they were so transformed; quite like a fairyland!)—for there was a thread hanging from the back of his collar, which Mrs. Weston was going to cut for him, but she had not got any scissors with her; so he thought to ask me if I had any, and of course, I was happy to be able to oblige him—I always carry a little pair of scissors with me, you know, for you never can tell when you may have use for it. So he borrowed it, but in all the flurry of the evening— such a delightful ball it was!—he forgot to return it; and if you will believe me, he actually came out of his way this morning, just to bring it to me—though it was of no importance, as I could have got it back from Mrs. Weston any time, and I daresay he must have been in a hurry to get back to his aunt and uncle in Richmond—but he would not go away without returning it. And indeed, it was only because he was so kind as to stop here to return my scissors, that he was leaving Highbury so much later than he intended—and that he happened to be coming by just at that moment, when Miss Smith was so much in want of assistance—"

She talked on a little further, about how fortuitous it was that Mr. Churchill had been detained (or rather, had detained himself, to return her scissors) just long enough to help Miss Smith; and how, after calling on them, he had walked a little way with her and Mama, and how charming he had been, and how attentive to Mrs. Bates, and how delightful the ball had been, and how wonderful it was that everything should always work out for the best.

Jane, though silent (for there was no need to speak, with two such inveterate talkers present as her aunt and Miss Nash), was caught up in a rapidity of thought. Her prudence in having refused to meet Frank by the Richmond road now appeared to her doubly fortunate. Had she gone, Miss Smith and Miss Bickerton would likely have seen them together; and from Harriet Smith, knowledge of their meeting would assuredly have spread, not only to Miss Nash and, through her, to Miss Bates, but worse, to Hartfield. Miss Bates might be too trusting ever to doubt her niece, but Miss Woodhouse's suspicions would surely be roused by such a circumstance. And those frightful gypsies! The very thought of them made her tremble. Suppose she *had* gone, and been accosted by them herself? She feared she would not have shown even so much courage as Miss Bickerton and Miss Smith. And if Frank had not been at hand to rescue *her*—if he had already left with Miss Smith—what would have become of her? Surely now he must admit the wisdom of her having stayed at home.

Frank, meanwhile—taking it for granted that the note he pressed into Jane's hand that morning had produced the desired effect—was worrying over what she would think of his failing to appear as promised. By the time he had got away from Hartfield, leaving Harriet Smith to Miss Woodhouse's care, it was nearly noon. He returned with all haste to the appointed spot, to find no sign of either Jane or the gypsies. Not being much given to alarm, he was possessed by no great uneasiness, lest his beloved had been run off with. He was confident he had given the culprits such a scare as would have persuaded them to depart at once, without committing further mischief. But that he should have kept Jane waiting—that she should have gone home, perhaps in anger, before he arrived—and after he had made such a point of her coming! From Richmond he wrote her a letter full of apologies. Not for the world, he said, would he have had her exposed to any danger or fright—else he might wish it were herself he had delivered from the gypsies, instead of Harriet Smith; her own darling self clinging to him as Miss Smith had done!

# Chapter Forty-One

**JANE WAS SURPRISED** to find, on receiving Frank's letter, that he quite relied upon her having gone to meet him on the Richmond road that morning. She assumed, however—as she told him in her reply—that he must now see how unwise such a course would have been.

Learning that she had not, in fact, attempted to meet him that morning, Frank felt a surprise equal at least to her own; and so far from agreeing with her as to the folly of the planned rendezvous, was rather annoyed at her persistence in condemning it. Always so cold, so correct, so over-cautious! She said she wished they might be able to meet, but would not run the smallest of risks to effect it. He began a letter of complaint to her in this style; but on reading over what he had written, he soon began to be quite ashamed of himself, recollecting the very great risk she ran in keeping to their engagement at all; and after reading over her own letter again—studying every passage and phrase which marked her affection for him—he took a fresh sheet of paper, and took up his pen once more, to compose a letter of such warmth, as would make this author blush to copy it down for your perusal. Whether the recipient of the letter blushed upon reading it, cannot be known; but it may be guessed that the protestations it contained, and the promise it gave of Frank's returning to Highbury within the week, furnished her some moments, at least, of real happiness.

Life, however, or some semblance of it, must go on; and June opened much as May had closed. The report, which around that time began to be in general circulation, that Mrs. Weston was expecting a child, was of a nature too predictable to excite much wonder in any of her neighbours, though the talking of it gave great pleasure to all. Jane, meanwhile, found herself still in company with the Eltons a good deal more than she liked. On those occasions when she did not spend some part of her day at the vicarage, Mrs. Elton called on her at Mrs. Bates's house. The vicar's wife was happily anticipating a summer visit from her sister and brother, and found great enjoyment in regaling her friends with the future exploring parties to be taken in the Sucklings' barouche-landau; always hastening to assure Jane that she would have the honour and delight of being introduced to the estimable couple when they came.

"And, my dear Jane," she said, "you really need have no fear of meeting my brother and sister. For all the magnificence of their home at Maple Grove, I assure you, there is nothing in the manners of either but what is highly conciliating. You will like them exceedingly; and I have not a doubt they will find you altogether charming. I shall have you with us very often while they are here. Selina, I know, will be perfectly enchanted with you; indeed, I may vouchsafe to say, so will they both. Oh, I assure you, you will frequently make one of our party, whilst they are here."

Another letter came from Helen Dixon, to announce that Colonel and Mrs. Campbell would remain in Ireland at least until August. Jane was again entreated to come, and again obliged to send her regrets. A thick packet from Margaret Devere arrived soon afterwards. She wrote:

My dear Miss Fairfax,

I hope this letter finds you in good health and spirits. I was surprised to learn, from your last, that you are resolved on remaining at Highbury, despite invitations from the Dixons and the Campbells to join their party in Ireland. I trust I may conclude from this that you are finding a great deal to enjoy in your present situation. Your attachment to your aunt and grandmother must be strong indeed, to resist such inducements to quit them.—It is almost enough to make one suspect that Highbury possesses some *other* attraction which holds you there. If so, I do hope for your sake that he is charming—rich—and *very* handsome!

As for me, I continue to improve my intimacy with Mrs. H. Today she was well enough, for the first time, to call at the Rectory. Their lodgings being but a short distance from here, she walked over with her son this morning. After giving her the sternest injunction, in the most affectionate manner, to send for him as soon as she felt the least bit fatigued—and urging me to enforce his command—he left us together, and went off to the carriage house.

I will not weary you (as I did in my last) with repeating the minute particulars of our conversation, though there was much in it of interest. Mrs. H. told me more about her own life, and *his*. She also spoke with splendid acuteness of painting—about which she has evidently learnt a great deal from J.; and of society—about which her observations are both penetrating and amusing, though her impressions of *the great world* have been formed mostly at a considerable remove. On the piety of our noble *patroness*, for example, she remarked, "'Tis an ornament of the spun-sugar variety: very pretty—but I fear it will not stand up well in the heat.'

We had been talking for some time when I perceived she was growing tired. I reminded her of her son's instructions, and was about to send a servant to summon him; but she would not hear of disturbing him—was not very tired at all—was sure he would come for her when he was ready—hoped I would not find her too troublesome, if she stayed until then. In vain did I remonstrate with her; and foreseeing that no argument was likely to induce her to allow me to call for him, short of telling her I was sick of her company (which of course I could not do), I begged she would lie down on my own bed until he should return; and to this she consented with little opposition, as she really was quite fatigued. I saw her comfortably settled upstairs; and looking in on her again after a time, I found her sleeping tranquilly, so I returned to the parlour and was soon absorbed in a book.

I know not how much time passed before J. walked in; but he was clearly astonished at finding me alone, and abruptly asked where his mother was. A little flustered, I replied, 'She is upstairs, lying down—she was tired.'

'Why did you not send for me?'

'She insisted I should not—she did not like to disturb you. I persuaded her to rest here instead.'

'She is not ill?'

'I do not think so. She was asleep when last I looked, but she appeared perfectly well.'

His features relaxed a little. 'I beg your pardon, Miss Devere,' he said. 'I daresay it seems foolish that I should be so anxious about her; but she has suffered a great deal of late—and it is so soon after my father's death. I could not bear it if anything were to happen to her.'

I assured him I did not think his anxiety foolish in the least. He was still standing; and after a little interval in which he appeared somewhat irresolute, turning his hat about in his hands, he sat down in a chair opposite me.

'I wish to thank you again,' he said, 'for all your kindnesses to my mother. Your friendship has been of real
service, I think, in raising her spirits.'

'It has been a pleasure to me,' I told him, with a sincerity
which I hope he could not doubt. 'Mrs. Hammond is a more
than agreeable companion.'

Another pause; then, 'I am happy to know she has won
your approbation. You have assuredly won hers.'

I cannot describe to you, Miss Fairfax, the wonderful
look he gave me just then; nor can I adequately express
how I felt when, after several moments had gone by in silence, he spoke again: 'Maggie, I—' he began. You may
guess what I felt, to hear him call me by that name, as he
had so many, many years ago!—But he did not go on, and I
know not what he intended to say; though I have imagined
many a sweet conclusion to that bewitching beginning! Just
at that instant, however, there was a movement on the
stairs: it was Mrs. H., of course, coming down to join us.
And I must confess to you that (in spite of my affection for
her) I should have been very glad if she had not interrupted
our *tête-à-tête* for just a little while longer! They stayed but
a few minutes more after this; then J., giving her the support of his sturdy, manly arm(!), escorted her home.

O, am I not the most ridiculous creature who ever lived?
I go through every day in such a state of trembling expectancy as I can hardly bear—feeling always as though I am
on the very brink of some tremendous, wonderful change.
After all that has happened since last summer, I cannot believe it possible that he will leave Weymouth without our
first coming to some explanation—to some understanding—
or perhaps (as I sometimes think), to blows! It cannot be
that he has returned after such a period, only to leave
again; surely we have been brought together, because we
are intended to be together. Yet I continue in this state of
suspense, day after day, month after month—and nothing
is changed. I know not how much longer we can go on as
we have done; but something *must* give way, somehow.
What is broken *must* be mended!

So occupied am I with my own concerns, I have almost
neglected to give you any account of my brother and Miss L.
I ought to tell you, to begin with, that Mary is very much
improved in information since last summer; for she has applied herself with laudable diligence to reading the books
Stephen recommends to her. She is not clever, to be sure,

but neither is she quite backward; what is more, she will do anything to please him, and so gets on reasonably well. He has taken considerable pains in teaching her; and certainly his efforts have not gone unrewarded. But how much greater would the reward be, if it were to come about that he has been educating a wife for himself! As yet, however, she is still but a schoolgirl in his eyes. He seems unable to see her for what she is: a rather pretty, sweet young woman, of *marriageable* age.

But, you may be wondering, what can *you*, my dear Miss Devere, possibly do to remedy this blindness? One step I have already taken—a *very* small one, as you shall see. My brother recently suggested we resume the little tours begun last summer for Mary's benefit—in which we were so fortunate as to have your society, as well as the Campbells, and Mr. Dixon, and—but I need not tell you who was with us then. Stephen proposed that the three of us should make a trip to Dorchester; which, he said, would offer an excellent backdrop for acquainting Mary with the history of James II, the popish plot, Monmouth's rebellion, the Bloody Assizes, &c. I hastened to point out to him that Mary's accompanying us last year, among a large party of friends, and with Colonel and Mrs. Campbell to act as chaperones, could give no occasion for suspicion to anyone; but that our continuing with such outings now, with none but the two of us to attend her, *might* give rise to talk—to *expectations* which would injure her reputation if not fulfilled. That she could have any such thing as a reputation capable of injury, or could even be the object of any expectations, appeared not to have occurred to him before—and to strike him now with some force; and when she called on me a little later that day, I observed he was thoughtful and abstracted, and seemed hardly to know how to conduct himself towards her. *That* was a most promising sign, I think you will acknowledge!

As for the next part of my plan, I have exercised all of my diplomatic powers toward persuading her father to bring her to the next assembly—she did not attend them last year, as you may recall. To gain the point, I'm afraid I was compelled to promise him I would dance with him at the very same ball; which, I confess, I shall find tiresome indeed. Now, do not you think me a most praiseworthy sister, Miss Fairfax, that I should be willing to make so great a sacrifice for the sake of my dear brother's happiness? Mr. L.

even agreed to allow Mary a new gown for the occasion—
which I then assisted her in choosing; and I think that, between us, we have chosen very well indeed. It is often said, I
know, that men attend but little to what any woman has on.
But I have observed that whenever a young lady, not absolutely plain, is arrayed in her best gown—with her hair
freshly washed and cut, and arranged in the most becoming
fashion—she is certain to draw the notice of any gentleman
worth caring about. He may not be able to tell if she wears a
silk gown or a muslin, or whether her hair be 'bobbed' or 'a
la Greque'; but you may be sure he will not fail to perceive
that she is looking very well altogether. And I am very much
mistaken, if such expedients should not prove as efficacious
in my brother's case, as in any other man's.

I find by the length of this letter that I have once again
trespassed on your good nature to an unpardonable degree.
Pray feel free to impose upon me as much as you like in
your next—which I hope I may look forward to the pleasure
of receiving soon; and I promise not to grumble at the postage, no matter how excessive. Thanking you once more for
your indulgence, I remain,

Yours most aff'ly,
Margaret Devere

# Chapter Forty-Two

**ON FRANK'S RETURN** to Highbury he was invited, with his father and Mrs. Weston, to dine with the Eltons at the vicarage. Jane was asked as a matter of course, and Mr. Knightley completed the party. It was on this occasion that Jane first began to fear Mr. Knightley's suspicions had been roused against them. Once, before dinner, she glanced at Frank and discovered him gazing at her with a decidedly warm expression. Disconcerted, she immediately averted her eyes. They alighted by chance on Mr. Knightley, whose own eyes were at that moment fixed on Frank. He then briefly turned them upon herself, with a serious questioning look, and turned away.

On another evening, she and her aunt were out walking when they met with Frank and Mrs. Weston, who were on their way Hartfield. Their two parties united, and soon met Miss Woodhouse and Miss Smith returning home from their own walk, accompanied by Mr. Knightley. Emma pressed them all to go in and drink tea with her father; and as they were turning into the grounds, Mr. Perry passed by on horseback. The gentlemen spoke of his horse.

"By the bye," said Frank to Mrs. Weston presently, "what became of Mr. Perry's plan of setting up his carriage?"

Mrs. Weston looked surprised, and said, "I did not know that he ever had any such plan."

"Nay, I had it from you. You wrote me word of it three months ago."

"Me! impossible!"

"Indeed you did. I remember it perfectly. You mentioned it as what was certainly to be very soon. Mrs. Perry had told somebody, and was extremely happy about it. It was owing to *her* persuasion, as she thought his being out in bad weather did him a great deal of harm. You must remember it now?"

"Upon my word I never heard of it till this moment."

"Never! really, never! Bless me! How could it be? Then I

must have dreamt it—but I was completely persuaded—"

In the shades of the broad avenue, Jane flushed: of course, she herself had written to Frank of Mr. Perry's carriage. The truth must have struck him at the same moment, for he turned somewhat abruptly to Harriet Smith, saying,

"Miss Smith, you walk as if you were tired. You will not be sorry to find yourself at home."

The subject was not so easily disposed of, however. "What is this? What is this?" cried Mr. Weston, "about Perry and a carriage? Is Perry going to set up his carriage, Frank? I am glad he can afford it. You had it from himself, had you?"

"No, sir," replied his son, laughing, "I seem to have had it from nobody. Very odd! I really was persuaded of Mrs. Weston's having mentioned it in one of her letters to Enscombe, many weeks ago, with all these particulars—but as she declares she never heard a syllable of it before, of course it must have been a dream. I am a great dreamer. I dream of everybody at Highbury when I am away—and when I have gone through my particular friends, then I begin dreaming of Mr. and Mrs. Perry."

Jane dared not look at him, but she was listening closely to all that passed; and she was astonished to perceive, from the tone of his voice, that he was more amused than alarmed by his mistake.

"It is odd though," observed his father, "that you should have had such a regular connected dream about people whom it was not very likely you should be thinking of at Enscombe. Perry's setting up his carriage! and his wife's persuading him to it, out of care for his health—just what will happen, I have no doubt, some time or other; only a little premature. What an air of probability sometimes runs through a dream! And at others, what a heap of absurdities it is! Well, Frank, your dream certainly shows that Highbury is in your thoughts when you are absent. Emma, you are a great dreamer, I think?"

Emma was out of hearing. She had hurried on before her guests to prepare her father for their appearance, and was beyond the reach of Mr. Weston's hint.

"Why, to own the truth," cried Miss Bates, much to Jane's chagrin, "if I must speak on this subject, there is no denying that Mr. Frank Churchill might have—I do not mean to say that he did not dream it—I am sure I have sometimes the oddest dreams in the world—but if I am questioned about it, I must acknowledge that there was such an idea last spring; for Mrs. Perry herself mentioned it to my mother, and the Coles knew of it as well as ourselves—but it was quite a secret, known to nobody else, and only thought of about three days. Mrs. Perry was very anxious that he should have a carriage, and came to my mother in great spirits one morning because she thought she had prevailed. Jane, don't you remember grandmama's telling us of it when we got home?"

Jane's consternation increased as her aunt talked on without pause.

"I forget where we had been walking to—very likely to Randalls; yes, I think it was to Randalls. Mrs. Perry was always particularly fond of my mother—indeed I do not know who is not—and she had mentioned it to her in confidence; she had no objection to her telling us, of course, but it was not to go beyond; and, from that day to this, I never mentioned it to a soul that I know of. At the same time, I will not positively answer for my having never dropt a hint, because I know I do sometimes pop out a thing before I am aware. I am a talker, you know; I am rather a talker; and now and then I have let a thing escape me which I should not. I am not like Jane; I wish I were. I will answer for it she never betrayed the least thing in the world. Where is she?—Oh! just behind. Perfectly remember Mrs. Perry's coming. Extraordinary dream, indeed!"

They were entering the hall. It seemed to Jane as though every eye must be upon her, every mind suspecting her. To cover her confusion, she busied herself with her shawl. The others had walked in already, but Frank and Mr. Knightley waited at the door to let her pass. She felt instinctively that Frank was trying to catch her eye, but Mr. Knightley was watching—watching, as she imagined, with acute interest. Steeling herself to an appearance of tranquillity, she passed between them into the hall, and looked at neither.

The rest of the evening was nothing but wretchedness to her. Frank seemed bent on mortifying her, and almost determined to betray their secret. After tea, as they all sat together around the large circular table, he urged Miss Woodhouse to bring out a box of letters she had made for her little nephews. Emma obligingly produced the alphabets, and she and Frank began amusing themselves in forming words for each other, or for anybody else who would be puzzled.

He placed some letters before Jane. Apprehensive, she

gave a slight glance round the table, and applied herself to
them. It took her but a minute to discover the word—it was
*blunder*. Though irritated that he should add to the risk of
exposure by this unnecessary acknowledgement, she
pushed the letters away with a faint smile. In doing so, unfortunately, she neglected to mix them with the other
letters, and Miss Smith at once took them up and fell to
work.

"Blunder!" she exclaimed when, with the aid of Mr.
Knightley, she identified the word. Jane, in the greatest
dread of Mr. Knightley's scrutiny, felt her cheeks burning.

Next there was some banter between Frank and Emma
over another word. "Nonsense—for shame!" Emma scolded
in a low voice, though with a smile of amusement on her
lips.

"I will give it to her—shall I?" said he in the same tone.

"No, no," Emma protested with eager laughing warmth.
"You must not; you shall not, indeed."

With much trepidation did Jane see him place another
word before herself, and entreat her, with an air of sedate
civility, to study it. Quickly perceiving the word to be *Dixon*,
she could scarcely conceal her indignation. Would nothing
make him understand how deeply such foolery offended
and disgusted her? Looking up, and seeing herself watched,
she blushed still more deeply than before. Saying only, "I
did not know proper names were allowed," she pushed the
letters away, and resolved to be engaged by no other word
that could be offered. She turned towards her aunt.

"Aye, very true, my dear," cried the latter, though Jane
had not spoken a word. "I was just going to say the same
thing. It is time for us to be going indeed. The evening is
closing in, and grandmama will be looking for us. My dear
sir, you are too obliging. We really must wish you good
night."

Jane was immediately up, and wanting to quit the table;
but others were also moving, and she could not get away.
Frank anxiously pushed another collection of letters towards her. The letters—had she cared to make sense of
them—spelled *pardon*; but she swept them away unexam-
ined. It was growing dusk; the light had nearly faded from
the room, and the candles were not yet brought in. She
looked for her shawl. Frank was looking too; and presently
she found he was laying it across her shoulders, and whis-
pering something in her ear—whether apology, entreaty, or

jest, she knew not. She was more angry with him at that moment than she had ever been, and would not stay to listen to anything he might have to say.

# Chapter Forty-Three

**PLEADING A HEADACHE,** Jane retired to bed as soon as they returned home. Her aunt attended her to her room, to wring out a cloth in cool water and press it to her throbbing temples. In consideration of her niece's aching head, Miss Bates offered only a subdued, affectionate good-night of about five minutes duration, and then left her to the unceasing tumult of her own thoughts. In her restless tossing, Jane heard ten o'clock strike, then eleven, then twelve. Finally she fell into a fitful slumber, visited by harassing dreams which she could hardly separate from sober reality. She awoke before dawn to acute misery.

Was she unreasonable to be so much incensed at Frank's behaviour? Was she judging him too harshly? She could not doubt the disclosure about Mr. Perry's carriage had been inadvertent. He *ought* to have been more careful; but she could hardly condemn him for an unintentional error. But to compound the indiscretion, by spelling out *blunder* with the alphabets—and then teasing her, and mocking Miss Woodhouse, with *Dixon*! She could hardly believe it of him, but it did look very much as though he were indeed encouraging Emma's appalling suspicions.

Nor was last night the first occasion on which he had seemed to take amusement in Jane's discomfiture. She had readily pardoned his previous offences—explaining them away under the general plea of 'high spirits' (spirits which, once, she had found so irresistible!) and assuming her own expressions of displeasure would be sufficient motive for him to rectify his behaviour. Now she experienced a keen anxiety. Suppose she and Frank were, in truth, unsuited to each other—unsuited in temperament, and in principles? Suppose the man she had come to know at Weymouth—the man she had fallen in love with—were but a fiction, an invention; and the Frank Churchill of Highbury—trifling, imprudent, at times even unfeeling—were the true man!

These were Jane's thoughts as she waited wearily for the

pale light of dawn to illumine her window; yet even as she questioned, feared, and doubted, she wished he might come to talk away her misgivings—to soothe her with every proof of affection he could evince. But he was to leave for Richmond early this morning—was perhaps, at that moment, already preparing for the journey. She would not see him today. It would be no long interval before he returned again to Highbury, certainly; but she hated the thought of their being parted, even for a few days, without some restoration of understanding between them.

Hard it was for Jane to keep her mind to anything that morning. She tried first to write a letter to Helen, but could find nothing of consequence to say. Next she attempted some knitting, but after dropping several stitches through inattention, put it aside. She sat down at the piano, and played the first measures of three or four songs; but each piece reminded her of Frank, and at length she walked away with a sigh to the window, to gaze abstractedly onto the wet street below. It had begun raining just after dawn. He would have an uncomfortable ride back to Richmond, she reflected.

As noon approached, however, the sky began to clear, and Mrs. Bates and her daughter resolved on going out for their daily walk, proposing to venture as far as Mrs. Goddard's, if they did not find the road very dirty. Miss Bates urged Jane to join them, as the day was quickly brightening and she would perhaps find it too hot to walk later; but she would not go. "She was still a little under the weather after her headache—she had not slept well—she was too tired to walk."

Staring absently at the glistening puddles on High Street some time after they left, a figure coming up the road drew her attention: it was Frank! A minute later he was in Mrs. Bates's small sitting room, a sheepish but not apprehensive smile on his face.

"How lucky to find you alone!" he said cheerfully. "I am come to take my punishment like a man, you see. I know I deserve a thorough scolding—so do your worst, whatever it may be, and I shall undertake to endure it with patient resignation."

His lighthearted mood, so utterly in opposition to her own, shocked her. She turned away from him in dismay. His smile faded.

"What is it?" he cried, crossing over to her in a few long

strides. "Surely you are not still vexed over my making such a stupid mistake yesterday?"

"You ought not to be here," she said tearfully. "My aunt and grandmother may return at any minute. You must go— you must go!"

"But I shall not go, until you have told me what the matter is. I am come on purpose, as I knew you were a little angry with me—and I did not wish to go back to Richmond without seeing you. The rain gave me an excuse to put off my departure, but I cannot delay too long; so you had better tell me at once."

Oh! how she wished she might tell him all the fears and agitations that pressed upon her—but it was far too hazardous to allow him to remain. After urging him again to go, however, she found he was in earnest in his intention to stay and hear what she had to say; and she could not but yield, though she hardly knew where to begin. After a little pause, in which she attempted to gather her thoughts, she said,

"Frank, you must—you must try to be more careful. If you continue as you have been, our secret is sure to be discovered."

"If you are referring to my foolish little slip about Perry's carriage—"

"The mention of the carriage was accidental, I know. But you made matters so much worse by your subsequent actions—which certainly were *not* an accident."

"What, do you mean the alphabets? You cannot really think anyone besides ourselves would guess the significance of the word *blunder*."

"Yes, I do! I have lately begun to feel that Mr. Knightley may suspect us; and I thought he observed me sharply last night, when Mr. Perry's carriage was being discussed—and then again, when Miss Smith unscrambled the word. And if *he* does not soon guess our secret, I fear Miss Woodhouse will."

"Oh," he replied coolly, "I should not be very surprised to learn that she has already."

"What!"

"Indeed, I nearly confessed everything to her myself, before I returned to Yorkshire in February; and—"

"You nearly confessed—!" Jane was staggered by this admission. "You would have confided our secret to Miss Woodhouse! Would have risked everything, to tell *her*—

when all this time we have been lying to everyone else! To your aunt and uncle—to the Campbells—to my grandmother, and aunt Hetty—to your father, and Mrs. Weston!"

Frank looked a little ashamed of himself, and replied in a defensive tone, "You know why the secret must be kept from my aunt and uncle. As for the Campbells—had they known of our engagement, they would certainly have insisted on its being conducted openly, or broken off; as would your grandmother. And Miss Bates, you must own, is not one to be safely entrusted with a secret. Nay, she would own it herself, good soul that she is. It does pain me—it pains me very much, to deceive my father and Mrs. Weston—to deceive anyone I care for. I dislike subterfuge as much as you do."

"Do you?" she asked. "I confess, Frank, it sometimes seems to me as if—as if you find a kind of perverse amusement in all of this; as if it were a sort of game to you."

"I wish always to be forthright and truthful in everything," he insisted. "Indeed I do! But my father, Jane—I do not mean to disparage him in any way—he is the best of men; but I fear our secret would be scarcely any safer with him, than with your aunt."

"But are these not precisely the reasons why we must exercise every caution?"

"I hope I am careful to take no chances which might betray our secret."

"Yet you would have told Miss Woodhouse."

"I very *nearly* did. But I did not."

She was silent. He appeared as discontented now as she was herself, and she was loath to say anything more; but there was another subject on which she felt compelled to speak, though a glance at the clock reminded her of the risk he took in remaining.

She began again. "As we are mentioning Miss Woodhouse, Frank, I feel—I must beg you, again, to be more constrained—more discreet in your behaviour towards her."

"Are you still jealous of my attentions to Miss Woodhouse?" he replied irritably. "You know very well they mean nothing, as I have assured you a hundred times."

"They may mean nothing to you; but I fear they mean a great deal to Miss Woodhouse. I truly believe she is becoming attached to you; and it is cruel to mislead her into thinking her feelings are returned."

He recoiled at the word *cruel.* "If I had the smallest idea that my attentions might be the means of injuring her, no selfish considerations should ever induce me to continue them. But I am perfectly convinced of her indifference."

"I see no evidence of it."

"Miss Woodhouse understands me. Our tempers are very like. Her easy playfulness suits me exactly. And our relative situations are such that—my attentions to her are a matter of course—are owed her; she accepts them in that light, and knows they mean nothing more. Plainly she is not the sort of young lady to be easily attached to anyone—and that she is free of any attachment to *me*, I can assure you. Indeed, I should not be surprised to learn—as I was saying before— that she had discovered our secret early on. From some hints she has given me, I have good reason to think she has found us out at least in part. If so, you can hardly imagine she would allow herself to entertain any serious feelings for me."

The clock chimed a quarter past twelve. They both knew he must not stay longer; and there was really nothing more to be said. She saw that his reasoning was not quite consistent. Had he not previously assured her that Miss Woodhouse would never guess their secret, because she believed Jane was in love with Mr. Dixon? But she despaired of making him see her point of view; and to debate the matter further would only be making them both more unhappy. She could not bear to part from him, however, in such discord. With a mournful sigh, she said,

"I am sorry if I have been disagreeable, Frank. The last thing I wish to do is reproach you. It is only that—I do so hate to be always deceiving people—always playing a part! It seems so wicked. It makes me miserable, and—rather cross, I fear."

At once, he rewarded her with a sunny smile. "Ah! But you must remember, Jane, what Shakespeare wrote: *At lovers' perjuries, they say, Jove laughs.*"

"I do remember it," she said gloomily. "It was Juliet who said it—and I know too well how *her* story ended."

# Chapter Forty-Four

**HELEN DIXON WROTE** again from Ireland, full of news. There was a welcome addition to their limited acquaintance at Baly-craig: a Miss Bartholomew, granddaughter to Mr. Dixon's elderly neighbours, had come to Ireland to live with her grandparents. Helen and her mother had called on the young lady already, and found her exceedingly amiable.

"Miss Bartholomew," wrote Mrs. Dixon, "is just nineteen, and is to inherit her grandfather's estate—a pretty little house, and a small but pleasant park. There is nothing extraordinary in her looks, but she is rendered almost pretty by a very pleasing manner. I do think we shall get on very well together; and were I not intending that our vicar, Mr. Axelrod, should marry *you*, dear Jane, I should certainly mark him out as Miss Bartholomew's future husband. As you have already refused the exemplary Mr. Devere, however, perhaps I ought to conclude your taste does not run to clergymen—in which case I may allow Miss Bartholomew and Mr. Axelrod to make a match of it after all!"

It seemed to Jane as if all the world were bent on making matches; or at least (recollecting Mrs. Churchill) all that part of the world which was not bent on thwarting them. Miss Devere sent another report from Weymouth on the progress of her own matchmaking.

"Marriages, as the say, are made in heaven," she wrote, "—but a little earthly assistance never comes amiss; and this most recent ball has, I think, opened my brother's eyes at last. Mary looked quite lovely and grown-up in her new gown, and Stephen was all but speechless when he beheld the transformation. He was also plainly irritated at the attentions paid her by Mr. M., the tutor, and complained to me of 'that fellow's presumption' in dancing with her a second time—though he himself had almost committed the impropriety of asking her for a third! I had need to remind him that they had already danced together twice—and that only an engaged couple might do more without remark.

" 'Engaged!' he exclaimed, then lapsed into a perplexed silence. Most encouraging, indeed!

"I believe my own dances with Mary's father (which, as I had previously agreed to them on her account, I could not escape) were of some use in provoking jealousy in a different quarter—for J., too, was at the ball. Mr. L. was, as usual, conspicuously attentive. Directly after my dances with him, I danced with J.; and he did not scruple at making some rather ungenerous observations upon the able attorney's dancing, and the cast of his complexion—which I could not but impute to the *green-eyed monster*. He said little else to me beyond answering my inquiries after his mother, whom I had not had any opportunity to see that day; and seemed in rather a cross mood altogether—which I set down (not unreasonably, I hope?) to the same cause. I should of course consider it beneath me to attempt to win any man's affections by *scheming* to make him jealous. However, if he should chance, in the natural course of events, to be *driven* to jealousy—well, far be it from me, Miss Fairfax, to quarrel with the workings of Providence!"

The letters from Ireland and Weymouth were a diversion, but could not long distract Jane from the painful anxieties about Frank and their engagement, which weighed upon her mind. His letters were frequent, and affectionate as ever; but they were notes merely, and concerned chiefly with reporting the state of his aunt's health, which seemed to vary greatly from day to day. Adding to her woes, Mrs. Elton continued to urge on her the necessity of finding a situation as soon as possible, repeatedly assuring her of her own unstinting efforts toward that end; and not all of Jane's gentle repulses could persuade the lady to give them up.

Had Mrs. Elton been able to gratify her vanity through the expected visit of her brother and sister, she might have found less time for bestowing these officious attentions on her protégée. But after being long fed with hopes of a speedy visit from Mr. and Mrs. Suckling, she and all the Highbury world were obliged to endure the mortification of hearing that they could not possibly come till the autumn. Mrs. Elton was very much disappointed. It was the delay of a great deal of pleasure and parade. Her introductions and recommendations must all wait, and every projected party be still only talked of.

"But then," said she one afternoon, "why should not we

explore to Box Hill ourselves? We can always go there again
with them in the autumn."

Jane had nothing to argue against it, nor did Mrs. Elton's
*caro sposo*; so it was very soon settled that they would go.
When word of their plan got about, it soon received an
enlargement—one might say, an improvement. Miss Woodhouse and Mr. Weston had themselves been contemplating
a similar expedition; and Mr. Weston, on hearing that her
brother and sister had failed her, proposed to Mrs. Elton
that the two parties should unite, and go together. Whatever Miss Woodhouse might think of this proposal (and
Jane suspected she was not overfond of the vicar's wife),
Mrs. Elton found it an eligible one, and very readily acceded
to it.

It was now the middle of June, and the weather fine; and
Mrs. Elton was growing impatient to name the day, and settle with Mr. Weston as to pigeon-pies and cold lamb, when
a lame carriage-horse threw everything into sad uncertainty. It might be weeks, it might be only a few days, before
the horse were usable; but no preparations could be ventured on, and it was all melancholy stagnation. Mrs. Elton's
resources were inadequate to such an attack. Her spirits
were happily revived, however, by a chance remark of Mr.
Knightley's, that she had better explore to Donwell instead.

"Come, and eat my strawberries," said he. "They are ripening fast."

If Mr. Knightley did not begin seriously, he was obliged to
proceed so, for his proposal was caught at with delight.
Donwell was famous for its strawberry-beds; but cabbage-
beds would have been enough to tempt the lady, who only
wanted to be going somewhere. She promised him again
and again to come—much oftener than he doubted—and
was extremely gratified by such a proof of intimacy, such a
distinguishing compliment as she chose to consider it.

Mr. Knightley was fortunate in everybody's most ready
concurrence; the invitations were all accepted with high expectations of pleasure. Jane and her aunt were to be among
the guests; and Mr. Weston, unasked, promised to get
Frank over to join them, if possible. In the meanwhile the
lame horse recovered so fast, that the party to Box Hill was
again under happy consideration; and at last Donwell was
settled for one day, and Box Hill for the next, the weather
appearing exactly right.

Under a bright mid-day sun at almost Midsummer, the

company collected at Donwell. It was an old and estimable property, its situation low and sheltered, with an abundance of timber in rows and avenues, which neither fashion nor extravagance had rooted up. Its ample gardens stretched down to stream-washed meadows, of which the Abbey, with all the old neglect of prospect, had scarcely a sight. The house was large, rambling and irregular, with many comfortable, and one or two handsome rooms.

The party were soon assembled round the strawberry-beds, excepting Mrs. Weston, who remained sitting indoors with Mr. Woodhouse; and Frank, who was expected every moment from Richmond. Mrs. Elton, in all her apparatus of happiness, her large bonnet and her basket, was very ready to lead the way in gathering, accepting, or talking—strawberries, and only strawberries, could now be thought or spoken of. The only interruption to her discourse—of which Jane, in her preoccupation, heard scarcely ten words—occurred when Mrs. Weston came out to inquire if her son-in-law were come. She was a little uneasy, she said; she had some fears of his horse. Jane, who had been worrying only that Frank's aunt might at the last minute keep him from coming—or that, if he did come, he would come but to multiply her distress—now remembered the earlier accident with his black mare, and took up Mrs. Weston's anxieties as well.

Mrs. Elton, after half an hour, grew weary of stooping in the heat and glare of the summer sun. Seats tolerably in the shade were found; and in short order she was importuning Jane about a situation, a most desirable situation, which she had received notice of that morning.

"It is not with Mrs. Suckling, nor with Mrs. Bragge; but in felicity and splendour, I assure you, it falls short only of them! It is with a cousin of Mrs. Bragge, a Mrs. Small-ridge—an acquaintance of Mrs. Suckling, and well known at Maple Grove. My dear Jane, you can scarcely conceive how charming! She moves in quite the first circles everywhere. I am wild that you should close with the offer at once—and I give you fair warning, I shall permit no demur. I cannot allow you to let such an opportunity as this slip through your fingers! Indeed, I am determined to write as soon as I get home this evening, to accept on your behalf."

With all possible energy did Jane assure her she would not at present engage in anything, advancing the same reasons she had given many times before. Still Mrs. Elton would hear no denial, would admit no objections. She insisted on being authorised to send an acquiescence by the morrow's post. Her pertinacity was too much for Jane; and at last, with a decision of action born of desperation, she proposed a removal. "Should not they walk? Would not Mr. Knightley show them the gardens—all the gardens? She wished to see the whole extent."

It was hot; and after walking some time over the gardens in a scattered, dispersed way, scarcely any three together, they insensibly followed one another to the shade of a broad short avenue of limes which, stretching beyond the garden at an equal distance from the river, led to a view at the end, over a low stone wall. Half a mile distant was a steep, wooded bank; from its base rose the Abbey Mill Farm, with meadows in front, and the river making a close and handsome curve around it.

It was a sweet view—one before which Jane, in a different mood, would have lingered long in admiration and pleasure. But if the sun did not oppress her, Mrs. Elton's ceaseless urgings did. Though by no means in doubt of her own powers of persuasion, Mrs. Elton was now enlisting Miss Bates in her cause as well; and even aunt Hetty's good-natured chatter, her profuse expressions of gratitude to Mrs. Elton, Jane at that moment found difficult to endure.

It did occur to her that her own gratitude ought be a good deal warmer than it was—and would undoubtedly have been so, had she in fact been seeking a situation. She could not help reflecting, as Mrs. Elton described in great detail the manifold advantages of Mrs. Smallridge's household, that it might be prudent to ponder what she should do, in the event she and Frank did *not* marry—for their marrying seemed to her now very far from certain. Indeed, the possibility seemed more and more remote with each passing day; and she felt they could not go on as they were very much longer.

*If Frank only knew how I am beset,* she brooded,—*if he could but see how I am tormented by remaining in this impossible position, he would—*

Indeed, if Frank did know all her unhappiness, what would he do? Release her from her engagement? Wretched as she was at present, fearful as she was for the future, it was terrible to imagine either present or future without him. Yet given all its attendant difficulties, perhaps he would be compelled to give up the engagement after all—or would simply tire of it. Perhaps she would soon find herself in need of a situation—in need of Mrs. Elton's patronage after all!

The next remove was to the house; they must all go in and eat;—and they were all seated and busy, and still Frank did not come. Mrs. Weston was uneasy; he had expressed himself as to coming, with more than common certainty: "His aunt was so much better, that he had not a doubt of getting over to them."

Mrs. Churchill's state, however, as many were ready to remind her, was liable to such sudden variation as might disappoint her nephew in the most reasonable dependence—and Mrs. Weston was at last persuaded to agree. Jane herself was growing steadily more alarmed, though she too knew the others were probably right in attributing Frank's absence to his aunt's ill health, or her ill humour. She was made the more uneasy by a conviction that, while he was being talked of, Mr. Knightley was sometimes looking at her. She was careful to betray no emotion on the subject; but she felt pressed and harassed on every side— and unspeakably weary of everything and everyone.

The cold repast was over, and the party were to go out once more to see what had not yet been seen, the old Abbey fish-ponds; perhaps to get as far as the clover, which was to be begun cutting on the morrow, or, at any rate, to have the pleasure of being hot, and growing cool again. Only Miss Woodhouse remained within, sitting with her father, that Mrs. Weston might be persuaded away by her husband to the exercise and variety which her spirits seemed to need. Jane went out with the others; but at the first opportunity she slipped away and, resolved on going home, returned into the Abbey. Meeting with Miss Woodhouse sooner than she expected, she gave a little start at first; but composing herself as well as she could, she said,

"Will you be so kind, when I am missed, as to say that I am gone home? I am going this moment. My aunt is not aware how late it is, nor how long we have been absent— but I am sure we shall be wanted, and I am determined to go directly. I have said nothing about it to anybody. It would only be giving trouble and distress. Some are gone to the ponds, and some to the lime walk. Till they all come in I shall not be missed; and when they do, will you have the goodness to say that I am gone?"

"Certainly, if you wish it," said Emma. "But you are not

going to walk to Highbury alone?"

"Yes—what should hurt me? I walk fast. I shall be at home in twenty minutes."

"But it is too far, indeed it is, to be walking quite alone. Let my father's servant go with you. Let me order the carriage. It can be round in five minutes."

"Thank you, thank you—but on no account. I would rather walk. And for me," she added tremblingly, "to be afraid of walking alone! I, who may so soon have to guard others!"

Emma replied, in a gentle tone of real compassion, "That can be no reason for your being exposed to danger now. I must order the carriage. The heat even would be danger. You are fatigued already."

"I am," she answered. "I am fatigued; but it is not the sort of fatigue—quick walking will refresh me. Miss Woodhouse, we all know at times what it is to be wearied in spirits. Mine, I confess, are exhausted. The greatest kindness you can show me, will be to let me have my own way, and only say that I am gone when it is necessary."

Emma had not another word to oppose, but watched her safely off with the zeal of a friend.

"Oh! Miss Woodhouse," said Jane in a sudden burst of feeling as they parted, "the comfort of being sometimes alone!"

# Chapter Forty-Five

JANE HAD JUST turned out at the end of Donwell lane when she saw Frank on the road ahead, riding towards her. They soon met.

"Jane!" said he, alighting from his horse. "Is the party broken up already?"

"You are very late, Frank; we expected you hours ago. Mrs. Weston has been exceedingly anxious."

"I thought I should not be able to come at all—indeed, I could ill be spared. My aunt was taken with a nervous seizure this morning, which lasted several hours. But where are you going?"

"I am going home."

"Home! When I have come so far, in all this heat, just for the hope of spending a few hours in your company!"

"I told Miss Woodhouse I was going home—I told her to tell the others. It would hardly do for me to turn around now and go back again."

"Well—it is no matter. I shall walk with you into Highbury. I am not much in a humour for visiting anyway; it is too hot. I had much rather have a quiet walk with you."

"No—you mustn't. You must go on to Donwell. They will all be very glad to see you."

"As you are not, I see."

"Oh, Frank! You know we must not be seen walking together, or we should be in danger of being found out."

"So you have said before; but I cannot see the harm in it. I am sure I have been seen walking about with Miss Woodhouse on any number of occasions. No one remarks it."

"Are you quite sure of that?"

It did not suit him to reply to this question. Instead he said, "Am I never to see you, then? Are we never to be alone? For once here is a perfect opportunity—and it seems you cannot wait to be rid of me! You are always glad to be rid of me, I think."

"Oh! how can you say such a thing! When you know very

well—"

"How can *you* be always so cold and prudent? If you felt any real affection for me—"

"If I—!" she exclaimed. "Certainly you can have no reason to doubt *my* affection!"

"I suppose by that you mean to say you have reason to doubt mine?"

"I mean to say that—that I have not been engaged in a very conspicuous—a very hazardous—a very hurtful flirtation with someone else. *I* am not the one who has been showing to the world a—a very decided preference for another person—on the pretext of concealing a secret—which *you* seem utterly bent on betraying!—Now, I must go."

"I will come with you," he insisted.

"No. You must not.—I will not allow it."

"You will not allow it! You *refuse* to allow me to walk with you?"

"Yes!"

He fixed her with one long, searing look; then he bounded up onto his horse, and thundered off toward the Abbey without a backward glance.

If Jane had been unhappy before, she was perfectly wretched now. And tomorrow they were to meet again at Box Hill, in the presence of all their friends! What would he say then? How would he conduct himself? Would he amend his behaviour in a single particular? Or would he, perhaps, decide not to come at all?

Frank, for his part, felt quite as thoroughly miserable as Jane did. Upon arriving at Donwell, he was so cross that even Miss Woodhouse began to think him a little disagreeable. He grumbled to her about the heat, and his long ride; and he soon found it necessary to go off by himself for a long while, before he could regain a degree of coolness and civility. When he came back, she was occupied in looking at views of Switzerland; prompting him, in his dejection, to express a hope of going abroad soon.

"As soon as my aunt gets well, I shall go abroad," said he. "I shall never be easy till I have seen some of these places. You will have my sketches, some time or other, to look at— or my tour to read—or my poem. I shall do something to expose myself."

"That may be—but not by sketches in Switzerland."

The sharpness of her perception again took him by surprise. Yes, she *did* understand him—he was quite sure that she did. But what did it matter, after all? What did anything matter, now?

"You will never go to Switzerland," she added lightly. "Your uncle and aunt will never allow you to leave England."

"They may be induced to go too. A warm climate may be prescribed for her. I have more than half an expectation of our all going abroad. I assure you I have. I feel a strong persuasion, this morning, that I shall soon be abroad. I ought to travel. I am tired of doing nothing. I want a change. I am serious, Miss Woodhouse—whatever your penetrating eyes may fancy—I am sick of England, and would leave it tomorrow, if I could."

"You are sick of prosperity and indulgence," said she. "Cannot you invent a few hardships for yourself, and be contented to stay?"

"*I* sick of prosperity and indulgence! You are quite mistaken. I do not look upon myself as either prosperous or indulged. I am thwarted in everything material. I do not consider myself at all a fortunate person."

"You are not quite so miserable, though, as when you first came. Go and eat and drink a little more, and you will do very well. Another slice of cold meat, another draught of Madeira and water, will make you nearly on a par with the rest of us."

"No—I shall not stir. I shall sit by you. You are my best cure."

"We are going to Box Hill tomorrow;—you will join us. It is not Switzerland, but it will be something for a young man so much in want of a change. You will stay, and go with us?"

"No, certainly not; I shall go home in the cool of the evening."

"But you may come again in the cool of tomorrow morning."

"No—it will not be worth while. If I come, I shall be cross."

"Then pray stay at Richmond."

"But if I do, I shall be crosser still. I can never bear to think of you all there without me."

"These are difficulties which you must settle for yourself. Choose your own degree of crossness. I shall press you no more."

"Well," he said at last, "—if *you* wish me to stay and join the party, I will."

She smiled her acceptance; and nothing less than a summons from Richmond was to take him back before the following evening.

They had a very fine day for Box Hill; and all the other outward circumstances of arrangement, accommodation, and punctuality, were in favour of a pleasant party. Everybody had a burst of admiration on first arriving at their destination; but in general there was a languor, a want of spirits, a want of union, which could not be got over. They separated too much into parties. Mr. Knightley took charge of Jane and Miss Bates; the Eltons walked together; and Emma and Harriet belonged to Frank. It seemed at first an accidental division, but it never materially varied. Mr. Weston tried to make them harmonize better; but there seemed a principle of separation among them, too strong for any fine prospects, or any cold collation, or any cheerful Mr. Weston, to remove.

At length, however, they were all required to sit down together. When they did so, Frank—who, in walking about with Miss Smith and Miss Woodhouse, had been remarkably silent and stupid—became suddenly talkative and gay, making Emma his first object. Every distinguishing attention that could be paid, was paid to her. To amuse her, and be agreeable in her eyes, seemed all that he cared for; and she gave him every encouragement. Jane observed the spectacle with mounting anger and disgust. Had Frank's design been to plague and offend her, he could not have done a more thorough job of it.

"How much I am obliged to you, Miss Woodhouse," said he, "for telling me to come today! If it had not been for you, I should certainly have lost all the happiness of this party. I had quite determined to go away again."

"Yes, you were very cross," she replied, "and I do not know what about, except that you were too late for the best strawberries. I was a kinder friend than you deserved. But you were humble. You begged hard to be commanded to come."

"Don't say I was cross. I was fatigued. The heat overcame me."

"It is hotter today."

"Not to my feelings. I am perfectly comfortable today."

"You are comfortable because you are under command."

"Your command?—Yes."

"Perhaps I intended you to say so, but I meant self-command. You had, somehow or other, broken bounds yesterday, and run away from your own management; but today you are got back again—and as I cannot be always with you, it is best to believe your temper under your own command rather than mine."

"It comes to the same thing. I can have no self-command without a motive. You order me, whether you speak or not. And you can be always with me. You are always with me."

"Dating from three o'clock yesterday. My perpetual influence could not begin earlier, or you would not have been so much out of humour before."

"Three o'clock yesterday! That is your date. I thought I had seen you first in February."

"Your gallantry is really unanswerable. But," (lowering her voice) "—nobody speaks except ourselves, and it is rather too much to be talking nonsense for the entertainment of seven silent people."

"I say nothing of which I am ashamed," replied he, with lively impudence. "I saw you first in February. Let everybody on the Hill hear me if they can. Let my accents swell to Mickleham on one side, and Dorking on the other. I saw you first in February." He whispered something to her, and then—

"Ladies and gentlemen," he announced, "I am ordered by Miss Woodhouse (who, wherever she is, presides) to say, that she desires to know what you are all thinking of?"

Some laughed, and answered good-humouredly. Miss Bates said a great deal; Mrs. Elton swelled at the idea of Miss Woodhouse's presiding; Mr. Knightley's answer was the most distinct.

"Is Miss Woodhouse sure that she would like to hear what we are all thinking of?"

"Oh! no, no," cried Emma, laughing. "Upon no account in the world. It is the very last thing I would stand the brunt of just now. Let me hear anything rather than that."

"It is a sort of thing," cried Mrs. Elton emphatically, "which I should not have thought myself privileged to inquire into. Though, perhaps, as the *chaperon* of the party—I never was in any circle—exploring parties—young ladies—married women—"

Her mutterings were chiefly to her husband; and he murmured, in reply, "Very true, my love, very true. Exactly so, indeed—quite unheard of—but some ladies say anything. Better pass it off as a joke. Everybody knows what is due to you."

Again, Frank whispered something to Emma, then declared, "Ladies and gentlemen—I am ordered by Miss Woodhouse to say, that she waives her right of knowing exactly what you may all be thinking of, and only requires something very entertaining from each of you, in a general way. Here are seven of you, besides myself (who, she is pleased to say, am very entertaining already), and she only demands from each of you either one thing very clever, be it prose or verse, original or repeated—or two things moderately clever—or three things very dull indeed, and she engages to laugh heartily at them all."

"Oh! very well," exclaimed Miss Bates, "then I need not be uneasy. 'Three things very dull indeed.' That will just do for me, you know. I shall be sure to say three dull things as soon as ever I open my mouth, shan't I?" (looking round with the most good-humoured dependence on everybody's assent) "Do not you all think I shall?"

"Ah! ma'am," said Emma archly, "but there may be a difficulty. Pardon me—but you will be limited as to number—only three at once."

Miss Bates, deceived by the mock ceremony of her manner, did not immediately catch her meaning; but, when it burst on her, it could not anger, though a slight blush showed that it could pain her.

"Ah!—well—to be sure. Yes, I see what she means," (turning to Mr. Knightley) "and I will try to hold my tongue. I must make myself very disagreeable, or she would not have said such a thing to an old friend."

Jane stared at Miss Woodhouse in horror. Miss Woodhouse, who had been so kind to her yesterday—Miss Woodhouse, whom she had even pitied for being the dupe of Frank's intrigues! That Miss Woodhouse did not esteem her aunt just as she ought, was by no means unknown to Jane; but that she could be, not merely uncivil, but openly, wantonly cruel to her, was what Jane would never have believed, had she not heard it with her own ears! Mr. Knightley was plainly indignant. Even Frank looked a little ashamed.

Mr. Weston, anxious to smoothe over any unpleasantness, immediately offered up a conundrum. "I doubt its being very clever myself," said he. "It is too much a matter of fact, but here it is: What two letters of the alphabet are there, that express perfection?"

"What two letters," said Emma, "express perfection! I am sure I do not know."

"Ah! you will never guess. I will tell you: M. and A.—Emma. Do you understand?"

Understanding and gratification came together. It might be a very indifferent piece of wit, but Miss Woodhouse found a great deal to laugh at and enjoy in it—and so did Frank and Miss Smith. It did not seem to touch the rest of the party equally; some looked very stupid about it, and Mr. Knightley gravely said,

"This explains the sort of clever thing that is wanted, and Mr. Weston has done very well for himself; but he must have knocked up everybody else. *Perfection* should not have come quite so soon."

"Oh! for myself, I protest I must be excused," said Mrs. Elton. "I really cannot attempt—I am not at all fond of the sort of thing. I had an acrostic once sent to me upon my own name, which I was not at all pleased with. I knew who it came from. An abominable puppy!—you know who I mean," (nodding to her husband). "These kind of things are very well at Christmas, when one is sitting round the fire; but quite out of place, in my opinion, when one is exploring about the country in summer. Miss Woodhouse must excuse me. I am not one of those who have witty things at everybody's service. I have a great deal of vivacity in my own way, but I really must be allowed to judge when to speak and when to hold my tongue. Pass us, if you please, Mr. Churchill. Pass Mr. E., Knightley, Jane, and myself. We have nothing clever to say—not one of us."

"Yes, yes, pray pass me," added her husband, with a sort of sneering consciousness. "I have nothing to say that can entertain Miss Woodhouse, or any other young lady. An old married man—quite good for nothing. Shall we walk, Augusta?"

"With all my heart. I am really tired of exploring so long on one spot. Come, Jane, take my other arm."

Jane declined it, however, and the husband and wife walked off.

"Happy couple!" said Frank, as soon as they were out of hearing. "How well they suit one another! Very lucky—marrying as they did, upon an acquaintance formed only in a public place! They only knew each other, I think, a few weeks in Bath! Peculiarly lucky!—for as to any real knowledge of a person's disposition that Bath, or any public

place, can give—it is all nothing; there can be no knowledge. It is only by seeing women in their own homes, among
their own set, just as they always are, that you can form
any just judgement. Short of that, it is all guess and luck—
and will generally be ill-luck. How many a man has committed himself on a short acquaintance, and rued it all the rest
of his life!"

His meaning was unmistakable. Jane, who had borne his
taunts in silence so far, now felt obliged to respond.

"Such things do occur, undoubtedly," she began, full of
anger and injury; but the very passions urging her to speak
stopped her throat, and prevented her continuing at once.
She coughed a little, endeavouring to subdue her emotions,
and Frank turned towards her.

"You were speaking," said he, gravely.

She recovered her voice. "I was only going to observe
that—though such unfortunate circumstances do sometimes occur, both to men *and* women—I cannot imagine
them to be very frequent. A hasty and imprudent attachment may arise—but there is generally time to recover from
it afterwards. I would be understood to mean, that it can be
only weak, irresolute characters—whose happiness must be
always at the mercy of chance—who will suffer an unfortunate acquaintance to be an inconvenience—an oppression
for ever."

He made no answer; merely looked, and bowed in submission. Soon afterwards he declared, in a tone of affected
liveliness,

"Well, I have so little confidence in my own judgement,
that whenever I marry, I hope somebody will choose my wife
for me. Will you?" (turning to Emma). "Will you choose a
wife for me?—I am sure I should like anybody fixed on by
you. You provide for the family, you know," (with a smile at
his father). "Find somebody for me. I am in no hurry. Adopt
her, educate her."

"And make her like myself."

"By all means, if you can."

"Very well. I undertake the commission. You shall have a
charming wife."

"She must be very lively, and have hazel eyes. I care for
nothing else. I shall go abroad for a couple of years—and
when I return, I shall come to you for my wife. Remember."

Jane had heard quite enough. "Now, ma'am," said she to
her aunt, "shall we join Mrs. Elton?"

"If you please, my dear. With all my heart. I am quite ready. I was ready to have gone with her, but this will do just as well. We shall soon overtake her. There she is—no, that's somebody else. That's one of the ladies in the Irish car party, not at all like her. Well, I declare—"

They walked off together. In half a minute Mr. Knightley joined them. Jane would rather not have had his keen eye regarding her just then; but luckily, he was too much occupied in soothing Miss Bates's feelings to take much notice of her. Fighting back tears, Jane could offer few words herself, to raise her aunt's spirits; but she endeavoured to show by a fond look, and a pressing of her hand, and by clinging affectionately to her, how very dear she was; dearer than ever, indeed, now that Frank had so betrayed and disappointed her. Aunt Hetty's generosity—her candour and forbearance in excusing Emma's insolence, and taking the blame onto herself—her praising Miss Woodhouse for always showing her so much attention, when her society must be so irksome, stood in sharp contrast to Frank's treachery. Her goodness only made Jane love her and cling to her the more.

They walked on together until they overtook the Eltons. Mrs. Elton had been handsomely abusing Miss Woodhouse to her husband ever since they separated from the rest of the party, and in the present company she scrupled not to continue. She gave her friends every opening to join in the censure, but to no avail. Jane, though aggrieved on her aunt's account and jealous on her own, would not utter a word against her; nor would Miss Bates. Mr. Knightley, however displeased he had been by Emma's remarks, was clearly no better pleased by Mrs. Elton's. Finding herself unable to enlist anyone but Mr. Elton in her cause, she wisely changed the subject.

"You must all spend your evening with us," she declared. "I positively must have you *all* come."

Mr. Knightley at once declined; and though she insisted he should not be let off, he was so steady in his refusals that she had at last to submit. But Miss Bates needed no persuading, and Jane, feeling she could as well be miserable at the vicarage as at home—and wishing, since she herself could not be happy, that her aunt might be made so—did not oppose her inclination.

The appearance of the servants, giving notice of the carriages, was a joyful sight. It was settled that the Eltons would leave Jane and Miss Bates at their house, and would send the carriage back for them at seven o'clock. It would be more than enough time, Jane calculated as she returned home and climbed the stairs to her grandmother's apartment, for Frank to come to her with some explanation—to send some message of penitence, at least, for his behaviour. That he would leave Highbury without offering any apology was impossible. Though it meant their secret must be revealed to her aunt—to her grandmother—to the whole world besides—he *would* come. He would come, and be contrite, and talk all her anger away. She was expecting him every moment. He would come and make everything right again. She held tightly to a hope that all might yet be mended, if he chose it—and to a belief that he *would* choose it. She intended she should not be too easily won over; but in her heart, she did intend to be won over at last.

# Chapter Forty-Six

**HE DID NOT** come. But, she reflected—having again followed her aunt into the Eltons' carriage, and cast one last look down the Randalls road as they drove off—he would surely come tomorrow, before he rode back to Richmond. No doubt he had put off calling till then, that he might have a chance of finding her alone. A tedious evening with the Eltons would have to be endured in the interim; but aunt Hetty's spirits were much restored by the prospect of the visit, which must be her present comfort.

The small party collected at the vicarage that evening seemed rather fagged after the outing to Box Hill; and had it not been for Miss Bates's desultory chat, they should all have been exceedingly dull. Just before tea, Mr. Elton was called out of the room on parish business; and Mrs. Elton then began to talk again of that desirable situation which, in spite of all Jane's emphatic declarations, that lady was still determined she should take. Finding her now still firmly, if somewhat abstractedly, opposing these designs, Mrs. Elton renewed her efforts with Miss Bates; between them, she believed, they would surely wear out Jane's resistance.

"Leaving aside Maple Grove, of course, and Mrs. Bragge's," said she, "I assure you, my dear Miss Bates, there is not such another nursery establishment so liberal and elegant in all my acquaintance."

"Indeed!" answered Miss Bates.

"Oh yes—no situation could possibly be more replete with comfort, excepting only Mrs. Suckling's and Mrs. Bragge's; but Mrs. Smallridge is intimate with both. A most delightful woman! Her style of living is very nearly equal to that of Maple Grove, and in the very same neighbourhood: only four miles away."

"Jane should like it of all things, I am sure. Imagine, my dear," (to her niece) "just four miles from Maple Grove!"

"And as for the children—why, excepting the little Sucklings and the little Bragges, there are not such elegant sweet children anywhere."

"I have not a doubt of it. The little Smallridges—most enchanting children, certainly!"

"Your niece will be treated with such regard and kindness! It will be a life of pleasure—nothing but pleasure, from one week to the next. And the salary—"

"I daresay it must be very liberal."

"Liberal! Why, my dear Miss Bates, even you and I, knowing how very much our sweet girl deserves, must think it quite equal to her merits."

In a low voice Mrs. Elton named a figure, and Miss Bates's hushed exclamations of "Goodness me!" and "Upon my word!" and "Can it be so?" told her she had hit her mark.

The vicar soon returned, apologising for his neglect; but old John Abdy's son, he said, had been most urgent in wishing to speak with him.

"Ah," said Miss Bates. "Poor old John! I have a great regard for him. He was clerk to my dear father twenty-seven years; and now, poor old man, he is bed-ridden, and very poorly with the rheumatic gout. I really must go and see him tomorrow. Perhaps, Jane, you will go with me to call on him? I suppose" (to Mr. Elton) "the son came to ask you about relief from the parish. He is very well to do himself, I know—being head man at the Crown, ostler, and everything of that sort—but still, I suppose he cannot keep his father without some help."

Such indeed had been the purpose of his call at the vicarage; and there was a general discussion about the ostler and his ailing father while Mr. Elton drank his tea.

"By the bye," said he, helping himself to a bit of cake, "John told me a chaise was sent out to Randalls this evening, to take Frank Churchill back to Richmond posthaste."

"Indeed!" said Mrs. Elton with a smirk. "Is it possible he has quarrelled with our good Miss Emma?—Perhaps he discovered she was plotting marry *him* off to Harriet Smith, and could not get himself away fast enough!—But why should he not go back on his own horse, I wonder?"

What Mr. Elton had learned from the ostler on the subject (being the accumulation of the ostler's own knowledge, and the knowledge of the servants at Randalls) was, that a messenger had come over from Richmond soon after the return of the party from Box Hill—which messenger, however, had been no more than was expected; and that Mr. Churchill had sent his nephew a few lines, containing, upon the whole, a tolerable account of Mrs. Churchill, and only wishing him not to delay coming back beyond the next morning early; but that Frank, having resolved to go home directly, and his horse seeming to have got a cold, Tom had been sent off immediately for the Crown chaise, and the ostler had stood out and seen it pass by, the boy going a good pace, and driving very steady.

Jane could scarcely believe what she heard. Frank had gone back to Richmond! Though he might have stayed—had permission to stay—he had chosen to go! Had he carved the words in marble, the message could not be more clear. There would be no apology, no reconciliation; she had been a fool to expect it. He was wearied of her, wearied of their engagement. He did not wish to be forgiven. He would not forgive.

He did not love her anymore!

After they had finished their tea, she took Mrs. Elton aside; and, with as much composure as she could summon, said that upon thinking over the advantages of the situation at Mrs. Smallridge's, she had resolved on accepting it. Mrs. Elton was ecstatic; and after praising her good sense—and confiding how she had known from the first that she should persuade her in the end—told her Mrs. Smallridge was in a great hurry, and could she be ready to leave within a fortnight? Jane gave a listless assent; then she went to tell her aunt what she had been saying to Mrs. Elton, and Mrs. Elton at the same moment came to congratulate Miss Bates upon it.

**JANE DID** lie down upon her bed that night; but she did not close her eyes. After a long and wretched night, she arose with the first light. Seating herself then in a chair by her bedroom window, she put down on paper the short letter she had spent most of the night composing in her head.

Dear Frank, (she wrote)

The events of the past few days have made it quite clear to me, that it will be best for us not to meet again. Perhaps it was never to be expected that any good could come from a connection such as ours, entered into so heedlessly, and maintained in such secrecy. At all events—as your sentiments on this matter were yesterday so plainly expressed as to be unmistakable—I must conclude that you would welcome a release from our engagement. Indeed, I feel it has long been a source of repentance and misery to us both. I therefore dissolve it, and free you to form another attachment more agreeable to your notions of happiness.

J.

With tolerable sang-froid, she folded up the letter, addressed it, sealed it, and locked it, for the moment, in her writing desk. Then she burst into tears, and wept inconsolably, till her eyes and nose were red, and her head ached.

Her grandmother and aunt were soon astir, and the three ladies ate an unwontedly solemn and silent breakfast together. Mrs. Bates and her daughter were almost as much affected as Jane herself; for though delighted with her great good fortune in obtaining such a superior situation, they could not but be sorry to part with her. After breakfast, Jane sat down to write the necessary letters to Helen Dixon and Colonel Campbell, her eyes filling with tears all the while.

"My dear,' said Miss Bates, her own eyes welling up in sympathy, "you will blind yourself."

"Dearest aunt," Jane exclaimed, gratefully taking up her hand, "Do not be distressed. It is only the trial of writing these letters—but I am nearly done. I will post them directly I have finished; and once I have sent them off, I know I will soon be better—I will soon be well."

"Colonel and Mrs. Campbell will be sorry to find that you have engaged yourself before their return."

"Yes—I am sure they will be; but I am only acting on what has long been intended. They will not fail to see that this is such a situation as I could not feel myself justified in declining."

After a few minutes, she took up both letters—adding to them, unobserved, the one which she had earlier shut up in her writing desk—and walked to the post-office; still sustaining a small, irrational hope, much tempered with despair, that the morning post would yet bring some word from Frank. She had posted the letters and was about to leave, when the post-mistress hailed her.

"Wait, Miss Fairfax—just a moment! Here is something come for you this morning, after all; I had quite overlooked it."

In spite of her throbbing head, Jane brightened instantly, and hastened to receive the letter which was held out to her. A quick glance at the direction, however, told her that it came, not from Frank, but from Margaret Devere.

She returned home bitterly dispirited. For her grand-mother's sake, and her aunt's, she endeavoured to repress her tears, but it was impossible they should not perceive her sorrow. Unable to sit still, moving restlessly about the room, at length she halted before the pianoforte. It was but a short time since it first arrived in their little parlour; yet how long ago it seemed! How rash and imprudent a gift she had then thought it—how greatly she had disapproved it—and yet, how foolishly happy it had made her! Surely Frank had loved her, truly loved her, then. What had become of all his devoted attachment?

And what was to become of the pianoforte?

"You must go," she said aloud with a deep sigh. "You and I must part. You will have no business here."

Miss Bates came up then, and wordlessly put a comfort-ing arm around her.

"Let it stay, however," said Jane, laying her head upon her aunt's shoulder. "Give it houseroom till Colonel Camp-bell comes back. I shall talk about it to him. He will settle for me. He will help me out of all my difficulties."

They expected no callers at that hour, and so were not aware anyone was come until they heard the tread of foot-steps on the stairs. Jane was disturbed by the sound, and instantly turned to withdraw.

"It is only Mrs. Cole, depend upon it," said Miss Bates. "Nobody else would come so early."

"Well," said Jane, decisively, "it must be borne some time or other, and it may as well be now."

Patty came in and announced, "Miss Woodhouse."

"Oh!" said her aunt, "it is Miss Woodhouse; I am sure you will like to see her."

Miss Woodhouse! The last person in the world she could bear to face now! "I can see nobody," said she, and in great haste retreated to her bedroom.

Her aunt followed her out just as Patty was opening the door to admit their guest. "Well, my dear," said Miss Bates,

"I shall say you are laid down upon the bed, and I am sure you are ill enough. I will tell her you are you extremely sorry to miss seeing her; but her kindness will excuse you. Indeed Jane, do lie down—you are quite worn out. A little rest will do you good, I daresay."

Jane, however, could find no more repose in her bedroom than in the parlour, and continued her restless movements. She could hear Emma and aunt Hetty talking together in the other room, the former speaking in soft tones of sympathy and concern, the latter replying with civility and gratitude. That her aunt could endure Miss Woodhouse's company; could talk even of her kindness, after yesterday's affront, was astonishing to Jane—or would have been, had she been less thoroughly acquainted with the unvarying sweetness of her aunt's disposition.

Her own sentiments regarding Miss Woodhouse were rather more complicated than Miss Bates's. She deplored the deception Frank had been practising on Emma, and had often felt both shame and pity on her account; but at the moment these nobler sensations were all but sunk in jealousy. What had Frank said? That Emma *understood him*—that their tempers were *very like*—that her easy playfulness *suited him exactly*! For all his jokes at Emma's expense, all his thoughtless trifling with Emma's feelings—no doubt he would end by marrying Emma Woodhouse after all!

She consumed almost nothing at dinner that evening, in spite of all Miss Bates's solicitous urgings. Everything put before her was distasteful. It was not until after dinner that she recollected Miss Devere's letter, still unopened in her reticule. Though without much feeling of interest, she retrieved and read it. It announced, in words of real, unselfish gratification, the success of her matchmaking scheme: Mr. Devere had yesterday made an offer of marriage to Miss Lodge—and had been instantly, joyfully accepted.

Jane could read no further; tears stung at her eyes and blurred the page before her. It must not be supposed, however, that in light of present circumstances, she regretted having refused the clergyman's proposals herself. Though she might wish she had been able to feel for him those feelings that a wife ought to feel for a husband, she had never felt them; she had been in love with someone else, and could not now wish to have acted otherwise than as she had acted. Mr. Devere was an excellent man, an exemplary man, and he deserved to be made happy; and Mary Lodge was a good-natured, unaffected girl, who loved him devotedly. It was in every way a match to be rejoiced in, not deplored.

And she did not deplore it, by any means. But she was seized by a very mournful conviction, that the affection and companionship accorded to others seemingly as a matter of course, were to be forever denied her. She was ashamed of herself, ashamed of her tears, ashamed she could not be unreservedly glad for Mr. Devere and Miss Lodge. If she was not granted their good fortune, it was because she was not worthy of it. She was an impostor. Her friends thought her possessed of every virtue; but she knew differently. She knew herself to be a deceitful, ungrateful, selfish, resentful, jealous creature. Was it any wonder Frank had come to despise her? Surely, it was not in his nature to be cruel or inconstant. Had she not seen proof enough of his goodness at Weymouth, in all his kindnesses to his old governess? Was he not loved and valued by his aunt and uncle—by his father and Mrs. Weston? Was he not held in high esteem by all who knew him?

No, Frank was not to blame for their present misunderstandings. If he had been thoughtless and hurtful in his conduct of late—if he had behaved badly—she herself had most assuredly driven him to it.

# Chapter Forty-Seven

**THE NEXT DAY** Mrs. Cole called with a prodigious piece of news; she had it from Mrs. Weston herself. An express from Richmond had been received that very morning at Randalls, to announce the death of Mrs. Churchill! Though her nephew had had no particular reason to hasten back on her account, she had not lived above six-and-thirty hours after his return. A sudden seizure, of a different nature from anything foreboded by her general state, had carried her off after a short struggle. The great Mrs. Churchill was no more.

Jane heard the report with a jolt—and was shocked to find how little attention she could spare to the contemplation of Mrs. Churchill's sufferings, and the grief of her husband. As Miss Bates and Mrs. Cole talked over the news, her thoughts flew to Frank; and she could only think what an alteration was effected in his circumstances by this event! It was Mrs. Churchill's pride, she knew, and not her husband's, which had stood in the way of their happiness. Her influence ended, no doubt Mr. Churchill would be easily persuaded to consent to any arrangement, any alliance Frank might propose. But it was too late. Too late!

"It is a sad event," said Mrs. Cole.

"A great shock," agreed Miss Bates. "A very great shock indeed. To think how we have always believed her complaints to be quite imaginary! For I must confess that I, for one, was convinced her illnesses were nothing but fancies; and indeed, Mr. Weston hinted to me more than once, just between ourselves—. Poor Mrs. Churchill! No doubt she has been suffering a great deal—more than anybody ever supposed; and continual pain, you know, *will* try the temper. It must be very terrible, to be always in some affliction; and I am sure we all ought to pity her, poor lady. My mother and I, thank heaven! have always enjoyed excellent health. Jane has now and then known a little indisposition, I am sorry to say; but of course, she is only too inclined to make light of anything of the kind. But Mama is really quite remarkably hale—save for a few aches and pains in damp weather, when the rheumatism is apt to bother her—which is only to be expected at her age, however; and indeed I am apt to feel a touch of it about the knees myself, when it is very damp; but only when it is *very* damp, because I have such a nice thick flannel petticoat—and indeed, so has my mother—which I daresay is at least partly responsible for her keeping in such good health. And she still sees very well, too, with the aid of her spectacles—which Mr. Frank Churchill was so kind as to fix for her when the rivet came out, and they have been just like new ever since. How grieved he will be over his aunt's passing! But he will be such a great comfort to his uncle—his only comfort now. Poor Mr. Churchill! I understand he was quite devoted to his wife. I hope his own health is not too much injured by the sad event, poor man. At his time of life, you know—! Even with all her faults, what will he do without her? His loss will be dreadful indeed. I daresay he will never get over it."

It was not until Mrs. Cole had left them, that Miss Bates first observed how very ill her niece was looking. Jane was in fact so much indisposed that it was soon judged necessary, though against her own consent, to call in Mr. Perry to examine her. The apothecary found her suffering under severe headaches and a nervous fever, to a degree which made him doubt the possibility of her going to Mrs. Smallridge's at the time proposed. Her health seemed for the moment completely deranged, her appetite quite gone; and though there were no absolutely alarming symptoms—nothing touching the pulmonary complaint which was the standing apprehension of the family—he was uneasy about her. He thought she had undertaken more than she was equal to, and that she felt it so herself, though she would not own it. Her spirits seemed overcome.

Happening to call at Hartfield later that same morning, Mr. Perry ventured to confide his opinion of Miss Fairfax's health to Miss Woodhouse. Her present home, he could not but observe, was unfavourable to a nervous disorder: confined always to one room—he could have wished it otherwise—and her good aunt, though his very old friend, he must acknowledge to be not the best companion for an invalid of that description. Her care and attention could not be questioned; they were, in fact, only too great. He very much feared that Miss Fairfax derived more evil than good from them.

Miss Woodhouse, with a genuine desire to be of use, wrote a note to Jane urging her to spend a day at Hartfield. However kindly intended, the invitation could scarcely have afflicted Jane more grievously, had it been sent on purpose to torment her—suggesting as it did so many painful circumstances to her mind, with which its author was inextricably connected. She refused it only by a verbal message, saying she was not well enough to write.

The following morning brought fresh trials. She wished for nothing so much as quiet and solitude; but was obliged instead to endure the many kind wishes and solicitous inquiries of all her friends. Mrs. Elton, of course, could not be denied—and Mrs. Cole made such a point—and Mrs. Perry said so much; and thus, in feeble smiles and faint thank-yous, was half the morning consumed. From Mrs. Perry, at least, she learned that a short letter from Frank had been received at Randalls. His uncle was better than could be expected, he wrote; and their first removal, on the departure of the funeral for Yorkshire, was to be to the house of a very old friend in Windsor, to whom Mr. Churchill had been promising a visit the last ten years.

Regardless of her indisposition, Jane had not neglected her early walk to the post-office that morning, thinking—hoping—that Frank might have managed, even in the midst of his present obligations, to send some manner of reply to her letter. That he had not done so, she had accounted for by supposing he was too much occupied with pressing family business to write. With Mrs. Perry's report, however, came the painful recognition that *she* was his only correspondent so slighted.

Mrs. Perry had just left them when another note was delivered from Hartfield. Miss Woodhouse wrote again, in the most feeling language, to say that she would call in the carriage at any hour Jane would name, to take her for an airing; mentioning that she had Mr. Perry's decided opinion in favour of such exercise for his patient. Feeling oppressed and persecuted to an intolerable degree by these attentions, Jane nonetheless roused herself to return a very brief note; saying, with her compliments and thanks, that she was quite unequal to any exercise. An hour later the persevering Miss Woodhouse called at Mrs. Bates's house in her carriage, in the hope that Jane would yet be induced to join her. Jane sent her aunt down to convey her refusal; but

Miss Woodhouse, having once made up her mind, was not easily deterred. At her behest, Miss Bates was in and out of doors, up the stairs and down several times, in attempts to persuade her niece; though even she could not fail to perceive that the mere proposal of going out seemed to make Jane worse. When Emma at last threatened to come upstairs herself and try her own powers of persuasion, Jane was compelled to extract a promise from her aunt, that she would on no account let Miss Woodhouse come up.

She thought this final rebuff must put an end to such insupportable kindnesses; but half an hour later, some arrowroot of very superior quality arrived from Hartfield, with a most friendly note from Miss Woodhouse, saying she hoped the gift might prove of benefit in stimulating Miss Fairfax's appetite. With an uncommon energy did Jane demand that the arrowroot be returned, as a thing she could not take; and she insisted, moreover, on her aunt's stating in reply, that she was not at all in want of anything.

Her fragile spirits could bear no more. Over the anxious objections of Miss Bates, she escaped from the cramped rooms, the confined little house, and struck out heatedly, walking down Broadway Lane towards Clayton Park. She did not slow her pace until she reached the lush, green meadows sweeping away beyond the fields and pastures of Farmer Mitchell. There she wandered mournfully among the nettles and daisies for much of the afternoon; and not before the irritation of her nerves had been a little tranquillised by the beauty and peace which surrounded her, did she return home to a dinner she could not eat.

As the days passed, her thoughts and emotions varied wildly from one moment to the next. In the morning, she would be full of indignation toward Frank, imputing to him all manner of faithlessness and misconduct; in the evening, she would soften towards him, and hold herself at fault for everything that had gone wrong between them. Before breakfast, she would be struck with the strongest feelings of remorse toward Miss Woodhouse; after dinner she would work herself into a perfect fever of jealous agitation at the thought of her. Having voluntarily chosen to contract an engagement in secret, she at times reproached herself for not accepting with a better grace the many difficulties which such an arrangement must, of necessity, entail. By and by she would condemn herself for having been so ready, whatever the motive, to deceive all her friends—for having consented to so dishonourable an arrangement at all.

Several days passed in much the same fashion, though with the improvement, at least, of no further overtures from Miss Woodhouse. Aunt Hetty fretted and fussed over her continually; but not all Miss Bates's bustle and worry could revive her appetite, or bring the bloom back into her pale, thin face. Still no reply came from Frank. However, he wrote twice more to Mrs. Weston, from whom it was learned that he and his uncle had already removed to Windsor.

All hope was now utterly extinguished. But when once this affair was truly over—when once she was actually installed in Mrs. Smallridge's household, in a new neighbourhood, and with new duties to occupy her—her health and spirits, she told herself, were sure to improve speedily. It was only the uncertainty—and the waiting—and the painful reminders of Frank meeting her at every turn, which so oppressed her mind.

Late one night, she wrote him another note, expressing her very great surprise at having received not the smallest answer to her last. "As silence on such a point cannot be misconstrued," she added, "and as it must be equally desirable to us both to have every subordinate arrangement concluded as soon as possible, I am sending you, by a safe conveyance, all your letters. If you cannot command mine so as to send them to Highbury within a week, please forward them to me after that period, in care of Mr. Robert Smallridge, Hazelwood Court, Henbury, Gloucestershire."

Frank's whereabouts in Windsor had been opportunely disclosed by Mrs. Cole; but Jane could not send her note there: should a letter from Miss Fairfax to Mr. Frank Churchill come into her hands, the Highbury post-mistress could hardly be expected to keep so interesting a piece of news to herself. With the hope that he had at least remembered to arrange for his letters to be forwarded from Richmond, she directed the note to "Miss Frances Cramer," at the address he had previously made use of there. She then gathered together all the letters he had ever written to her and, weeping quietly, wrapped them up in a tidy parcel to be returned to him.

As early as possible on the following morning, she walked out to despatch her letter at the post-office. The parcel she entrusted to a tradesman who, passing through Highbury regularly on his route to London, was often employed by its residents to carry packages to town. The accomplishment of these errands did not accord her quite the full measure of relief which she had anticipated from them; but she ventured to hope she would be rational again before very long.

Two or three days afterwards, she determined it was time to begin preparing for the removal to Gloucestershire. Miss Bates attempted to dissuade her, repeatedly saying she was much too weak even to consider making the journey as yet. But Jane, though far from convinced herself, hastened to assure her aunt that dread of the change hanging over her was more to blame for her present ill-health than anything else; and that, once settled in her new situation, she would soon grow accustomed to it, and would be quite well again.

Miss Bates and her mother were now gone out for their morning walk, planning to call on Mrs. Cole in their way. With the prospect of at least half an hour's solitude before her, Jane retired to her bedroom to begin the requisite sorting and packing of her belongings. She had not got beyond looking through the small stack of books lying on her little bedside table—deciding she would take two of these with her to Gloucestershire, and leave two behind—when Patty came into the room in search of her, and announced,

"Mr. Frank Churchill."

# Chapter Forty-Eight

**SO LITTLE EXPECTATION** did Jane have of ever seeing Frank again that, with a slight start at the sound of his name, she could only look blankly at Patty, and wonder what she meant by uttering it.

"I told the young gentleman," said Patty, "that Mrs. Bates and Miss Bates was out; but he said he wished to speak to *you*, Miss, if you was at home—said he wished to speak to you most particular. So I made free to show him into the parlour, as I thought you wouldn't refuse to see him. Shall I tell him you'll be right out, Miss?"

It took a few moments for Jane, after comprehending that Frank was indeed in the house, to recover the power of speech. What could he mean by coming here? Did he doubt he was truly released from their engagement, without the ceremony of a personal interview? Could he have any apology to offer now, for his past behaviour?—Or was he, perhaps, coming to break the news to her, that he was engaged to Miss Woodhouse?

"Yes," she said tremblingly, as this last tormenting idea entered her mind. "Yes, tell him I will see him, Patty. Tell him I—I will be out in a moment."

It was, in truth, a little longer than that before she made her entrance; for she felt so faint and weak at the prospect of the meeting, that she feared her legs would give way beneath her. She had slept little, and taken very little nourishment, for many days past; and she now found it necessary to sit down fully five minutes, before she felt able to walk out with any degree of steadiness. At last she did emerge, to find Frank gazing out the window with an unusually sober countenance. She gave a little cough, and he started towards her eagerly. At the sight of her, however, he halted abruptly, an expression of profound shock on his face.

"Good God!" he cried. "How ill you look, Jane!"

This was not a very promising beginning; for what lady,

however little vain, likes to be told she is looking ill—
especially by a gentleman flush with health and vitality, and
handsome enough to break her heart ten times over? She
responded in a querulous tone.

"Why are you come, Frank?"

So truly shocked was he by the alteration in her appearance, he could not immediately return her any answer. She
looked as pale and thin and drawn, he thought, as if she
were suffering under some grim wasting illness; and *he* had
done it—he was to blame! Till that moment, he had never
wholly understood how deeply his thoughtlessness—his impudence—his willful disregard for her feelings had injured
her.

She was leaning heavily, he perceived, on the back of a
chair for support. He stepped across to her and took her
arm, saying gently, "Sit down, I beg you. Do not fatigue
yourself."

Though strongly inclined to resent this unlooked-for and
much-belated solicitude, she was really too weak to oppose
him, and allowed herself to be led to the sofa and placed
upon it. When he had settled her there to his satisfaction—
tenderly setting an extra cushion behind her, that she
might be as comfortable as possible—he remained standing,
penitent, before her.

"I am come, Jane, to ask your forgiveness," he said feelingly, "and to endeavour, by every means in my power, to
persuade you not to end our engagement."

The application took her so much by surprise that she
found herself again without any capacity for speech; and
he, in very great earnest, went on,

"I know my conduct these several months past has been
disgraceful—reprehensible. I cannot express how deeply it
mortifies me to reflect on it. When I think how I have tried
your patience, and abused your trust—when I see you looking so ill, and know it is my own doing—all my own doing—!
These are impressions which will not soon fade from my
mind—evils I will not soon learn to pardon."

She was very much affected, and hardly knew how to reply. He spoke with evident sincerity, yet it seemed too
sudden a change; she knew not how to believe it. After a
pause, she began,

"When you sent no reply to my letter, Frank, I could only
conclude—"

"Your letter!" he broke in. "That terrible letter, telling me you wished to dissolve our engagement, was delivered on the very morning of my poor aunt's death. I had time to send a few lines only in reply; but I wrote them within the hour—trusting, under the circumstances, they would be enough to satisfy you."

"You wrote—within the hour! But I never received any reply!"

He nodded gravely. "A few days passed after I had written, and I was disappointed when I did not hear from you again. But I was not at all uneasy. I was too much occupied—and I own, too cheerful in my altered prospects, to be severe. I made excuses for your silence. Then my uncle and I removed to Windsor; where, yesterday, I received your second letter, and the parcel of my own letters all returned to me. It was clear, from what you wrote, that my reply had never reached you. Oh, Jane! how I raved at the blunders of the post—until I discovered the blunder was my own! From the confusion of my mind, and all the duties falling on me at once, as a consequence of my aunt's passing, my answer, instead of going out with all the other letters being sent that day, had been by mistake locked up in my writing desk!"

"Then—you never intended—?"

"No."

She felt herself in some danger, then; but she *would* remain firm. It would be easy, all too easy to forget the misery of the past few months—to resume their engagement once more; but would anything really be altered if she did? She thought back again over those months, purposely reminding herself of all his misdeeds.

"I did try," she said, "on more than one occasion, to make you understand—to make you see how you were hurting me by your conduct—how you were hurting others. But you went on, heedless—flirting openly with Miss Woodhouse, though I remonstrated with you again and again—making sport of her, and provoking me, with those horrid jokes about Mr. Dixon. You repeatedly acted without discretion, or prudence—at times, it seemed to me, even without feeling—and were wont to accuse *me* of coldness, if I refused to do something you wished because I felt it would expose us to suspicion."

"I know—I know. I plead guilty to it all! I have behaved abominably; to you, to Miss Woodhouse—to everyone. I have been selfish, and capricious, and incautious. I have been, indeed, utterly and completely wrong, from beginning to end; and I can offer nothing in my defense—nothing whatever. I can only beg your pardon, with all my heart—and pray that, somehow, you may find it in yours to forgive me."

Little satisfied with his reflections, he walked over to the window and looked out, without seeing what he looked on. Speaking rather to himself than to her, he said,

"To promote your comfort and peace of mind, ought to have been my first object. Having placed yourself, for my sake, in such an awkward and painful position, you had every right to expect I would do anything—take any burden upon myself—rather than add to your cares. I ought readily to have submitted to any wishes of yours, even had they been unreasonable."

He turned back to face her. "And they were not in the least unreasonable—I acknowledge they were not, though I was such a brute as to think them so then, and to resent. I did truly believe—I still do believe, that Miss Woodhouse entertained no feeling for me beyond friendship. I should never have gone on as I did, had I not been fully persuaded of her indifference. But I knew that my manner to her was offensive to *you*—and that alone ought to have governed my behaviour. I can only say, not to excuse myself, but—"

He halted.

"To—extenuate?" she supplied, a somewhat alarming susceptibility beginning to steal over her.

"Yes—to extenuate, I hope, in some small measure—I can only say that the separations and the delays—the uncertainty of how long it might be, before we could hope for any change to our advantage—were, to me, beyond bearing; though no doubt it did not appear so to you. You once accused me of treating the secrecy of our engagement—the need for concealment and deception—as a game; and I confess I did exactly that. It was the only way I could contrive to endure the frustration I felt, without being driven absolutely to despair. But for all my impudence, Jane, I really was very miserable. And though it ought not to have been so, my wretchedness drove me to act ungenerously—unjustly, toward you; and made me disgracefully insensible of all that you were suffering on my account."

"Then at Donwell, Frank—when I said you must not walk home with me. You were so unreasonable; so violent! And at Box Hill—oh! I shall never forget it—you said, 'How many a man—'"

"Please," he broke in, "I pray you—do not repeat what I said that day. It cuts me to the soul to remember it. What must you have thought of me, for speaking such hateful words?"

"I thought you were angry. I thought you repented—deeply repented—of our engagement. And when I learned you had gone back to Richmond that evening, though you might have stayed over till the morning—though you might have tried to see me again before you left—it seemed but a confirmation of my worst fears."

"I *was* angry. I thought you overcautious. I believed *myself* the injured party—injured by your coldness, as I saw it. I left Highbury that evening, only because—because I would be as angry with you as possible. How utterly foolish—worse than foolish, it seems to me now! But even then, I always meant we should be reconciled in time. I was a very great fool; but still, I was not so much a fool as to think I should be happier without you. I never conceived you would so readily take me at my word; that you would be so precipitate as to acquiesce in the schemes of that—detestable woman; whose whole treatment of you, I must beg leave to say, has from the first filled me with the strongest indignation and loathing! How you can have borne with it so sweetly, so patiently, is a matter of no small wonder to me! However," he was forced to add, "when I consider how shamefully I have treated you myself—when I think of the sweetness and patience with which you have suffered all my own ill usage—when I think of how I hope to be forgiven—I suppose I ought not to quarrel with any degree of forbearance toward Mrs. Elton.—Be that as it may—you must believe me when I tell you I never had the smallest wish of ending our engagement. And I pray my explanation, deficient as it is, has begun to—to make you think better of ending it yourself?"

He gave her a look of appeal which was difficult to resist; however, after a brief but painful interval of solemn reflection—a good deal of it centred on Miss Emma Woodhouse—she shook her head, and said tearfully,

"No—no. It is better as it is. We have done nothing but make each other miserable, since the first moment we entered into this rash engagement."

"Has it really," he asked, crestfallen, "been nothing but misery to you, Jane?"

"I cannot pretend there have not been moments—. But

they have been too few; far too few. No," she repeated, "it is better as it is. I will go to Mrs. Smallridge; and you—" (with a little sob) "—perhaps you will marry Miss Woodhouse."

"Marry Miss Woodhouse! Is that what you are thinking?" His hopes somewhat renewed by this revelation, he could not here repress a smile. "My dearest girl! I confess to a—a very warm regard for Emma Woodhouse—I think her a very charming young lady; but I do *not* want to marry her. There is only one young lady whom I wish to marry—only one, whom I have ever wished to marry—and she is most decidedly *not* Miss Woodhouse."

How powerfully she longed to yield to his persuasion! "But the idea of going on as we have been," she said, "of continuing in this deception—is horrible to me. I cannot endure it any longer!"

"You will not have to endure it any longer," said he. "My uncle has given his consent to our engagement."

She stared at him in disbelief. "What! So soon after Mrs. Churchill's death! No—how can that be, Frank? You only mean, I suppose, that you expect he will give it eventually."

"I mean, he *has* given it."

She could only listen, amazed, as he explained, "You may imagine my shock, Jane, when I received your last letter— when I discovered my own unsent letter in my writing desk last night. How angry, how offended I knew you must be, at my seeming indifference! I was almost wild, thinking what was to be done—how such a wrong was ever to be put right. I knew another letter would not answer. I had to see you—I had to come to Highbury at once. But I saw that I must speak to my uncle first. Without his sanction, how could I expect you would listen to me again? Only the most profound desperation, you may be certain, could have prompted me to such a measure, at such a time; but I *was* desperate. I went to him directly, and laid the whole before him. Circumstances were in my favour; my poor aunt's death had softened away his pride (independent of her, you know, it never was very much); and before I left—and more easily than I could have dreamt—I had obtained both his pardon, and his blessing."

With this disclosure he saw her resolve breaking down, and his spirits rose still higher. In an unsteady tone which belied the sternness of his words, and with a shaky smile which betrayed his anxiety, he said,

"Now, madam, tell me plainly—do you mean to honour

your promise—or no?"

"Oh, Frank!" was all she said.

And then she was crying, and his arms were around her, and he was tenderly embracing her, and kissing her, and murmuring the sweetest of endearments and apologies; and she was filled with such a painful joy, such a blissful sense of release from every affliction which had weighed upon her for so many months, that she felt the happiness of it was almost too much to bear.

After a little time, they sat together on the sofa, both feeling rather spent, and both exceedingly joyful; but neither yet perfectly comfortable, nor quite able to believe in their present felicity.

"But Frank," she soon felt the need to inquire again, "are you really quite sure—? Are you altogether certain you would not be a great deal happier with Miss Woodhouse?"

Some minutes more were required for him to reassure her, in the most delightful manner possible, that he cared nothing for Miss Woodhouse, nor for any other young lady, and that his affections were entirely her own. Then,

"I really ought to be going back to Windsor, Jane," he said, though showing very little inclination to depart. "I must not trespass on my uncle's goodness, after such indulgence as he has favoured me with. But there is one other point," he added hesitatingly, "which it is necessary to mention before I go. When my uncle granted his consent to our marriage, he made one demand—only one—which I know you will not think unreasonable. He only conditions that, out of respect for my aunt's memory, we should not yet make our engagement a matter of public knowledge."

Jane looked a little uncertain at this, fearing it meant a continuation of that dreadful secrecy they had been under for so long—and even for a moment (it cannot be denied) entertaining a suspicion that he had never spoken to his uncle at all. Frank, seeing the expression on her face, and guessing at her thoughts, hastened to add,

"Of course, you may tell your grandmother and aunt; and I shall stop a few minutes at Randalls on my way out, to acquaint my father and Mrs. Weston with our engagement."

These assurances set her mind at ease. "I fear, Frank," she said, "the Westons will be very angry with us when they learn of it."

"They will be very angry with *me*—on one account, at any rate. And I suppose (on the same account) they will insist on enlightening Miss Woodhouse as to our situation."

"And I'm afraid Mrs. Elton must be informed as well, if I am to be released from my promise to Mrs. Smallridge."

"Mrs. Elton!" he could not refrain from exclaiming. "That overbearing, interfering—. Yes, I suppose she must be told, too; though it would not surprise me a bit if she were to have you spirited off to Bristol anyway, utterly regardless of your own wishes in the matter—all the while congratulating herself on having got you so admirably situated at last."

Jane laughed shakily, and he went on, "And when once my father, and your aunt, and Miss Woodhouse, and Mrs. Elton have all been told, I have no doubt the news will be all over Highbury before nightfall—which is hardly what my uncle intended. But," he concluded with a very cheerful resignation, "I suppose it cannot be helped."

And thus it was that Miss Bates and Mrs. Bates, and Mr. Weston and Mrs. Weston, and Miss Woodhouse, and Mrs. Elton—and through them, all the other good citizens of Highbury—were shortly to learn that Miss Jane Fairfax and Mr. Frank Churchill had long been secretly attached to one another, and engaged to be married. But in fact, the first person to receive an inkling that anything momentous was afoot, was Mrs. Bates's servant, Patty; who was much amazed when her young mistress, a few minutes after Mr. Churchill had taken his leave, came down to the kitchen, looking still extremely weak and wan, but uncommonly happy.

"Patty," said she to their faithful servant, "Is there any cold meat left from last night's dinner? I am so very hungry!"

# Chapter Forty-Nine

---

**OLD MRS. BATES** was, at first, greatly shocked and
displeased to learn that her granddaughter had for many
months been practising a deception on all her friends; and
Miss Bates was so astonished when she heard the news
that she actually could not utter a word for nearly a minute.
But altogether, they were both so fond of Jane—thought so
highly of Mr. Churchill—were so relieved to see Jane smiling again, her appetite restored and her health mending—
that she suffered scarcely a reproach from either; and they
soon began to look upon the match as a blessing of no
small estimation.

Mr. and Mrs. Weston, when apprised of the engagement,
laid the greatest part of the blame with Frank; their displeasure was directed almost entirely at him, and that (as
he had predicted) chiefly on Miss Woodhouse's account. It
had been their darling wish that the two might be attached
to each other, and they had been fully persuaded it was so;
nor would they, at the outset, credit Frank's assertions that
the young lady's affections were not engaged. When once
they heard from Emma's own lips, however, the assurance
that she did not care for Frank, and had suffered no material injury in consequence of his duplicity—well, they were
both so fond of Frank, and thought so highly of Miss Fairfax, that their forgiveness was not long withheld either.

As for Miss Woodhouse, she wished the couple might be
very happy. Yet while she really was *not* in love with Frank,
she could not directly subdue a little feeling of resentment
over the manner in which he had imposed upon her.

"I must say," she told Mrs. Weston, "that I think him
greatly to blame. What right had he to endeavour to please,
as he certainly did—to distinguish any young woman with
persevering attention, as he certainly did—while he really
belonged to another? How could he tell what mischief he
might be doing? And how could *she* bear such behaviour!
Composure with a witness! To look on, while repeated at-

tentions were offering to another woman before her face, and not resent it? That is a degree of placidity, which I can neither comprehend nor respect."

Miss Woodhouse's bitterness was perhaps the more acute owing to some recollections of her own indiscretions, which entered into her mind at that moment. She had long regretted having ever imparted to Frank her thoughts about Jane and Mr. Dixon; and the conviction that these ungenerous suspicions must surely have been repeated to Miss Fairfax, made her present mortifications the heavier. And who can say but that she might not have still other, private causes for mortification, when reflecting on the follies and delusions of the spring and summer just past? At all events, I am certain no one will be much surprised by Emma's indignation at having been so thoroughly misled. To discover one has been taken in is never agreeable; and the discovery is perhaps the more painful to those of us who, like Emma Woodhouse, have been accustomed to congratulate ourselves on possessing a capacity for seeing farther, or deeper, or more clearly than our companions.

"I cannot say," she continued, "how it has sunk him in my opinion. So unlike what a man should be! None of that upright integrity, that strict adherence to truth and principle, that disdain of trick and littleness, which a man should display in every action of his life."

Mrs. Weston (who, though hardly pleased herself with Frank's conduct, really loved him very much) felt called upon to defend her son-in-law; and she urged Emma not to judge him too harshly.

"I am to hear from him soon," said she. "He was here only a quarter of an hour, and in a state of agitation which did not allow the full use even of the time he could stay. But he told me at parting that he should soon write; and he spoke in a manner which seemed to promise me many particulars that could not be given then. Let us wait, therefore, for this letter. It may bring many extenuations. It may make many things intelligible and excusable which now are not to be understood. I must love him; and now that I am satisfied on one point, the one material point, I am sincerely anxious for it all turning out well, and ready to hope that it may. They must both have suffered a great deal under such a system of secrecy and concealment."

"*His* sufferings," replied Emma drily, "do not appear to have done him much harm."

Even before Mrs. Weston had received Frank's promised letter, Mr. Weston resolved that they should pay a call on their daughter-in-law-elect. His wife at first demurred; she wished merely to write to Jane instead, and to defer the ceremonious call till such time as Mr. Churchill could be reconciled to the engagement's becoming known—as, considering everything, she thought such a visit could not be paid without leading to reports. But Mr. Weston thought differently; he was extremely anxious to show his approbation to Jane and her family, and did not conceive that any suspicion could be excited by it; or if it were, that it would be of any consequence.

"Such things always do get about," he observed—and not wholly without foundation, for he himself had already told the secret, in strictest confidence, to Mrs. Cole, Mr. Perry, and Miss Smith.

So the visit was duly paid. It was a visit which Jane, conscious as she was of having acted wrongly, had been living in some dread of; and so great was her distress and confusion when it took place—so little did she feel herself deserving of any consideration—that she was scarcely able to speak a word to either of them. After an awkward quarter-hour, Mr. Weston left them to attend to some business at the Crown. Then his wife, on the plea of Jane's recent illness, invited her to take an airing in the carriage with her. She declined it at first; but on being pressed, finally yielded.

In the course of their drive, Mrs. Weston, by gentle encouragement, overcame so much of Jane's embarrassment, as to bring her to converse on the important subject. Apologies for her seemingly ungracious silence in their first reception, and the warmest expressions of the gratitude she was always feeling towards Mr. Weston and herself, must necessarily open the cause; but when these effusions were put by, they talked a good deal of the engagement. On the misery of what she had suffered, during the concealment of so many months, Jane was energetic.

"I will not say," she stated with visible emotion, "that since I entered into the engagement, I have not had some happy moments; but I can say, that I have never known the blessing of one tranquil hour."

"You felt yourself wrong, then," said Mrs. Weston, "for having consented to a private engagement?"

"Wrong! Oh! yes—how could I not feel it? The consequence has been a state of perpetual suffering to me; and so it ought. But after all the punishment that misconduct can bring, it is still not less misconduct. Pain is no expiation. I never can be blameless. I have been acting contrary to all my sense of right; and the fortunate turn that everything has taken, and the kindness I am now receiving, is what my conscience tells me ought not to be.

"I pray you," she went on after a moment, "do not imagine that I was taught wrong. Do not let any reflection fall on the principles or the care of the friends who brought me up. The error has been my own—entirely my own; and I do assure you that, with all the excuse that present circumstances may appear to give, I shall yet dread making the story known to Colonel Campbell."

There was another little pause before she added, "One natural consequence of the evil I involved myself in, was that it made me so unreasonable. The consciousness of having done amiss exposed me to a thousand inquietudes, and made me captious and irritable to a degree that must have been—that I know was hard for him to bear. The misunderstandings that resulted, so painful to me as they were, were largely of my own creating. I did not allow, as I ought to have done, for his temper and spirits—his delightful spirits—and that gaiety, that playfulness of disposition, which, under any other circumstances, would, I am sure, have been as constantly bewitching to me, as they were at first."

There was more then to be said about Frank; the subject was nearly as gratifying to Mrs. Weston as it was to Jane. They talked of Frank's lively mind and engaging manners, his open, cheerful temper, and the depth and warmth of his attachments; and Mrs. Weston heard with pleasure some part of the history of her acquaintance with him at Weymouth. There was considerable relief to Jane in this conversation, pent up within her own mind as everything had so long been; and her companion was very much pleased with all that she had to say. Mrs. Weston had not a doubt of her being extremely attached to Frank; and under the circumstances could readily forgive her, for having allowed her affection to overpower her judgement.

After another interval, Jane began to speak of Miss Woodhouse, whose name she could not mention without a blush. All her jealousy having been done away, an unmixed sense of shame now prevailed respecting her conduct toward that young lady. It was perfectly clear to her now that

Emma Woodhouse had been in no way to blame for all she had suffered these several months past; that she had, in fact, behaved towards her of late with the utmost charity and goodwill; and that all her recent overtures of friendship had been spurned with hardly even a decent pretence of civility.

"I hope," Jane now told Mrs. Weston, "that whenever you have an opportunity, you will thank Miss Woodhouse for me—I am sure you cannot thank her too much—for every friendly wish, and every endeavour to do me good, which she offered during my illness. I am but too sensible," she added with a still deeper blush, "that she has never yet received any proper acknowledgement from me, for all her kindness."

Jane's thanks—though to her own mind unpardonably behindhand, and miserably deficient—when conveyed to Emma by Mrs. Weston that very afternoon, were not received ungraciously. Indeed, Miss Woodhouse was quite as ashamed of her own conduct toward Jane, as Jane could be of her conduct toward Miss Woodhouse.

"If I did not know her to be happy now," said Emma to her friend, "which, in spite of every little drawback from her scrupulous conscience, she must be—I could not bear these thanks; for, oh! Mrs. Weston, if there were an account drawn up of the evil and the good I have done Miss Fairfax! Well, this is all to be forgotten. You are very kind to bring me these interesting particulars. They show her to the greatest advantage. I am sure she is very good—I hope she will be very happy. It is fit that the fortune should be on his side, for I think the merit will be all on hers."

Mrs. Weston, though pleased to find Emma so ready to forgive Miss Fairfax, could not be satisfied until she had procured an equal pardon for her son-in-law. With this in view, she forwarded to her, very soon after receiving it, Frank's explanatory letter; and Emma was obliged, in spite of her previous determination to the contrary, to do it all the justice that Mrs. Weston foretold. The letter must make its way to her feelings. Every line relating to herself was interesting, and almost every line agreeable. Though it was impossible not to feel that he had been wrong, yet he had been less wrong than she had supposed—and he had suffered, and was sorry—and he was so grateful to Mrs. Weston, and so much in love with Miss Fairfax, that there was no being severe; and had he entered the room at the moment she finished reading his letter, she must have shaken hands with him as heartily as ever.

Her friendliness towards the engaged pair was now so complete as to induce her to pay a call on Jane at her grandmother's house, on a morning when, as it happened, Jane was already occupied with a visit from Mrs. Elton. Mrs. Elton having, of all Jane's friends, perhaps the least cause for resentment, had initially been the most resentful of any. The necessity of keeping her engagement a secret from her nearest relations—from her guardians—from her dear friend Mrs. Dixon—from all her other friends and neighbours at Highbury, was perfectly intelligible to Mrs. Elton. But that Jane should have thought it necessary to keep *her* in the dark too! She, who had been such a staunch friend, since the very first moment of their acquaintance! Who had favoured her from the first with such uncommon attention—honoured her with the utmost intimacy and unreserve—exerted herself so unstintingly on her behalf! Mrs. Elton could hardly have conceived of so much ingratitude, and was, for a time, very angry indeed.

But Jane, feeling herself so greatly to blame, was truly and properly penitent; and Miss Bates's—flattery it cannot be called, for there was nothing in it of design or dishonesty; but her oft-repeated praise for Mrs. Elton's benevolence—her perpetual thanks for Mrs. Elton's many kindnesses—her perfect reliance on Mrs. Elton's magnanimity, by appealing to that lady's *amour-propre*, did much to smoothe her ruffled feathers; and ultimately, she too decided to forgive. There was satisfaction to her, as well, in imagining the humiliation Miss Woodhouse must feel, whenever she should hear of the engagement. How shocked, how chagrined she would be, to learn of the defection of the young man, whose attentions she had shamelessly encouraged—whose attachment to her, she had plainly never doubted—whom she had, quite obviously, wanted for herself!

Miss Bates was out when Patty entered the parlour to say that Miss Woodhouse was waiting downstairs. Mrs. Elton had been reading, to Jane and her grandmother, the handsome letter she had that morning received from Mrs. Smallridge, releasing Jane from her commitment. Glad of the interruption, Jane directed Patty to beg Miss Woodhouse to walk up; but immediately afterwards, desirous of showing Emma every possible attention, went out to meet her on the stairs. She came eagerly forward with a blush of consciousness, and an offered hand; and said, in a low, but very feeling tone,

"This is most kind, indeed! Miss Woodhouse, it is impossible for me to express—I hope you will believe—excuse me for being so entirely without words."

Emma looked gratified by this reception, and expressed her own goodwill by a very, very earnest shake of the hand. They then walked together into the parlour; and Jane was pleasantly surprised to find Mrs. Elton greeting the newcomer with unusual graciousness. One reason for her good humour soon became evident, however: it was being in Jane's confidence, and fancying herself acquainted with what was still a secret to other people generally, and to Miss Woodhouse in particular. While Emma was paying her compliments to Mrs. Bates, Mrs. Elton, with a sort of anxious parade of mystery, busied herself in folding up and putting away Mrs. Smallridge's letter, saying to Jane, with significant nods,

"We can finish this some other time, you know—and, in fact, you have heard all the essential already. I only wanted to prove to you that Mrs. S. admits our apology, and is not offended. You see how delightfully she writes. Oh! she is a sweet creature! You would have doted on her, had you gone. But not a word more. Let us be discreet—quite on our good behaviour. Hush! You remember those lines—I forget the poem at this moment:

> For when a lady's in the case,
> You know all other things give place.

Now I say, my dear, in our case, for lady, read—mum! a word to the wise. I am in a fine flow of spirits, an't I? But I want to set your heart at ease as to Mrs. S. My representation, you see, has quite appeased her."

And again, on Emma's turning her head to look at Mrs. Bates's knitting, she added, in a half whisper,

"I mentioned no names, you will observe. Oh! no; cautious as a minister of state. I managed it extremely well."

It was a palpable display, repeated on every possible occasion. When they had all talked a little while of the weather and Mrs. Weston, she said to Emma, "Do not you think, Miss Woodhouse, our saucy little friend here is charmingly recovered?" (with a side-glance of great meaning at Jane) "Do not you think her cure does Perry the highest credit?"

And when Mrs. Bates was saying something to Emma, whispered farther, "We do not say a word of any *assistance* that Perry might have; not a word of a certain young physician from Windsor. Oh! no; Perry shall have all the credit.

"I have scarce had the pleasure of seeing you, Miss Woodhouse," she shortly afterwards began, "since the party to Box Hill. Very pleasant party. But yet I think there was something wanting. There seemed a little cloud upon the spirits of some. However, I think it answered so far as to tempt one to go exploring again. What say you both to our collecting the same party again, while the fine weather lasts? It must be quite the same party, you know—not one exception."

Soon after this Miss Bates came in, and was thrown into a perplexity in speaking to Miss Woodhouse, from doubt of what might be said, and impatience to say everything. After some disconnected ramblings, there were a few whispers to Mrs. Elton, expressing a more than commonly thankful delight toward that lady for being there; then Mrs. Elton, speaking louder, said,

"Yes, here I am, my good friend; and here I have been so long, that anywhere else I should think it necessary to apologise; but, the truth is, that I am waiting for my lord and master. He promised to join me here, and pay his respects to you."

"What! are we to have the pleasure of a call from Mr. Elton? That will be a favour indeed! for I know Mr. Elton's time is so engaged."

"Upon my word it is, Miss Bates. He really is engaged from morning to night. There is no end of people's coming to him, on some pretence or other. The magistrates, and overseers, and churchwardens, are always wanting his opinion. They seem not able to do anything without him. 'Upon my word, Mr. E.,' I often say, 'rather you than I. I do not know what would become of my crayons and my instrument, if I had half so many applicants.' Bad enough as it is, for I absolutely neglect them both to an unpardonable degree. I believe I have not played a bar this fortnight.—However, he is coming, I assure you; yes, indeed, on purpose to wait on you all." And putting up her hand to screen her words from Emma, "A congratulatory visit, you know.

"He promised to come to me as soon as he could disengage himself from Knightley; but he and Knightley are shut up together in deep consultation. Mr. E. is Knightley's right hand."

At this, Emma remarked, "Is Mr. Elton gone on foot to Donwell? He will have a hot walk."

"Oh! no, it is a meeting at the Crown, a regular meeting. Weston and Cole will be there too; but one is apt to speak only of those who lead. I fancy Mr. E. and Knightley have everything their own way."

"Have not you mistaken the day?" said Emma. "I am almost certain that the meeting at the Crown is not till tomorrow."

"Oh! no, the meeting is certainly today," was the abrupt answer, which denoted the impossibility of any blunder on Mrs. Elton's side.

"I do believe," she continued, "this is the most troublesome parish that ever was. We never heard of such things at Maple Grove."

"Your parish there was small," said Jane. "It is proved by the smallness of the school, which I have heard you speak of, as under the patronage of your sister and Mrs. Bragge; the only school, and not more than five-and-twenty children."

"Ah! you clever creature, that's very true. What a thinking brain you have! I say, Jane, what a perfect character you and I should make, if we could be shaken together. My liveliness and your solidity would produce perfection. Not that I presume to insinuate, however, that some people may not think you perfection already. But hush!—not a word, if you please."

It was an unnecessary caution; Jane was wanting to give her words, not to Mrs. Elton, but to Miss Woodhouse. The wish of distinguishing her, as far as civility permitted, was very powerful, though it could not often proceed beyond a look.

Mr. Elton made his appearance. His lady greeted him with some of her sparkling vivacity.

"Very pretty, sir, upon my word; to send me on here, to be an encumbrance to my friends, so long before you vouchsafe to come! But you knew what a dutiful creature you had to deal with. You knew I should not stir till my lord and master appeared. Here have I been sitting this hour, giving these young ladies a sample of true conjugal obedience—for who can say, you know, how soon it may be wanted?"

Mr. Elton was so hot and tired, that all this wit seemed thrown away. His civilities to the other ladies must be paid; but his subsequent object was to lament over himself for the heat he was suffering, and the walk he had had for nothing.

"When I got to Donwell," said he, "Knightley could not be found. Very odd! Very unaccountable!—after the note I sent him this morning, and the message he returned, that he should certainly be at home till one."

"Donwell!" cried his wife. "My dear Mr. E., you have not been to Donwell! You mean the Crown; you come from the meeting at the Crown."

"No, no, that's tomorrow; and I particularly wanted to see Knightley today on that very account. Such a dreadful broiling morning! I went over the fields too," (speaking in a tone of great ill-usage) "which made it so much the worse. And no apology left, no message for me. The housekeeper declared she knew nothing of my being expected. Very extraordinary! And nobody knew at all which way he was gone. Miss Woodhouse, this is not like our friend Knightley! Can you explain it?"

Emma protested that it was very extraordinary, indeed, and that she had not a syllable to say for him.

"I cannot imagine," said Mrs. Elton, (feeling the indignity as a wife ought to do,) "I cannot imagine how he could do such a thing by you, of all people in the world! The very last person whom one should expect to be forgotten! My dear Mr. E., he must have left a message for you, I am sure he must—not even Knightley could be so very eccentric—and his servants forgot it. Depend upon it, that was the case: and very likely to happen with the Donwell servants, who are all, I have often observed, extremely awkward and remiss. I am sure I would not have such a creature as his Harry stand at our sideboard for any consideration. And as for Mrs. Hodges, Wright holds her very cheap indeed. She promised Wright a receipt, and never sent it."

"I met William Larkins," continued Mr. Elton, "as I got near the house, and he told me I should not find his master at home, but I did not believe him. William seemed rather out of humour. He did not know what was come to his master lately, he said, but he could hardly ever get the speech of him. I have nothing to do with William's wants, but it really is of very great importance that I should see Knightley today; and it becomes a matter, therefore, of very serious inconvenience that I should have had this hot walk to no purpose."

After this Miss Woodhouse rose to take her leave, and Jane attended her out of the room, and went with her downstairs, where Emma said with a smile,

"It is as well, perhaps, that I have not had the possibility. Had you not been surrounded by other friends, I might have been tempted to introduce a subject, to ask questions, to speak more openly than might have been strictly correct. I feel that I should certainly have been impertinent."

"Oh!" cried Jane in some confusion, "there would have been no danger. The danger would have been of my wearying you. You could not have gratified me more than by expressing an interest. Indeed, Miss Woodhouse," (speaking more collectedly), "with the consciousness which I have of misconduct, very great misconduct, it is particularly consoling to me to know that those of my friends, whose good opinion is most worth preserving, are not disgusted to such a degree as to—I have not time for half that I could wish to say. I long to make apologies, excuses, to urge something for myself. I feel it so very due. But, unfortunately—in short, if your compassion does not stand my friend—"

"Oh! you are too scrupulous, indeed you are," cried Emma warmly, taking her hand. "You owe me no apologies; and everybody to whom you might be supposed to owe them, is so perfectly satisfied, so delighted even—"

"You are very kind; but I know what my manners were to you. So cold and artificial! I had always a part to act. It was a life of deceit! I know that I must have disgusted you."

"Pray say no more. I feel that all the apologies should be on my side. Let us forgive each other at once. We must do whatever is to be done quickest, and I think our feelings will lose no time there. I hope you have pleasant accounts from Windsor?"

"Very."

"And the next news, I suppose, will be, that we are to lose you—just as I begin to know you."

"Oh! as to all that, of course nothing can be thought of yet. I am here till claimed by Colonel and Mrs. Campbell."

"Nothing can be actually settled yet, perhaps," replied Emma, smiling again, "but, excuse me, it must be thought of."

The smile was returned as Jane answered, "You are very right; it has been thought of. And I will own to you (I am sure it will be safe), that so far as our living with Mr. Churchill at Enscombe, it is settled. There must be three months, at least, of deep mourning; but when they are over, I imagine there will be nothing more to wait for."

"Thank you, thank you. This is just what I wanted to be assured of. Oh! if you knew how much I love everything that is decided and open!—Good-bye, good-bye."

# Chapter Fifty

**JANE REFLECTED WITH** great satisfaction on this visit from Emma Woodhouse, and that afternoon sent Frank a most cheerful account of their meeting. Miss Woodhouse had treated her not merely with civility, but with the warm cordiality of a true friend; and Jane felt she had never before rightly estimated Emma's good nature.

She was, however, still living in dread of Colonel Campbell's reply to the news of her engagement. She had spent one entire evening writing her explanatory letters to the Colonel and his wife, and to Helen; and of the latter's forgiveness, she was almost too confident; but she was equally certain of the Colonel's being deeply hurt by her deception. She feared the Colonel might particularly resent her conduct, as being the cause of injury to his friend, Mr. Devere; and in writing to him, she thought it owed to her own character, and to her respect for him, to explain that she had become engaged to Frank only after rejecting the clergyman's proposal. However, she could not but acknowledge that she had been prompted to refuse Mr. Devere, by the consciousness of feeling that for Frank Churchill—though without having then the smallest expectation of marrying him—which made it impossible for her to marry any other man. She could only venture to hope that the engagement of Mr. Devere to Miss Lodge would serve in some degree to lessen the blame, to which she might otherwise be liable on that gentleman's account.

When she had done writing these painful and difficult letters, her spirits were so much depressed that she had need to read over Frank's last letter again, to prevent her feeling altogether dejected. She had not seen him even once since the day of their reconciliation; but he wrote every day, and in his latest letter had expressed a strong hope of being able to come to her again very soon.

About this time reports arose in Highbury to surpass, in the minds of many of its inhabitants, even the anticipation of another visit from Mr. Frank Churchill. Shortly after Miss Woodhouse had paid her congratulatory call on Jane, the whole neighbourhood was made happy by the arrival of a new baby at Randalls, and the assurance that Mrs. Weston was well, and her daughter flourishing. A further bit of news soon followed, which was, that Harriet Smith was gone away to have a bad tooth attended to in London, where she was to be the guest of Mr. and Mrs. John Knightley. The very next occurrence to distract—nay, astound—the good folk of Highbury, was the announcement of an engagement between Miss Woodhouse, and their own Mr. Knightley!

Mrs. Weston, as Emma's dearest friend, was the first to be told of the engagement; and she deemed it an auspicious connection in every respect. Indeed, said she, in one point of the highest importance, it was so peculiarly eligible, so singularly fortunate, that it now seemed to her as if Emma could not safely have attached herself to any other creature. Never would Emma have consented to forsake her poor father—and how very few of those men in a rank of life to address her would have renounced their own home for Hartfield, as Mr. Knightley had declared himself ready to do! It was a union of the highest promise of felicity in itself, and without one real, rational difficulty to oppose or delay it.

Mr. Weston had his five minutes share of surprise when his wife told him the news; but he, too, quickly saw all the advantages of the match. "Of course, it is to be a secret, I conclude," said he. "These matters are always a secret, till it is found out that everybody knows them. Only let me be told when I may speak out. I wonder whether Jane has any suspicion?"

He went to Highbury the next morning, and satisfied himself on that point. He told her the news; and Miss Bates being present, it passed, of course, to Mrs. Cole, Mrs. Perry, and Mrs. Elton immediately afterwards. Miss Woodhouse and Mr. Knightley engaged!—it was of all things most wonderful. Before long, all of Highbury was buzzing with it.

To Jane, the engagement was a matter of considerable delight. She had always held Mr. Knightley in the highest regard—was now overflowing with goodwill toward Miss Woodhouse—and, upon reflection, felt them to be very well matched, and almost certain to be happy together. Further, if there had lingered in her mind any little doubts regarding Emma's attachment to Frank, this news put an end to them at once. It was a circumstance, indeed, to gratify every feeling; and she took an early opportunity of calling on Emma at Hartfield, where she was received with the friendliest welcome.

"Little did I suspect, Miss Woodhouse," said Jane as she and Emma walked out together in the shrubbery, "when you were lately offering me congratulations on my engagement, how soon I should be called upon to congratulate you on your own! And perhaps it had all been settled already, when I saw you then?"

Emma admitted that it had.

"I hope you will allow me to say," Jane went on, "how very pleased I was when Mr. Weston told me the news, and to wish you every happiness—though of your happiness with so excellent a husband, I think, there can be little cause for doubt."

Emma thanked her with a most becoming warmth. "No, indeed," she said, smiling. "There can be no doubt at all as regards *my* future happiness; though with so very unworthy a wife, there may be some question as to *his*."

To this, Jane of course objected; and Emma concluded, still smiling, but with an unaffected humility Jane had never before seen in her, "But I mean to deserve him better in future; and I am sure no woman on earth could have a stronger motive, or a truer wish to change, than I have now."

In general, it was a very well approved match. Some maintained they had always detected a faint something—a little hint of a partiality, either on the lady's side, or on the gentleman's. Many others, though not prepared to claim such prescience, were content to declare the engagement the most natural and proper thing in the world; and the only wonder was, that it hadn't come about long ago. Some might think him, and others might think her, the most in luck. One set might recommend their all removing to Donwell, and leaving Hartfield for the John Knightleys; and another might predict disagreements among their servants; but yet, upon the whole, there was no serious objection raised, except in one habitation, the vicarage. There, the surprise was not softened by any satisfaction. Mr. Elton cared little about it, compared with his wife; he only supposed "she had always meant to catch Knightley if she could;" and, on the point of living at Hartfield, could daringly exclaim, "Rather he than I!"

But Mrs. Elton was very much discomposed indeed. "Poor Knightley! poor fellow!—sad business for him. She was extremely concerned; for, though very eccentric, he had a thousand good qualities. How could he be so taken in? Did not think him at all in love—not in the least. Poor Knightley! There would be an end of all pleasant intercourse with him. No more exploring parties to Donwell made for her. Oh! no; there would be a Mrs. Knightley to throw cold water on everything. Shocking plan, living together. It would never do. She knew a family near Maple Grove who had tried it, and been obliged to separate before the end of the first quarter."

Frank at last turned up in Highbury one morning, quite unexpected either by Jane or the Westons, and with leave from Mr. Churchill to stay over till the morrow. In honour of the occasion, Jane was invited to spend the day at Randalls, where she and Frank passed most of the morning walking about out of doors, in a state of great mutual happiness. Together they talked over the likely particulars of both the near and the distant future. Though Jane had as yet received no letter from the Colonel in reply to her own, she thought it unlikely the Campbells would remain in Ireland beyond August. Frank had already persuaded Mr. Churchill that they should themselves remove to London when the Campbells returned to it, and continue there till they might carry Jane back with them to Enscombe. He had some hope too (he told her), of his uncle's being soon induced to pay a visit at Randalls; he wanted to be introduced to her.

"But we were introduced," said she in surprise, "at Weymouth."

"My poor uncle does not recollect it. His memory is not good, I'm afraid; and the strain, on that occasion, of being called upon to learn several names and faces at one time," he added with a grin, "I suppose caused him to forget them all."

After they had thoroughly discussed their plans and wishes, and exchanged such sweet words and tokens of affection as lovers must do, they went back into the house, where they found Mrs. Weston sitting in the drawing room with Miss Woodhouse and her father. Jane met them both with pleasure. Frank, too, was extremely glad to see Emma again, though plainly there was a degree of confusion—a number of embarrassing recollections on each side—a consciousness which at first allowed little to be said. When Mr.

Weston joined the party, however, and when the baby was fetched, there was no longer a want of subject or animation. While Jane was admiring little Miss Weston, she was pleased, before long, to perceive that Frank had drawn Emma aside, and was talking to her with every appearance of ease and friendliness.

Mrs. Weston began to give an account of a little alarm she had been under the evening before, from the infant's appearing not quite well. She believed she had been foolish, but it had alarmed her, and she had been within half a minute of sending for Mr. Perry.

Frank caught the name.

"Perry!" said he, trying, as he spoke, to catch Jane's eye. "My friend Mr. Perry! What are they saying about Mr. Perry? Has he been here this morning? And how does he travel now? Has he set up his carriage?"

Jane, though trying to seem deaf, could not avoid hearing him.

"Such an extraordinary dream of mine!" he cried. "I can never think of it without laughing. She hears us, she hears us, Miss Woodhouse. I see it in her cheek, her smile, her vain attempt to frown. Look at her. Do not you see that, at this instant, the very passage of her own letter, which sent me the report, is passing under her eye—that the whole blunder is spread before her—that she can attend to nothing else, though pretending to listen to the others?"

Jane was forced to smile completely, for a moment; and the smile partly remained as she turned towards him, and said in a conscious, low, yet steady voice,

"How you can bear such recollections, is astonishing to me! They will sometimes obtrude—but how you can court them!"

She could not be really angry, however; and he had a great deal to say in return, and very entertainingly. The rest of the day passed most agreeably; and on the following morning, just after Frank had stopped in at Mrs. Bates's house to take his leave before returning to Windsor, Mrs. Goddard called with news of yet another noteworthy event: the engagement of her parlour-boarder, Harriet Smith, to Mr. Knightley's tenant—the young farmer, Robert Martin.

"You may imagine my surprise," said Mrs. Goddard, "when Mr. Martin came to see me yesterday, to apply for information of her relations or friends. Some months ago, indeed, I had thought there was more than a little liking there—on his side at least; but nothing ever came of it, and I had long since concluded it to be no more than a passing inclination."

"But now he has asked, and she has accepted!" said Miss Bates, clapping her hands together in delight. "I am so pleased! She is such a sweet, pretty girl—and he is an excellent young man; I hear nothing but good of him from Mr. Knightley. And once last winter, you know, he did me a very great service—you recollect it, ma'am," (to Mrs. Bates) "—I had turned my ankle on my way home from calling at Hartfield; and I really don't know what I should have done, Mrs. Goddard, if Mr. Martin had not come along just then, and helped me home. Indeed, now you mention it, I do recall a rumour afloat last year that he was quite taken with Miss Smith. Do you remember my telling you about it, Jane, last autumn, when you first arrived? She spent two months with the family at Abbey Mill Farm last summer, on a visit to the Miss Martins, with whom she was very intimate; and everything seemed then in a very fair train. But, as you say, nothing came of it—until now! But how *did* it come about, I wonder? For is not Miss Smith in town just now?"

"She is indeed—she has been staying with Mrs. John Knightley this fortnight. But it seems Mr. Martin was going into town on business of some sort a few days ago, and Mr. Knightley asked if he would bring some papers to his brother. Mr. Martin, of course, was happy to oblige such a good friend; and when he made the delivery, Mr. John Knightley asked him to join them all that evening to Astley's—which he did; and he dined with them the next day as well. It was then, as he told me, that he found an opportunity of making his proposals to Harriet."

"Ah!" said Miss Bates with real satisfaction. There had been little enough of romance in her own life, but she was always ready to take pleasure in the romances of her neighbours. "Is it not wonderful how these things come about! Here it is, not a twelvemonth since Mr. Weston married Miss Taylor—and already there is a little Miss Weston come; and but a few months ago that Mr. Elton married Mrs. Elton—who has proved such a very agreeable addition to our little circle. And now our own dear Jane is engaged to Mr. Frank Churchill (who is quite a hero of ours, you know); and Miss Woodhouse to Mr. Knightley—surely there is not a better man to be found anywhere than Mr. Knightley; and now sweet little Miss Smith and good Mr. Martin are to be married too. And of course I must not forget Miss Campbell and Mr. Dixon, who were married last autumn at Weymouth. Now, who could have foreseen any of it, only a year ago?"

"I am exceedingly pleased with the match," said Mrs. Goddard. "Robert Martin is a respectable, sensible, industrious young man, quite comfortably circumstanced, and with every prospect for greater prosperity in the future. I am extremely fond of Harriet; but just between ourselves, her parentage is such that—well, I am sure she could not do better."

Listening to all that Miss Bates and Mrs. Goddard said, Jane did remember what her aunt had told her, so many months past, about Miss Smith and Mr. Martin. She also remembered Mrs. Elton's claim that Harriet had been in love with Mr. Elton; and her own fear that Mr. Knightley's kindness, on the night of the ball at the Crown, might lead her into a hopeless attachment to that gentleman. She was very glad, therefore, both for Miss Smith's sake, and for Mr. Martin's—who, by all accounts was a very deserving young man, and very much in love with her—to hear of this happy ending to her history. There might be something yet unexplained in these twists and turns of the young lady's affections. But in fact, the solution to the mystery might be no more than that she had liked Mr. Martin from the first; and had decided in the end—failing any more elevated offer to which she might (perhaps with Emma's encouragement) have been bold enough to aspire—that she liked him still, quite well enough to marry him.

# Chapter Fifty-One

**HELEN DIXON, BEING** a young woman happily wed to the husband of her choosing, could not wish anything less for her dearest friend. Thus the letter she sent in answer to Jane's was full of affection and congratulation, and breathed not a hint of reproach. She did not in the least resent that the secret had been kept from her. She did not like to speak ill of the departed, she wrote, but of course, if Mrs. Churchill *would* be so unreasonable as to object to her nephew's marrying Jane, merely because she had not a fortune or a title, what else could they have done? She had always liked Frank Churchill—thought him handsome and agreeable—and was sure he and Jane would be very happy together. Helen and Ned were both delighted that she was not to go out as a governess after all; and they were already planning that she and Mr. Churchill should come and spend the whole of next summer with them at Balycraig.

The generosity of this reply, though no more than she expected from her beloved Helen, was a great comfort to Jane. Colonel Campbell's letter, which arrived by the same post as his daughter's, was written in rather a different tone. In opening, he had some stern words to say to his ward regarding her deception. He owned himself hurt and disappointed by her actions. He could scarcely believe that she, whom he had always credited with principles of the strictest rectitude and honour, should have found it possible to practise such duplicity, not only towards those with whom she had lived almost as a daughter for so many years, but towards her own relations as well. Jane wept as she read these reproofs, so thoroughly merited. But as the Colonel's letter continued, his very great affection for her (aided, perhaps, by the recollection of a few youthful indiscretions of his own) so much overcame his displeasure, as to cause him to grant that even the most estimable individual might stray from the straight path, once or twice in a lifetime; and to allow that her age and inexperience, and the extraordinary nature of the circumstances in which she had been placed, though they could not excuse, might lessen somewhat the guilt of the offence. He referred but once to her refusal of Mr. Devere—leading her to conclude that the latter's recent engagement had indeed spared her some censure on *his* account, at least.

Colonel Campbell's understanding words brought on a fresh flow of tears, though these were tears of relief; but as she read on, she again grew anxious. He felt it incumbent upon himself, he wrote, to express some very grave misgivings as to the character of the young man she intended to marry—to whom, in his own mind, he assigned by far the greater part of the blame attached to the whole affair—and some fears for Jane's future happiness with him on that score. He had nothing to say against Mr. Churchill's person, manners, or situation in life; they had all liked him very well at Weymouth. Without question, the gentleman had fortune, charm, and good looks enough to turn any young woman's head; and the Colonel had not a doubt but that hers *had* been turned—for it was certain this plan of deceit could never have originated with herself. He urged her to consider carefully whether she really wished to entrust her future well-being and respectability to a gentleman whose principles it was only too easy to suspect. She need make no positive decision as yet, however. He and Mrs. Campbell would be returning to London before the first of September. If, by that time, she found that she had better not marry Mr. Churchill, he would engage to take whatever steps might be necessary to extricate her from a connection, into which she had perhaps found herself drawn before time had been given for due deliberation. But whatever her final resolution, (he concluded), he hoped Jane knew she could always rely upon his friendship.

These exhortations, and the Colonel's scruples about Frank—which were not, as she was forced to admit to herself, entirely unreasonable—made her very uncomfortable for a time. But a little reflection brought a brighter view: if Colonel Campbell could pardon *her* wrongs on the grounds, as he said, of her age, inexperience, and circumstances, no doubt he would soon see the justice in pardoning Frank on the same grounds. When he learned how Frank had, at the first, proposed entering into some profession by which he might earn his bread, without reference to his guardians and their fortune; when he learned that she herself had rejected this idea, thereby rendering secrecy necessary—she felt sure the Colonel would recognise that Frank's share in the blame was not so heavy as he now supposed it to be. Indeed, when given the opportunity to become better acquainted with all the excellencies of Frank's character, he *must* be disposed to excuse that one great error into which they had both fallen. These fortifying thoughts—together with a very kind and forgiving message from Mrs. Campbell, appended at the bottom of the Colonel's letter—were so encouraging as to allow Jane to appear at breakfast that morning with a more than tolerably cheerful countenance.

It was not long, however, before she discovered another cause for anxiety. It had been some time, she realised, since she had received a letter from Margaret Devere. Was it possible that Miss Devere—who had always treated *her* with such perfect unreserve—had somehow heard of her engagement, and was angry she had concealed it from her? Luckily, Jane's suspense on this point was not of great duration. The day after receiving Colonel Campbell's letter, she wrote a lengthy letter of explanation and apology to Miss Devere. When she carried it off early the next morning to the post-office, the post-mistress handed her a packet from Weymouth, containing the following letter:

My dear Jane,

I know you will forgive the liberty I now take of addressing you, for the first time, by your Christian name; for such a story as I have to relate I really cannot introduce with a cold and ceremonious *Dear Miss Fairfax.* So kind a friend as you have shown yourself to be these past months—so interested and sympathetic a party to all my nearest concerns—I would not now deny you (or, I might say, spare you) the fullest possible account of my present happiness. What follows, then, are all, or nearly all the particulars, of the reconciliation lately affected between myself, and Mr. James Hammond.

Two days ago, Mrs. H. called on me at the Rectory. After conversing for a little while on one or two indifferent subjects, she began to talk (as she often does) of *him*; and at length she ventured to communicate something of her regret that so worthy a man as her son 'should have no better object to bestow his affections on, than his poor old mother.' I said, in reply, that I wondered Mr. Hammond had never married; and she confided to me that many years earlier—before he had attained his present great success—he 'had fallen in love with a young lady, who had broken his heart.'

She did not know all the circumstances; but she gathered, from some comments he had once made, that the woman in question had been much above him in station; that her family had disapproved of the match; and that the lady herself had been only too ready to give him up. She believed he had never got over this early disappointment.

Here was intelligence, you may well conceive, of some consequence to me. 'The lady only too ready to give him up'! Knowing as I did how very *un*ready the lady was (for it was impossible the lady could be any other than myself), I could only conclude that she misunderstood, or misremembered, what her son had said on that point. Betraying, I hoped, no emotion beyond what a friendly regard might occasion, I expressed my sympathy for what he had suffered. I told her I was the more disposed to pity him, as I had gone through a like experience myself.

'When I was seventeen,' said I, 'I fell in love with a young man: poor, and occupying then a humble position in life, but certain to rise; for he was possessed of mind, character, and abilities, greatly superior to any other man of my acquaintance. Indeed, in the sixteen years that have passed since that time, I have never seen his equal. But my father thought him beneath me, and forced us to part. My heart, too, was broken—and I have never married, simply because I have never met any other gentleman who could make me cease to regret for a moment what I had lost in him.'

What, you may wonder, was my motive in revealing so much of my history and sentiments to her? What could I hope to gain by it? Merely that she should repeat to her son every word I had said. In this I was spurred on by the knowledge that he was nearing the completion of his commission; and I thought at least to make a *push* of some kind, before he should leave Weymouth, and my chance be lost forever. I was persuaded Mrs. H. had grown fond of me during these many weeks of our acquaintance, as had I of her; and sometimes of late I flattered myself that she wished he and I might become attached to each other. It appeared to me that, in so plainly disclosing to me the state of his affections, she might be hoping to awaken in me an interest hitherto (as she supposed) unfelt. By the same reasoning, I thought it likely she would recount to him the tale of *my* unhappy love affair, with the aim, perhaps, of inspiring in him some feeling of tenderness toward me. Though I was far from certain what would result from such a scheme, I be-

lieved it must precipitate *some* sort of confrontation—or illumination—or resolution; or perhaps (as I half-feared) it
might have no effect whatever—which would in itself be a
resolution of a kind, if hardly a satisfactory one to me.

You will perhaps deem it beneath me, to engage in a
stratagem of this nature. But I protest—are we women always to sit by passively, whilst Fate orders our wretched
lives for us, and do nothing to help ourselves to happiness?
I would not stoop to injure another creature merely to benefit myself; but should I injure myself, to the benefit of no
other creature? Should every earthly joy be sacrificed on the
altar of punctilious morality? I say, Nay!

(Forgive my ranting.—I have done.—And if I have not
shocked you quite beyond redemption, I shall proceed with
my story.)

That same evening, my brother was gone to Ashdale Park
at the behest of Lady P. I had eaten an early dinner in solitude, and had just settled myself with a book, out in our
little side garden, when I heard someone knocking—indeed,
pounding—at the front door. A few moments later, James
Hammond stood before me.

'The servant said I would find you here,' said he. I was
piqued by his abruptness; but before I could say one word,
he demanded, 'What sort of plot are you hatching, Miss
Devere?'

'I beg your pardon?' said I.

'Why have you been telling such stories to my mother, as
you know to be utterly false?'

'I have not the honour, sir,' I responded (throwing into
my voice as much of a chill as possible), 'of understanding
what you refer to. I am not aware of having told Mrs.
Hammond anything that was untrue.'

He made a sound something between a growl and a
groan, and looked very much as if he should like to throttle
me. 'I refer,' said he, 'to that fanciful bit of invention—that
barefaced rewriting of history, with which you so charmingly
regaled my mother this morning. I refer to that—that *fairy
tale*—wherein *you* are the ever-faithful princess, pining in a
tower for her lost love—banished from her life by the malevolent devices of an evil king.—What I wish to know is,
whether there is some method to your madness? Or are you
simply deluded? Is your memory faulty? Or perhaps, Miss
Devere—perhaps you think *now* that you were a little too
hasty in severing our connection sixteen years ago—now,

that is, that I have amassed wealth enough to answer even *your* immoderate requirements.'

I felt a cold fear clutch at my breast. 'There must be some mistake—some dreadful mistake—'

'Yes, indeed; the mistake was mine—for being so half-witted as to believe all the empty professions of love, which you once so liberally bestowed upon me. I know not what your purpose was in trifling with me *then*; I suppose you were merely amusing yourself at my expense. What hours of diversion it must have afforded you, to make the poor drawing master (pathetic dupe that I was!) fall in love with you.'

'But I never—! My father—'

'Of course—your father, knowing you better than I did, arranged a far more advantageous match for you. What I cannot understand is why *that* marriage never did take place. Perhaps the fortunate gentleman discovered your true character before it was too late, and extricated himself. Or perhaps *you* broke it off—thinking to catch someone still richer?'

My feelings just then cannot be described. I tried to collect my thoughts to make some coherent reply, but they were spinning round frightfully in my head, and I could not seem to get hold of them.

'But—did you never get my letter?' I asked finally.

'Oh! yes, madam,' he replied. 'I had the *honour* of receiving your letter. Indeed, I owe you thanks for it—I have carried it with me these sixteen years, as an invaluable reminder of the treachery of the female heart.'

I felt my pulses throbbing all over me, as a faint glimmer—a horrifying suspicion—began to grow in my mind. 'Do you mean—have you the letter in your possession now—at this moment?'

'I keep it always near my breast, as a sort of—talisman,' he said, pulling a yellowed, much-creased sheet of paper from the inside pocket of his coat.

'May I see it?'

At this he looked surprised, and a little wary. He hesitated, doubtful; then he unfolded the letter, and held it out to me. Trembling, I took the paper from his hand, and stared at it for some time before I could begin to see or understand what was written on it. For there, in such language!—cold, haughty, almost heartless; without a single softening word of solicitude or regret—the writer of the letter stated that she had lately received, from an unexceptionable gentleman of rank and property (a friend of her brother's, and well known to her family), a very eligible offer; which, upon reflection, she had decided to accept. 'I now realise, sir,' she wrote, 'that my father was perfectly right to send you away. I am fully persuaded that you and I should never have suited. Indeed, with prospects so very indefinite, it was presumption in you to address me at all; and preposterous in *me* ever to have contemplated risking all my future happiness, for a pauper.' And the letter was signed, *Margaret Devere*. But (I need not tell you) it was not my letter!

Aghast, I read it through twice more, till I was quite mistress of its contents. Then I looked up at James, telling him, in a voice scarcely above a whisper, that I had not written it. His angry demeanour changed at once to one of astonishment. 'What!' he exclaimed, snatching the letter from my hand and gazing on it in disbelief.

''Tis not even my handwriting,' I murmured stupidly.

After a long silence, he raised his head; and those extraordinary eyes of his stared back at me with an expression of such bleakness and pain in them, as should have wrung my heart on his account—had it not been already quite thoroughly crushed on my own. 'But,' said he, 'if you did not write it—?'

I raised my hands in mute, helpless bewilderment.

'Your father?' he suggested.

'Perhaps, but—no. No, I am sure he would not.—It must have been—Richard.'

'Your elder brother?'

I nodded. 'It can have been no one else. He must have intercepted my own letter, somehow, and—sent that one in its place.'

He stood, stunned again into silence. Consequently he appeared struck by a new idea, and said, 'But you said you did send me a letter?'

'I did.—I did send a letter.'

He seemed unable to find words with which to articulate the next question in his mind: What did *your* letter say? But I knew what he was thinking. 'I wrote—that if you would come to Scotland for me—I would run away with you—and marry you at once.'

'Good God!' he cried. Another silence followed. Then, 'Oh, Maggie,' he said. 'Maggie!'

I have never fainted in my life; but I should have at that moment, so overpowered was I by a flood of emotions—save that, in an instant, he had crossed the little distance that separated us, and caught me up in his arms. Together we fell to our knees—I weeping—he very nearly so—and clinging to each other 'as orphans in the storm'. After sixteen years—reconciled, reunited—restored to each other at last!

After a long time, he tenderly raised me to my feet and led me over to the little garden bench, where we sat together in the soft, mild radiance of an early summer evening, in a state which is not to be described. At first, we said little; but at length we began to talk over the past.

What conceivable motive my brother could have had for perpetrating so grievous a crime, he declared to be a matter of wonder to him. That any one of my family should disapprove of our attachment could hardly surprise him much; but my father had already forbidden him to see me again, and warned him from the premises; and furthermore had banished me to Scotland. Did not my brother think these precautions adequate for my protection?

'Perhaps he thought it likely,' said I, 'that on the strength of such an encouragement from me, you might follow me to Scotland.'

'He would have been right to think so,' he admitted. 'Still—he might have been content merely to prevent your letter from reaching me, without committing the further outrage of substituting a forged one.'

'He could perceive as well as anyone else, I suppose, that you were not a man to be easily deterred.'

'No; nor should I have been—had it not been for the rumours circulating in the village immediately afterwards, that you were on the verge of making a very great match, and were gone to your sister's home in Scotland, to be joined there by your future husband. And I should never have credited *those* reports,' he acknowledged, 'had I not received a confirmation of their truth in that letter.'

'The rumours,' said I, 'must have originated with my brother as well.' I explained to him that my brother had indeed been attempting to arrange a match for me, with a friend of his—a man of large fortune, who had been staying at my father's house earlier that year, and who, presumably, admired me a great deal. Mr. M. was a person for whom I could never have felt the least esteem or affection, even had I not been already attached to someone else. Young and inexperienced as I was, I felt I had good reason to mistrust his character; and his insincerity and affectation of manner made him every way repugnant to me.

I had not been exiled to Scotland a week before he and Richard followed me there; and a few days later Mr. M., finding me alone, made his solemn declaration. I rejected him with equal solemnity; and, to my happiness, he departed the house that very day. In his rage, Richard revealed to me that he owed a very large sum of money to Mr. M.—a debt which was to have been forgiven, had the marriage taken place.

As I had thwarted his plans, however, he was obliged to own his profligacy to my father, and beg to be extricated from his difficulties. Those difficulties proved serious indeed; and were only to be alleviated through the sale of some valuable property, as well as the next presentation to a family living, which had been intended for my younger brother. My father was furious when the disclosure was made to him, and was taken ill soon afterwards. Indeed, he was never altogether well again, so greatly disappointed was he in his eldest son's character. Threatened with disinheritance, my brother promised to reform—and did redeem himself sufficiently, in my father's estimation, to be suffered to continue as heir to the estate.

'But for the evil he has done us,' I told James, 'I never will forgive him.'

He was as little disposed to forgive Richard as I was myself—but he confessed it might be more difficult still to forgive himself, for having been so easily taken in by that letter. Not for the world would I have seemed to blame him, yet I could not help admitting to some surprise, that he had ever believed I could write it.

'It does seem incredible to me now,' said he. 'Knowing you as I did, I ought to have felt how impossible it was that you could have written anything so arrogant, so unfeeling, to anyone—and to me especially. But the truth is that my pride was injured, mortally injured, by the abuse I had received at your father's hands. I will not bother to repeat to you all he said to me—the affronts and accusations he heaped upon me; but the suggestion that my real object was to raise myself, by marriage, far above the station to which I had been born—and to obtain your few thousand pounds for myself, into the bargain—I confess cut me deeply. With so firm a knowledge in my heart of my own integrity, I ought not to have been so easily provoked; my judgement ought not to have been so easily deranged. And indeed, I believe I could have borne with almost any reproaches he might have cared to utter against *me*; but the affronts to my family I could not bear. He spoke with the utmost contempt of my father's occupation—of my father himself—a man he had never met—a man endowed with every virtue which could make him truly worthy of esteem! These slanders I could not suffer impassively; and I own, some part of the resentment I felt towards your father recoiled onto you, and coloured my perception—my feeling for you—so that I could not judge rightly. Attribute it, if you would be charitable, to the passions of youth. They can be my only excuse.'

'But perhaps after all, James,' said I after a period of silent contemplation, 'it was for the best.'

At this, he would have objected violently; but I checked him, explaining, 'Had you married me then, with scarcely a shilling to call your own, you must have given up painting—for you would have been compelled to turn all your energies to earning our bread; and who can say that you would not in the end have come to resent me for it—to regret that we had ever met? And I should have come to hate myself, too, for being the means of extinguishing all your bright hopes—for keeping you from ascending to that eminence which I knew you to be destined for—and which you did finally achieve.'

'But though we could not obtain your father's approval,' he protested, 'we might have kept to our engagement. Indeed, even had we obtained his consent, we should have had to wait until I had money enough to support you. Had I only trusted to your affection, we might have been married as soon as I began to be a little known in my profession. The wait, I grant you, would have been long; but still—'

'But without my father's sanction—and kept apart as we must have been, unable to see each other—without any means even of communication—do you really think we should have had the prudence to wait?'

He acknowledged that we probably should not, and fell into a perplexity of unhappy reflections; until I roused him by asking, whether he had known me to be living at Weymouth when he accepted Lady Paget's commission? He admitted that he had.

'When she first opened the subject with me,' he said, 'she made mention of a Mr. Devere, who was the rector of St. Alban's. It was natural to guess he might be a connection of yours, and not very difficult to find out the rest. In truth, it was chiefly owing to your presence here that I was persuaded to come.'

'Though you believed I had used you so ill?'

'Ah, Maggie!—the heart is a stubborn, unmanageable organ. I had thought my love for you long dead—had done everything in my power to conquer it; but when faced with the possibility of seeing you again, I discovered it had only been in a kind of sleep. Reawakened, it proved as strong as it ever had been. If anything, it was grown stronger.'

'Then you did wish to see me again? But you were not very friendly, when we met that first day in the church.'

'Nor, I shall not scruple to point out, were you.'

'You were not the only one who had cause for anger, you know. I had offered to sacrifice everything for you—and never heard from you again!'

'Did it not occur to you that I might never have received your letter?'

'Yes—but I had not thought it would need any invitation from me, for you to find out where I was, and pursue me—if you wished to. Of course, I had no idea then of what my brother had done. When you didn't come, I told myself you were only waiting until you were more favourably circumstanced—until you could better afford to marry. But ultimately, I was forced to conclude that you had forgotten me very quickly: 'Out of sight is out of mind,' as they say. Even so, I should have met you again last summer with the greatest pleasure—had you not been from the outset so cold and remote.'

'It was my intention, when I first saw you, to be cool, distant, and polite. I meant not to display any emotion toward you at all—not to show you by any outward sign that you still had power over me. I wished to prove to you that you were nothing to me; that it was altogether a matter of indifference to me, whether we met or not.'

'But if your aim was to win me back—?'

'I had no such aim; at least, not in the beginning. Rather, I had been hoping I might find you so altered as to shatter to bits that passion which still tormented me. What I found instead—even after the lapse of so many years—and though you were indeed changed, from a girl to a woman— was that you were yet the same person I had fallen in love with—only more beautiful, more captivating than ever.'

'There were times,' I said, 'when I did think I perceived something of the old feeling in you—in the way you looked at me, and spoke to me; but it would vanish in a moment, and you would abruptly turn cold and quarrelsome! You confounded my every attempt to understand you.'

'But recollect, you were the woman who had once spurned me (as I believed) in the most heartless fashion. I did mean to be uniformly cool in my demeanour; yet whenever I was in your company, I found myself drawn to you—drawn into betraying some part, at least, of the attraction I still felt toward you. Then I would curse myself, and resolve to make you feel the sting of my resentment. At the same time, there was something so delicious, even in quarreling with you—and I found myself caught again and again.'

I told him of my suspicions about his setting up the studio in Weymouth; and he acknowledged they were correct.

'There was no need whatever for me to remain here, once I had inspected the church, and agreed to terms with Lady Paget. Had it not been for you, I should have gone back to my studio in London to execute my commission. You kept me here, quite against my will. I spent fifteen years endeavouring to hate you—to forget you; but my heart was always constant, in spite of my best efforts. No woman ever inspired in me half the fascination—one-tenth of the tenderness I felt, and feel, for you—dearest Margaret!'

Having now endured an engagement long enough to suit the notions of the most fastidious matron who ever drew breath, we are determined we shall wait not one week more. He is gone today to Dorchester for the license, and we are to be wed four days hence—this very Saturday! "But O! methinks, how slow this old moon wanes! She lingers my desires..."

I am well aware, my dear friend, that this long, long letter will cost you a pretty fortune in postage; I hope you may find some small recompense in its contents. As Voltaire said, *'Le secret d'ennuyer est celui de tout dire.'* I trust I have quite mastered this dubious art of telling all—and thereby succeeded, perhaps, in boring you most thoroughly. There is more, much more, which I could tell you; but were I to scribble a hundred sheets, I could never convey half the joy I am feeling.

I must not forget, however, before I close, to convey my brother's and Mary's thanks for the warm good wishes which you were so kind as to send them, through me, in your last letter. With every hope for your own health and happiness, (and my respects to your good grandmother and aunt), I remain,

Your affectionate friend,
Margaret Devere

# Chapter Fifty-Two

**THE READER WILL** now expect to be informed that Frank Churchill and his bride lived, forever after, a life of perfect contentment, affection, and domestic harmony. That expectation notwithstanding, I must acknowledge that there was, in the early months of their marriage, a little uneasiness between them from time to time. Frank's inability to comprehend at once that he had a wife who would willingly give up her own pleasure to his, caused him sometimes to continue practising those little deceptions which he had so often and so successfully employed with his aunt, to achieve his desired ends.

But this was only at first, and only in trifles. In all important matters, he invariably consulted Jane's feelings and inclinations before his own; for he never did forget what his selfishness during those months of their engagement had cost her. Moreover, though he had occasionally shown, during that same period, an irritability which might have boded ill for her happiness in wedlock, he was naturally of a very easy disposition; and, I am happy to say, gave his wife but little cause to complain of his temper. As for Jane, she loved her husband so dearly as to be ready to forgive him almost anything—and most certainly to forgive those minor lapses in truthfulness to which he was, for a time, now and then still liable.

Less than two years after they were united in matrimony, good old Mrs. Bates died; and Jane proposed to her aunt that, as she was now alone in the world, she should come and live with them at Enscombe. Miss Bates demurred most earnestly: she was not alone, she protested. "Though she missed her dear mother most acutely—the best mother in the world—such a great loss to her, and indeed to everybody who knew her—she could never be alone, with such kind friends and neighbours as she had always been so fortunate to possess in Highbury. Not a day passed, that she did not see Mrs. Goddard, or Miss Nash, or Mrs. Cole, or

Mrs. Perry—or indeed all four; and Mr. and Mrs. Weston continued so attentive—and the Eltons were as amiable as ever—and the Hughes, and Otways, and Coxes, too, were always so friendly and obliging! Then either Mr. or Mrs. Knightley called at least once in every week, very often twice. She had been invited twice last month to Hartfield, to dine with Mr. Woodhouse; and they sent over such bountiful quantities of game, fruit, &c., just as they had been wont to do whilst her mother lived. And as her dear nephew was so exceedingly generous in the frequent gifts he sent—more than ample to meet every other need—she really did not want for anything, and would not think of imposing herself on them."

After much affectionate pressing, however, from both her niece and nephew, and with assurances of the elder Mr. Churchill's concurrence in their wishes—"which was really so excessively good of him, and she was so grateful for his civility, and so desirous of expressing her thanks to him in person"—she was at length persuaded to pay them a visit in Yorkshire. While staying there, she met again unexpectedly with Mr. Bradley—the former curate of her late father, for whom (as she once confided to Jane) she had so long ago entertained a very tender regard. Mr. Bradley, widowed three years earlier, was visiting a married daughter who had settled in Yorkshire. Her husband, as it happened, was the vicar of Enscombe parish. Mr. Bradley's friendship with Miss Bates was quickly renewed; and friendship was soon succeeded by warmer sentiments. After a ten weeks' reacquaintance, the happy pair were married by his son-in-law at Enscombe church, and travelled home to a handsome manor in Kent, carrying with them all the good wishes of their assorted Yorkshire relations. Monkworth, Mr. Bradley's seat, was less than twenty miles distant from Highbury; so to every other blessing which this late union could bestow upon the cheerful and deserving Miss Bates, was added the further one of being able regularly to visit the town which had for so long been her home, and to which she retained so many ties both of memory and friendship.

Following the death of his wife, the elder Mr. Churchill seemed, remarkably, to begin growing younger. Not a twelvemonth after the marriage of Miss Bates and Mr. Bradley, old Mr. Churchill astonished the world, by making an offer of marriage to a respectable and very attractive widow of about two or three and forty, living on a modest jointure in a neighbouring parish. She was delighted to accept; and, as she was a good-humoured and sensible woman, and seemed genuinely fond of Mr. Churchill, she was cordially received by his nephew and niece at Enscombe. Though remarrying rather late in life, and with three grown children by her first marriage, this lady within another twelve-month's time presented her husband with a strong and healthy infant son; and Frank, for so long his uncle's nearest male relation, found himself displaced by this young olive branch, who became the heir of Enscombe. (And it is well for us, reader, that he did; for where would be the moral of our story if, through deceptions and stratagems, Frank Churchill had obtained for himself not only a beautiful, virtuous, loving and beloved wife, but a great fortune and a splendid estate as well?)

This event was initially somewhat of a shock to Jane and Frank, who had by that time a daughter of their own, and another child expected. Jane, however, was quickly reconciled to their new circumstances. She had never been easy with the prospect of great wealth, and could cheerfully, but for Frank's sake, live without it; and she loved old Mr. Churchill too well not to rejoice in his happiness. Frank, though sincerely glad on his uncle's account, was, for a short time, downcast on his own; but as he found the old man still meant to provide for him—that he was still to have, if not a great fortune, at least a competence—he too was soon reconciled, both to the change in his position, and to his new aunt and cousin.

When the young heir was about a year old, Frank and Jane removed with their own son and daughter to a small property near Weymouth, endeared to them both as the place where their attachment had first arisen. Over the years they made regular journeys from thence, to visit the Churchills in Yorkshire—the Bradleys in Kent—the Westons in Highbury—the Campbells in London—and the Dixons in Ireland; with all of whom they continued on the closest terms of affection and esteem. They periodically received all these friends in Dorset as well; and were even occasionally honoured (after the death of Mr. Woodhouse made it practicable for them to be sometimes away from Highbury) by a visit from George and Emma Knightley—with whom, in time, they also formed a lasting intimacy. And with both the Deveres and the Hammonds, they enjoyed for the rest of their lives a mutual friendship of the warmest and most abiding nature.

The enduring conjugal happiness of James and Margaret Hammond cannot be doubted. They too settled near Weymouth, close to her brother and sister, in a house overlooking the sea. With her husband's encouragement, Margaret began first to assist him in his work, and then to take commissions of her own—eventually becoming a portraitist of some distinction in her own right. Old Mrs. Hammond, cherished by both, lived with them; but for some time she missed her old friends from Oxfordshire, and was particularly lonely during that portion of the year which her son and daughter spent in London, though having no desire to go there herself. Through Jane and Frank Churchill, she was introduced to Mrs. Nesbit, who still resided at Weymouth, and was now in great measure restored to health. Each lady found in the other a most agreeable companion; and between them, they took excellent care of little Zeus— by that time grown into a very regal cat indeed.

The former Miss Lodge's worshipful view of Mr. Devere was a little tempered by marriage; gradually ripening into a more mature affection and esteem. Indeed, after some months of wedlock she was already grown so little awed by her husband, as to now and then challenge his opinions, and even to express some of her own. And Mr. Devere, after a period of adjusting to this new state of affairs, was actually heard on occasion to allow, that it was not so very bad a thing for a wife to have a little independence of spirit, and a mind of her own.

### ❧ THE END ❧

Printed in the United States
93135LV00003B/35/A